The Sagitta Mishap

by

Hugh Chare

Publication Data

The Sagitta Mishap © Copyright 2010 Hugh B. Chare.

Book and Cover design by Hugh B. Chare.
The front cover illustration includes works by John Boyden and PK Baldwin, and they are used by kind permission of John Boyden Photography and PK Baldwin.

ISBN: 978-0-9824184-4-4

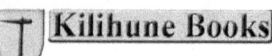 Kilihune Books

Preface

This is a work of fiction. Any resemblance in the featured characters to actual persons, living or dead, is purely coincidental.

As far as I know, the United States Navy did not and does not have a Sagitta missile program and did not and does not have a joint program with the Central Intelligence Agency to deploy missiles on civilian vessels, and the United States Air Force did not and does not have an Auriga missile program. Also, as far as I am aware, United States Air Force Plants are numbered 01 to 85; no Air Force Plant 97 is known to me.

My thanks to Vittorio for helping me with my Italian and to Valerio for inspiration.

Contents

Prologue

DATE-TIME 11/14 – 13:18 COPY 01 OF 03
UTAH EXPLOSION
        BC – Utah Explosion, MST, 2018 · FL ·
Deadly Explosion Reported in Utah Rocket Factory · FL ·
By Bernard Rasmussen · FC ·
Salt Lake City Star
WHITE'S VALLEY, UTAH – A deadly explosion rocked the Utah mountains today and destroyed a building. The explosion was heard in nearby Tremonton and felt in communities as distant as Logan and Brigham City. It is feared that the lives of thirteen men have been lost in the explosion, but there remains little in the way of clues for investigators. The company, Locomotive Springs Technologies, a division of Waterway Chemicals, Inc. of Houston, says that it is searching for survivors, but that the chances are slim. It promises a full investigation into the cause of the accident. The United States Air Force also promises a full and thorough investigation to determine the cause of the incident. UOSH will also be sending investigators. This is the second such explosion in Utah in recent times, the previous being almost a year ago in December 1987 at the nearby Morton Thiokol plant.
AP-BA-11-14 1345MST ·FL ·

Incident

Bernard Rasmussen read through his piece again and then sent it off. He had been on the road since the early morning, first out into the Utah hills to look at the scene of the destruction and then back to his office to file his story with the wire services. One thing about the remote location, it would be a while before the TV stations had their talking heads on the ground, and uplinks would be difficult. He had received no help from the company when he had tried to file his story from the site, only stonewall tactics as they tried to keep the press and broadcast media away.

He wondered what his editor would choose to do with the story, just run it as a one-day wonder or give him the freedom and time to try and find out just what did happen. He was sure that the Air Force would be unwilling to share much, if that is they could agree in the first place who had jurisdiction. UOSH, the Utah Occupational Safety and Health office, would try and do the standard workplace review, but the number of people they could use would be limited because he was certain that the Air Force would hide behind the need for access to classified materials and the Air Force would claim that it had jurisdiction. He had already promised himself that he would go back out to the mountains later in the day to get some pictures. There was a hill overlooking the site from which he could get a good view. The pictures ought to add something to the story.

He had tried to get some local colour and background from a diner in Tremonton, but people were only just coming in, and no one knew anything. He supposed that the people who had been at the plant at the time of the explosion were either still there or had gone home. He did learn that the workforce was drawn from northern Utah and southern Idaho. There was competition for labour between the Locomotive Springs Technologies plant, LST for short, and the Morton Thiokol plant due west of Tremonton. That was truly a big rocket plant made famous by the fact that the Space Shuttle boosters were made there. They had had their own problems with the press and the broadcast media first after the Space Shuttle Challenger explosion over Florida and then again after the 1987 incident at their factory in Utah.

Sometimes he wished that the population were not so heavily influenced by the Mormon Church. Because they had a prohibition on alcohol, it made it difficult to follow the usual practice of meeting people in bars and plying them with liquor until their tongues loosened. He would either have to find the non-practising Mormons or those outside the church who might be found in a bar, or try another approach by taking meals at the small local diners. Whatever they might think about alcohol, even the Mormons had to eat. Even though he actually came from Pennsylvania, his name of Rasmussen, was accepted quickly, and people assumed that he was a local boy who had made good. His editor had pointed out to him that Rasmussen was not an uncommon name for that part of the country, and he had already capitalised on that in past stories.

Bernard tried to find out what he could about previous accidents and explosions in rocket factories. There was the Morton Thiokol explosion of 1987. Before that, he had heard of a fire at the Morton Thiokol Space Division factory that made boosters for NASA. He called one of the research assistants and asked her to get whatever information she could on those incidents and any others that she could uncover. He was particularly interested in which step of the process the different fires had occurred. He also needed a book on the general process for making rockets so that he would have some idea of what to talk about with any contacts he might make. He was a little sceptical about actually getting anything useful; he had not really had occasion to use the research department before, probably to his own detriment.

Colleen, the researcher, was back within the hour. She had information on the earlier fire; it was in 1985 and was a mixer fire at the Morton Thiokol Space Division, the operation that produced solid rocket boosters for the Space Shuttle. The more recent fire was in later manufacturing stages and involved a whole MX missile stage, or Peacekeeper rocket segment. As for books, she had been unable to turn up much yet.

"Keep looking, will you please?" Bernard asked her. "Also, can you get me something on who is in this business and where they are?"

"I'll keep looking," she promised. "I do know that in the solid rocket business that apart from LST, there are Morton Thiokol, Hercules, Aerojet, CSD and Atlantic Research"

"Who's CSD?" he asked.

"The Chemical Systems Division of Pratt & Whitney," she explained. "They have a factory near San Jose. Aerojet has a factory near Sacramento. You know about the Morton and Hercules plants here in Utah, and the only other significant one is Atlantic Research in Arkansas, but I gather they're better known for tactical rockets."

"How come you know so much about this?" Bernard asked.

"I'm interested," she started. "I always wanted to do an exposé on the sins of some of the really big aerospace companies, like Boeing, McDonnell Douglas, Lockheed, Martin Marietta, General Dynamics or some other. I also know a little about the rocket industry because it's so important to the economy of Utah. Perhaps with this incident, I'll learn a little more."

"If I get the go-ahead from our lord and master to investigate this story, would you be prepared to help me?" he asked.

"Okay," she said amicably if not enthusiastically.

"Well, great," he said. "I'll be back in touch as soon as I've seen the editor and convinced him that this is worth pursuing. Meanwhile, see what else you can dig up for us in the archives, would you?"

"Okay, Bernard," she said and left. Bernard could not help thinking as she left that she had a nice arse. He guessed her age at about thirty-five and wondered if she was married. He had seen no ring, but that was not always a definitive indicator.

When Colleen arrived home, her partner, Isabella, was preparing dinner.

"How was your day?" Isabella asked.

"Okay," Colleen replied. "I was asked today to do some research on you."

"On me, how?"

"Well, not you exactly, but LST and the incident out in the desert."

"Oh, and what did you find out?"

"I called Sigourney in Washington, and she called a friend of hers in the Pentagon, and I got the basics."

"What's next?"

"I think Bernard, the reporter, wants to do something more in-depth, and I'll have to keep providing him with something to earn my keep as a researcher. But, I promise I'll tell you whatever I tell him."

"Do you think he'll find out what happened, because we've no idea as far as I've been able to learn?"

"Maybe, but I don't altogether trust Bernard and his methods," Colleen explained. "I'll have to tread very carefully."

"As long as you don't tell him that we're living together," Isabella pleaded. "I couldn't face a reporter digging into my private life."

"Nor me," Colleen agreed. "I'll be careful, I promise. So what's for dinner?"

"Muqueca."

"How much did you make?"

"Probably enough for six, but I'll take some for lunch tomorrow."

"I'm hungry, is it ready?"

"Just about, set the table, and I'll serve," Isabella replied.

*   *   *

"Have you seen this piece in the paper, James?" asked Katrina.

"No, what?" he asked.

"Some explosion in a rocket factory in Utah," she replied. "It sounds really bad, thirteen *ouks* got killed, shame."

"May I see?" he asked, reaching for the paper. Katrina handed him the paper and pointed to the appropriate article and picture.

"Wow, big detonation!" commented James. "The reporter says explosion, but this lot detonated. They're talking about survivors, but unless they were a long way off, there won't be any."

"That bad?" she asked.

"You remember the ore train that hit the magazine truck near Kitwe and the Kafironda accident?" he asked.

"*Ja,*" she replied.

"As bad as those," he explained.

"Who was the company?" she asked.

"Locomotive Springs Technologies, some division of a Houston-based outfit called Waterway Chemicals. Apparently, they make rockets for the Air Force," he read from the article.

"So, what's the plan today?" Katrina asked.
"I'll go to the outplacement office and see if there's anything for me and make some calls," James thought.
"It's been a month now," she commented. "Do you ever get disheartened?"
"Sometimes," he admitted. "But I keep reminding myself that everything takes longer than you want, and I console myself with the knowledge that Waterford Industries is footing the bill and paying us at least for the next five months."
"True, but I do get concerned," she admitted. "I'm sorry that I can't do more to help."
"It's fine, *Suikerbossie, alles sal reg kom*," he promised.

James drove to Irvine and the offices of the outplacement agency. He had been referred to them when the company he had been running had been sold to an English company. The English company had moved their own president over, and it was obvious that there was no room for James in the new organisation. So, he had taken the outplacement and was now busily looking for something else. At the office, there were no messages waiting and no mail, so a slow start to the day. James sighed and found a desk, and started to call people he knew to see if any of them had opportunities, or more particularly knew of opportunities that might be available. He had to admit that it would be easy to become disheartened. For the first time in his career, he was actually looking for a job, rather than taking an opportunity offered to him. It was a new experience for him, and he found it rather unsettling. There were others in the office who had mapped out plans of campaign and set timetables with goals and dates, but James found that difficult to do. He was much more used to assessing opportunities and risks and deciding whether he would take the risk or not; setting life goals was something quite alien to him.

He had often thought about the life goals that others had set for themselves and wondered how any plan could survive the first unexpected opportunity. Perhaps they would just forego the opportunity because it did not fit "The Plan". That struck him as particularly boring and lifeless, because who knew where an opportunity might lead. When he had first gone to Africa to work in a copper mine, he had had no notion of ever coming to the United States nor of working in the aerospace industry. Since coming to the United States, they had had the chance to live and work in several states, and James had successfully managed companies in a variety of industries. None of those things had been in any 'Plan'. Still, he thought, it must work for some because they laboured mightily over them.

At about noon, he gave up for the day and drove home to Orange. Katrina had half expected him home and had made a picnic lunch, which she suggested that they take to the Santiago Oaks Regional Park just a little further up the valley. Although it was mid-November, the weather was still reasonable, in the mid-seventies, and the sun was shining, making it warm enough for an outdoor lunch. The park had in it some really nice oak trees and was hardly used at all, so was very quiet. James had heard tales of mountain lions in the park but had yet to see one or evidence of one. He did not doubt that they were there and thought that it would only be a matter of time and more pressure from housing development before they became obvious.

"How was the morning?" Katrina asked him.

"*Nikis,*" was his comment, an old expression from their Zambian days meaning nothing.

"Have you thought about approaching one of the big aerospace companies?" she asked.

"You mean people like Boeing, MacDac, Lockheed and the rest?" he asked.

"Yes, are they any good?" she asked him in return.

"They are large, but I don't think I'm that suited to be buried somewhere deep in a large company," he thought. "I'm sure that they all have divisions or operations I could run, but I think I'd rather stay one tier down like Waterford Industries was and supply those guys."

"Maybe tomorrow will bring something," she said encouragingly.

"*Ja*," he agreed. "Anyway, what's for lunch?"

The next day, James was back in his temporary office, going through the motions of being serious about finding a job. He had sent off letters and résumés by the score, but did not seriously expect much in the way of returns. It was very rare to get a job by applying through the mail at the level he was, and opportunities did not present themselves every day. Word of mouth and contacts, one's network, were usually far more productive. James had worked his network as best he knew how and was really waiting for results. He was making a point of calling people to follow up on his initial contacts, but also trying hard not to be a nuisance. He had called all the headhunters he had either used in the past or who had contacted him with some opportunity, to let them know that he was available and what the circumstances of his change in employment had been. Most of them already knew, as they kept well abreast of events in the industries they served, particularly acquisitions and divestitures. Those were two events that often led to changes in management and were therefore opportunities for the headhunters, or executive search firms, as they preferred to be called.

He had had brief interviews with two of those headhunters who were looking for operations managers for different companies. Neither of those opportunities had appealed, and both had seemed a long step back from where he had just been. He saw his challenge of the moment as being patient enough to wait for the right opportunity and not panic and jump at the first opportunity that came along. He had the protection of his contract with Waterford Industries, which had given him six months to find a job. With just over one month already gone, there were still five months of pay still coming in, so no need to panic, yet.

On Friday, James received a telephone call from a headhunter who was doing a search for a division manager for an aerospace company. The division was quite small, only just over one hundred people, far fewer than the 2,200 people in six divisions that he had just been running. The headhunter described the company and the job, and James identified it as being one of his previous suppliers. The headhunter admitted that James had correctly identified his client and then went on to ask James his real question: did James have any recommendations of people to call who might be genuinely interested in the job? As James had viewed this particular supplier as generally lacking in just about every aspect of business, he was loath to recommend any of his friends or even casual acquaintances for the job. He suggested a couple of names of people that he knew in different companies who might welcome a change or the chance to move up the ladder, and promised to keep it in mind if anyone occurred to him at a later date.

At about four in the afternoon, there was a party for one of the outplacement victims who had landed a position. She was signing on with Disney and was destined for Paris and Euro Disney. Her abilities with French had paid off, and she was excited about the move. On the downside, four other people had shown up in the morning, all from the same company and all affected by an acquisition that placed the highest value on the greatest asset, the people. Unfortunately, in their case, that meant the people from the acquiring company and not the acquired company. James went home happy for the woman going to France and feeling for the foursome that had just arrived. Perhaps his own luck would change soon, and they would have a placement party for him before the end of the year.

*   *   *

Bernard Rasmussen, armed with his camera and a large telephoto lens, drove north from the freeway up Magpie Canyon and then a jeep trail until he came to the LST fence, then he hiked up until he was at the highest spot he could find, looking down across the valley to the LST plant buildings. He could see the factory, some of which was laid out below him and some of which was hidden from view in side canyons. The crater was very evident, even if it was partially obscured by a small canyon wall. He took pictures of that and all the buildings around it. He could just make out damage to some of the other buildings and saw that there were a number of people on the ground who he guessed were making a search of the area for pieces, fragments of the building or the rocket or any other clues that they might come up with.

9

His editor had liked the idea of an in-depth story and had told him to keep digging to see what he could unearth. He had not managed to get back to the scene later in the day of his first visit, so here he was in the snow four days later, freezing to death and hoping to get the one picture that would reveal all. That was a fond hope, but one never knew. He could see groups of cars and pickup trucks around the crater and the people scouring the ground for clues. They did not seem to him to be doing that in a very systematic way, but perhaps there was more logic to their methods than he could see. He had tried to keep the sun to his left and behind him and not let it catch the lens of his camera and therefore give him away, but he was sure that someone would spot him soon enough, so he quit while he was ahead and worked his way back to his car.

He drove back into Tremonton and stopped to get something to eat at a burger joint. Most of the other people in the place looked like farmers, but there was a small group in a corner that was obviously discussing something other than farming. They kept looking around furtively as if they expected someone to overhear. Bernard got his burger and sat close to them, but with his back to them so he could feign disinterest. He had been right about their furtive behaviour. They were discussing the accident at LST, and all had different opinions as to what had happened. They all shut up fast when the door opened and a couple of Air Force officers came in. Bernard noted a lieutenant colonel and a captain. He did not know enough about the different arms of the Air Force to know where these two came from or even if they were in any way associated with the rocket plant, but it seemed reasonable to assume that they were. They got hamburgers and sat close to Bernard, eating and, between bites, discussing football. The colonel must have had money riding on the Chicago Bears because he was most interested in the captain's predictions for the upcoming game. Bernard did gather from the conversation that the colonel had a high regard for the captain's views on football. He decided that it might be a good opening and turned to the officers.
"Say, sorry to overhear you guys, but my money's on the Bears against the Bucs," he started.

"You think?" the colonel replied.

"Sure, I've followed those guys for a while now, and I'm predicting they'll beat the Bucs twenty-seven to fifteen," he elaborated.

"Twelve points?" the captain scoffed. "Maybe six, but not as much as twelve!"

"Well, Dick, look what they did to the Redskins this weekend," the colonel suggested. "They creamed those guys!"

"And, the last time they met the Bucs, they beat them twenty-eight to ten," Bernard added.

"Yes, but that was a home game," Dick objected. "This next one's in Tampa."

"I'll give you that," Bernard agreed. "And I think the home-ground advantage will give the Bucs something, but not enough."

"Glad to hear you agree with me, er, I didn't catch your name?" the colonel asked.

"Bernard," he replied. "I gather that the captain here is Dick, and you sir?"

"Bill, are you from Tremonton?" the colonel replied and asked.

"No, just passing through on my way back to Salt Lake. I peddle for a company that sells woodworking machinery," Bernard lied, hoping that his cousin would cover for him if anyone checked up on him. He presumed that any mention of newspapers would drive these two away faster than a skunk at a picnic.

"Do you pass through here regularly?" Bill asked.

"Yes, I've a pretty standard route," Bernard confessed.

"Okay, we'll see you here the same time next week and see who is right," Bill promised.

"Do you two guys work around here?" Bernard asked.

"Unfortunately," Bill replied. "But we are under the gun right now. You may have seen the news items about the incident at the LST plant, well, we're from there!"

"That looked pretty bad," Bernard commented. "I'm sorry for you guys if you have to deal with that."

"We'd be fine if it weren't for all the help we're getting right now from everybody and their brother," Bill complained.

11

"I imagine that there's a lot of interest," Bernard commented. "Are you taking a break from there right now? I would have thought that the pressure would be on to be at the site full-time?"

"Hell yes," Bill confirmed. "But we've just come from a meeting with brass at Hill. As for the rest, we can't move for people and the press; don't get me started on the press, bunch of bloody vultures all hovering around to be in on the kill when they pin the blame on some poor bastard!"

"I don't know, Bill," Dick said. "I think the TV station people are worse; they're forever shoving microphones in your face and trying to look important and intelligent when they're on camera."

"You're right about that, Dick," Bill agreed. "You know, Bernard, we've got some people from one of the networks camped outside our gate just waiting for people to go off shift and see if they can get anything out of them."

"Sir, we'd better go," Dick interrupted. "We've an appointment with the colonel from San Bernardino at ten."

"Right," agreed Bill. "We'll see you next week, then Bernard and see if your predictions are good!"

"Hey guys, I've just realised that next week is Thanksgiving, so it'll have to be two weeks from now," Bernard said.

"So, what's your prediction for the next game?" Bill asked.

"Bears over the Packers, sixteen to zip!" Bernard predicted.

"Sixteen points?" Bill and Dick both asked.

"My money will be on it," Bernard promised.

The two Air Force officers left, and Bernard paid his check and then went out to his car. The men that he had first noticed had not all gone, and two remained in deep discussion. They asked Bernard whether he was with the Air Force because he had been talking to the officers, but he assured them that he was just an innocent traveller who had an interest in football. With that, they both left in their pickup trucks, leaving Bernard to wonder why they had asked him about being with the Air Force. He also mulled over in his mind why the Air Force officers should have gone to Hill Air Force Base and what was in San Bernardino.

His editor was pleased with the pictures and told him to cultivate the Air Force officers and, if possible, find some contacts in the surrounding towns that might be willing to talk. He agreed with Bernard that bars were as good a place to start as anywhere. Although this was largely Mormon country, there were still bars and not all the LST employees were likely to be paid-up members of the church. Bernard called Colleen and asked her if she had any more information. She did, she had lists of all the programs the different companies were involved in and basic descriptions of the rockets and their sizes. Obviously, she had been busy! Perhaps the research department was useful after all, and he had been a fool not to use their resources before.

"Where did you get all this stuff?" Bernard asked.
"Well, I called a classmate of mine who's in Washington, and she called a friend of hers at the Pentagon and voilà!" she replied.
"So what is the program that we're most interested in?" he asked.
"I don't know," she admitted. "I couldn't find out much; my source suggested that it might be the Auriga program, which is a competitor to the Morton Thiokol and others' SICBM or Midgetman."
"What's an SICBM?" he asked.
"I gather it's a small intercontinental ballistic missile," she explained. "I understand that it's got one warhead that is nuclear and can probably hit anywhere in the Soviet Union in a matter of minutes."
"How big is it?" he asked.
"I understand that it's a few stages and that all the stages could be made by LST. The first stage weighs about twenty thousand pounds, and the other stages are all progressively slightly less," she replied.
"That's pretty big," Bernard commented.
"Oh no," she demurred. "The Space Shuttle booster is over a million pounds, and the first stages that Morton makes for the Air Force and the Navy are both close to ninety or a hundred thousand pounds. The Morton first stage of the Midgetman is about twenty thousand pounds, so it makes sense that this Auriga missile should be in competition with the Midgetman."
"Does this Auriga or the Midgetman go in a silo?" he asked.
"I wasn't able to find that out, but I suppose it must because that's the way the Air Force deploys their missiles," she said. "My contact told me

that she couldn't get any more information, and she was only guessing as to the program. Everything you have there is in the public domain. I'm uneasy about digging too deeply and abusing the trust of friends."

"Don't you wonder why the Air Force has two programs for something?" he asked.

"Yes," she agreed. "But it was explained to me that the Congress gets involved and they like to abuse their committee positions by funnelling funds and work to their own Congressional Districts. Then they also wrote a bunch of laws about competition, which are in conflict with common sense."

"I take it that the government makes it all more complicated than it really needs to be," he commented. "And, because it's more complicated, it's more expensive and takes longer to get anything done!"

"I suppose so," she agreed. "But what do they care? They get paid no matter what and forget about trying to unseat one of them after they're elected. To them, it's just numbers on paper, and it's only us poor idiots that have to pay the taxes to keep them in the manner to which they quickly accustom themselves."

"You're right about that," Bernard agreed. "It pisses me off how everything they do and say is calculated to work towards re-election!"

Well, we won't change it bitching about it," Colleen laughed.

"You're right, Colleen," Bernard agreed. "I think that's enough for the day. I've about had it, and I'm hungry. Do you fancy getting a bite to eat?"

"Okay," she said. "I'll just get my coat and meet you at the elevator."

Well, things might be looking up, Bernard thought. She was a little older than he, but what the hell! Here it was a Friday night, and she apparently did not have a date, or her regular boyfriend, if she had one, was unavailable or something.

Over dinner, Bernard asked Colleen about herself and learned that she was a journalism major from Utah State. She liked being a researcher. It gave her the opportunity to look into all kinds of things. She shared a small house on the east side of Kaysville, just into the benches. Then she shifted the conversation to him.

"You're not married?" she asked him.

"No," Bernard confessed. "I've had a few steady girlfriends, but they all seem to want things that I'm not sure I do."

"Such as?" she asked.

"Well, children for one," he explained.

"There's nothing wrong with you not wanting children," she agreed. "You've no idea how many people keep asking me why I'm not married and when am I going to get married and have children."

"And you're not married?" Bernard asked, looking for confirmation.

"No, I was engaged once to a young guy when he had just come back from his mission. But I soon saw that his notion of a life wasn't quite mine, and I called it off," she replied.

"Look, I don't want you to think I'm being overly pushy," Bernard started. "But can I buy you a drink somewhere?"

"No, thank you, Bernard," she said. "I really have to be going; my partner is expecting me."

"Let me just get the check then," Bernard offered. He also digested the partner snippet and decided that she was living in sin with some man and did not want to discuss it.

When Colleen arrived home, her partner, Isabella, who had been working late at her office, was still up, and she asked about the day and the evening. Colleen gave her a quick summary of the day and what she had learned through their friend Sigourney in Washington. Isabella suggested a couple of other avenues that she might try, none of which were traceable back to her and all of which were in the public domain. It was really just a question of knowing where to look and what to ask about.

"I think Bernard fancies me and is trying to hit on me," Colleen commented.

"Well, he's going to be disappointed, isn't he?" Isabella stated.

"Oh my heck, yes," Colleen laughed. "I wonder why men all seem to assume that you'd be enormously thrilled to go out with them?"

"It's part biological and part societal," Isabella thought. "They're trained at an early age to expect that everyone will be bowled over by their charm, masculinity and whatever."

"Well, Bernard thinks he has it!" Colleen laughed. "I almost feel sorry for the guy."

Interviews

When James went to the office the following Monday, there was a message from someone called Charles Evans at Taylor and Baldwin, a large search firm from Chicago. It was one that James had not used in the past, but he had heard of them. They were typically better known in the chemical and food industries. James called the number and asked to speak to Evans, who took his call immediately.

"Hi James, do you go by James or Jim? This is Chuck Evans. I was given your name by Ron Pearson, and he suggested I call you," he started.

"That was kind of Ron," James commented. "I go by James generally. What may I do for you?"

"It's rather more along the lines of what we may be able to do for you," Chuck laughed. "I gather from Ron that you are free at the moment?"

"Yes," James agreed. "I was running Waterford Industries until the sale, and the new owners brought their own guy over from England, and there really wasn't the need for two leaders."

"Sure, I've seen it before," said Chuck. "Well, here's the deal. We have a client who has asked for confidentiality at this moment, who is looking for a senior executive to run an aerospace division of about two hundred million in sales annually."

"When you say aerospace, what are we talking about?" James asked.

"Well, it's pretty high-tech stuff with a diverse set of technologies," Chuck hedged.

"Where is the operation?" James asked.

"Can't really say just now," Chuck apologised. "But look, I've got your résumé and it's pretty impressive. Why don't you hop on a plane to Chicago tomorrow and come and see us on Wednesday morning, and we can talk about things. There'll be a ticket waiting for you at the American counter at John Wayne for the seven o'clock flight tomorrow morning. We've also got you a flight back on Wednesday afternoon, so you'll be home for Thanksgiving."

"I could do that," James agreed. "Is there anything else I can tell you in the meantime?"

"Not at the moment, this is kind of a rush job, and I'd rather do everything here. I'll see you Wednesday, then at eight, just check in with the receptionist at our building on Michigan Avenue, and she'll direct you where to go. We'd like you to stay at the Fairmont, in fact, I'll make a reservation for you when we hang up and don't worry about the charges, we'll cover all that," Chuck elaborated.

"Fine," James agreed. "I'll see you Wednesday at eight."

With that, Chuck hung up, and James called Katrina to tell her the news. Katrina wanted to know who the company was and where the job would be, neither of which questions James could answer. He then called Ron Pearson and thanked him for the referral and asked if Ron had any ideas as to who it could be. Ron speculated for a while and then remembered something that Evans had inadvertently let drop and had immediately tried to cover up and gloss over. Ron told James that some kind of accident had prompted the change. James suggested to Ron that the LST explosion might be a possibility, and they then both went off to research the operation. James came up with the information first. The size was about right; the Missile Systems Division of LST was somewhere around two hundred million in revenues, the technologies were varied, anything from composite case construction to mixing of propellants to machining of metallic parts.

James had met the president of LST before, but otherwise knew little else about the details of the company. He found what he could about the company and its various divisions and made himself up a dossier to take with him and read before the Wednesday meeting. Obviously, there was only a chance that this was the client, but it seemed a pretty good bet. He called Ron back and they traded information. Ron had managed to acquire an organisation chart and said that he would fax it to James before lunch. He also suggested picking up the 10-K and 10-Q reports of the parent company, Waterway Chemicals, a Houston-based company; they would tell him more about the company. Even better if he could find it quickly, the proxy would give him management information. Ron went on to say that they might be jumping to the wrong conclusion. The accident had only occurred about a week earlier, and for the company to be already looking for a new leader seemed unlikely, but if it were true, they were moving extremely rapidly. If it really were true, then someone had dropped a clanger, as the Brits

17

would say and needed to be moved out fast. James thanked Ron for his time and input and then called a friend he knew in the securities business and arranged to have copies of the various 10-K and 10-Q reports delivered to him at the Fairmont in Chicago. James stopped by the office of the counsellor that he had been working with him and gave her the news that he had an interview in Chicago. She wished him luck and asked him to keep her informed.

At home that afternoon, James told Katrina about his telephone conversations with Ron and their suspicion that it might be LST that was looking for a new manager. Katrina wondered why they just did not promote someone from within, as that had to be cheaper than flying potential candidates all over the country. They went back over the newspapers for the past week that they had to see if there were any further stories about the accident, but found little. It was almost as if everything had dried up, and after the initial burst of publicity, a lid had been put on the situation.

"What do you think about moving to Utah?" James asked Katrina.
"I'm not sure," she temporised. "Where in Utah?"
"Let me get an atlas and show you where I think it is," he suggested. "If I'm right about this job opportunity, the job would be in the northern part of the state, somewhere near Idaho, and I suppose we would live somewhere between Brigham City and Salt Lake City."
"Is it cold?" she wondered.
"I'm not sure, probably not as cold as Wisconsin," he thought. "I went a few times to the Bingham Canyon mine when we first came here, and it never struck me as too bad."
"Utah, isn't that all Mormons?" she asked.
"I'm not sure," he admitted. "It's where the whole Mormon religion ended up after they were hounded out of Missouri, but what proportion of the population is Mormon, I've no idea."
"Mormons, aren't they the ones that don't drink and have more than one wife?" she continued.
"They aren't supposed to drink," he confirmed. "And as for polygamy, I think that's rather gone away these days."
"Just don't get any ideas if we go there!" she warned.

"I wouldn't dream of it," he promised. "I've enough on my plate with one *ou frou*, I couldn't manage any more."

"Less of the *ou frou* stuff," she threatened. "And just what do you think you're doing?"

"I'm just exploring," he said.

"Well, keep doing what you're doing and we'll be forced to see if you can satisfy this *meisie*!" she promised.

The next day, James drove down the 55 freeway to the Orange County airport and collected his ticket from the American Airlines counter. The flight to Chicago was a little under four hours, so put him into O'Hare just after one in the afternoon. He debated about taking one of the trains into Chicago, but decided to be extravagant and take a taxi. At the Fairmont, his package of information was waiting, and he took it to his room to read. He called Katrina to tell her that he had arrived. She had news for him.

"These *ouks* you're going to see must be serious, James," she said. "You've had four phone calls today from people you've worked with, all telling me that they've been contacted by this search firm."

"Brother," commented James. "Taylor and Baldwin must have worked hard to find all the people I've worked with in the past."

"Well, I suppose it's a good thing," thought Katrina. "At least you'll get good reports from the people they called. But I thought they did reference checking after the interviews?"

"Normally, yes," James agreed. "This is a little unusual, but they said they were in a hurry."

The Taylor and Baldwin offices were only a short walk from the hotel, which was just as well, because it was cold. The wind was blowing from the southwest and seemed to cut right through the coat that James was wearing. He had almost forgotten what winter could be like in the Midwest, and this was only late in November. James had wondered if he might see other candidates for the job at the hotel, but with the swarm of 'Bright Young Men' that he saw in the lobby of the hotel, there was no way to know which of them might be of interest. As promised, the receptionist in the building directed him to the appropriate floor, and he was met off the elevator.

"James, hi, Chuck Evans," was the greeting. Chuck was a sincere-looking person about his own height and weight, but a little older. Chuck led the way to a conference room and introduced him.

"Larry Hill, meet James Martin. James is the guy that Ron Pearson recommended we call regarding the Delta project," he explained.

"Pleased to meet you, James," Larry said. "Have a seat, coffee or something else?"

"Coffee would be fine, thanks," James assured them. Larry struck him as appearing even more sincere than Chuck Evans, if that was possible, the kind of person who would tell you what he thought you wanted to hear, but from whom you would never actually get any real answers. Answers might be given that sounded plausible, even believable, but they were always questionable.

"Sorry, we can't be more specific about the assignment yet," Larry apologised. "We'll need clearance from the client before we reveal who and what it is."

"I understand," said James. "Apart from the fact that it is aerospace and has revenues of about two hundred million, what else can you tell me?"

"Well, there's about thirteen hundred employees at the site, and it's non-union," Chuck offered.

"How many times do you get asked if you make glassware?" Larry asked.

"Quite a few," James admitted. "I usually take the time to explain the difference between Waterford Industries and Waterford Crystal, but there are times when the question seems a little redundant."

"I guess that could be aggravating," Larry agreed. "But I suppose there are other companies that are diverse, like Kaman with helicopters and guitars, Moog with actuators and the music synthesiser and the big French glass outfit, what's it called?"

"Saint-Gobain," James offered.

"That's it. Anyway, tell us a little about yourself, James?" asked Larry.

James went through a brief version of his career to date, beginning with the most recent and going back in time. They were particularly interested to learn how he had adapted to new situations with different technologies. He spent some time explaining the technologies of the different companies he had worked for and the challenges presented in

20

each case. They also wanted a more detailed explanation of his familiarity with explosives and what he had actually done with them. The conversation then switched to the types of customers that Waterford Industries had and to what level he had dealt with those customers, merely at the buyer level in purchasing or at the engineering and program management levels. They seemed particularly impressed that he had been to meetings of the different aerospace associations and mingled, if only peripherally, with the chief executives of major aerospace companies.

He was asked all the usual questions about leadership style, perceived strengths and weaknesses, things he felt he could improve, etc, etc, all of which he was sure were just thrown in to see how he handled the idea that he might actually be wrong occasionally. James had long ago come to the conclusion that people with what he called CEO disease knew in their hearts that they could never be wrong; that is what made them, in their minds at least, good CEO material. Whether or not they were looking for this level of ego for this job or whether they just wanted someone to kick ass, take names and generally sort things out, he could not judge yet. They then asked about his ability and willingness to move, and he assured them that that would not be an issue. Finally, they asked if he had any questions.

"Obviously, you can't tell me yet who your client is, but perhaps you could explain the hurry?" James asked. The other two looked at each other, and he got the impression that they were mentally drawing lots to see who would answer that one. Apparently, Larry won or lost.
"There have arisen circumstances that make it expedient for the company to make certain changes, including but not limited to management changes," Larry intoned.
"That sounds like a legal speech," James joked.
"In a way it is," Larry agreed. "I'm really sorry we cannot be more specific, but the circumstances dictate more than the usual degree of circumspection."
"The company doesn't happen to be LST, does it?" James asked. He caught the momentary look of alarm in the eyes of both of them and knew that his guess was right. Larry might be sincere, but he would

make a poor CEO. He just did not have the ability to believe in his own infallibility. Chuck was just a poor poker player and wore his emotions on his sleeve.

"We could not possibly engage in any speculation as to the identity of the client," Larry explained. "Would you be free for an early lunch before you fly back to Orange County?"

James was reminded of a Zambian Army colonel he had known once who was a master at changing the subject. Perhaps Colonel Mulanga and Larry Hill had both been to the same school of dissembling, but Larry did not have the charm that the colonel had, nor the ability to make the subject change seem like the natural course of the conversation. He dropped the subject and enthusiastically endorsed the idea of lunch.

Over lunch, Larry told James that the next step would be for him to meet the client. They would arrange that and also disclose the identity of the client after they had reported back on the results of their interviews. Larry made it sound as if they were presenting a slate of three or four candidates for the client to interview. James then asked if the client might not be missing some really good talent because of their drive for speed. The others agreed that that was certainly a risk, but they felt comfortable that they would be presenting the client with options that were feasible. When they parted, Chuck promised to call James on Monday with news and possible details about the next step.

From the O'Hare airport, James called Ron Pearson and then Katrina and reported on his morning. He told them both about his question about LST and the reaction he got. For Ron, that confirmed their suspicions, and he promised to call James over the week. He planned to call a couple of friends of his and see what he could find out about the operation and the people who were there. James already had the 10-Qs, 10-Ks and the proxy, so he knew who the senior management of the parent company was, but unfortunately, those documents did not reveal much about the local management. On the plane ride back to Orange County, James read through the annual report carefully and noted the comments about the different divisions, particularly the rocket operations. He knew now who he would be likely to meet the following week and trusted that Ron could come up with some background.

James and Katrina spent a quiet Thanksgiving. James cooked dinner while Katrina watched and gave advice. They had received three invitations to dinner at friends' houses but had decided to spend it quietly on their own. James was not ready to talk about his potential opportunity yet, and he was sure that any conversation would have been quickly steered in that direction by their friends, who were all well-meaning and concerned. He and Katrina did discuss it, though, and at length. They had been through a few job changes and the related moves before; the biggest being the move from Zambia to the US in the mid-seventies. Katrina told James that if he thought that would be the best move for them, then she was in favour. Her only concern was what Utah was like as a place to live.

*   *   *

"Colleen, how was your Thanksgiving?" Bernard asked.
"Replete with family squabbles and swarms of obnoxious children," she commented. "How about you?"
"I spent it with my cousin and his family," he said. "I've sort of borrowed my cousin's identity for a while when I schmooze the Air Force," Bernard explained. "I figured they wouldn't talk to a reporter, but if I can be in the woodworking machine business, I'm harmless. Maybe you'd better dig up some stuff for me on home woodworking shops and the kinds of equipment people use?"
"I can do that," she promised.
"His Holiness, the editor, has given me the green light to cultivate the colonel and see if we can't get something out of him," Bernard commented. "Maybe I can work on his football fantasy and get him exposed to some real money; that might put him in an awkward spot."
"I thought they were all supposed to be such straight arrows?" Colleen asked.
"I think they're straight as long as there's a superior around, if not, then they're probably pretty human!" Bernard thought.

23

"I heard a rumour from a friend in Logan that the LST problem started in a mixer," Colleen said.

"A mixer, what are we talking about, a cement mixer type thing, a bucket and wheelbarrow, or what?" Bernard asked.

"I'm not sure," she admitted. "Why don't I dig a little and see what kind of mixers they are. Oh, and wasn't the Morton problem in 1985 a mixer problem?"

"I don't remember," he admitted. "I wonder what those mixers look like?"

"I heard another rumour," she added.

"What?" he asked.

"I heard that LST's parent company engaged a headhunter to replace the current boss of that division," she elaborated.

"Where did you hear that?" Bernard asked, a little agog that she had managed to get such information.

"Well, I've a friend who let something drop about a panel of possibles being interviewed this week," she explained.

"Colleen, you're a marvel!" Bernard exclaimed.

"Just doing my job," she said, downplaying her achievements.

"You're enjoying this assignment, aren't you?" he asked.

"You bet," she confirmed. "It'll be even better when we can get some hooks into someone from the site."

"Well, we'll see," Bernard promised.

As she left the office, Bernard watched in admiration. She had a way about her that was alluring and seductive. He had a really hard time believing that she was not married and wondered if there was something in her personality and makeup that made her impossible to live with. He weighed up her assets and liabilities, and all he came up with were assets. She was really attractive, well put together, had her own house, had a job, and was intelligent. Ah, maybe that was the problem. She was intelligent, not just a girl with big hair who would have had six kids before she was twenty-five. She probably scared the shit out of most of the Mormon guys who, in his opinion, just wanted baby machines. Well, perhaps that was a little unjust. His own cousin only had two kids and did not want any more. He simply could not afford any more.

James got a phone call on Monday afternoon from Larry asking him if he would be available to go to Salt Lake City for an interview with the client. Larry disclosed that the client was Waterway Chemicals, the parent company of LST, but that the first interview with the company would be at the LST level. Larry had made reservations for James to fly on Tuesday morning to Salt Lake City for an interview at two on Tuesday afternoon. He also advised that he had made reservations at a hotel in Salt Lake City and to prepare for possible follow-up interviews on Wednesday. It looked as if they were trying to narrow down their slate of candidates quickly. As his interview was not until two and he was scheduled to arrive at ten, James had a couple of hours to kill, so he called Steve, a college classmate, who worked at Kennecott and suggested lunch. Steve said that he would pick James up at the airport and drive him into the city to the hotel where they could get lunch.

James went home and gave Katrina his news. She had been busy and had got maps and brochures about Utah from the AAA office in Anaheim Hills, and wanted James to show her on a map exactly where the factory was. He had to admit that he was not certain, but knew that it was somewhere towards the north of the state, near the Idaho State line and northwest of a town called Tremonton. That put it in a fairly remote part of the state, away from any major conurbation, which brought up the obvious question of where they would live if they actually moved to Utah. James said that was a question he would bring up with the LST people.

The Delta flight to Salt Lake City left from Orange County and was a little under two hours. For the most part, it followed the I-15 freeway north from Las Vegas until just before Salt Lake City, then it took a more westerly path as it entered the approach pattern. Their descent into the Salt Lake airport took them over the Kennecott mine of Bingham Canyon, and James wondered how Steve was doing. He had not seen him for a few years since he had essentially moved on from the mining industry into more industrial and aerospace-related companies.

25

Steve was there to meet him at the gate, a little heavier than before and with a lot less hair. Steve laughed about that and commented that his hard hat usually covered the evidence.

"There's a lot of *oukies* in suits hanging around," James remarked.

"It's Tuesday and the day for young guys to leave on their missions," Steve explained. "That's why there are so many people. They're all seeing little Jimmy off to convert the world. Check the badges and you'll see, Elder Smith or whatever their name is."

"What about girls? Do they go on missions, too?" James asked.

"A few," Steve replied. "They are usually older than the guys, and they're not elders but sisters. Anyway, that explains all the people!"

"Wow, *maningi bantu*," James commented on the number of people there were in the terminal.

"Remember, James, this is Utah, and big families are the norm, the only place where a BMW is actually a Chevy Suburban!" Steve laughed.

"What?" James asked, a little puzzled.

"BMW, basic Mormon wheels," Steve explained. "Three rows of seats and three or sometimes four to a row."

"What about you?" James asked.

"Only two, both girls," Steve replied. "I can't afford any more."

The drive into the city centre was quick, not too much traffic and no snow. At the hotel, James noticed a man and a woman looking at all the people coming in as if they were looking for someone. Apparently, he did not fit the bill, for whatever reason. He and Steve found the restaurant and talked about mundane matters until the food came.

"So, what brings you to Salt Lake?" Steve asked.

"Keep this under your hat," James cautioned. "I've got an interview this afternoon with LST."

"So, they're replacing the division manager where they had the accident," Steve commented.

"Right," James agreed. "What do you know about them?"

"They've got a reasonable reputation in the state," Steve began. "But they do hire and fire like a typical aerospace company, a program dies and then it's one week's notice and you're out of here!"

"That's a little 60s, don't you think?" James asked.

26

"True, but there are times when I think I've stepped back twenty or thirty years here," Steve laughed.

"But what about living here, what's that like?" James asked.

"Actually, not bad at all," Steve thought. "I like to ski and the skiing is the best. The education system's not bad, the weather is okay, not southern California, but much better than Hibbing or the Upper Peninsula."

"What about the Mormon influence?" James wanted to know.

"Actually, apart from some odd elements of their belief system, it's not too bad," Steve commented. "Their basic ethic of work and family is fine, and their welfare system beats the Federal or State welfare systems every way possible. I wish the Feds could do on ten per cent what these guys can. My only real beef is that their women tend to be treated as servants to the men, but all the wives I've met go along with that, so I figure it's their *indaba*."

"So, you have no problems living here?" James pressed.

"On balance, no," Steve admitted. "I've lived in worse places and met far worse groups of people. There are few problems with alcohol or drugs, except the abuse of prescription drugs and over-the-counter things like cough medicine."

"Why cough medicine?" James asked.

"Alcohol," Steve replied. "It's a covert way to drink without being caught at the State Liquor Stores by the local Bishop, or your neighbours who will shop you to the Bishop."

"How does that work?" James asked, curious about the liquor laws.

"Well, the State runs stores for the sale of booze. The stores all seem to me to be in the less desirable parts of town and are cash only, no checks, no credit cards," Steve explained.

"Maybe that's to protect the fallen Mormons from having their names traced," James laughed.

"Maybe, but if you go to buy booze, remember to take cash!" Steve advised.

"So how are things at Kennecott?" James asked.

"We're about to be sold again," Steve told him. "BP is rumoured to be having talks with RTZ about selling off the Minerals Division to them."

"What will that mean for you?" James asked.

"Less dickheads and more mining guys," Steve laughed. "My sense is if RTZ buys us, they will invest, whereas BP is going through one of your classic diversify/consolidate cycles. They have woken up to the fact that they're an oil company and they're getting focused back on oil, not a bad thing to do really."

"Could you run me over to the LST offices?" James asked. "They're on 9th South."
"No problem, what are you doing tonight?" Steve asked.
"I'm not sure; do you have a number where you can be reached?" James asked.
"Sure, here's my card, and my home number is on the back," Steve said, handing over a card. "If you're ready, we can go?"

At the LST offices, James checked in at the lobby and was directed to the ninth floor, where he was met by another receptionist. He had noticed someone he knew leaving the foyer when he first arrived downstairs and guessed that he was another of the potential candidates. The receptionist ushered him into the boardroom, where there were three men, all probably in their early sixties, all with grey hair and all with a little middle-aged or old age spread. One of them, James, already knew from his attendance at various aerospace association meetings. He was Robert Warner, the president of LST.
"James, please have a seat. Let me do the introductions," Robert said. "This is John Robertson, our CFO, and this is Ken Butler, our VP of HR. Thanks for coming on such short notice."
"It was no problem," James assured them.
"We gather that you're looking for a position right now," Ken asked.
"Yes, after the sale of Waterford Industries, the Brits brought over their own president, and there really was no spot for me," James explained.
"I've met the guy," Robert commented. "A complete moron, trust me, you're better off out of there. Once I heard that he had come over and that you were out, I was looking for an opportunity to get you into our organisation. This turned out to be that opportunity. I just wish it hadn't involved the deaths of the poor guys out there in the desert."

"So, tell us a little about yourself," invited John. For the next three hours, James talked and answered questions about his career to date, his life, his aspirations, strengths, weaknesses, etc, etc.

They then asked James if he had any questions, and he started with the obvious ones: why was the position open, and what had happened to the incumbent? Robert took that one and went through a summary of the events following their accident. He pitched it as an LST-driven change, but James got the impression that both the corporate office and the customers were not happy and had directed the change. He did learn that Dean Anderson, the incumbent, was on paid leave and would depart the company as soon as a successor had been named. They were most anxious to get back into production and to find out what had gone wrong and caused the fire and subsequent explosion.

At close to five, Robert indicated that he wanted to wrap things up, and he had one final question.
"You have an active secret clearance?" he asked.
"Yes, or at least I suppose it's still active. I doubt that Waterford has deactivated it yet because I'm still on their books."
"Well, we can get that transferred over easily enough," Robert commented. "And we'd better get it upgraded to TS."
"What are your plans for dinner?" John asked.
"I have none," James said.
"Would you join Robert and me for dinner then?" John continued.
"I'd be happy to," James assured him.
"Okay then, why don't you give us a few minutes? Becky will show you to an office where you can admire the view and wait. We'll pick you up on the way out and go straight to the restaurant," Robert said.

James waited in a nearby office and made a quick telephone call to Steve to tell him that he would be busy that evening after all. When Robert came to collect him, they took the elevator down to the basement and the parking that was there. From there, they drove to the restaurant that was perched on what they called the benches, which James learned was actually an old beach from the ancient lake that once filled most of the valley. Apparently, earth movements had allowed most of the water to drain away, leaving the current Great Salt Lake, with inlets but no outlet, hence the salinity.

Over dinner, James asked again about the management change, and Robert admitted that it was a directed change, one that he had come to realise was necessary. He was concerned with the operations at the Missile Systems Division and said that what they really needed was a new broom to sweep away the old attitudes. That was going to be quite a task because many of the division management had been there for years and would be resistant to change. John wanted to know if James had had any experience with rocket propellants before, to which the answer was an obvious no, but James reminded him that he had dealt with explosives before, from his days as a mining engineer, so nitroglycerin was not unknown to him, nor were the headaches that came as a result of handling it.

The following day, LST sent a driver to pick James up at the hotel, and they then picked up Robert and drove north to the factory site. Their drive took them past Ogden and Brigham City, then Tremonton and the split between the I-15 and I-84 freeways. From Tremonton, it was only a short ten miles up the hill until they turned off the I-84 freeway onto a side road that went north into the hills. James commented to Robert that it was a little different to driving in the LA basin. There, there could be up to eight lanes of traffic in each direction, all doing either seventy-five miles an hour or five miles an hour, whereas in northern Utah, it was two lanes in each direction with perhaps one car or truck every five minutes. The other difference was the snow. It was falling, not heavily, but enough to accumulate on the road, and it was cold enough that it was not melting. James wondered how much there would be when they left to go back to the airport and whether the Utah Highways Department ploughed the freeway or not.

The LST gate was about three miles into the mountains and screened from the freeway by some hills. Once inside the gate, they stopped briefly at an office to sign in and then drove around the site. Considering that there were supposed to be 1,300 people at the division, they were not at all evident. Obviously, because it was a three-shift operation, a number would be off at that time, but even so, there seemed to be too few people. Robert pointed out that a lot of the operations people were scattered in small groups around the factory, which was laid out in accordance with the quantity/distance rules for separation of buildings that had explosives in them. That brought to mind a question that James had been puzzling about for some time. Why were there thirteen people killed in the accident? He asked about a typical mix crew and learned that it would have been less than half that number, including the driver of the delivery truck. So, what had happened that there were twice as many people as expected? Robert said that that was one of the answers they were trying to get, that, plus what had actually caused the explosion.

They drove to the site of the recent explosion and looked over the crater and the debris field around it.

"I suppose it was fortunate that the hills directed the blast up and to the south and therefore away from the other buildings," James commented.

"Yes," Robert agreed. "We're lucky in that the topography favours isolated buildings, lots of nice little hills and canyons in which to put high-risk operations."

"Was there much other damage?" James asked.

"A few windows out here and there and some cracks in masonry walls, and we did get some debris from the blast that came through the roofs of a few buildings," Robert replied. "I think we were lucky that it was this mixer and not one of the others that are less shielded by natural revetments."

"How much was in the mix?" James asked.

"Well, if all the constituents were in the mix bowl, then about 8,800 lbs," Robert estimated.

James quickly did the conversion to kilos, as his own explosives experience had all been in Africa, where they used kilos instead of pounds. "So, about 4,000 kilos?" he asked.

"I suppose so, yes," Robert confirmed. "You think in terms of kilos then?"

"When it comes to this," James confirmed. "The biggest shots I ever set off were 120 cases of dynamite at 25 kilos per case underground and the equivalent of 400 cases in a surface mine. I once blew up a building to get rid of it and did not use anywhere near that amount! I almost wrote myself off, too, because I didn't anticipate how far the shrapnel would go as the steel in the building came apart!"

"I suppose we all learn from our mistakes," Robert laughed.

"Yes," James agreed. "But, there are times when the margin between mistake and disaster is thin."

"Well, that's the plant," Robert said. "I suppose we ought to leave before too many people become curious."

"So, what's the next step?" James asked as they drove back to Salt Lake City and the airport for his flight home.

"Could you be in Houston on Friday?" Robert asked. "You'll probably have to stay overnight. Is that okay?"

"Of course," James agreed. "When, where and how?"

"We'll make a reservation for you and have a ticket available at the Orange County airport. When you get to Houston, rent a car. Here's the address of the office and the directions. When you get there, ask for Jane Lewis, she's the VP of HR," were the instructions that Robert gave. He then added, "I expect you'll also meet John Hiller, our CEO and perhaps Mark Green, the CFO. Call me after you're done! Here's my home number in case you run late. Don't worry about the time when you call, I'll be up."

"Okay," James agreed. "Any words of wisdom or advice when dealing with those guys?"

"Just remember that they're chemical guys and don't do much in the way of government contracting. We're the only significant part of the business that is involved with the government, and there are times when they would rather not be. So if a potential buyer came along with the right money, we'd be gone," Robert commented. "Anyway, good luck on Friday, I'd like to have you on our team!"

From the airport, James called Katrina and gave her a rundown on the day and told her that he would be going to Houston on Friday for the next round of interviews. He also told her that they were talking about upgrading his security clearance, which probably would mean people would be calling their friends and neighbours with odd questions about their drinking and sex habits. That had happened before, and a couple of their friends had called to ask what it was all about. James did wonder why they needed to upgrade the clearance to top secret, but supposed that it had something to do with the fact that the company made ballistic missile segments, and therefore was perhaps a little more sensitive than most of the programs he had been involved with at Waterford Industries.

*   *   *

On Friday morning, Bernard and Colleen reviewed their situation. Colleen had been tipped off that the potential candidates for the new manager were going to be put up at a particular hotel in Salt Lake City, a place that she found disturbing because it always seemed to her to be decorated in some man's warped dream of a French hotel of less than seemly repute. She and Bernard had camped out in the lobby for a couple of days and had studied the comings and goings. They had picked out three possible candidates and had confirmed names with the desk clerk that Bernard knew. It was a quick job to contact one of the search people that Bernard had used in the past, who lacked integrity and tie names to current employers and occupations. They had seen many others that were possibles but had dismissed them for various reasons. They had actually looked over James Martin, but as he came in with a Kennecott employee, having arrived in a Kennecott truck, concluded that James was in no way connected to LST.

Bernard had wondered about the normal crew size for mixing operations and decided to ask the Air Force lieutenant colonel what the standard crew size was. He and Colleen drove north to Tremonton to meet the Air Force at the diner they frequented. He had talked over his plan of attack with Colleen and had asked her to wear something tight that would draw attention. She tried out a couple of different looks and they agreed on a red sweater, black skin-tight pants and knee-high boots. Colleen had also researched the home woodworking machinery business, and they both were now quite conversant with the machines and their functions. The snow that had fallen earlier in the week had been ploughed from the road, but it had accumulated on the hills, and the Wasatch Front range was covered in a heavy blanket of new snow.

Colleen confessed that she had toyed with the idea of calling in sick so that she could go skiing, but had decided to wait until the weekend.

When they arrived in Tremonton, the Air Force was already at the diner. They waved Bernard over, and he introduced Colleen as his assistant.

"Nice to meet you, Colleen," Bill said and then quickly dismissed her from his mind and attention. "Bernard, you must have a great crystal ball; your predictions on the Bears, Buccaneers and the Bears-Packers games were right on. I made out big time!"

This conversation confirmed Bernard's assessment of the colonel. He was a dedicated and avid gambler. Any normal man would have spent a little more time sounding out Colleen to see if she was attached or not, or at least have gazed in mute admiration, as Captain Dick was now doing. She had stopped all the conversation in the diner when she had walked in and taken off her coat, and there were now wives muttering things about scarlet hussies and kicking their husbands under the tables. For the men there without wives, they just looked.

"So how much did you make?" Bernard asked.

"I was a little conservative, so I only put down a couple of grand," Bill bragged. "But it returned in spades. I probably made fifteen grand! Next time, I think I'll push the boat out a little further!"

"What do you gentlemen do?" Colleen asked.

"We work at the LST plant up the road," Dick replied, because Bill had been lost to the conversation with Bernard about football, point spreads and odds.

"What do you do there?" Colleen asked.

"We make sure that they adhere to the contracts and oversee safety matters and security," Dick said.

"Were you there when they had that accident?" she asked.

"Not at that particular time, but shortly afterwards. It wasn't pleasant," he replied.

"There were thirteen people killed, weren't there? That's terrible," she asked, seeking confirmation.

"Thirteen, yes, and we don't know why there were thirteen there. There should have only been four or five at the most. We're still trying to understand the whole thing," Dick admitted.

"How did it happen?" she asked.

"A mixer blew up," he replied.

"A mixer, what like a KitchenAid?" she asked.

"Almost, but not quite the same," he said. "Actually, it's a Baker Perkins mixer. They also make mixers for bakeries. So, in a way, yes, just like a food mixer, only bigger, six hundred gallons bigger!"

"Does anyone else use that kind of mixer?" she asked.

"I guess bakeries would," Dick thought. "I've never really thought about it."

"Hey, Dick, we need to go!" Bill interrupted. "We have to meet those Canoe U pukes at eleven."

"Remember, Bill, Bears will lose to the Rams in LA by a twenty-point spread!" Bernard predicted.

"I hope you're wrong, but I'll put my money on it that way," Bill said. "See you next week! Bye!"

"What did you learn?" Bernard asked Colleen after the two Air Force officers had left.

"The accident was a mixer that blew up, and there should have only been four or five people there, so they have two mysteries to solve," she replied.

"Do you know what kind of mixer?" Bernard asked.

"Yes, it's made by some company called Baker Perkins, we should look them up. It's like a food mixer, like a Kitchen Aid, only bigger, much bigger. He said six hundred gallons," she replied.

"Do we know what goes in the mixer?" he asked.

"I've no idea, but I'm sure we could get a general idea," she promised.

"What and where is Canoe U?" Bernard wondered. "Is that a program or something?"

"I'll see if I can find anything out," Colleen said. "Can we get out of here now? Some of these guys give me the creeps. They look as if they're the product of marrying a little too close to home!"

"That's only because you're dressed like their image of a scarlet woman," Bernard laughed. "But you're right, let's get out of here."

As they drove south from Tremonton, Bernard suggested to Colleen that they try the slopes at Snowbasin.

"I'd love to," she said. "I put some of my gear in that bag that I put in the trunk."

"Great," Bernard said. "In the season, I always keep some gear in the trunk, you never know when it might be needed. We can rent boots and skis at Snowbasin."

"And who'll pay?" she asked.

"I think the paper can stand a little gear rental and a couple of lift passes," Bernard assured her.

"Okay, fine! How good a skier are you?" she challenged him.

"I think I'm pretty good," he laughed.

"I'll beat you down any slope you pick!" she dared him.

"You think so?" he asked.

"I know so!" she reiterated. "Twenty dollars says so!"

"Fine, you're on!" he said, accepting the challenge. "And no excuses like 'they're not my regular skis, so I'm not used to them', we take things as we find them, agreed?"

"Agreed! But I'll beat you anyway!"

"Back to LST for a minute," Bernard interrupted. "I'm not sure which part of the Air Force our two officers work. Do you think you could find out?"

"I think that should be simple enough," she thought. "I'll call my contact in Washington this weekend."

"Do you have many contacts in Washington?" he asked.

"A few," she admitted. "I know one at the Pentagon, a Congressional staffer and one at the Smithsonian; she's a researcher like me."

"Well, that might be useful in the future," Bernard thought.

"Maybe," she temporised. "Anyway, I'll try and find out how the Air Force guys fit in their organisation."

"Great," Bernard thanked her. "Okay, here's Ogden. Let's find some lunch and then go skiing."

*   *   *

James flew to Houston and made his way to the Waterway Chemicals head office in the downtown area. They had a tower not far from Pennzoil Plaza, but it was nowhere near as striking as the Pennzoil building; it was more like a small version of the First City Tower, without the vertical offset cuts, making it very plain and utilitarian, but serviceable and functional. It was still a lot of steel and glass, but with no particular architectural cachet. James parked in the office parking and checked in at the reception desk. He was quickly passed on to the twentieth floor and another receptionist who guarded and controlled access to the executive suites of the chairman, president and the other officers. James was shown into the boardroom and given coffee. He had only to wait about five minutes before a side door opened and a woman came in. She introduced herself as Jane Lewis, the Vice President of Human Resources.

"Welcome to Houston," she said. "Have you been here before?"

"A few times," James replied.

"What brought you to Houston?" she asked.

"The Offshore Technology Conference," he explained. "When I ran Waterford Industries, we had operations that were involved in different businesses, including some that supplied to offshore rigs and pipeline companies."

"Ah, I see," she commented. "So now it's rockets. What do you know about rockets?"

"Not much, I admit," James said. "But I imagine that there are people who understand the technicalities well enough; what I can offer is direction and organisation."

"Well, we need that," she said. "What about employee relations?"

"I have managed, in the past, to get the people that worked for me to do things they didn't think were possible," he replied.

"John Hiller will be here in a moment," she promised. "He's a chemical guy, more accustomed to dealing with process plants, tankers and large volumes of fluids than bits and pieces. Rockets are one of those other products that we have that really don't fit into the mainstream of the company."

They were interrupted by a man who came in through the same side door that Jane had used. He introduced himself as John Hiller and then sat down to talk to James about the company and what they were doing. His knowledge was either encyclopedic, or he was amazingly good at making things up on the spur of the moment. James rather thought it was the former because too much fit with the information he had picked up from the annual reports that he had read. Occasionally, John would turn to Jane, who made a comment, and James wondered a couple of times how much of that was rehearsed.

Finally, they turned the tables a little and started to ask James about his work experience and his successes and problems. The interview proper went until five, and then John suggested that they get an early dinner. He told James that Jane would take care of him until dinner, including getting him checked into a hotel. He said that they would be joined at dinner by Mark Green and Costanza Albertini, the president of their shipping company. That rather puzzled James. The CFO, he could easily understand, but the shipping company? Perhaps he was a confidante of John Hiller and his advice was sought, or he was the only other executive available at the time. Before they left the office, Jane asked James about his citizenship and security clearance. James told her that he had become a citizen in 1984, and for security, he told her the same thing that he had told Robert Warner. Jane repeated what Robert had said in that she said that it should be easy enough to get it transferred over and that they would need to upgrade it to top secret.

Dinner was at a beef restaurant; they were in Texas after all, and most of the other diners were in the oil and chemical businesses, judging by the snippets of conversation that James could pick up. Their own conversation ranged from James's career and experiences to his views of the world in general. They were particularly interested in his experiences in Zambia and how he had dealt with incidents with explosives. James thought that was reasonable enough because the ingredients for solid rocket motors combined to form what were essentially explosives. James learned quite a lot about the company and the various subsidiaries, which ranged from basic chemicals to paints and adhesives, plus the less obviously related businesses of fibres and rockets.

The shipping company did not only ship the company's feedstocks and chemical products, but also had a general cargo business with a fleet of small freighters around the world. It was the one part of the business not generally run from the United States. It was headquartered in Italy, and the ships were all registered in Malta, typical of the various flags of convenience used in the shipping business. Costanza split his time between Leghorn, or Livorno as he preferred to call it, and Houston. Costanza really did know a lot about ships and shipping. He knew not only their own fleet but also seemed to have an encyclopedic knowledge of shipping in general. He asked James about his trip to South Africa, and he demonstrated his breadth of knowledge by recalling things about the Union Castle line and was able to tell James what had happened to the various boats, which had been sold to breakers' yards and which had been re-flagged, at least temporarily, before also ultimately landing up at breakers' yards. The RMS Pendennis Castle that James had travelled to Africa on had been taken out of service by Union Castle in 1976, only seven years after James had taken his trip. The vessel was sold to Filipino-owned Ocean Queen Navigation Corp., with the idea of converting it to a cruise boat. The Pendennis Castle was moved to Hong Kong to a shipyard for refit in August of 1976, but was not put back into service by the Filipino company. They then sold the boat to a Liberian Company, Kinvarra Bay Shipping, who renamed it Sinbad 1, but it remained laid up. Finally, it was moved from Hong Kong to Kaohsiung, Taiwan and the breaker's yard. James was saddened to hear about the ignominious end of the boat and told a few stories about his trip, but commented that the age of the jet aircraft, particularly the wide-bodied Boeing 747, had quickly spelt the death of mail boats and passenger traffic.

Costanza then asked James if he had ever been to Italy, and James explained that his sister lived near Viareggio, on the coast, west of Florence. That set off a whole discussion about Tuscany and places of interest that they had both been to, from Pisa to La Spezia. He asked James if he spoke any Italian, and James admitted some knowledge but did not go as far as claiming fluency.

After dinner, John began to tell James what they expected of him. First, he told James that the job was his if he wanted it and to work out details of compensation, etc, with Robert Warner. He then started to elaborate on his views of what was wrong with the current organisation and how he thought it should be changed and improved. James thought that it was undermining the authority of Robert Warner a little, but then Robert had shared some of the same concerns.

Jane told James that he would find Ken Butler, the LST VP of Human Resources, supportive, but that if he ever had any concerns to call her directly. James hoped that he would never find himself in that position. Running to the corporate office for help had never been James's style, and he did not want to start now. He asked Jane if she knew the human resources manager at the Missile Systems Division. He noticed the look that she exchanged with John and was then not surprised when she told James that Gene Bonds, the current manager, was less than stimulating. John then reinforced his earlier comments and told James that if he had to make replacements, then he should do so, and sooner rather than later. He told James that Ken Butler or Jane would help him with any issues that arose because of severing of senior staff.

Later that evening, James called Robert Warner and told him that the Houston interview had gone well. Robert already knew and asked if James could be in Utah on Monday to meet and discuss terms of employment. He suggested that James make his own travel arrangements and bring Katrina so that she could look around the area and perhaps do some house-hunting. He told James that he could submit an account for all his travel-related expenses at the end of the week. Then James called Katrina and had a much longer conversation. He gave her the news and then asked if she would be ready to go to Utah on Monday for a house-hunting trip and general tour of the area. Katrina had done some homework and had gathered information on Ogden, Brigham City, Logan and Tremonton, all towns where they might possibly live. Although Ogden was the furthest from the factory, it probably offered the most in terms of services and in diversity, being only about fifty per cent Mormon. James then went through the whole interview and dinner with her, and they talked about what he should ask for in a package. He had learned from his previous jobs and knew a little more now about what to ask to be included, from relocation assistance to change of control protection. He told her when he would be home the following morning and promised to take her out for a celebratory dinner when he got home.

*   *   *

"Hello," Bernard said rather blearily as he answered the telephone. He looked at his bedside clock and saw that it was nine in the morning.

"Good morning, Bernard," came the overly cheerful voice of Colleen. "I trust you slept well?"

"I suppose you've called to gloat?" he muttered. "I wasn't at my best form the other day, and I think the slopes could have been better groomed."

"Excuses, all Bernard," she said. "I have my twenty dollars, and I'll give you the chance to win it back sometime, or would you like to increase the wager?"

"No, no, that's fine," he said, knowing that he could never race Colleen down any kind of ski slope with any hope of beating her. "What's up?"

"Well, here's a mystery for you," she began. "Canoe U."

"Yeah, what is that?" he asked.

"It's the rather less than polite term given by other members of the armed forces for the Naval Academy," she explained.

"So Bill and Dick were going off to meet Navy guys?" he asked, seeking confirmation.

"Probably," she confirmed. "I suppose it's possible that a graduate of the Naval Academy would go into another service, but not likely."

"So what was the Navy doing at LST? I thought all their business was with the Air Force," he asked.

"I called my friend at the Pentagon," she said. "And she said that they might be just there for an inter-service information exchange, like something she called JANNAF."

"What's that?" he asked.

"Apparently, it's the Joint Army Navy NASA Air Force committee; it's an inter-agency committee for exchange of ideas and technologies in the propulsion business," she explained. "My friend was going to check to see if there were any formal JANNAF meetings in Utah this week, but even if there weren't, that doesn't mean anything because they could be just swapping ideas."

"Okay, thanks," Bernard said. "What about who Bill and Dick work for?"

"We'll have to wait until Monday for that," she said. "My sources don't all do weekend searches."

"What are you doing this weekend?" Bernard asked, hoping for something like a date.

"I'm going skiing with a friend," Colleen replied. "We're driving up to the Tetons in a few minutes and will be back late Sunday night."

"Oh, okay," he said, disappointed but not sure what else to say. "Have fun, see you Monday."

"Okay, Monday. Oh, by the way, the mixers we are looking at have two blades that I understand precess around, whatever that means, and I gather that clearances between the blades and the mix bowl can be a big issue. Maybe that's the problem here?" she suggested.

"Thanks, I'll look into that. What was the name of the company that you said made the mixers?" he asked.

"Baker Perkins," she replied. "They make mixers in Michigan, I think, and then there's an outfit called John Day that makes mixers in Kentucky. I suppose they're probably very similar, but I don't know."

"Great, thanks again for the info. See you Monday," he said, then hung up. So, he thought to himself, she already has a friend and wondered what kind of friend, serious boyfriend or just a skiing buddy?

Bernard got up and fixed himself some breakfast, then sat down and doodled for a while, trying to work out the odds of the next football games that the Chicago Bears would be playing. He wanted to set up the colonel and get him in a position of being considerably in debt, but with an escape in case things did not go according to plan. He had been fairly good at assessing the games that the Bears played and had managed to make some money for himself, but never enough to attract the attention of the IRS. He listed the bookies that he could lay off the bet onto and the amounts that each might take. He wanted to get the colonel into the hundreds of thousands so that he would have a strong incentive to cooperate. That meant some risk on his part, as the guy might just get really cold feet and go all honest on him and confess his sins to his superiors. That would not serve Bernard at all; he needed a desperate colonel willing to tell anything if it would get him a way out of a big loss. He decided to let the colonel win the Lions game, and then he would set him up for the Vikings game, which would be the last game of the regular season.

He then listed the questions that he wanted answered. What program was involved in the incident? Why were there thirteen people at the site instead of the more normal four or five? Who was at fault, the operators or the management? Could the management have anticipated the problem, and if so, what should they have done differently? Was anyone likely to be prosecuted under the Utah work safety rules? How soon would they be back in production? How much would it cost to get back into production, and how much did the company lose during the downtime? Would the company have to pay any penalties to the Air Force for delays? Would the company bill the Air Force for downtime on the program and for the remediation work? Who was going to pay for the new building they would probably need, after all, it was an Air Force plant. The LST plant was actually Air Force Plant 97, managed by LST, much in the same way that Morton Thiokol managed Air Force Plant 78.

Bernard realised that his list was probably far from complete and perfect, but with answers to those questions, he could make a pretty good story. In fact, he could start writing it now in terms of headings and storyline and just fill in the details later. His spin on the story was going to be unfeeling management who were after production and profits at any cost, even at the cost of human life. That was always a good seller. He then realised that he knew nothing about the management of the company and who might have to take the fall. He then made a list for Colleen to research on Monday, including the names, titles and backgrounds of the LST corporate management and the local Missile Systems management. He wondered if he could work in the collusion of the Air Force in substandard work and systems and blame them as well. To do that, he would need to know how the Air Force was organised and which part of the Air Force had responsibility for what. Because it was the military, he doubted if it was straightforward, but believed it was likely to be convoluted with no clear lines of command and responsibility. That had been his experience in Vietnam, with chaos ruling and politicians exacerbating the issue by interfering with local command decisions. Even after the lessons of Vietnam, he doubted whether things had really changed, so disorganisation was a good possibility.

The Wasatch Front

James and Katrina flew to Salt Lake City on Monday morning and checked into the hotel. Katrina had an appointment with a realtor from Ogden at noon, so she took the car and drove north to meet him. James took a cab over to the LST offices and met with Robert Warner to negotiate the terms of his employment. The upshot of the discussions was a base salary of $150,000, with a bonus opportunity of 55% of the base, plus a car and the usual employee benefits, such as pension, health care, etc. They also agreed to pick up James's house in California, in the event that he could not sell it in a reasonable time and to provide for a relocation package. James also asked for a similar relocation package in case the company was sold or he was terminated without cause within three years. He was concerned lest the division lose most of its business through contract cancellations for reasons other than non-performance or fraud. In his mind, there was always the possibility that the US and the Soviet Union could come to some agreement on arms reductions, and then the contracts that LST had would be at risk. Robert dismissed that as a fond hope and readily agreed to a protection that he thought would never actually be exercised. They then had a long discussion about change of control protection and finally agreed on a parachute, not exactly golden, but at least a silvery bronze. Robert promised that stock options were likely to be forthcoming in the near future, and James would be included in the list. He could not promise exact numbers as the corporate office in Houston determined that, but he said that he would do his best to make it worthwhile.

With the basics of employment out of the way, Robert called in Ken Butler, and together they drove north to the operation. Robert explained to James that Ken was coming along to take care of the removal of Dean Anderson. He would supervise the office clear-out and the termination. At the plant offices, Robert led the way to a conference room where the managers were convened. He introduced James as the new Vice President and General Manager of the Missile Systems Division. Robert then introduced the team. James had an organisation chart and made himself some notes as the introductions went around the table. James wondered if he was supposed to make any kind of speech, but was relieved to hear that a plant tour had been scheduled and that they were to leave immediately. The operations manager, John Plackett and the safety manager, John Entwistle, went along with them on the tour. James spent most of his time listening as they described mixing and casting operations and the difference between live and inert operations. They made a stop at the Air Force offices, where Robert introduced James to Lieutenant Colonel Bill Ridings and to Captain Dick Melling. James promised to return soon and get to know these two better, as he would have to work with them in the coming months or years.

During the drive back to Salt Lake City, James asked for opinions on the management team. Robert made comments about each of the team and Ken added the occasional remark. James was concerned about the general lack of engineering depth in the team. Apart from the engineering manager, Allan Black, the balance had degrees in liberal arts subjects. That in and of itself was not a great worry, but James was concerned that they would lack the basic education and training to understand issues that arose; this was, after all, a fairly technical business. He asked Robert how that circumstance had arisen, and Robert was a little hesitant at first and then admitted that he had given Dean Anderson too much of a free hand in hiring, firing and promotions. Dean apparently had the notion that once the engineering had been done, any fool could build it. Regrettably, that was beginning to show in the performance of the operation, and things were cropping up that indicated problems that were fairly deep-seated. Obviously, James would have his work cut out for him!

As they passed Brigham City and then Ogden, James asked for their views on which town would be better to live in. Robert said that any of the towns along the Wasatch Front would be fine, but pointed out to James that, as he was not a Mormon, he might find it easier to live in Ogden, which had a higher proportion of other faiths than most of the other cities and towns along the Front. The other option was the city of Logan, a little off the Wasatch Front, generally a little colder than the Front but a university town with an active social scene. For the commute, Robert told James that if he stopped by the office in the morning, they would have his company car for him.

When they dropped James at the hotel, Robert suggested that he and his wife take James and Katrina to dinner. He said that he would stop by at seven and pick them up. James and Katrina had met Betty, Robert's wife, at one of the aerospace functions they had been to. Katrina's take at the time was that she was nice enough, but a little gushing at times, which made her hard to take. Now James had to break the news that they would be having dinner together, and he had no idea if there would be anyone else there to relieve things. When James reached their room, Katrina had a lot to tell him. She had spent the better part of the day looking at houses in Ogden. The realtor had made the same comment that Robert had made and recommended Ogden for the Martins over Brigham City, Tremonton or Logan. Katrina had found a house that she wanted James to look at and perhaps make an offer on. It was on the benches above Ogden and not too far from the mouth of one of the canyons. James told her about his day and the dinner engagement. Fortunately, Katrina had brought something other than jeans and jackets, so she had something to wear when they went to dinner. She was a little nervous at having to spend the whole evening making small talk with Betty, but supposed that she would survive. One thing James needed to do before he forgot was call the outplacement office in Irvine and tell them his news. He spoke to his counsellor and gave her the news that he had been hired and that he had actually already started and would miss the normal placement party that they would typically have. She understood and wished him well.

Dinner turned out not to be as bad as Katrina feared it might be. Apart from Robert and Betty, there was also Jane Lewis from Houston. She was in Salt Lake City with her husband, who had a small speciality sporting goods company and who was demonstrating some new skis. He had been unable to join them that evening because he was meeting with several clients whom he hoped would place large orders for new skis. James introduced Katrina to Jane, and they started to discuss the trials and tribulations of relocation. Jane told them all about some of her real estate ventures in various cities around the United States and how only one of them had actually returned any real value. Still, she was happy now in Houston, had her children off to college and was enjoying life. She did tell them that breaking into a corporate position in Waterway Chemicals had been quite a crusade, and she was not sure whether she would want to do it again. Oil men and Texans, in her view at least, saw women as being either barefoot and pregnant in the kitchen, or as gracing the arm of some older executive as he showed off his latest trophy. Katrina looked at Robert a little in alarm at this last pronouncement, but it appeared that it was a conversation that had been repeated many times before. Perhaps the knowledge that her husband's business would keep them comfortably no matter what Waterway Chemicals did made her bolder than she would otherwise have been.

*   *   *

"Bernard, did you hear that LST hired a new guy?" Colleen asked.

"No, who, what, when and where?" he replied.

"Apparently, they hired some guy from LA who started yesterday," she elaborated. "I gather he's from aerospace but not rockets."

"Okay, so get his name, where he worked before and whatever else you can find out about him," Bernard instructed.

"I also heard that they let the last manager go," she added.

"Who, that guy Anderson?" he asked.

"Yes, Dean Anderson," she confirmed. "Now, among the ranks of the happily unemployed. But I doubt that he is going to talk much. I would think that his severance will also include a gag clause."

"You're probably right," he complained. "We'll have to find a way to push his buttons and get him talking. Is he LDS?"

"I don't know," she admitted. "I'll find out."

"What about the Air Force weenies, who do they work for?" he asked.

"Ah, yes," she started. "My contact in Washington tells me that they are the honchos of the Air Force Plant Representative Office, AFPRO for short, and report to the Contract Management Division of the Air Force, and that is based out of New Mexico, Kirtland Air Force Base to be precise."

"So, they're not the real customer?" Bernard asked.

"I suppose not," Colleen agreed. "I gather that the customer is the Ballistic Missile Organization, BMO for short, which is based at Norton Air Force Base in San Bernardino, and BMO is part of Air Force Systems Command."

"Okay, that explains the one comment that one of them made about meeting a colonel from San Bernardino. What else do we know?" he asked.

"The contracts are generally fixed price," she added.

"What does that mean?" he asked.

"As I understand it, it means that LST and the Air Force agree on a price and then anything that LST can make by reducing costs is theirs, unlike Cost Plus contracts, where the Air Force would pay all costs no matter what and some kind of fee on top, sometimes fixed sometimes tied to some kind of performance criteria," she explained.

"So does that suggest cost-cutting and corner-cutting by LST? Who negotiates all this stuff?" he wondered.

"Beats me," she admitted. "But there's a whole raft of things called FARS, or Federal Acquisition Regulations, that seem to cover just about everything."

"I suppose these FARS are as screwed up as the Income Tax Code?" he suggested.

"Oh, undoubtedly," she agreed. "I can't imagine the Congress making anything simple and straightforward, then there'd be no jobs for the boys that are lawyers, accountants and lobbyists!"

"God, what a mess," he thought. "No wonder hammers cost $250 each if the Air Force buys them! Anything more on the Navy connection?"

"Not that I can find out," Colleen admitted. "My contact in Washington had nothing on that at all. No JANNAF meeting, nothing. Maybe they were just looking to see if their programs ran any better than the Air Force programs. You know what the services are like, jealousies and envy abound!"

"Okay, well, we'll run that to ground at some time. Meanwhile, what else did you find out about mixers and what goes in them?" he asked.

"I'm still working on that," she said. "I hope to have something by the end of the week."

"Okay, keep at it, I'll see if I can't work out a winning strategy to put Colonel Bill into a delicate situation!" he laughed.

James drove north from Salt Lake City to the plant and was pleased to see that the badge he had been issued along with the car granted him access to the facility. He was asked if he had any matches, lighters or other fire-producing devices about his person, which he gathered was a standard question for a propellant factory. He did wonder how smokers managed and thought that he would ask someone later. He found his new office and reintroduced himself to Heather, the secretary there. Heather had a list of regularly scheduled meetings that he probably should attend, but also commented that anything could be changed to suit his wishes, except the regular reviews with the customers who came in from California or Washington. Because he had stopped in Salt Lake City to pick up the car, he had missed the early morning operational meetings, and the next scheduled event was not until after lunch; it was a progress review of the incident investigation. James then went on a walkabout to see where everyone else was situated. He quickly found the production and program office and was surprised to learn that the engineering offices were in separate buildings and divorced from the balance of the staff.

The incident investigation review was interesting. The members of the team included the resident Air Force lieutenant colonel, Bill Ridings, an Air Force colonel and a lieutenant from San Bernardino and a Navy lieutenant commander from Washington. For the company, there was the safety manager, the engineering manager, Tom Manning, the Engineering VP from the corporate group in Salt Lake City and several others, mostly technical. Progress had been made, and it was now clear that for some reason, two mix teams and their foremen had been at the mixer building on the day of the explosion. That accounted for the unusually large number of people, but the reason for their presence was still a mystery. There was another person there who under normal circumstances would not have been there, and that was an engineer, Michael Miller, by name. Miller apparently had earned the reputation of getting himself involved in processes that he would normally have no occasion to oversee or even investigate. The school of thought presented

50

at the meeting was that this was a young man anxious to improve himself who took any opportunity to learn that presented itself. James, however, caught the look of one of the technical people who apparently did not totally subscribe to this view. James decided to see him later and find out what the minority report might be.

As for the explosion, the general consensus was that the evidence seemed fairly conclusive that it was blade-to-bowl contact, which suggested a foreign object. Whether that foreign object was something that had broken off the feeding systems of the mixer and fallen in, or whether there was some other explanation, was yet to be determined. James asked to see the failure tree analysis and was disturbed by the fact that they did not have one: he asked how they could reach any kind of conclusion without such an analysis and told them that he wanted to see a tree by the next meeting. Tom Manning protested that a tree was hardly necessary because they knew what the failure mode was. James asked them all to humour him and create the tree; it might, after all, suggest mechanisms by which the event had actually occurred.

James then asked if all the debris from the explosion had been found, mapped and collected. That had been done, so he asked if they had made any attempt to reconstruct the mixer from the debris. That drew derisory laughs until he pointed out that it was routinely done with plane crashes. He admitted that they did not have the resources of the NTSB, the National Transportation Safety Board that investigates plane crashes, among other incidents, but suggested that it might be worthwhile to at least examine the debris. What he was looking for was evidence that the inspection port had either been open or closed at the time of the explosion.

He also suggested that, if blade-to-bowl contact was the source of ignition, then perhaps there were three scenarios they should be examining: first, a failure of some piece of equipment or measuring device that had allowed a foreign object to fall into the bowl, second, an accidental introduction by one of the crew and third, a deliberate introduction by one of the crew.

51

This latter drew immediate protests. How could James imagine that anyone would do that deliberately, knowing that it meant certain death? James suggested murder or murder/suicide. That was greeted with more disbelief and horror, but James pointed out that this was an investigation and all possible avenues of thought should be followed and run to ground, no matter how bizarre they may seem. He reminded them all that the explosion in 1940 at the Hercules Kenville factory was never fully understood and that, perhaps because of the era, Nazi sabotage was suspected, so they should not dismiss any possibility. James also asked if it was possible that a thin film phenomenon might be the cause, rather than an actual blade-to-bowl contact. That set off another debate, mainly about the little-understood phenomenon of thin films and how they formed and if they could, in fact, ignite. But it was a much safer subject to debate than accidental or purposeful introduction of a foreign body into the mixer. James told them to add thin-film phenomena to the failure tree and give him some experimental data; at least that would disprove the hypothesis.

After the meeting, Bill Ridings went back to report to whomever he reported to on these matters, and James went back to his office to review the pile of paper that sat on his new desk. He spent the afternoon variously looking at papers, then asking Heather what was normally done with each item. A great deal of it was just for information, and James asked Heather to sort it out for him in the future and only give him things he needed to sign or items that clearly demanded attention. He would try and cut down on the amount of information-only paper that came into the office in the future. He then met with Entwistle and scheduled a test that would give him access to the live area buildings. The safety rules were quite straightforward and largely common sense. There were a few technical questions, but nothing really unusual or out of the ordinary; it certainly was not as comprehensive as the Blasting Licence examination he had taken in Zambia many years earlier.

James then asked Heather to have Allan Black, the engineering manager and John Plackett, the operations manager, come to his office. When they were there, James asked John, "When the detonation occurred, how much damage was done to other buildings and facilities?"

"Not too much," John replied. "The canyon in which that building was situated deflected most of the blast up and forward."

"What damage was done to equipment in other buildings?" James persisted.

"I'm sorry, I don't know what you mean," John temporised.

"Were any of the machine tools or mixers, or any pieces of equipment, jolted out of alignment or out of true?" James explained.

"Oh," John replied. "I don't know."

"Well, I suggest that you stop work on all processes until you have checked on all our machine tools, mixers, autoclaves and the rest to see that they are still properly installed and aligned," James instructed.

"But, you can't do that," John protested. "The Air Force won't let us just stop work."

"They'll like it even less if we produce a mountain of scrap!" James commented. "I want you and Allan to contact riggers and whoever else you might need and start checking everything out, beginning tonight."

"But, we don't have the budget for that," Allan protested.

"I'll worry about that," James assured them. "I would like to see a basic plan by tomorrow afternoon that lays out all the machinery that we have and the schedule for checking it out and bringing it back online."

"How will we set priorities?" John asked.

"I'll get Simon Wilmott to help you set them," James promised.

"But that means I'll have to work late," John whined.

"I'm sorry, but it comes with the territory," James remarked. "I'll get hold of Simon and Ron Hilliard as soon as you're gone and set things up for setting priorities and accounting for the work."

James did just that, after they had gone, and told them what he expected. There were a few protests from Simon initially until he also saw the point of potentially building scrap. Then he was on board and went off in search of John and Allan with fire in his eyes. He was going to make sure that everything was as it should be and quickly at that.

James's task for the evening, when he went back to the hotel, was to look over the files of his staff and set up a series of interviews and reviews to see who he would keep and who he would let go. But first, he thought that it would be a good idea to find a hotel in Ogden so that his commute would be a little shorter. It would also give him a sense of what commuting was likely to be like if they bought the house in Ogden. Basing himself there, while they looked, placed Katrina closer to the houses and would let her take a look around Ogden as well. He called Robert Warner and suggested that he move to Ogden, and Robert agreed that it was a good idea. They also discussed the day and James's impressions of his staff and who he had concerns about. Robert then commented that he had ruffled the feathers of Tom Manning a little, but agreed with James that, as it was now his Division, if he wanted a failure tree analysis, he should get one, and was surprised that it had not already been done. James also asked for some Human Resources help to go through the files of the dead employees, looking for clues, no matter how obscure, that might point to any instability that could lead to scenario number three. He reasoned that if the measurement devices and instrumentation were as stable as everyone said, then it suggested either an accidental or deliberate introduction of a foreign object. Robert did not like the sound of that; it was the kind of thing that the press would love, so he asked James to keep his findings, if any, very close to the vest for now.

The next day, James and Katrina moved to the Marriott hotel in Ogden. It was a reasonable enough hotel and convenient for Katrina as she pursued her house hunting. It was also a little closer to the plant for James, so cut down his commute. Before he left for the plant, James went with Katrina and the realtor to look at the house she had picked out. James liked it. It sat up on one of the benches, and the views around were the mountains to the east and the Great Salt Lake to the west. Far out over the lake, they could see the Promontory Peninsula and, to the south, more mountains with a faint distant view of the mountains that surrounded the Bingham Canyon mine. The house was two levels and surrounded by what the realtor called Scrub Oak, thick, low bushes that provided good ground cover and low landscape maintenance. James left Katrina doing a more thorough review of her checklist of items she wanted in a house, and he drove out to the plant.

*   *   *

"James Martin!" Colleen announced to Bernard on Wednesday morning.

"Who?" Bernard asked, confused. "Who's James Martin?"

"He's the new GM and Veep of the Missile Division of LST," she explained.

"So, where's he from?" Bernard asked.

"According to this blurb we just received from LST, he was with a company called Waterford Industries until recently. Apparently, this Waterford is not the glass company but some aerospace systems house based in LA. I'll find out more about it, Bernard," she promised.

"So, any missile or rocket background?" he asked.

"Not that this blurb says," she replied.

"Okay, Colleen, put your spies to work and see what you can turn up on this guy," he instructed. "Meanwhile, I have a heavy lunch date in Tremonton with the good colonel!"

"Good luck," Colleen wished. "Are you sure that you're doing the right thing here?"

"What do you mean?" he asked.

"Well, it seems pretty nasty to set the poor bastard up like this. Are you sure this isn't blackmail?" she asked.

"Blackmail. That's such a nasty word," Bernard laughed. "No, I wouldn't call it blackmail, just a little nudge here and there!"

"Well, I think it's blackmail, what you're planning, and I don't think we should do it," she commented.

"Getting cold feet?" he asked.

"Not cold, downright frozen!" she stated quite categorically. "I think you should not do whatever you have in mind."

"Maybe you're right," Bernard admitted. "What if I just let him win and make him grateful enough that he volunteers things without coercion?"

"I'd feel the tiniest bit better about that, but I still think we've gone too far," she persisted.

"Okay, okay, I'll behave," he promised, knowing that he had no intention of keeping that promise, no matter what arguments she came up with. To him, the story was too important. "Tell you what, why don't you send me a memo detailing what you've dug up so far and then drop out of the case and move on to something else, so that whatever happens you won't be involved?" he suggested.

"That sounds almost as if you're going ahead with your nefarious scheme no matter what!" Colleen challenged. "I'll send the memo and copy His Holiness, and put myself on another assignment. I'm out of this!" she announced and then stalked out of his office.

Bernard left the office muttering. He had hoped to use Colleen's skill as a researcher for a little longer, and he had also fantasised about getting her into bed. Oh well, that looked as if it were a non-starter. Still, he had his strategy set now. The result of last night's game had confirmed his status as a prophet, and he was fairly certain he could predict the next game. So now was the time to let the colonel win more than a little.

In the diner in Tremonton, Bill was already there, on his own, and he was delighted to see Bernard.

"How do you do it?" he asked.

"What?" Bernard asked.

"You've been right every game this season," Bill marvelled. "How do you do that?"

"I've a great crystal ball!" Bernard laughed.

"But how did you manage to get the spread just right, 23 to 3, so twenty points just like you said?" Bill wondered.

"Lucky, I guess," Bernard admitted. "So what did you make on the game?"

"I picked up a cool fifty grand!" Bill whispered. "God only knows how I'm going to hide it from the wife and worse, the IRS!"

"Where did you place your bets?" Bernard asked.

"In Vegas," Bill told him.

"Well, that's the first problem," Bernard commented. "If you did it through a legitimate betting agency, then they will report the transaction to the IRS, so you'll have to come clean about it to them. As far as your wife is concerned, does she do your taxes, or read the returns that you do?"

"No, she just signs them, and I send them in," Bill explained.

"So that shouldn't be a problem then," Bernard promised. "Why don't you let me place the bets for you? I can do it so that the IRS won't get to hear of it."

"Really?" Bill asked. "You can do that?"

"Sure, I do it for myself, what's another bet or two added to my own?" Bernard assured him.

"Okay, so what's your prediction for the game against the Lions next week?" Bill asked.

"I see it as a close game," Bernard commented, truthfully, actually, because he had had difficulty seeing how this one would play out. "I can't give you the point spread, but my money's on the Bears to win, but not by much!"

"Okay, see what kind of odds you can get for me for the Bears to win and let's add to that a win by a single point!" Bill said rather grandly. "If the odds are good, I'll put the fifty grand I won last week on the bet."

"Wow, that's more than I would go!" Bernard said, impressed by the amount and the gutsy way Bill was looking at things.

"What the hell, why not?" Bill asked, grinning.

"Yes, but if I'm wrong and you lose, the IRS will still come looking for you for the taxes on that fifty grand," Bernard warned him.

"We're not going to lose!" Bill said quite firmly. "Just do it!"

"Okay, you're the boss," Bernard agreed. "I'd better be going so that you can get back to your salt mine. Oh, I read in the paper that LST hired a new guy for the operation. What's he like?"

"Fucking Limey!" Bill spat out.

"What, not a US citizen?" Bernard asked.

"Oh, he's a citizen right enough, I've seen his passport," Bill assured him. "But, he talks like a fucking Limey, comes across as a supercilious bastard, asks a lot of questions and then looks at you as if he doesn't believe you when you answer his stupid fucking questions. He's got enough of them, too, probably carries around a book of endless questions to piss everyone else off! I wouldn't want to work for the guy! You know, he even suggested that our explosion might have been a deliberate act!"

"How do you mean, deliberate act?" Bernard asked.

"Well, I suppose it's an option. If we had blade-to-bowl contact, then there either had to be major misalignment of the mix axes, or there had to be some foreign object in there. The only ways to get a foreign object in there are for something to break, something to be accidentally dropped in or for some asshole to actually commit suicide by deliberately dropping something in. But who in their right mind would do that? It's a recipe for certain death!" Bill elaborated.

"So where's he from?" Bernard pressed, keeping that last nugget to himself for now. He would use it later when he had some leverage on the good colonel.

"Some contractor called Waterford Industries," Bill replied. "I checked with a counterpart of mine in LA, and they do all kinds of mechanical and electro-mechanical systems for planes, helicopters, ships, you name it."

"No rocket experience?" Bernard asked.

"No, probably doesn't even know which end the flame comes out of," Bill laughed. "He does have the reputation of firing people, though. Where he came from, he went through a few division managers. As I said, I wouldn't want to work for the bastard. Why the fuck did Anderson fuck it all up by having an accident? You know the fucking Air Force is probably going to re-assign me now, probably to Thule or somewhere equally attractive!"

"Really, why?" Bernard asked.

"Anderson's fuck up reflects on me. It's like a Navy puke running a ship aground. No matter who else fucked up, if you're the captain of the ship, you take the fall!" Bill moaned.

"I'm sorry to hear that," Bernard said, quite truthfully, because if he did not make his move soon, he would have to start all over with another officer. "When might this happen?"

"Probably in the New Year. I have to go for a review and a hearing in the middle of January. My career's probably stalled right here with not much chance of making bird colonel and forget flag rank!" Bill complained bitterly. "But hey, I need to go, I must get back because I still have meetings that I'm supposed to be interested in!"

"Hey, good luck with your review," Bernard told him. "Who knows, it may not turn out as bad as you think."

"Fat chance," Bill said.

On his drive back to Salt Lake City, Bernard reflected upon his discussion with Bill and thought of several new angles he could use for his story. He could use an unfeeling, vindictive Air Force, or a justly concerned Air Force weeding out a less-than-performing officer. He would have to see how events shaped to see which path he would take. Life was good, and he now had the colonel in a vulnerable position where he might actually welcome some additional income and therefore be more prepared to take a greater risk. He wondered if the colonel and the investigative board would take seriously any suggestion of a 'deliberate act' and his mind ran off in all kinds of directions. Suicide was his best candidate for a possible motive, but then again, murder was always a possibility, and in his opinion, there was enough inbreeding in those people that mental instability was a good possibility.

He wondered if he could get Colleen interested in coming back to the project if he pitched to her the potential of a murder mystery. He would dangle out the bait and point out that they had all missed the Mark Hofmann story, but here was one almost as good; the only thing missing was any conceivable angle that involved the Church. Maybe he could even work that in if he could find one of the crew who believed in Blood Atonement! That would be a scoop worth going after. He disliked almost everything about the Church; to him, the idea of those people calling themselves Saints was laughable, and their pervasive control of almost everything in the State, including his own newspaper, was frightening. Anything that he could do to embarrass the Church, he would do. Bernard wondered what Colleen's position on the Church might be. She was apparently single and well-educated, so he guessed that she was not a practising member of the Church, even if she had been raised in an LDS family. She might even share his view, or even better, she might have strong opinions about the suppression of women within the Church and be looking for a vehicle to lash out at them. It was worth considering, and he thought about how he would pitch the idea to her.

*   *   *

James and Katrina made an offer on the house, and it was accepted. With that done, she went back to California to put their existing house on the market and start getting things ready for a move. James promised to be back in California on the weekend to help. Then he focused his attention on the new job and started to call in each of the managers for meetings. He confirmed his fears and concluded that he needed to change the Manufacturing Manager, the Safety Manager, the Quality Manager, the Human Resource Manager and a couple of lower positions in manufacturing. He also had decided that he needed to create a new position, that of Matériel Manager. He considered himself fortunate that there was depth in the program and engineering organisations, and he could draw from them without loss of continuity. He would need to go outside for the human resources and quality positions. He just saw no real candidates inside the company. That done, he put the wheels in motion with Ken Butler from LST and set a timetable for when he wanted to make the changes.

James then got program briefings from the different program managers. He learned that they had a program with the Air Force, the Auriga missile, which was supposed to be a potential competitor to the Migetman or SICBM, the Small Intercontinental Ballistic Missile. They had another program, based on the Auriga case size, known as Auriga Type B. It was similar in size to the base Auriga but had a different propellant system and a different set of firing lines and guidance systems; they were also making as many inert segments as they were live segments. James was curious as to why there were so many inert segments. They could not be fired, and he could not think of that many uses for cases filled with what was essentially just filler. Bernard Zaun, the Program Manager, either did not know or was disinclined to discuss it; he just told James how many of each segment were at which stage of manufacture. Having learned from past experience, James also got various foremen and managers to take him around and actually show him pieces and supplies that they had on hand. What was recorded and written did not always reflect what it actually was!

Allan Black, the engineering manager, gave him a quick lesson in propellant chemistry, and he learned of the two major classifications that they used, Class 1.1 and Class 1.3. To James, the difference was that whereas Class 1.3 explosives and propellants would burn and explode, Class 1.1 explosives and propellants would detonate. What that really meant to him was that a Class 1.3 explosion in a building might leave the building frame at least partially intact, but a Class 1.1 explosive or propellant would leave a nice crater in the ground and little else. Most of James's past experience with explosives would fall into the Class 1.1 grouping. The mining companies were not interested in slow burns; they wanted massive, instantaneous explosions to get the most effect from shock waves in the rock. Allan told him that the Auriga Type A for the Air Force was mainly in Class 1.3, but the Auriga Type B was definitely a Class 1.1, driven by the oxidisers added, the nitroglycerine and nitrocellulose mix and the HMX, HMX being another explosive that otherwise went by the description of cyclo tetramethylene-tetranitrate.

Colonel Ridings called him incensed that James had issued a stop-work order on all the programs. It was only after James explained that continuing to work with equipment that might be out of alignment could cause scrap, which would put all the programs late, that he began to see the light. Then James told him what the plan of action would be once he got the details from his people. It was only after James hinted that he might even take the credit for issuing the stop work order that he began to really warm up to the idea, and by the time the conversation was over, he had actually thought it up on his own and had instructed James to take the action. He rang off, telling James that he would be calling his own Command with the news and the plan of action, and he would be calling the BMO and the Navy program offices.

The security officer from the Air Force AFPRO contingent asked James to call in on him one day, and they went through forms that James supposed had to do with transferring his clearance and upgrading it. He also went through a briefing that dealt with document control, general communications and travel restrictions. That was not as limiting as it could have been and mainly listed countries that James should not visit under any circumstances, none of which were on his list of places to go anyway, and a list of countries to which travel was permitted but with notice and pre- and post-travel briefings.

On Thursday, James received a call from Robert Warner asking him to be at the Salt Lake City airport at six the following morning. He was to report to the fixed-based operator, the FBO, that the company used to hangar their plane. Robert explained that they had a briefing at the Pentagon at one in the afternoon on Friday. He also promised to drop James off in California on the way back, suggesting Ontario rather than Orange County. James then called Katrina and told her that he would be flying into Ontario and promised to call with further details.

At six on Friday morning, James found his way to the FBO and met Robert. LST had a Lear 55, which was very nicely appointed. They had the Lear to themselves, and as soon as they were aboard, they took off. James had flown in Learjets before and had always enjoyed the ride. Once in the air, Robert told James that they were going to meet with a group of people at the Pentagon, one to introduce James and two to get and give an update on the programs they were working on. James asked why that would not be done in San Bernardino, where BMO was located, and all Robert would say was that the meeting would include people other than the BMO folks. The pilots had catered lunch on the plane, or rather brunch, because they had left early and would not be landing before eleven thirty local time and still needed time to get to the Pentagon for the one pm meeting. They landed at the Washington National Airport, taxied to an FBO where a Navy car met them and drove them to the Pentagon.

James had been to the Pentagon before and had always been fascinated with the rings and levels coding. It was like a road map to find one's way around. He had had to identify himself at the door and give his Social Security Number, which the guard had entered into a computer, apparently checking him off against a list of approved visitors. They were escorted to a briefing room where James was introduced to the assembled group. There was no reciprocal introduction of the others present. Bill Ridings, the Air Force lieutenant colonel from the site, was not there, but there was an Air Force officer present, a brigadier general who had missile wings on his uniform. James wondered if he was from San Bernardino or the Pentagon. There were quite a few Navy people in the room, one of whom was Lieutenant Commander Reinsch, who had attended the incident investigation meetings at the plant. There were also some civilians, or at least people dressed in civilian clothing. They could be contractors or Pentagon employees. Finally, an aide came in and announced Admiral Keene, who came in and took charge of the briefing. The admiral fit James's idea of an admiral. He was short but in good shape, he had short grey hair and very dark piercing eyes.

"Gentlemen," he began. "This is a classified briefing of a special access program. Mr Simonds, have all those present been identified and vouched for?" he continued.

"Sir, I have identified all present, and the only person present who is new is Mr James Martin of LST, who has the requisite clearances and is vouched for by Robert Warner, the president of LST," Lieutenant Simonds replied. James guessed that Simonds was the admiral's aide.

"Very well, welcome, James," started the admiral, apparently warmly. "We are here to discuss the Sagitta Program, which you know as Auriga Type B. The existence of Sagitta is classified and should not be shared with anyone beyond this room. Now perhaps you'll tell us just what the problem is at your factory and why one of our mixers blew up!"

"Admiral," James began. "I have been on the job since Monday and can only repeat what seems to be the early consensus of the investigating team. The detonation was most probably caused by blade-to-bowl contact, either directly or by a foreign object. That detonation led to the destruction of the building and the deaths. We cannot yet establish why there were more people present than would normally be the case, but I will find out."

"You will find out?" the admiral asked.

"Yes, sir," James promised.

"I understand you've stopped everything at the plant for a while?" the admiral asked, not taken in at all by the fact that Colonel Ridings had called his Command, giving them the news and portraying it as his order, which news had then been passed up the line to the Pentagon. The admiral knew better than that and had already sidelined the colonel in his own mind as being a typical clone of the Contract Management

Division of the Air Force, who could probably do no real good but could also do no real harm.

"Yes," James confirmed. "They had done no checking to ensure that the detonation had not shaken anything off its foundations or misaligned any of the pieces of machinery, equipment or major tooling that we use."

"How much time will we lose because of that?" the admiral asked.

"Actually, no more than we were going to lose anyway because of the mixer loss," James promised. "We have carefully scheduled all the checks, and we have an army of riggers on site right now making sure everything is as it should be. Simon Wilmott, our manager of programs, has taken the lead and is doing a very good job. He understands the issues and would rather incur small delays than potentially build a factory full of scrap and thus major delays."

"When will you be back in production?" the admiral pressed.

"We have two live first-stage segments in final inspection," James replied. He then added, "We have another two stages in casting and a further two cases in winding. We have the equivalent number of second and third stages in production and can deliver two full-up missiles this month and another two next month. We do have an equivalent number of inert stages, and these can be built faster than the live stages because we can use a different set of mixers."

"How much mixer capacity do you have?" the admiral asked.

"We have three mixers that are capable of handling the propellant," James replied. "With those three in operation, I can produce three sets of segments every two months, down from the two a month that was the previous rate. But before we go back into production with those mixers, I want to run some additional checks to see that blade-to-bowl contact will not be an issue."

"How long before you can start casting again?" the admiral wanted to know.

"I would say two to three weeks," James estimated. "I would like to see some data on the verticality of the mixer axes and also want to review the sensors and feed mechanisms to see if we can work out where the problem arose."

"Okay, that tallies with the information I have already received from Lieutenant Commander Reinsch," the admiral commented. "You'll be seeing a lot more of her in the next few weeks!"

"Fine, sir," was really the only reply that James could give.

"What about other pieces of the missiles?" the admiral asked, prompted by a question written on a small piece of paper that had been slipped to him by one of the other people present.

"We are actually ahead of the previous production schedule with completed nozzles and have a further ten throat billets in manufacture now, enough for just over three missile sets, we have another filament winding machine about to come online, the first articles have been done and bought off, we have insulation packages for three each of each stage in inventory and that line looks to be in good shape," James reported.

"What about raw materials?" the admiral pushed, referring again to his note.

"We have enough aluminium powder for the next six months and plenty of ammonium perchlorate, we have deliveries of the nitroglycerine nitrocellulose mix regularly scheduled, we have the capacity to grind HMX as we need it and have enough on hand to satisfy demand for the foreseeable future and we have enough carbon fibre to wind thirty segments, ten of each," James elaborated.

"I presume that by aluminium you really mean aluminum," the admiral joked, then he asked. "No shortage of ammonium perchlorate then?"

"No," James confirmed. "Probably by the sheer luck of poor planning, we have some years' supply on hand. Since the PEPCON explosion, it seems that we have been regularly approached by the other missile manufacturers to release AP, but our contract rating is such that we are compelled to retain it. I do have a concern with agglomeration and am working to see what we can do about better desiccation," James explained.

"What do you mean, better desiccation?" the admiral asked.

"Ammonium perchlorate is hygroscopic, and if too much water is involved, it clumps and then we have to regrind it and reclassify into the appropriate size fractions," James explained.

"So, you're trying to keep the water out?"

"Yes, sir," James confirmed. "The better job we do of keeping the material dry, the easier it is to use in the future."

"Isn't that one of the reasons that the plant was located in Utah, the low humidity?" the admiral asked.

"Yes," James confirmed again. "But, there is still a level of moisture in the air and temperature variations will cause condensation, even of small amounts of water. I think we can do a better job of husbanding our raw materials."

"Did you hear that, Walter?" the admiral laughed, commenting to one of the civilians. "He wants to better husband the stuff. That's the first time I've heard that expression in one of these meetings. Young man, come back and see me regularly, I think we may get on well!"

"Does anyone else have any questions?" the admiral then asked, and another civilian, or a man dressed in civilian clothes, perked up.

"Can you explain to us the variability that exists in the grains of the third stages, as compared to past experience?" he asked. "And will this lead to variability in performance or premature failure?"

"At the moment, no, I cannot explain that," James admitted. "But, I believe we changed inspection systems from x-ray film to computer-aided tomography three months ago and surmise that we may be seeing artefacts that we have never been able to see before, but that have always been there," James replied.

"Check it out, will you, James," the admiral asked, giving the questioner a withering look. "Does anyone else have a question that it is reasonable to assume that Martin actually has had time to find answers to?"

"Admiral, with respect," the questioner interrupted. "My customer is most concerned about this and needs an answer, but I accept that Martin may not know now, but we might expect a briefing in a month's time."

"Okay, give us a briefing on that in a month and as for restarting production, you can have your three weeks, but keep us in the loop. We don't want to lose another mixer!" the admiral warned. "When can you have a replacement mixer online and ready to go?"

"We can have it running in six months if we get the funding for the replacement," James promised. "I checked with Baker Perkins, and they can have a mixer in three months, and then the balance of the time is to install, test and do a first article on a mix."

"Piece parts and ordnance?" the admiral added.

"We have enough thrust vector actuation packages for twelve missile sets," James commented. "And, we have ordnance train sets for the same sets and have not cut back production levels."

"Very well," the admiral grunted. "Thank you, gentlemen. I'll be expecting an update here next month, and Robert, give him the money for another mixer. We'll work out payment details with the Air Force Property Management people at Wright Pat. We can be sure that they'll make it as complicated as they can, but if we're paying, they'll play ball. Okay, then anything else? No, good, then Commander Collins will see you out of the building."

"Thank you, Admiral," Robert said. On that note, he motioned to James to follow, and then they left.

"That's it?" James asked when they had left the room.

"That's it for now," Robert corrected him. "If we don't perform and meet those numbers you gave the admiral by the next briefing, we can expect all kinds of help!"

"Are those numbers correct?" Bernard Collins asked while they were walking back towards the main exit.

"Yes," James replied. "The reported numbers that are fed through the Air Force have some discrepancies, but I actually had a look at each item to find out where we are and have given you the real numbers. Now, I need to get our systems checked so that the system numbers match the real numbers."

"You've been busy!" Robert commented.

"I just asked a lot of questions," James laughed. "It's easy when you don't know anything!"

"I was surprised at the question on grain defects," Bernard commented. "But I suppose contractors have to prove their worth once in a while, and it's a question that has come up a few times over the past few months."

"So, he wasn't a Navy guy?" James asked for confirmation.

"No," Robert explained. "In the rocket business, there is usually a contractor that makes the stages, and then there is another contractor that does the integration. The Navy likes Lockheed Missiles and Space, the Air Force used to like Martin Marietta, but they also seem to not be able to take a leak without TRW telling them how to do it!"

"Where are these missiles deployed?" James asked. "It seems to me that they are too small for submarines. Why use a single warhead shot when you can get one with ten? They are a little large for most surface ships, unless, of course, you put in special launch tubes."

"We don't know," admitted Robert. "At least I don't know, perhaps Bernard does, but it's a special access program which probably means that they've got everything compartmentalised to hell and we'll never be told."

"If it makes you feel any better, James, I don't know," Bernard also admitted. "It's all need to know and I have no need to know!"

When Bernard had seen them out of the building, James asked the other question that had been in his mind.

"Will we get funding for another mixer?"

"I've already run it through corporate with ROM numbers, but you might get some definite numbers and submit a capital request," Robert replied. "There'll be no issue with the money, particularly as the admiral just said he'd pay, but corporate will want real quotes for their files."

"Okay, I'll do that," James promised. "Most of the money will be for a new building, though."

"I know," Robert agreed. "You may have some permitting issues with Utah, but I don't think so; it's pretty straightforward, we're just replacing a building with a like facility. The only snag may be code changes since the mix building was originally put up."

"I may have to go for code exemptions to keep control systems as near as possible, like or at least greatly similar to the other buildings," James commented. "I don't like the idea of too much variability in control setups."

"You're right there," Robert agreed. "All we need is another incident brought about by the fact that controls are so different that we create a problem, rather than fix one!"

The one item that James had not brought up with Robert was that he was sure he had seen Costanza Albertini in an anteroom, apparently waiting for someone. What he was doing there, James could only speculate upon. Perhaps the shipping company had contracts to haul Defense Department materials, but James thought that unlikely, as the shippers were supposed to be US-owned with US-flagged vessels and US crews. The Waterway Shipping Company might be US-owned, but all the vessels were flagged in Malta, and Costanza had said that the crews were a regular United Nations.

At the FBO at Washington National, James called Katrina and gave her an arrival time of 6:37 pm, which the pilots assured him that they would meet. He also told her which FBO they would be using. On the plane heading for California, there were so many questions that James wanted to ask Robert, but as the pilots were definitely not on the need-to-know list, he held his tongue. Robert did say that he would come out to the plant in the middle of the following week, and there was a secure briefing room that they could use for conversations. By secure, he meant that it had cypher locks and an electronic screening system to blank out any attempts at eavesdropping. Satisfied for now, James then turned to more mundane, if that was the right word, matters of staffing and which of his people he wanted to replace and why. Robert had a few questions, but basically left it in his hands. He said he realised that that had got them into trouble with Dean, but that he also trusted James to make good and sensible decisions. He had also checked on James's background and knew what his record was like in the way of replacing division managers and senior staff. He was envious of the team that James had built at his previous company and asked what it would take to do the same at LST.

They touched down and taxied into Atlantic Aviation and pulled into their ramp slot at 6:36 pm, one minute early. Robert got off with James to say hello to Katrina and then left to go back to Utah.
"So, how was Washington?" Katrina asked.
"Quick," James laughed. "We flew in, met a bunch of *ouks*, explained what we knew about the incident and then left."
"Did you miss me this week?" she asked.
"Always, *Suikerbossie*," he confirmed.
"I've got a little surprise for you when we get home," she promised.

"What, or are you going to keep me in suspense?" James asked, intrigued.

"You'll just have to wait and see," she told him. "It won't hurt you to wait for once!"

Throughout the drive home, James tried to imagine what Katrina had in mind and what the surprise might be. Obviously, it had nothing to do with selling the house in Orange; she would have shared that information with him immediately, so what was it?

Investigations

James flew back to Salt Lake City on Sunday night, smiling. Katrina had obviously missed him during the previous week, and they had made up for lost time and opportunities over the weekend. She could be very inventive when it came to bedroom matters, and James wondered a little if his inane grin, as he remembered things, would be noticed by his fellow travellers. He now struggled to get his mind off his wife and back to the more mundane matters of work. They had to make a living after all!

On Monday morning, James was in the factory early. He had left his hotel just after five in the morning and was in the plant a little after six. He had had to slow down a couple of times on the drive north as passing truck drivers had flashed their lights at him, warning him about Utah Highway Patrol cars further up the road. Although the speed limit was generous, the UHP were not known for allowing excessive speeding, even though traffic was light and the road was generally clear and empty. In the factory, James wandered around and found the foremen from manufacturing in the cafeteria. They were getting breakfast and doing the shift changeover. The night shift team was passing on any information that might be relevant and important to the incoming day shift. James was greeted with slight suspicion, but then accepted, and the conversation continued. After the day shift team left to organise the work planned for the day, a couple of the night shift team lingered, and they were happy just to talk to someone who would listen.

At his regular meetings with his staff, James then heard the other side of the story and was saddened to realise that they had no clue about what was really happening in the factory. The manufacturing manager, who was on his list for replacement, had absolutely no idea where things stood, and his deputy had only vague notions. They clearly did not follow James's dictum of walking the floor first thing in the morning, each and every morning, to find out what was happening. There was obviously much to do! It was as well that he had taken the time the

71

previous week to wander around because he might have been misled enough to give the admiral erroneous data. Simon Wilmott gave a report on the state of the checking process, and they had uncovered a couple of minor shifts of equipment that were quickly corrected. They were spending a little more time on the mixers, but had already confirmed that the mixers used for the Air Force were fine, and they were back in production on that program.

James then met with Simon and the facilities engineers and went through his concerns about the Navy mixers. Finally, he got tired of hearing about what they did not know and suggested that they all repair to a mixer building and actually look at the machinery and decide what checks they should run. It was a little shocking to realise that some of the engineers had only ever been in the building once in their time at the company. He did get a basic description of the building and facilities from George Wheelwright, one of the manufacturing engineers who was there checking on ingredient addition.

"We have in this building the standard Baker Perkins 600-gallon vertical axis mixer. It has two stainless steel blades and a stainless steel bowl that is secured to the mixer frame from below," he explained. "The main oxidisers, nitroglycerine and nitrocellulose, are added to the bowls in another building, and the bowls are transported here on special carriages. In this building, we add the other ingredients, including the AP, the aluminium powder, the HMX and the binders."

"How are they metered?" James asked.

"There are weigh bins for the larger amounts," George replied. "And there are flow meters or measured beakers for the lesser amounts."

"What sensors or other devices are in the in-stream flow that could break off and get into the mix?" James continued. George then gave an explanation of the control and metering technologies, and he actually had drawings and schematics that showed what he was talking about.

"How often do we check the circularity of the bowls and the sweep arc of the mix blades?" James asked.

"Obviously, we spec the bowls round with a tight tolerance," George replied.

"Fine, but what about in use? How often do we check for out-of-round?" James pressed.

"I'm not sure," George admitted. "I'll have to check the operations procedures."

"What about the sweep arc of the blades?" James asked. James thought about how bizarre and incomprehensible this conversation would be to someone who was either not familiar with the process or did not have a technical background. The whole conversation would sound like a foreign language.

"I don't know how we'd check sweep arc," George confessed. "I always thought that that was a facilities issue."

"Maybe, but you run the process, so you should know," James commented, realising as he said it that it sounded cruel, but George needed to appreciate that things would now be different. "As for the sweep arc of the blades, I can think of a few ways to do the job, many of which will be influenced by the verticality of the mixer axis. Perhaps you should discuss it with some of these facility guys, and all of you give me some proposals next week."

"Yes, sir, I'll do that," George agreed a little reluctantly. Now he was committed and had to come up with a solution to a problem he had thought about before but had not been able to solve. He also now had a boss whom he suspected knew how to do the job and who was giving him no clues. It was the kind of test that he really did not like.

"What about tools, manual sampling devices or other things?" James asked. George went through the list of tools generally stored in the buildings and showed James the shadow boards where they were kept. Unfortunately, two of the items were missing from the shadow board of the building they were in, and it took a little while to find them and restore them to their proper places.

"What about personal items being dropped into the inspection ports?" James continued.

"Well, this is an empty pockets building," George explained. "And spectacles or safety glasses should be fitted with lanyard restraints when working here."

"Static electricity?" James wondered.

"The use of conductive shoes or legostats is mandatory here," George explained. "The floor of the main level is actually covered with lead to avoid sparking, so conductivity is not always the best. But, on the ladderways and catwalks, it's fine."

"Any clue what Michael Miller was doing here?" James asked.

"No," George admitted. "You know, there was something odd about that guy. He seemed to me to want to know too much. It was almost as if he were writing a book. You should check through his desk and locker someday and see what's in them."

James then told George and the facility engineers what he expected in terms of checking the alignment of the main axes of the mixer and even suggested how they might do this. When he asked for an explanation of the actual operation of the feed mechanisms and the sensors that were installed, he was a little appalled that they first looked to George and then to a foreman to explain all the items. He voiced his displeasure to the facility engineers after the foreman had departed. He told them that he wanted to see schematics of all the systems and that he expected them to actually see that the schematics matched the physical systems. He got the impression from the foreman that they had to occasionally bypass various steps and procedures because it was not physically possible to do what the instructions required. He wanted that cleared up and no flow charts of processes with open loops, no mismatches between as-designed and as-built systems, or at least none that had not been captured and properly recorded. All in all, he was not thrilled with the general level of engineering discipline in the manufacturing side of the business. And that was only after a few days' observation; heaven only knew what might turn up with more scrutiny. He was amused to overhear a comment afterwards that "He used the 'F' word three times in one sentence!" Well, sensibilities offended or not, perhaps they would look at their jobs more seriously and start taking a real interest in what they were supposed to be doing.

Their next stop was the case winding facility. They had one machine online and running, and the second was actually in the qualification process. James was interested in the tooling, and Simon described the process of tool assembly and disassembly. Both were done from the inside because they wanted the exterior of the finished tool to be as smooth as possible with no projections or hollows. The first segments were easy to bolt together because the bolts were reachable, but it quickly became the situation that someone had to crawl inside to bolt on additional segments. James was reminded of the tubbing used to line shafts and tunnels in unstable ground in mining and for underground railways. Those were significantly larger and were put in place with machines. He quickly realised that the constraint was that everything had to go in and come out of one of the holes at the end of the case, the fore and aft polar bosses. Fortunately, the aft polar boss, where the nozzle attached, was large enough that everything would fit through it. He did make a suggestion to Simon about creating an arm that could be inserted through the boss when someone was inside, and upon which the segments could be placed for withdrawal, reducing the risk of dropping them and damaging the insulation layer of the case windings themselves.

Simon described the case manufacturing process and showed James the insulating rubber that went onto the mandrel first, then the filaments that were used to actually wind the case. They used a carbon fibre that had been pre-impregnated with a resin and a specific pattern for the winding. The finished wound case was moved to a large autoclave for curing, and then the tooling was removed and cleaned and prepared ready for the next case. James asked Simon to work with the engineers and give him a concept for a retractable arm by the following week.

*   *   *

"Here's your book," Colleen announced to Bernard.
"What book?" he asked.
"The one on rockets that you said might be useful," she elaborated.
"So, you're still talking to me?" he asked.
"I'm just doing my job," was her retort. "It doesn't mean that I approve of what you're doing!"
"Okay, okay," Bernard said, trying to smooth things over a little. "What's the book?"

"Rocket Propulsion Elements by a guy by the name of Sutton. First published in 1949, this one's much newer, 5th edition published in 1986," she explained.

"Wow, thanks, Colleen, how much do I owe you?" he asked.

"I took the money out of petty cash and left a chit to your name," she replied. "So you agree with His Holiness on whether or not this is covered."

"Okay, okay," Bernard muttered. He then opened the book and started to page through it. He had to admit that nearly all of it was over his head. But, it would be useful to garner technical terms from both for use in his articles that he had mapped out in his head and to talk to the Air Force guys about when he saw them next. Just before Colleen left the room, he asked her what she thought about the notion of a deliberate act to set off the mixer fire.

"What do you mean?" she asked.

"Well, the colonel said that the new guy, Martin, had suggested that it might have been a deliberate act," he replied.

"But that would be crazy," she said. "From what I've heard about this stuff, once it goes, it goes, and there's no putting it out, so it would have been suicide! Did he actually say that it might have been a deliberate act?"

"Well, I guess not exactly. I gather that he said that as they did not know what the cause was, and that if it was what he called blade-to-bowl contact, then something had to get in there. So, the options were something broke and fell in, something was dropped in accidentally, or something was dumped in there deliberately," he explained. "What do we know about all the people who were there? Any of them have financial or marital problems?"

"How on earth would you find that out?" she asked.

"Well, there has to be gossip in any of the small towns those guys came from, so maybe someone has an idea," he suggested.

"I'll get a list of those that died and see if we can find something," she promised.

"I thought you'd given up on me?" he asked.

"Look, if some dickhead kills himself and others in the process, then it's a human interest story that is worth investigating. It's a lot more palatable than trying to blackmail your stupid wayward colonel!" she said.

"So, you'll help?" he asked, seeking confirmation.

"I'll dig up what I can about those that died and see if there's anything out there on any of them," she promised. "I may need some cash to spend a little time in Idaho," she added.

"No problem," he agreed. "I'll sign for whatever you need."

That evening, Colleen related her conversation with Bernard to Isabella and asked her what she thought about the notion of a deliberate act. Isabella said that it sounded like the colonel was taking things out of context and that it sounded as if James Martin had merely suggested that they not eliminate all the possibilities in their investigation. She reminded Colleen that in police investigations, the good ones were run with no possibility, no matter how absurd it might sound, of being eliminated without some reasonable evidence or explanation. She had to agree that it seemed unlikely, but according to all the engineers, the likelihood of something breaking off and falling into the mix was also a very remote possibility. They were at the point of almost admitting that they really did not know, and the next step was to consider a restart of the operation and risk another explosion caused by the same kind of mishap. The statistics suggested that this was an extremely remote possibility, but without an actual explanation of what happened and, therefore, the knowledge of what to change or correct in the process, what choice did they have?

Isabella did not like the idea of Bernard trying to blackmail the colonel, but she was not sure how to proceed. She did not want to make overly public her relationship with Colleen. Life in Utah for an apparently single professional woman was difficult enough; life as an openly gay professional woman would be difficult indeed. She and Colleen discussed it and decided to let things go for the moment, and if they felt that things were likely to become too difficult, then they would re-examine their situation then.

*   *   *

77

Robert Warner called James the next day and told him that he would be bringing Isabella da Silva to the plant later. She was a Human Resources manager at the Salt Lake City office, and he thought that she might be able to help James look into the personnel files of those killed in the incident and particularly that of Michael Miller. Because they were not sure what they might find in the files of Miller, Robert Warner had picked Isabella because she had a security clearance, and her viewing potentially Secret documents would not present a reporting problem.

James then went through his replacement list and told Robert that he wanted to place blind advertisements for the jobs of Matériel Manager and Quality Manager. He actually had someone in mind for the Matériel Manager job, but wanted a backup in case he was turned down. James also told Robert that he wanted to replace Entwistle, the Safety Manager and Plackett, the Operations Manager, with internal people. He had identified a propellant chemist for the safety job and Simon Wilmott of Program Management for the operations job. Robert told him that they could discuss it all when he was out at the plant later that day.

After the regular morning meetings, James went to the engineering department and asked which was Miller's desk. Allan Black showed him the desk. It was off in a small annexe on its own. Allan told James that Miller had been happy to accept what seemed to everyone else a less-than-desirable slot. It was away from the mainstream and probably lonely if you desired company. As James thought about that, he had a different view; if Miller was up to no good, then it was the perfect spot. Allan told him that they had just shut the door to the annexe after the incident, and no one had been in there since. James asked about Miller's wife, and Allan told him that that was strange. She had been called about the incident, and when he had visited the house, she was gone with no forwarding address or anything. They had been renting a house in Logan, and the landlord, whom he knew, said that they had been good tenants, always paid their rent on time and left the house in good repair, left the furniture, appliances and everything, just nothing personal. Allan speculated that perhaps they had been having marital problems and that she had just left, relieved to be out of the relationship. Still, he found it a little strange that no one had come forward to claim the belongings of Miller that were at the plant, particularly as Roberta Miller, the spouse, had taken everything personal from the house.

James sat down at the desk and looked around. It was ordered and neat. There were small piles of papers stacked on one side; a telephone was on the other side, and in the centre, a piece of Plexiglass with a sheet of paper on it. James looked at the paper, and it looked like a letter that had been drafted. It was addressed to someone in England and seemed to be an itinerary for a trip around old buildings and estates, because there were cities, castles, granges and halls mentioned. Allan told James that, as best they understood events, Miller had been in the office and had received an urgent call from the mix building. He had dropped everything and had gone there, and some time thereafter, the incident had occurred. Allan then excused himself and went back to his work, leaving James to ponder. Looking around the space, there was little on the walls that gave any apparent clues, just a map of the facility and posters of castles and country mansions, some of which James recognised as being in England and Wales. There were no pictures of family on the desk; there were no other personal items of any kind, either on the desk or in the drawers that he could see. For all intents and purposes, it looked as if Miller was all work.

James took a quick look through the papers on the desk and in the drawers. George had been right. It was almost as if the guy was trying to write a book. There were schematics, flow charts, formulæ, process instructions, drawings of buildings and tooling and in general everything that one would need to know to make a missile. The only thing noticeable by its absence was the precise propellant formula. James sat back and looked at it all again, hoping to get some general sense of what the man was like and what he might have been doing. After about five minutes, he gave up. Whatever secrets the work area might have, they were not being revealed to him.

He was interrupted in his browsing by a call from his office. Heather told him that Robert Warner had arrived with Isabella da Silva. He asked Heather to bring them to the engineering department. When they arrived, Robert excused himself for a few minutes and went to talk to Allan, leaving Isabella with James. He asked her to sit and then asked her to tell him a little bit about herself. Isabella told him that she had a BS in business from UC Berkeley and an MBA with a Human Resource specialisation from Stanford. She lived in Kaysville with a roommate, liked to ski and had worked briefly for one of the large aerospace contractors before moving to Utah and joining LST.

James asked her if Robert had told her what the assignment was, and she assured him that she had been fully briefed and was interested to get started. James then asked her to pull the personnel files on all those who had died and go through them carefully to see if there were any common denominators that might provide a clue as to why two teams were in the building that day. He also asked her to review the files of those people who might normally have been team members but who were off that day for whatever reason.

He also asked her to box up everything that she could find in the space that Miller used and to thoroughly examine the desk and the filing cabinet for any papers that had fallen down the backs of drawers or that had been placed deliberately on the undersides of the desk or its drawers. James also told her to take all the posters off the walls and the plant map, and anything she might find underneath them. She looked at him a little strangely but nodded yes. She then asked about any computer accounts that Miller may have had, and James told her to check into that, and while she was about it, check the telephone records for all calls made from the phone in that office. He told her to get the phone forwarded to his secretary so that if any calls happened to still come in for Miller, then either he could take them or Isabella could. He doubted whether there would be anything of value to learn, but they should cover all bases. James told her that he would have someone clear out Miller's locker and bring everything to the office.

Robert and Allan joined them, and Isabella was introduced to Allan. He told them that there had been a few personal items of Michael Miller that had been left in the remote control bunker that serviced the mix facility that had blown up. Those had been boxed and sent to the plant's Human Resources office. James told Isabella to get hold of that box in particular because he wanted to see what was in it. James called Heather and asked her to open up the vacant office that was opposite his, and that Isabella would be using it. He told Isabella to get everything, once it had been boxed up, moved to that office so that she could work with the minimum of disturbance or without too many curiosity seekers.

While they left Isabella to her task, Robert and James went back to the main offices and to the security of the screened room. There, they could discuss the programs without fear of being overheard, either physically or by electronic means.

"James," Robert began. "I wanted to tell you what little I know about the Sagitta Program. As you know, we have a contract for the Air Force Auriga first stage. My guess is that the Auriga is actually going to go nowhere and that Midgetman will be the preferred small missile. As you now know, Sagitta is a Navy program, contracted through the Air Force, that is similar in size to Auriga, masquerading as Auriga B, but it is a black program, and they wanted to limit exposure, so all three stages are done here."

"That much I have discovered. Why would the Navy buy a single warhead missile?"

"I've really no idea. But, I think there's more to this than it being a simple Navy program. Some of the guys you saw last week in Washington are actually CIA. I happen to have seen one of them before at a classified briefing on Soviet missile technology."

"So, do you think the Air Force is fronting for the Navy, which is actually fronting for the CIA?"

"Maybe, but that prospect is scary. Normally, strategic missile arming codes are a presidential thing, and I wonder if the CIA would even bother with normal protocols."

"If the Air Force cancels Auriga and goes with Midgetman, how will the Navy cover the existence of the Sagitta program here?"

"I'm not sure. My guess is that they would probably say that it is an experimental missile and would continue to fund it and try hard to keep a lid on it all."

"Do you think the Sagitta goes on a boat?"

"That I don't know. The Midgetman is slated to be deployed on a special vehicle, the Hard Mobile Launcher and Auriga is going on a similar vehicle that's actually a heavily modified off-highway truck, so I suppose the Navy might be thinking along the same lines, except, of course, that they already base missiles in submarines, which are mobile anyway. My best guess is something like old oil rigs that are parked off in the ocean with launch canisters on them."

"Why would you think that?"

"Well, through our Escape Systems Division, we're also providing a whole series of gas generators to a company called Ocean Systems West, whoever they really are and through our Fastener Division, we're the supplier of an inordinate number of explosive bolts to another weird company called Ocean Parameters," Robert explained.

"So, they're probably blind companies to disguise the true customer, just as we do here with the major components we have to buy from the outside for Sagitta?"

"I'm pretty sure of that. The gas generators being purchased come in three sizes, and the numbers match the number of missile segments we are building live and inert. The one set of generators is about the right size for a canister launch, but there are two other sets of gas generators whose purpose I haven't figured out."

"Have you told Dave Desjardins and Walter Green about your suspicions?"

"No, I haven't really had anyone on the staff to discuss this with until now. I know you worked on some spooky stuff in the past and at least know what a black program is."

"Anyway, you think the missiles will be deployed off something like an oil rig?"

"Yes, there was a notion to put Peacekeepers out on rigs, but that idea was shelved; perhaps that was just a blind for the real program that is Sagitta!" Robert suggested.

"I suppose there could be some sense in that," James thought. "But if the rigs are static, there's really no difference between them and a silo in Wyoming or North Dakota."

"True, but they're in different places. And, who knows, perhaps they're thinking about old rigs in the North Sea, Persian Gulf or China Sea!" Robert added.

"I would have thought security on rigs outside the US would have been an almost impossible task?"

"Yes, but if each rig only has one missile and there are range destruct features in the firing lines, then any security threat has the ultimate fix, just destroy it, and the resulting heat of combustion will melt off the warhead, messy environmentally, but no nuclear detonation."

"That doesn't bear thinking about!"

"Anyway, James, that's all I know," Robert said. "Let me know what you turn up in your investigation, and let me know what you think of Isabella."

"Before you go," James switched to the other topic they had to discuss. "We should talk about the changes in the management that we talked about earlier."

"Okay, you gave me the bare bones over the phone. Could you go over them again?"

"I want to replace John Plackett in operations with Simon Wilmott from the Programs Office; I'll drop the position of Manager of Programs and just have the three guys report to me directly. I also want to replace John Entwistle in Safety with John Edwards from Engineering, and I want to go outside for the Quality and Matériel slots."

"Do you need a Matériel Manager?"

"I think so. I've looked around at all the stuff we have, and my bet is that if we manage inventory a lot better, we can give you $15 to $20 million a year in extra cash over and above operating earnings."

"I'd like that! When can you start?"

"I've already been working with Ken Butler on blind ads, but as I explained before, I have a candidate for Matériel Manager lined up and he will be here next week for a look around. Will you be available next week?"

"Yes, Ken already had me penciled in for some time; do you have a résumé that I can take with me?"

"Yes, I'll get one when you leave. I'm also not too sure about Gene Bonds in HR."

"Why don't you take a look at Isabella while she's here? She's looking for a move up, and we've nothing in the Corporate Office open at the moment."

"Okay, I'll do that, and about the others?"

"Work with Ken on packages for them. What are you thinking of?"

"Well, it's not their fault that they're not performing. They're simply in the wrong jobs and don't have a clue. I shouldn't punish them for that and let them go for poor performance. I think we should give them a reasonable outplacement package and help them find something better suited to their education and abilities. Let's face it, English Majors and Social Studies Majors are interesting but not much use in a technical job that requires some level of fundamental understanding."

"Okay, James. I'll go along with that." Robert agreed. "So, in aggregate, you won't even be up by one slot?"

"No, with the elimination of the Manager of Programs slot and the creation of Matériel Manager, it nets out," James confirmed.

"Have you seen anything of the Navy lieutenant commander yet?" Robert asked.

"No, I received a phone call earlier to say that she would be here tomorrow and wants to meet with me and then wants somewhere to sit while she's here."

"I've no doubt that'll piss off Bill Ridings, but she's the customer, so not much he can really do. I suppose she's already talked to them about what she plans to do while she's here. Should be interesting! On a completely different note, you really shook some of the guys up when you brought up the possibility of a deliberate act," Robert commented.

"Sorry about that," James replied. "But, I needed to be sure that the investigation team wasn't rushing to conclusions. Personally, I can't imagine why anyone would deliberately set off a mix bowl full of explosives, but without data to disprove the hypothesis, it has to stay as a possibility."

"You like to have data, don't you?"

"We're in an engineering business, and opinions are fine, sometimes the only thing when the data is insufficient or inadequate, but there's no excuse for not pursuing whatever data there might be," James explained. "Well, keep it up, and I'll see you in Salt Lake on Friday," were Robert's parting words.

*   *   *

Bernard drove north to Tremonton to meet with Bill Ridings. He thought that Bill ought to be really happy because his prediction had been right, the Bears had beaten the Lions in a close game with only one point deciding the winner. He had called Bill from a pay phone in Salt Lake City the day before and suggested the meeting with the added incentive of receiving the winnings. He had given Bill a clue as to how much it was by telling him what the aggregate of the odds turned out to be. Now his greatest concern was that Bill would be satisfied with whatever he had made from this game and wager nothing, or very little, on the next game. At the Tremonton diner, Bill waved Bernard over and could hardly contain himself.

"Do you have my winnings?" he asked, almost before Bernard had had a chance to sit down.

"All here," Bernard promised, patting a small leather satchel that he had been carrying. He had been quite nervous about carrying that much money around.

"All $100,000 of it?" Bill asked, with eyes almost as round as golf balls.

"All, plus your original $50,000," Bernard promised again, and he slid the satchel over the table to Bill, who opened it up and looked inside, then rifled the bills that were in there. His counting was interrupted by the waitress, who wanted to know what he wanted to eat and drink. Bill ordered, and Bernard echoed his order, and she went away. Bill was grinning like a Cheshire cat, and Bernard was afraid that he might actually start pulling the money from the satchel and start counting it on the table. Fortunately, reason and common sense prevailed, and Bill put the satchel next to him on the bench seat and pretended that it was of no great import. Bernard had also given him all the betting slips so that he could see where the bets had been laid off to and how much each bet was, and what the odds were. There was some variation in odds

85

but not too much of a spread, with only two obvious outliers where the bookies had got it completely wrong.

"So, what's your prediction for the Bears-Vikings game next week?" Bill asked.

"Tough one," Bernard stalled. He was now wrestling with the moment of truth. He, in fact, had a pretty good idea of how that game would go and had bet his own money on the Vikings. But, if he wanted to paint Bill into a corner, now was the only chance to do it, if he was going to leave him with an option in the post-season games. He really wanted Bill to come out ahead when it was all over, if only to make it more difficult for him to own up to his command structure that he had betrayed confidences. Bernard reasoned that if Bill actually came out ahead, then he was just as likely to forget the whole episode and put Bernard and his questions out of his mind. If, however, he left him with nowhere to turn, then he could just throw himself on the mercy of his command structure and shop him. Bernard did not fancy the idea of anyone looking for him, particularly not the government.

"So, what do you think?" Bill repeated.

"Bears to win over the Vikings by one," Bernard blurted out. Now he was committed, and it remained only to see how committed Bill was. Bernard soon found out. Bill pushed the satchel back across the table.

"Let it ride!" he whispered.

"You're sure? All of it?"

"Sure!"

"What if I'm wrong?" Bernard asked. "If we lose, then the people I lay the bets off onto will want to collect, and the bill will be huge!"

"Don't worry," Bill assured him. "You've been right up till now, why should this time be different?"

"I've been lucky so far," Bernard temporised. "My lucky streak can't go on forever!"

"Just do it, Bernard, I'll take my chances!"

"Okay, you're the boss," Bernard apparently reluctantly agreed, then continued. "How are you doing with the aftermath of the accident?"

"Well, we have an investigation team, but so far it looks just like a really bad accident; they do happen from time to time in rocket factories," Bill commented. "I just wish it hadn't been on my watch!"

"Nothing more on the deliberate act?"

"No, it was a legitimate question. I think he just asked it to make us all step back a little and make sure we weren't jumping to conclusions too quickly. The fucking Limey was right. If there was blade-to-bowl contact, then either the bowl was out of shape, or the mixer axis was bent, or something got in there. For something to get in there, it either had to break or be dropped in either accidentally or on purpose. I hate to admit it, but he was right to force us to consider the possibility. Supercilious Limey prick!"

"Does your boss understand that it's not your fault?" Bernard asked.

"My boss, hah, that idiot!" Bill spluttered out. "How the hell he put up two stars I'll never know."

"I'm sorry, what's a two-star?" Bernard asked, a little confused. He had thought that Bill would report to a colonel or a general and was not sure just what a two-star actually was.

"Sorry, a two-star general is a major general. He's probably mad at me because it may reflect upon his career as well and shorten the odds even further of him ever putting up a third star," Bill explained.

"What does the third star mean?" Bernard asked.

"Well, with flag ranks, one star is a brigadier, two a major, three a lieutenant and four a full general," Bill explained.

"Oh, right, but I vaguely remember something about Eisenhower and five stars," Bernard recalled. "Can you still get five stars?"

"Technically yes," Bill confirmed. "But, only if we are at war. The last five-star alive was Omar Bradley."

"Was there ever an Air Force five-star?" Bernard asked, curious now.

"Yes and no. There was Hap Arnold, but he was actually Army. There was no independent Air Force back then. There were five Army and four Navy five stars in World War two," Bill explained.

"I get lost with all the different parts of the Air Force and the ranks of the officers," Bernard laughed. "I'll bet it's hard even for you to keep track sometimes!"

"I've given up," Bill spat out. "After this incident, all I'm looking for is a way out that gets me as much as I can in a place that is as comfortable as it can be."

"Well, I'd better be getting on," Bernard said. "I've got accounts to see and places to go to. I'll see you next week, say Wednesday?"

"Fine, call me before you come up. Maybe we should switch places to meet. Some of these people are beginning to wonder why we keep meeting," Bill thought.

"What about somewhere in Brigham?" Bernard suggested.

"I could manage that, even better, if we met late in the afternoon, I could stop somewhere in Ogden on my way home, there's more choice there, and we could even find a place to get a drink, I'll get out of uniform before I come," Bill suggested.

"Okay, I'll call you next week, Tuesday or Wednesday morning and tell you what, where and when," Bernard agreed. "I'll see you!"

At his office, Bernard called Colleen and asked her if she had found anything on the people who had died in the incident. She told him that, although she had not done a truly in-depth search, her efforts to date had yielded nothing. The community where most of them lived was fairly small, and she had finally found someone willing to talk, and there had been nothing of note; in fact, it was worse than that, there had not even been small items of concern. All involved had been just regular citizens, active in their church, PTA and other groups. Even Miller had been involved with the local Stake House and had been regarded as a quiet but good member of the Church. So Bernard wrote that off as a waste of time and pondered his next moves.

*   *   *

Late in the day, Isabella came to see James. She had collected together all the materials that Michael Miller had had in his desk, filing cabinet and locker and was now beginning to catalogue it all. She had also pulled the personnel files on each of the incident victims and had reviewed them; nothing in any of them raised any red flags.

"So, you found nothing of note?" James asked.

"Not yet," she replied. "But, I'll look again to be sure."

"Let's take a look at what you found in Miller's locker," he suggested.

Isabella led the way to the office she was using and showed James the items she had pulled from the locker. There were the usual coveralls, hard hat, conductive boots, legostats, safety glasses, all of which must have extras because he should have been wearing similar items when he went to the mix building before the incident. One thing he found that was a little out of place was an Ian Allan book. James wondered quite what Miller was doing with a book that listed named British steam locomotives from the fifties and early sixties. When he was much younger, James had had a similar book and had used it to refer to when spotting steam locomotives, a not uncommon hobby for British boys of that era.

"Where are you from?" James asked. Her English was very good, but slightly accented, and he could not place the accent.
"Brazil," she replied. "My family has a large orange plantation, a sugar plantation and a *cachaça* distillery in the interior. I was sent to the US to get a business degree and an MBA. Unfortunately for the plantation, I rather liked it here and stayed. My brother now takes care of the plantation, which, as it turned out, is fine with everyone."
"What's *cachaça*?" James asked.
"It's a spirit distilled from sugar cane juice. It's not rum which comes from molasses, but from the sugar juice itself," she explained.
"Are you a citizen?" James asked.
"Oh, yes. I came to the US in 1972, when I was eighteen, got my bachelor's in 1976, my master's in 1979 and became a citizen right after that."
"Have you been back to Brazil since?"
"Lots of times. I try and go back once a year to visit with my family and see how the business is doing. My brother is actually doing a pretty good job, though it galls me to admit it!"
"What did you do before you came to LST?" James asked.
"After my bachelor's, I got a job with a small aerospace contractor in Pico Rivera. They wanted a human resource assistant who could speak Spanish. Well, I speak Spanish as well as Portuguese, so I fit the bill. I think I also meant points to them in terms of ethnicity and sex. While I was with them, I started on my MBA, then left and finished it up at Stanford. My dad funded that. I think he was hoping I would go back to Brazil. With my MBA, I then looked around and found Waterway Chemicals, which started me looking at cost-benefit analyses of

different benefit packages. That introduced me to Ken Butler, who lured me away to the frozen north where I discovered skiing."

"So you ski?"

"Oh yes! I love the challenge. It was a little difficult at first because I'd spent almost no time in the snow, just one or two trips to Big Bear when I lived in Southern California. But now, bring me a new big storm and I'll find a way to get out onto the slopes."

"You know that Jane Lewis's husband has a sporting goods company, don't you?"

"Yes, I actually signed on with him as a professional tester, so I get my skis and gear for nothing, provided, of course, that I actually use them and send in reports. That's the worst part of it, having to do the reports."

"How are you going to manage the commute from Kaysville?"

"It's further out here than I realised, but it'll be fine once I get past Ogden."

"Michael Miller, what can you tell me about him?" James asked, switching back to their original reason for meeting.

"He's from Pennsylvania, degree in chemical engineering from Penn State, came out here after a short stint with an anodising firm in Pittsburgh, came here in early 1988, married, no kids, rented a house in Logan, no reports of anything untoward. According to some people in Engineering, they went to a Stake House in Logan and were fairly active," she summarised.

"Next of kin?" James asked

"He listed his wife and a cousin, Geoffrey Miller, in England. As you know, the wife disappeared and the address he gave us in England turned out to be one of those places that hold mail for you, so we have had no contact with any family members," she explained.

"Okay, let's start with the easiest things. He would have graduated from Penn State when?" he asked.

"198," she replied.

"Do you know anyone at Penn State or who graduated from Penn State around then?" he asked.

"No, I'm afraid not," she admitted.

"Well, the school offices are closed, but let's try this," James said. He consulted a small book on his desk, then picked up the phone and dialled a number. It obviously rang and was answered because he then asked. "Mike, how's the market for high-priced plumbers these days?" Isabella listened to the one side of the conversation that she could hear and made notes.

"So, Michael Miller graduated in 1985 from Penn State," she confirmed.

"Agreed, but there's one small nagging detail. Michael Miller was injured in a bicycle accident and walked with a very slight limp. After he graduated, he went to work for a small anodising firm in Pittsburgh, then he quit, and Mike lost track of him. He was single, and his parents had died in a car crash three months before he graduated, and there were no siblings. Did our Michael Miller have a limp at all?"

"I'll find out," Isabella said. She picked up the telephone and called three people, then she confirmed what James suspected. "Michael Miller had no limp; in fact, he had been seen once or twice jogging in the hills above the plant."

"So who was our Michael Miller?" James asked.

"We don't know that there was another Michael Miller," she objected. "He may have recovered completely from his injury or found ways to cope so that he could jog."

"Perhaps," agreed James. "But, for the sake of argument, let's assume not."

"I don't suppose there were two Michael Millers who graduated at the same time?" she asked.

"Not according to my source," James confirmed.

"How would your source know one guy out of how many?" she challenged.

"I gather the class size was under a hundred, and Miller was an avid cyclist whom my contact knew and rode with," James explained.

"I can't believe it would be that easy to find that out," she commented and then asked. "When we hired him, surely we ran a check?"

"We may have done. What would it have shown? Michael Miller graduated Penn State in 1985, transcript attached, check for ID. Our man has an ID that shows Michael Miller. Why would we check further? If we had checked with the placement office at the university, they would have told us about the anodising firm in Pittsburgh, but how many people report their moves after their first jobs? It's only because I happen to know someone from Penn State who graduated at the same time that I was able to find out about his physical condition."

"Wouldn't there have been a class photo?" she asked.

"Perhaps, but do you want to bet that our man and the original look enough alike that any difference would be put down to a poor photograph?"

"What about fingerprints or something?" she asked.

"Well, as he was supposedly born in the US, and he had no security clearance and as far as we knew, he had no criminal record or military service, there would be no fingerprints on file anywhere. For people born here, it's not like it is for you and me, when we got our Green Cards, they took fingerprints and again when we became citizens; for native-born citizens, that is not done unless there is a need, like criminal activity, military service or security clearances."

"Has anything like this ever happened to you before?" she asked.

"Not quite the same, but résumé padding, yes. I once interviewed a guy who claimed to have done all kinds of things in Africa. The only problem was that I had been there at the time he was supposed to have worked miracles and knew that he had done nothing of the kind. It was a shame, really, because he might have been useful if he hadn't lied."

"What do we do now?" she asked.

"I think we need to look carefully at all the documents he collected and try and work out what he was really doing here," James commented. "I doubt that we'll ever find out who he really was."

"Do you think he was a spy?" she asked, looking towards the door almost as if she was afraid of being overheard.

"I don't know," he admitted. "Maybe he just wanted to disappear from a bad domestic situation, maybe he was running from the Mob, maybe it's the FBI Witness Protection Program. We just can't rule out any possibility."

"What do we do now?"

"I think it best if we keep it between us for now," James commented. "Unless we have specific evidence that Miller was up to no good, it serves no purpose to tell anyone anything."

"What will we need to go to someone with suspicions?" she asked.

"I think if you catalogue all those documents and there's something there that doesn't belong, we'll decide then."

"Okay, Mr. Martin," she promised.

"Please call me James," he suggested; then he asked, "If Robert brought you up here, how are you getting back to Kaysville?"

"I'd rather hoped that someone here could give me a lift," she replied.

"I'll drive you to Kaysville," James offered. "Are you ready to go?"

"If you are, yes," she said. "Let me just call a friend of mine, then you can drop me in town and I'll get a ride home with her."

James drove to Kaysville to drop Isabella off, and to pass the time, they talked about Brazil. James was interested in the orange plantation and in the distillery. He was intrigued by the *cachaça,* and she explained that much of it was used in a popular drink in Brazil, the *caipirinha.* She promised to make some for him and for Katrina one day and guaranteed that he would like them. After he had dropped Isabella outside a restaurant in Kaysville, James dove back to the hotel in Ogden and called Katrina. She was working through the process of selling the house, and they had actually had an offer. They talked a little about the offer and what the final net result would be for them. The housing market was still hot, and people were still queuing up for new developments. The press was predicting a continued strong market in 1989, so buyers were actually quite keen.

"When will you be home?" Katrina asked.

"I've got a meeting in Salt Lake early Friday afternoon and will fly to Orange County right after it," James replied.

"Call me when you leave, and then I'll be at the airport to meet you," she promised.

Lieutenant Commander Reinsch

Lieutenant Commander Reinsch arrived at eight the next day. She first checked in with the AFPRO Office and then made her way to James's office.

"Good morning, Commander," James welcomed her.

"Please call me Josephine," she invited. "I don't wish to impose, but orders are orders."

"I understand," James acknowledged. "How do we explain your presence here?"

"The cover story is that I'm doing a review for the Navy of other missile systems so that we can develop a manual of best practices," she explained.

"Okay," James agreed. "How may we best answer the questions you have?"

"Could we take a tour and walk through the process?" she asked.

"Of course," he agreed. "We have a regular production meeting first, which you might wish to sit in on. After that, we could do the tour, and then we have an office for you. Do you have a winter coat and boots? We'll have some walking to do between buildings, and it's cold out there."

"I have them with me," she replied. "In fact, I left them with your secretary, Heather. Is there somewhere I can change?"

"Of course," he said and then called out. "Heather, could you take Lieutenant Commander Reinsch to somewhere where she can change clothes?"

When she returned, now dressed in khaki fatigues, boots and carrying her overcoat, James led the way to the meeting where the production schedule was reviewed.

After the meeting, there were a few items that James wanted to actually look at in person. He was still not satisfied that the production control office actually knew what was going on. He was impatient to make his changes and wanted to make his announcements, but had promised Robert Warner that he would make no announcements until after their meeting on Friday. He worked out a tour route that would show

Lieutenant Commander Reinsch the process and also answer his own questions. "Should we ask Colonel Ridings to join us?" he asked.

"I suppose we should," she thought. James called the AFPRO office and arranged to meet Bill Ridings at the case winding facility. James gave the tour of case winding and explained mandrel construction, filament winding and then curing and mandrel removal. They saw a first-stage case in winding, a second-stage case prepared and ready for the autoclave cure and a third-stage case which had been cured and from which the mandrel tooling was now being removed. The lieutenant commander wanted to know where the carbon fibre and the polar bosses came from. James told her that they bought carbon fibre from two suppliers and that the polar bosses were machined on-site from forgings they purchased. That fit in nicely with the next step on the tour, which was the machine shop, where various components were made. From there, it was a quick walk to the nozzle facility, where they could see a number of nozzles from the different stages in various stages of manufacture. It was an odd combination of metal parts, tape-wrapped carbon fibre parts and elastomeric pieces for the seal that allowed the nozzles to move.

The last part of the tour was in the live areas. That is, it was the area where propellants were prepared, mixed and cast. As James had not authorised the restart of mixing for the Sagitta or Auriga Type B program, the only real activity was for the Air Force Auriga program. The lieutenant commander was interested in the processes generally, so she suggested that they tour all the live areas. They toured the mix buildings for Auriga and watched ingredient addition and mix operations. Then they went on to the mix buildings for the Auriga Type B propellant, where they found George Wheelwright, who was running some tests to see if the bowls were, in fact, round and if the blades actually went where they were supposed to.

"George, hi," James interrupted the work. "How's it going?"

"Hi, James. Well, all the data we have indicate that the bowls are all well within the circularity spec, and our initial results from the tests we are running now show that the blades prescribe the arcs that they are supposed to, so the probability of direct blade to bowl contact is very low," George explained.

"What about the mixers themselves? Are they vertical?" James asked.

"Two of the three were within three seconds of arc, which would make the maximum excursion from the prescribed path to be about ten thou and the third was out of plumb by about ten seconds of arc, or about 50 thou excursion. That one we shimmed back to plumb," George replied. "But even at that, there still would have been more than adequate clearance, and more than the spec calls for."

"What about the metering and inspection equipment and ports?" James asked.

"We've added lock wires to all the nuts that have any route to the mix bowl itself, and we've changed out a couple of the sensors to more robust ones that don't need as much manual adjustment," George elaborated.

"So, what was the possibility that something broke and fell in the mix that exploded?" Josephine asked.

George looked at James, who then made the introduction. "George, this is Lieutenant Commander Reinsch of the Navy. She will be here for a while observing our process."

"Well, it's conceivable, Ma'am," George replied. "I have identified three possible items that there was a possibility of failure with. I have modified those items on the remaining mixers, but I have a difficult time believing that something actually broke and fell in. I've talked to a couple of my friends at Hercules and Thiokol, and they have similar types of equipment and have no history of failure with those items."

"What about something being dropped through an inspection port?" she asked.

"That's always a possibility," George admitted. "But the procedures call for any spectacles, hand tools or the like to be lanyarded."

"Do you think procedures were followed?" she asked.

"Ah, that question I can't really answer," he said. "The CCTV cameras don't cover all the areas that people could go, and our review shows no evidence of anything untoward."

"Why were there so many people here?" she asked.

"That we don't know," he admitted. "It's possible that the crew were showing Miller the process, but why the second crew was there, we don't know, and obviously we can't ask them."

"Did you know any of them?" she asked.

"Only casually," he admitted. "We were never encouraged to spend much time out here or to get to know the crews."

"Has that changed?" she asked.

"Yes," was all George would say on that topic.

"Perhaps we should talk to the operations management about adherence to procedures?" Josephine suggested.

"I've done that," James commented. "They all assure me that they adhered rigidly to all processes and procedures."

"My own review confirms that," Bill added. "We routinely conduct reviews and audits of the procedures and whether or not they are being adhered to."

"I'm sure that your staff does its job," Josephine commented to Bill. She caught James's eye and clearly wanted to continue that discussion, but away from the Air Force colonel. James got the impression that she was being polite to a superior officer, but that she actually had little time for him. They quickly went through a casting building, but as there was no casting going on, it was a quick tour. Bill then excused himself and said that he had to get ready for the one o'clock investigation review. James suggested to the lieutenant commander that they get some lunch in the cafeteria and then go to the investigation review. Over lunch, she asked James what he thought about the issue of the workers following the procedures. James was careful with his reply, but did tell her that operational discipline when he had arrived had not been to the standards that he would accept. He told her that he was working to amend that and that management changes were in the works.

The investigation review brought nothing really new, just a formal presentation of the data from the bowl examinations and the blade excursion information. The team did have failure trees, and some of the branches had been closed because there were either data that ruled them out or tests on similar pieces of equipment that failed to produce a catastrophic result. Josephine sat through the meeting and made some notes, but asked no questions. James then asked what would happen if the ingredients were mixed in incorrect proportions. The consensus was that nothing of import would happen during the mix cycle and that the issue would be after the fact, when the propellant failed to set up after casting, or the ballistics would be wrong upon ignition. No one could come up with a scenario that suggested ignition in the mix bowl.

James asked how the reconstruction of the mixer was progressing, and they told him that it was being worked on. They did have a concern with their ability to identify all the parts, and he suggested that they get help from Baker Perkins. After all, he pointed out, the NTSB was undoubtedly going to ask for Boeing's help to reconstruct the Pan Am 747 that had just been blown out of the sky over Lockerbie in Scotland. That led to another discussion, but this one was not about LST and their problems but about the Middle East and the continuing conflict between the Israelis and their neighbours.

James left the lieutenant commander with Simon Wilmott and went off to Salt Lake City to meet with Ken Butler. They had details to work out before James made his announcements the following week. Ken was a little concerned that it was getting close to Christmas, and he was uncomfortable severing people just before the Holidays. James pointed out that the severance packages they had worked out were far in excess of what had been the company practice before he came, which in his opinion belonged in the Fifties and perhaps Sixties, but certainly not in the Eighties. Ken had to admit that they were now generous enough to give anyone a reasonable start at looking for a new job. He was worried about the cost, but James pointed out to him that another incident would cost them far more, both in lost revenue and in additional costs.

When James called Katrina that afternoon, he was happy to have a normal conversation about life. Katrina had organised the movers, and the van would be at the California house on the 2nd of January. She expected them to be packed and loaded that day, so that she and James would leave that evening and start on their drive north. Katrina finally changed the subject and asked, "When do you get to Orange County on Friday?"

"I'm on a Delta flight that gets in at 5:05," James said. "You should probably check the arrival time because there is snow in the forecast, and there might be a few delays."

"I'll pick you up at the curb," she promised. "I've missed you! You need to spend some time with me."

"I'll be there," he promised. "Is there anything that we need to do this weekend?"

"The only thing you need to do this weekend is devote yourself to satisfying me," she said. "I've been on short rations lately, so you have some making up to do!"

"You're not the only one," he laughed. "I've begun to think that I'm living like a monk here. I miss you."

*   *   *

Bernard looked over his notes on the LST incident and realised that he actually did not have much. He wondered if he was putting too much emphasis on information he might or might not be able to get from Bill Ridings. He still did not know much about the incident, except that it was in a mixer building and that current thinking was that it was something called blade-to-bowl contact. What precisely had caused this contact was, as yet, unknown and given the fact that the building and all that was in it was gone, it was unlikely that they would ever really find out. He had had Colleen follow up a little on the personal stories of the people who had been killed and had drawn blanks all around. None of those involved had any dark histories; in fact, they were all remarkably bland. Even Miller had checked out as being a regular at one of the local Mormon churches. His enquiries about the Navy people being on site had led nowhere. All in all, he was getting to the point of abandoning the whole idea of a story. If he did that, he would also let Bill Ridings off the hook with his betting and hedge the bets with a Bears' loss.

Bernard left his office and went to find Colleen. He had to get directions because he had actually never been to the research department.

"So, Colleen, what's up?" he asked.

"I'm working on a follow-up story on Bangerter's pumps," she replied.

"I'm sorry, what?"

"The pumps that the State Government installed to drop the lake level by pumping water into the western part of it, where it evaporates," she explained.

"Is that going to be one of those great projects that turns out to have been not really necessary?" he wondered.

"I'll let you know when I've finished my research," she promised.

"Have you heard anything more about the incident out at LST?" he asked.

"No," was all she would say.

"I wonder if I'm not missing something?" he said.

"What about your scheme with the Air Force colonel?" she asked.

"I'm even starting to wonder if he actually knows anything at all," he said. "He's so focused on his football and what he might do with the rest of his life that I think he's checked out already."

"Has he been given another assignment? Maybe he's FIGMO?" she wondered.

"He's what?" Bernard asked, intrigued.

"Fuck it, got my orders," she explained.

"Oh," he laughed. "No, I don't think he's got another assignment yet; he doesn't talk to his command people until January. Well, I'll just have to keep digging."

Later that evening, Colleen related her conversation with Bernard to Isabella, and Isabella wondered if they should not tell someone in the Air Force that Bill Ridings might be being set up for blackmail. Colleen was not sure. To date, Bernard had not actually done anything, except earn Bill some money, which he might or might not declare to the IRS. Isabella suggested that if Bernard actually went ahead with his plan, then she would put it into James's hands and let him decide what to do. Colleen thought that was a good idea and then asked, "What's he actually like?"

"Who, James Martin?" Isabella asked.

"Of course, James Martin, who else?" Colleen confirmed. "You've spent some time with him now, what's he like?"

"Difficult to categorise," Isabella commented. "He's obviously not American, even if he is a citizen. He seems to be nice enough."

"Nice, that's not exactly very descriptive!"

"I'm hedging. I'll give you a better description in a few days."

"Would you trust him?"

"I think so. I sense that he doesn't have much time for mediocrity or fools."

"If we have to confide in him, how do you think he'll react?"

"He can keep a secret. He certainly doesn't let the people out at the plant know what he's thinking, unless he wants to!"

"Okay, well, let's see what Bernard does and then decide," said Colleen.

*   *   *

On Friday, James left the office and drove to Salt Lake City to be in time for a luncheon appointment with Robert Warner. He was surprised to see Jane Lewis and Ken Butler there as well; he had thought that it would have just been he and Robert. Jane explained that she had come to review succession plans with Ken, so the changes that James wanted to make were of interest. James went through his reasoning for the changes fairly quickly and then laid out his new organisation chart. As he had previously explained to both Robert and Ken, he was going to replace John Plackett in Operations with Simon Wilmott from Programs and John Entwistle in Safety with John Edwards from Engineering. There were interviews set up the following week for the Quality and Matériel slots. He wanted to move on the Operations and Safety positions immediately, so had drafted an announcement for internal use and a press release for external use. Ken explained the outplacement packages they had put together, and Robert and Jane both approved them. Robert asked about the Human Resource position and if he thought that Isabella da Silva might be suitable. James did not want to commit himself yet, but he commented that even with the very little he had seen of her work, she was no worse than Gene Bonds! The meeting finished up with Ken promising to be at the plant at eight on Monday morning to handle the terminations and the introductions to the outplacement firm they had decided to use.

With the meeting over, James was free to go and was early for his flight to Orange County. He checked with Delta, and there was a flight at about three that got him in just after four. Fortunately, there was space, and he was able to switch flights. He called Katrina to let her know and she was thrilled that he was coming in early. The scheduled time might have been a little over two hours, but the actual time was a little under one hour and forty-five minutes. James rather suspected that the airline padded the schedule a little in case of traffic delays in the LA basin or weather delays in Salt Lake City.

As the plane descended over the San Bernardino Mountains, James looked at the smog inversion layer that sat over the LA basin. He had seen it many times before but the phenomenon never ceased to fascinate him. It was like descending through a definite layer, from clear air to murky air. Once in the murky air, it looked clear enough, but he knew that if you went back above it, it was really murky. The rest of the descent into Orange County was simple enough, with touchdown at four pm on the dot. The airport was a mess. Construction had started on a new terminal building. For James that was a shame. Gone would be the walks out onto the tarmac with the instructions that 'your plane is the third line down, second plane back', now it would be sterile gates with numbers accessed by jetways. Still, he supposed, it was progress and most people would regard it as an improvement from the current circumstance.

He had no baggage to claim, so walked out to the curb and waited for about five minutes until he saw Katrina driving towards him. He waved, and she pulled over for long enough to let him get into the car, then she was off.
"Hi sweetie," she said. "How was the flight?"
"Fine," he commented. "It was uneventful, which is always good, we left on time and arrived a little early and it was smooth enough. How are you?"
"Happy now that you're here," she replied. "How come you're early?"
"We were done in Salt Lake quicker than I thought, and I was able to get an earlier flight," he replied.
"Well, I'm glad," she announced. "I've missed you this past week!"

"I've missed you too, *Suikerbossie*," he said. "It seems like it's been a long week."

"It's been too long," she laughed. "I've got plans for you when we get home."

"Looking at this traffic, that may take a while," he complained.

"I think I'll cut over to Jamboree and forget the 55," she said. "I'm sure that it'll be quicker."

"You're right," he agreed. "So, what have you been up to?"

Katrina then told him all about her week and what she had been doing. She was ready for the move now, and they were really just waiting for the close on the house in Utah, so that they could actually move.

Katrina was right. The drive up Jamboree took a lot less time than the drive up the 55 would have. The freeway was a slow-moving parking lot, and the worst was yet to come. The rush hour started at about three thirty and continued until almost six. After that, it slackened off a little, except at the intersections with the 5 and 22 freeways. Their route would not take them as far north as the 91 freeway, but that would be another bottleneck. Once home, she wasted no time and dragged James off to a bath and then the bedroom. Later, their passion spent for the moment at least, Katrina suggested that they might go out for dinner. She wanted to go to Moreno's, a Mexican restaurant on Chapman Avenue, not too far from where they lived. Moreno's was in an old Quaker Meeting House and had long had a reputation for good food. Since they had lived in Southern California and discovered the restaurant, it had become a favorite of both Katrina and James. It was a short enough drive past the fire station, then the gravel pits that had once been the Santiago Creek, until they reached Chapman Avenue, from there it was a short drive west to the restaurant.

Over dinner, James told Katrina about his week and the changes he was about to make in the organisation. She listened, as always, and then told him that she had every confidence that he knew what he was doing. She asked about Isabella and Josephine, and James was able to tell her very little apart from the very basic information that he had. He told her that Robert was hinting very broadly that he might consider Isabella as a new Human Resources manager to replace Gene Bonds, the incumbent. James then asked her about the movers and the house sale. The house sale was proceeding well, and she foresaw no issues. There had been home inspection people through, and there were no items to be corrected or fixed.

For the movers, they would be at the house at eight on the morning of January 2nd, with an expected load out and depart the same day. She had not made a hotel reservation for that night deciding to pick a place to stay depending on how they felt. She had made a reservation in Saint George for the night of the 3rd and another in Nephi for the night of the 4th. The movers had promised to be there to unload on the 5th. James had worked with the realtors in Utah and had a walk-through scheduled for December 30th, when he would also pick up the keys. He had arranged with the realtor to transfer the utilities so that they would not lose heat in the house over the Christmas break.

That brought everything up to date, so they then talked about other things. Katrina had heard from her parents, and they were planning to plant more grape vines, these grapes being a Chardonnay variety rather than the Hannepoort grape that they already had. She had also joined a gym and was working out three times a week, and wondered what there might be in Ogden. She was combining weight training with aerobic exercise and said that she could already feel the difference in her general well-being. She laughingly told James about her new workout gear that included a thong leotard. James was intrigued and wanted to see, so she suggested that they pay the bill and go, and she would model it for him.

*   *   *

Bernard Rasmussen sat at the bar of the club he frequented and pondered his next move. The football game between the Bears and the Vikings was not until Monday evening, and although he was confident about the result, he had to consider the possibility that the Bears might actually win. In that case, he would have to change his approach to the colonel. He mulled over ideas that he had for just basic investigative journalism and kept finding that he was running into blank walls. He knew about the Air Force program at LST, but even there, only the basics. He had not been able to cultivate anyone at the plant from the company, and he began to think that he had placed too much emphasis on his single approach. Next to him was a group of people who had obviously just come back from the ski slopes. Judging by their conversation, they had had a good time, drunk too much and were now talking about the following week. As Bernard overheard snatches of the conversation, he realised that they were talking about the rocket business and about LST in particular. Now he paid attention and gathered that they were from California and were in town to conduct some kind of surprise audit of the LST plant. He heard the terms LST, Navy, first stage, mixer, Auriga Type B, Air Force, AFPRO and a few others, none of which made any sense. He finally turned to one and asked them where they were from. That was a mistake because they all then stopped talking and left.

Now Bernard had something to ponder. What he knew about the LST programs was that they involved the Air Force and a missile called Auriga. But, these people had mentioned something completely different; something called Auriga Type B and the Navy in the same conversation. That was the second time that he had heard a reference to the Navy with regard to LST, but his and Colleen's research had turned up nothing about the Navy. He thought about the name Type B and wondered what it meant. He paid his tab, left the bar and went to his office. Now he sat down and thought. The Air Force rocket program was the Auriga; perhaps that was another variant. Bernard looked up Auriga and learned that it was a constellation, from the Latin auriga or charioteer, so was Type B a different rocket program and was it, in fact, a Navy rocket? But why had he heard nothing about it? It was something to follow up on Monday!

Bernard wondered if he should call Colleen and ask her if she had ever heard of this Auriga Type B program or if she could find out if it even existed. Since she had told him that she had no interest in his schemes, he had been reluctant to spend too much time with the research people. He was after the story, no matter what it might take, whereas they, or at least she, seemed to have qualms about how he got information. It was really frustrating not having access to anyone in Washington. All his contacts were local and singularly ill-informed about the rocket industry, even though it made up quite a large part of the employment base of the state. The friends he had at Hill Air Force Base were all part of the logistics centre there and had nothing to do with the rocket business. If he had wanted to find out something about brakes for an F-16 fighter plane, that would have been simple enough, but the rocket people were really secretive. Bernard sighed, closed up his files and decided to go home. There were days when he wished that he were back in Pennsylvania. Utah was nice enough, but there were things he missed. That thought made him pause, and he went back into his office and called Delta Airlines and made reservations to go to Philadelphia for the Christmas break. Perhaps while he was there, he would look and see what the opportunities might be at one of the Philadelphia papers.

*   *   *

Monday morning, early, James arrived at the plant to find Isabella already there. She must have set off from Kaysville really early to be in the office before he was. Also, there was Lieutenant Commander Reinsch. She had stayed the weekend in Logan, so she had had a shorter drive. She asked for a few minutes of James's time. He showed her into his office and closed the door.

"What may I do for you?" James asked.

"I just wanted to let you know what my interim report to the admiral will say," she told him, then went on. "I can find no evidence of anything other than a mishap, source unknown."

"I would agree with that," James concurred. "But I'm not satisfied with the unknown, are you?"

"No, but I have to confess to being unable to see any rational scenario that would cause such an event," she said.

"All the data we have and the trials, tests and research we have done all point away from a misaligned blade causing blade to bowl contact or from contact with a broken piece of feeding equipment or measuring device," James went on.

"What does that leave?" she asked.

"Something dropped in through an inspection port," he suggested.

"I agree, but the real question is accidentally or deliberately," she added.

"In that I also agree. I've got Isabella da Silva from our corporate HR group in Salt Lake City scouring the files to try and find some clue as to why there were so many people there and if that had any bearing on the event," he commented.

"I'd like to meet her," she said.

James got up and left the office for a minute, and returned with Isabella. "Isabella da Silva, Lieutenant Commander Reinsch," he said, making the introductions. "The Commander shares our curiosity and puzzlement as to the number of people in the mix building and the source of ignition."

"I understand from James that you are reviewing files, looking for clues?" Josephine asked, seeking confirmation.

"Yes, I've done a quick scan of the personnel files and found nothing of note, and now I'm wading through the materials that we found in Miller's desk and locker," Isabella explained.

"Was there a lot?"

"Yes, screeds and screeds," Isabella confirmed. "I'm cataloguing everything and then I'll start to try and look for relationships or anomalies."

"How long will that take?"

"I'm not sure, but it won't be a short task; there's just so much paper."

"One of the things we are looking into is why Michael Miller had so much information stored in his work area and what he was actually doing," James added. "It seems to us that he was going well beyond his area of responsibility."

"Perhaps he just wanted to learn," Josephine suggested.

"Perhaps," James agreed. "It's gratifying to think that we had such a dedicated employee."

"But, you don't altogether agree?"

"I'm not sure," James admitted. "I suppose I'm a little suspicious by nature and wonder if there were not some other reason."

"Perhaps he was going to write a book?"

"Perhaps," James agreed. "It's also possible that he was trying to be the next engineering manager and was working to broaden his view of the process; we just don't know."

"Okay, what about the new mixer?" Josephine asked.

"It's on order," James confirmed. "Delivery is promised by March 25th. Our issue will not be the mixer, but getting a building ready in time. We have cleared the site of the old building and are re-digging the pit. I've decided to work through the bad weather by putting up a temporary enclosure over the site. I've brought in heaters so that we won't be bothered by the ground freezing, especially when we come to cast the pit and the foundations for the building. We have the steel on order, the insulation, the catwalks and ladder ways, the electrical gear and the rest of the feeding, measuring and ancillary equipment."

"You've done a lot," Josephine commented.

"The people here have," James said. "All I did was sign a bit of paper. We had the building design from the other mix buildings and the schematics, so all we have to do is replicate what was there."

"Is everything still available? I mean, are all the system items still in production?"

"No, not all," James confirmed. "We've had to make a few substitutions and I've got a team going through the process instructions to see what is affected."

Management changes

Heather interrupted the meeting to let James know that Ken Butler had arrived. James excused himself and asked Heather to get Simon Wilmott and John Edwards, and to get John Plackett and John Entwistle. He then told Lieutenant Commander Reinsch that she would undoubtedly hear later that day about management changes and that the first two he was making were in Operations and Safety. She guessed that the two new managers would be Wilmott and Edwards, and just wanted to know in which job each would be. She knew Simon Wilmott as he had taken her on the tour, and she had been impressed, so approved of his choice. She suggested to Isabella that they get some coffee, and they both left. As they left, Ken Butler came to the office and joined James.

The first of the new management changes to arrive was Simon Wilmott. James asked him in and offered a seat.
"Simon," he began. "I'm making some changes in the organisation and I would like you to take over Operations."
"Okay," Simon temporised. "What does that entail?"
"I want someone with a technical background in Operations, and I'll give you a free hand to do whatever reorganisation you think is necessary," James explained.
"A free hand?" Simon asked, looking for confirmation.
"Yes," James confirmed. "I don't think there's enough adherence to the processes and procedures, and in some cases, I suspect that they could not be followed even if you wanted to because they are not well written or have open loops in them or unworkable situations."
"That I would agree with," Simon said. "What about Programs?"
"I'll have the three program managers report directly into me, but my second in command has got to be the Operations Manager; that's where it all begins and ends for me," James explained. "I'm also going to create a new function, that of Matériel. I'll pull purchasing, warehousing and production planning into that group."
"Oh, who'll run that?" Simon asked.

"I'm interviewing now," James explained. "But, it won't be anyone from here. I'm looking for experience outside this operation because I want to bring in MRP disciplines, and we quite frankly just don't have any."

"Okay, when do I take over Operations?" Simon asked.

"Now," James said. "I'm going to relieve John Plackett now and have arranged for outplacement for him. And, so that you will know, I'm also replacing John Entwistle."

"Good idea," Simon agreed. "If I were you, I'd ask John Edwards to take that job. He'll do a better job of looking at the process from a safety point of view and worry less about the slogans and statistics!"

"Thanks for the input," James told him. "Could you ask whoever is out there to step in here?"

John Plackett came in and sat down, looking back and forth between James and Ken. James told him why he was there, and he was actually relieved, particularly after Ken told him in broad terms what the outplacement help would be. They left the office together to finalise things, and James asked Heather to bring in John Edwards. He had a similar conversation with John Edwards as he had had with Simon Wilmott, and John left eager to take up the reins of his new assignment.

Although he did not like the idea of keeping John Entwistle waiting, James let him sit until Ken returned. Separations were always better if there was a witness. He told John that he was being replaced, and John was at a loss to understand why. James explained that he had changed the job description for Safety Manager, and one of the requirements was now a technical qualification, either degree or Professional Engineer. Ken then took over and escorted John off to explain the finer points of outplacement to him and witness the turnover of his badge, files and company property.

James then asked Heather to call a special staff meeting at which he would announce the changes. There was a little surprise when James made his announcements. The team had been expecting something since the incident, but had not anticipated the replacement of the Operations manager by someone other than his deputy. Taking people from Programs and Engineering was a new tactic that none of them had thought of. He was asked if there would be further changes, and James told them that he was looking for a Matériel manager and would be restructuring the operations department to consolidate purchasing and the other functions related to the acquisition of materials and parts under the new department. What he did not tell them was that he was also looking for a new Quality Manager and that the Personnel Manager's job was also in jeopardy. That could come later. What James was concerned about now was the melding of the new management structure into an actual team.

Heather interrupted the meeting and told them all that there was an audit team from one of their customers waiting in the lobby. James told her that he would come and see them. When he arrived at the lobby, he was greeted by a crowd of twelve people, all complaining loudly about being kept waiting. The team leader introduced himself as Bob Blake and told James that they were there to review the operation, particularly in light of the recent incident.

"Mr. Blake," James began. "Could you give me some idea of the scope of this audit?"

"We're concerned that LST is not following its own procedures and that this may have contributed to the incident," Blake explained.

"I see," James said. "How do you plan to execute this audit?"

"We'll break our team into four sub-teams, one will review planning documents, one will review the workplace, one will interview operations people, and the last will look at the management structure," Blake elaborated.

"I see," James said. "How long do you anticipate that this will take?"

"We're planning to be here three weeks, or rather this week until the Christmas break, then we'll be back in January for another two weeks," Blake explained.

"I see," James said again. "I would like a briefing at the end of each day and a review of your work before you submit your findings to the company."

"I guess I can do that," Blake demurred. "I have my instructions to do our audit and then brief you on our findings, and then follow up on the CARs that will be generated, and I will brief the program office."

"So, you're assuming that there will be corrective action requests?" James asked.

"I fail to see how there will not be," Blake challenged. "There has been an incident here with destruction of property and fatalities; it's hard to imagine that all is copasetic."

"I see," James said yet again. He then suggested to Blake that they convene a pre-audit briefing with his staff, and they could assign escorts to the various teams and then see what issues might be uncovered. On their way to the conference room, they met Lieutenant Commander Reinsch. James made the introductions, and Blake asked her what she was doing there. She reacted by asking what business it was of his. James thought that he had better defuse this fast, so he told Blake that the commander was there doing a review for the Navy because the Navy was trying to develop a set of best practices. Blake snorted at that and commented that it was hardly likely that a facility that had just had an incident that resulted in the destruction of a building and fatalities would represent any best practices. James bridled at that but let it go. Blake was just one of those auditors who had to let you know just how powerful he was and how miserable he could make your life.

The management team was still assembled in the conference room, so the audit team simply joined them. Many of the audit team were known to the LST management because they had been to the plant before. Only Bob Blake and his deputy were new to them, and they were introduced as being from the Customer Quality department of the customer. The others were purchasing, engineering and quality people who had had various dealings with the LST plant team. James sensed some friction between most of the audit team and its leader, Blake, and wondered if he had not been brought in especially for this audit. Blake introduced his team and told the others what he intended to do, and asked for contacts to be assigned. They also wanted workspace and telephones. James asked Heather to arrange with the different departments for space and desks, and also telephones. Blake then asked James for an overview of the operation and an organisation chart. James happened to have an organisation chart that he had drawn up for the announcements of the management changes, so gave them a copy. It only took a minute or two before one of the more regular visitors noticed the changes and asked about them.

James commented on the changes that had been made but gave no further explanation. He was about to give an overview of the operation when Heather came in and quietly told him that three inspectors from UOSH, the Utah Occupational Safety and Health department, were in the lobby and wanted access to the plant to conduct a workplace review. James excused himself from the meeting and asked Simon Wilmot to take over while he went downstairs to deal with the UOSH people. Before he went, he also asked Simon to assign people to the various sub-teams to act as liaisons and to get requested information. As for the UOSH people, it had been expected that UOSH would conduct an investigation of some sort after the incident, and it had surprised everyone that it had been this long before they arrived. That was explained by the team leader, who cited manpower shortages for the delay. James asked them what their work schedule and requirements would be. He then asked Heather to get George Wheelwright to come to the lobby. He explained to the UOSH team leader, Kim Wheelwright, that they had another audit team that had just arrived, which was much larger and which would be requiring resources, but that he would be assigning a person to them to act as a guide and who would get whatever information they needed to conduct their review. Kim Wheelwright understood and told James that he would give him a quick review at the end of each day and a full debrief when they had completed their review. James waited with them until George arrived, and then he explained to George that the UOSH team was to get whatever access they wanted and whatever documents they might need to see, but he cautioned the UOSH team that there were certain documents that they would not be able to review because of their classification. The team leader understood and asked if those documents were likely to reveal much in the way of work practices. Both James and George assured them that they would not. They included details of propellant formulation and such, and, although the formulation did impinge upon types of mixers, etc., generally it would be quite feasible to conduct a workplace review without such access.

That all done, James went back to his office and called Robert to let him know what was happening. He had just hung up the phone when Heather came in, grinning from ear to ear.

"You missed the slap down in the conference room," she announced.

"I'm sorry," said James. "What?"

"Somebody, my guess being our Navy lieutenant commander, must have called the brass in Washington, because Blake got a call from his president and got an earful about his attitude!" she explained.

"Great, now that means he'll be really negative," James commented.

"No," Heather disagreed. "He's been recalled and they are sending another guy to head up the team, he'll be arriving at two, so he must have got his marching orders and a plane ticket pretty smartly!"

"How do you know all this?" James asked.

"Blake was instructed to hand the phone over to his deputy, who then apparently was told to put the phone onto speaker and their president told the rest of them that they were there to try and help, not just nitpick and that they were to be constructive in their review and not just write up gigs for the sake of appearances," she explained.

"Where was Blake while this was going on?" he asked.

"He had already left," she said. "He burned out of the parking lot in a cloud of smoke and was headed to the airport."

*   *   *

Bernard Rasmussen called Colleen and asked her if she would call her contact in Washington and ask her about a Navy program called Auriga Type B. Colleen was curious and asked him where he heard that name, and was not surprised to learn that it was in a bar. Bernard told her about the conversation that he had overheard and the fragments that he had picked up. Colleen asked him if he was sure of the name, and he repeated it for her. She said that she would call her contacts and see what she could find out. She was in Bernard's office twenty minutes later.

"I called Washington," she said.

"And?" he asked.

"Denials all around," she said. "No one knows anything about the Navy having a program called Auriga Type B, never heard of it, don't know anything about such a program, can't imagine what you were thinking."

"So, it's real?" he asked.

"Who knows," she said.

"Do you know anyone in any of the Congressional Delegations?" he asked.

"Yes," she admitted. "I actually know a couple of staffers."

"Call them and ask them why the Navy is denying the existing of an expensive ballistic missile program," Bernard suggested.

"May I use your phone?" she asked.

"Be my guest," he said and passed the phone over the desk to her. She called a number and had a brief conversation with someone. When she put the phone down, she looked at Bernard and said, "Well, maybe you have a story here. My contact wanted to know where we had heard of Auriga Type B, then he clammed up fast and changed the subject as quickly as he could."

"So, it's real?" Bernard asked.

"It looks like it," she admitted.

"I don't know why I didn't think about Congressional staffers earlier," Bernard complained. "We all know that neither they nor their lords and masters can keep their mouths shut. I suppose we need Congressional oversight on some of the Defence budgets, but it seems to me that if you tell them anything and then tell them that it's secret, they can't wait to tell someone just to let them know how important they are!"

"How do we confirm it?" she asked.

"Normally we'd follow the money, but I bet it's buried under some weird appropriation," he complained. "I'll just have to see if I can't bluff our good colonel and at least check his reaction."

"Be careful," she warned.

"Why, what can they do to me?" he asked. "I'm protected under the First Amendment.",

"Well, just be careful," she repeated.

Bernard turned his attention then to the football match scheduled for that evening. He had given a prediction to the colonel, and he wanted to review the betting. His personal prediction was for a Bears loss in a close game with the Vikings, but had told the colonel to look for a Bears win. Now he was no longer certain, and he wanted to review the teams again, who they were actually going to field and how it might play out. He checked the weather forecasts, and nothing indicated that the game might be called for bad weather, but he was still interested because some teams did better or worse depending on the weather. Temperature, rain and snow all affected how people played. He ran his predictions a dozen times and always came up with the same result, a Bears loss. Well, he would have to live with it now. All his bets were placed, and the colonel's money had also been placed. All he could do now was wait. Bernard thought about Colleen and decided that she must have a boyfriend already, which was why she had no interest in him. Well, he reasoned that was only to be expected. He had resigned himself, some time ago, to the fact that his success rate with women was mediocre at best. He was better at picking sports team winners than women, but it did get a little lonely at times. He could not understand why it was so difficult; he was not unattractive, moderately well compensated and had a passable personality, if not pleasing, so what was wrong?

*　　*　　*

That evening, Colleen wondered how to broach the subject of Navy programs with Isabella and decided to just tell her what they had learned, without asking for comment.

"Bella," she began. "I don't want you to comment on what I'm about to tell you, but you just need to know."

"Know what?" Isabella asked.

"Today Bernard told me that he overheard some guys talking in a bar, and they were talking about doing an audit at LST, and they mentioned Navy programs and rockets, and one mentioned the words Auriga Type B. Bernard asked me to call Sigourney, and she knew nothing, so then he asked me if I knew any of the Hill staffers. I called one guy I know and asked him about Auriga Type B, and he reacted. Bernard now thinks he knows that there is something at LST which is under the radar, and he plans to confront the colonel about it. If you need to let anyone know, just don't tell them you heard it from me," Colleen explained.

"Well, a whole bunch of people did show up to do an audit today," Isabella admitted. "I've never heard of anything called Auriga Type B. The only programs we have are Auriga and some small space motors for putting satellites into higher orbits. Maybe the Type B is a little different to the basic Auriga, but we are doing that for the Air Force, not the Navy. But I'll pass on your warning and let Martin decide what he needs to do, if anything. That's why he gets paid the big bucks. So, what's for dinner tonight?"

*   *   *

The next day, Isabella got to the plant early and found James wandering the halls. She had learned that it was his practice to manage by wandering around. She had also learned from his stories that it had been his practice long before Peters had popularised the term in his book *In Search of Excellence*. James had told her that working in a mine, the only way to find out anything was to wander around. She told him that she had something that she needed to tell him, but she needed to do it privately. James suggested the cafeteria, which was open, but at that time of the morning, there were never that many people there.

"So, what's up?" he asked.

"My roommate told me something last night," she replied. Then she glanced around to see who might be there and who might be listening. James told her not to worry, just to tell him normally whispered confidences and closed doors attracted attention.

"Well, Colleen, my roommate, told me that she has been working with this reporter, and he overheard some guys in a bar on Friday night, and they were talking about doing an audit here," she started.

"You know that we had that team show up yesterday?" he asked.

"Yes, it's probably the same team," she agreed. "One of them was shooting his mouth off and mentioned LST, the Navy, first stage and Auriga Type B."

"So, what did he do?" James asked.

"Apparently, Bernard, the reporter, had Colleen call some people she knew in Washington and ask about the Navy and Auriga Type B," she explained.

"And?" he prompted.

"She drew a blank with her normal contact, but a Congressional staffer reacted to the name Auriga Type B and then changed the subject fast," she continued.

"So what does this guy Bernard plan to do now?" James asked.

"Apparently, he's got some scheme to confront the colonel from the AFPRO office and ask him if it's true that there's a program here called Auriga Type B," she explained.

"Well, I suppose I could let Bill know that he might get a call," James suggested.

"There's more," Isabella said.

"Really! What?" James asked.

"Apparently, our colonel has a gambling habit, and the reporter Bernard is trying to set him up for what sounds like blackmail," she explained.

"Blackmail for what?" he asked.

"He wants a story," she explained. "And he thinks that he may be able to use the colonel's gambling habit as the lever to get him to tell all about the incident."

"But, there's really nothing to tell," he commented. "We still don't know why the mixer blew up, and there really is no story there."

"That may be true," she admitted. "But, now he's got this new approach about a phantom program called Auriga Type B."

"You've seen the program files," James commented. "I'm sure that you will stay silent on this."

"Yes, but I thought I'd better warn you that Bernard, the reporter, is going to start nosing around," she said.

"Thanks," he said. "Well, I suppose I'd better go and call Bill and tell him to expect a call from the reporter. That'll make his day!"

"What about the gambling problem?" she asked.

"I think that's the Air Force's problem," he commented. "I'm not sure I want to get involved in that. But, if you hear anything else, please let me know, we don't want swarms of reporters and cameramen knocking at our front gate!"

When Isabella had gone, James went in search of Lieutenant Commander Reinsch. He had first thought of talking to Bill Ridings, but decided against it. He was not on the need-to-know list for the existence of the Sagitta Program; to him, it was Auriga Type B and was being delivered to a Special Programs Office of the Air Force. Letting him know that a reporter might be calling to ask questions about the program would raise flags and cause the colonel to wonder what the real story was. It was better to keep the information within the circle of those who already knew, and that included the lieutenant commander. He found her in the office they had assigned her, going over her notes. James asked her to follow him, and he led the way to the secure room, where he told her what he had been told. She was annoyed that the contractor had been so indiscreet in such a public place. She agreed with James that there was no need to signal to the colonel that Auriga Type B was anything other than a special Air Force program. Then she left to talk to her office in Washington and alert them that someone had talked out of turn and they had a leak that needed plugging.

*   *   *

It was not until Wednesday that Bernard met with Bill Ridings. They arranged to meet in a club in Ogden, and Bill was apprehensive, to say the least. He had put all his winnings on the Bears to win, and they had lost by one point! He paid his "membership" fee and found a booth in a quiet corner of the bar and waited. Needless to say, he was not happy when Bernard arrived.

"What the fuck happened?" he asked.

"Hey, the odds finally got me, and I was wrong," Bernard replied. "You can't blame me for your losses. I warned you to get out and not do this!"

"Bullshit, all you did was ask if I was really serious," Bill commented.

"So, do you have enough to cover the losses?" Bernard asked.

"What do you think?" Bill asked. "Do you think I'm made of money? How the hell did I let myself get talked into this?"

"Well, there is a way out," Bernard ventured.

"How, another one of your great predictions?" Bill asked.

"Look, I'm sure of the outcome of the New Year's Eve game against the Eagles," Bernard promised. "But I'll want something from you before I give you the word."

"What, what the hell could you want from me?"

"A guy I know is related to one of the guys who died in that accident," Bernard lied. "He wants to know the real story, what the hell actually happened?"

"What do you mean?" Bill spluttered. "I can't talk about the accident or the investigation."

"Can't or won't?" Bernard pressed.

"What the hell can I tell you?" Bill asked, looking for some indication of where this conversation was going.

"All the guy wants to know is what happened so he can decide whether or not to sue LST," Bernard promised.

"What do I get?" Bill asked.

"The chance to double your money," Bernard promised.

"Double or what?" Bill wanted to know.

"Well, I really quite like you, Bill and I'll get you out of this," Bernard said. "The deal is you tell me what happened, I'll tell you how to bet on New Year's Eve, and I'll even throw in the chance to come out even if my prediction is wrong."

"How in the hell are you going to do that?" Bill wanted to know. "You must be out as much as I am."

"Actually, no," Bernard smirked. "I bet the other way and made out on the Vikings game!"

"You bastard, you set me up," Bill said, lunging across the table. Bernard evaded the lunge skillfully and pushed Bill back into his seat.

"Look, asshole, I could call up your CO and tell him what a risk you are with your gambling habit, or you could just go along and come out even or way ahead, not a bad deal, I think, what's it to be?" Bernard demanded.

"That's blackmail," Bill protested.

"Nasty word, blackmail," Bernard said. "I'm not trying to blackmail you. I would be just doing my citizen of the week bit by letting the Air Force know that one of its officers can't walk past a betting shop without risking his livelihood!"

"You prick!" was all Bill could think of to say.

"Look, just have a drink and be rational," Bernard suggested. "I'm not asking you to reveal state secrets, just what the hell happened."

"There's nothing to tell," Bill said dejectedly. "There was an explosion, most probably caused by blade-to-bowl contact, most likely as a result of a foreign object in the bowl. We just don't know what and how."

"Why were there so many people there?" Bernard asked.

"We don't know," Bill admitted. "The company doesn't know, we don't know, and I don't see how we'll ever find out because the only people who really knew are all dead."

"What's Auriga Type B?" Bernard asked, changing the subject completely.

"What?" Bill asked, trying to appear confused.

"Auriga Type B," Bernard repeated, but realised that this was a hopeless task because the confusion on Ridings's face was real enough. Bernard concluded that the colonel just knew nothing about it. He was not to know that the colonel's confusion was real enough, confusion about where Bernard could have heard of the Type B variant.

"Auriga Type B?" Bill asked, who by now had his emotions under control.

"Yes, Auriga Type B, a program you have at the plant," Bernard explained.

"We've got nothing by that name," Bill said, more comfortable now that he was on ground that he actually knew something about. "We've got Auriga and Sat motors 978, 988 and 998, but that's all."

"What's a Sat motor?" Bernard asked.

"A small motor you attach to a satellite to move it to higher orbits," Bill explained. "They're also called PAM motors, or payload assist motors; they're mostly for commercial use, but the military buys a few now and then."

"Ah, maybe Auriga Type B is one of those PAMs then?" Bernard suggested.

"Hey, could be, I don't know," Bill expostulated. "I've never heard of Auriga Type B either at the plant or at CMD Headquarters."

"So, what really happened in the accident?" Bernard asked again.

"Look, I told you, we don't know," Bill said. "As I said before, we think something got into the mix bowl, but we don't know what or how."

"Are they back in production?" Bernard asked.

"Will be soon," Bill replied. "We've been through all the processes and procedures, we've checked equipment, we've talked to the other guys in the missile business, and as far as we can tell, we've done everything to make a restart as safe as possible.

"So, no story there?" Bernard asked.

"What do you mean, no story?" Bill asked.

"Nothing, just my guy wondered if you all hadn't concocted a story to cover up some major screw-up," Bernard said quietly, kicking himself for almost slipping up and breaking his own cover story.

"No, no story, we just don't know, and it'll probably never happen again, which will be all the more confusing, because then we'll never actually know," Bill said.

"Okay then," Bernard said. "See, that wasn't so hard."

"So what about my bets and debts?" Bill now demanded.

"The smart money is on the Bears to beat the Eagles, and I'm putting my money on that," Bernard replied.

"Sure, you'll give me that little titbit and then bet the other way," Bill said accusingly.

"No, straight up, in fact, if you want to come to Salt Lake tomorrow or Friday, I'll place the bets with you," Bernard promised.

"You know, I think I'll just do that," Bill said. "I don't trust you one bit!"

"What's Auriga Type B?" Bernard asked again, looking to try and catch Bill off guard.

"Look, asshole, I told you, I never heard of anything called Auriga Type B, we've got Auriga, no type A, B or C," Bill said belligerently. "Give me a break, will you? There's nothing out there by that name."

"Then why did one of the audit team that's at the plant now use the name?" Bernard asked.

"Who knows?" Bill shrugged. "Maybe they were talking about another plant."

"No, LST, Navy and Auriga Type B all in one breath," Bernard explained.

"Well, that's more bullshit," Bill scoffed. "There are no Navy programs at LST."

"But when we first met, didn't I hear you say something to your junior something about Navy pukes?" Bernard challenged.

"Sure, but they were there to tour the plant and look for best practices," Bill explained. "In fact, we've got some hot young lieutenant commander out there now doing the same thing. We do that sort of thing all the time, believe it or not, we are actually looking to do things the best way!"

"What really happened in the accident?" Bernard asked again.

"Look, drop it, will you?" Bill said. "I've told you and told you what we know and what we don't know. Tell your guy that his relative died in a really bad accident that we don't understand and let it go."

"But, if you don't understand why, then how can you restart the process?" Bernard asked.

"Look. I've told you. We've checked everything goddamn thing we can think of, and it all checks out fine. We can't think of any reason why we should not restart," Bill protested.

"Yes, but if you get it wrong, more people die," challenged Bernard.

"That's about as likely as the next flight you take out of Salt Lake going down on takeoff," Bill scoffed. "Look, there have been aircraft accidents where they really never found out why, and the planes are still flying and not dropping out of the sky. Once in a while, shit happens!"

"Okay then, if you say so," Bernard reluctantly let it go. He knew that he had exhausted Bill as a source and that anything else he wanted to develop for his story would have to be through other channels. Perhaps he should go to Washington and meet with the staffer that Colleen had contacted. He might be prepared enough to deny everything over the phone, but face-to-face, he would have to be a really good poker player to put one over on him. Bernard prided himself on being pretty good at reading people, which is why he was sure that Bill knew nothing about this Auriga Type B.

"So, do you want to come to Salt Lake tomorrow or Friday?" Bernard asked.

"Friday afternoon, say two at Temple Square," Bill suggested.

"Fine, I'll be there," Bernard promised.

"You'd better be," Bill said threateningly. "If not, I'll come looking for you with an M-16!"

"Hey, calm down, we can fix this," Bernard promised. "You'll have nothing to worry about."

"I'd better not!" Bill said. "I'm off, I'll see you Friday, Temple Square at two, then asshole."

After Bill had gone, Bernard sat for a while and reflected. Perhaps his whole approach to this story had been wrong. Perhaps he should change the focus now to a greedy company unwilling to find out why something blew up and going back into operation for the sake of profits, and exposing people to risks. He also thought about the mysterious Auriga Type B. Maybe he was mistaken, or maybe it existed but had nothing to do with LST. He thought that he might just cold call the plant the next day and ask for the Auriga Type B Program manager and see what happened. People often inadvertently reveal things when asked the simplest questions. All in all, his cultivation of Colonel Ridings had been a waste of time. He had got nothing more than the standard company press releases that promised investigation and disclosed nothing.

*   *   *

Robert Warner called on Thursday afternoon to tell James that he had finished his discussions with Bill Evans, James's candidate for Matériel Manager and that Bill was on his way out to the plant. Robert was impressed and asked James how soon they could have Bill on board. That was something that James was going to discuss with Bill after he had had a chance to see the place and learn what it was that James wanted him to do. James called Simon Wilmott, Allan Black and John Edwards and made sure that each of them would have some time with Bill. It was not as if they would be interviewing Bill, but rather James wanted them and Bill to get a sense if they could work together. Bill arrived, and Heather brought him to James's office.
"Nice view," he said. "Can you ski those hills?"
"I've never tried," James admitted. "You know skiing's not my thing."
"How the hell are you, James?"
"I'm fine, and you?"
"Can't complain. So, what's the story here?"
"We've got classic defence contractor thinking," James explained. "They think that because they can progress bill it's a good idea to buy all the

124

stuff they can, the problem is they then have really no idea how much stuff they have or where it is."

"So, no MERP disciplines?" Bill asked, referring to MRP II or manufacturing resource planning.

"None!"

"What do you want me to do?" Bill asked.

"Set up a real Matériel function and get a handle on the amount of stuff we have here. Buy only the amounts we really need in a reasonable time frame, unless we have to buy mill runs, free up some cash and create a real master schedule," James explained.

"Okay, free hand?"

"Free hand," James agreed.

"What's the rest of your team like?" Bill wanted to know. "I'll need to work closely with the production guy to understand flows, process steps and times to work out a master schedule,"

"I just made some changes," James told him. "Here's an old org chart and a new one. I'm probably also going to change out the HR wanker and the quality guy."

"Sounds like old times," Bill laughed. "Do these guys hate you yet?"

"I'm sure that some do," James admitted. "Some have commented that it was about time, so not everyone is unhappy."

"Do I get to meet any of the rest of the team?" Bill asked.

"Of course," James assured him. With that, he called Heather and asked her to escort Bill to Simon Wilmott's office with the instruction that he should be brought back to James's office after his visit with Wilmott, Black and Edwards.

Bill was back just after five, and he and James talked for a while before leaving. James called Ken Butler and set up an appointment for Bill to see him on Friday, when they would conclude the employment details. Normally, this would have been done at the operation level, but James wanted to keep Gene Bonds out of the loop. He was leaning more and more toward replacing him, and Isabella da Silva was looking like a good replacement.

*   *   *

125

On Friday afternoon, Bernard Rasmussen and Bill Ridings met in Temple Square at two. Bill had driven down and parked away from the square and had walked over, lest someone see his car and recognise it. He had also changed out of his uniform and was in jeans, a heavy plaid shirt and a ski jacket, just another Utahn going about his business. Bernard led the way to his contact, where bets were placed and betting slips received. It was all very underhand and quiet because gambling, particularly of this sort and with this much money, is definitely frowned upon in Utah. Bill was able to confirm that Bernard actually handed over some of his own money and that he was betting on the same outcome as he had given him. Mollified for the moment, Bill suggested a drink, but Bernard declined and they went their separate ways. Bill chose to have a drink anyway and spent some time at one of the restaurants that had a 'private club' attached, 'private club' being the vehicle for selling drinks in the sometimes stifling atmosphere of Utah. It cost Bill $5 for the club membership, but after that, he was left alone with his thoughts and his drink.

*   *   *

While the wagering was in process, James met with Lieutenant Commander Reinsch, and she told him that she would be back on January 4th. She had passed on his warning about loose tongues, and that was being addressed as they spoke. It had been Blake who had blabbed, and he was now being interviewed by all and sundry and generally getting the fear of God put into him. After Lieutenant Commander Reinsch had gone, James met with his staff and told them that he would be back for a few days the following week but that he would not be back after the New Year until the 6th. He would be in the process of moving. He told them that he would call in for important messages, but stressed important. On that note, he left for the airport to go back to California for Christmas. At the Salt Lake airport, he called Katrina and confirmed his flight number and arrival time. She promised to be at the curb of the Orange County Airport to meet him, but warned him that traffic was heavy already and that the trip home could be slow.

Christmas break

"Hi, Sweetie, how was the flight?" Katrina asked when she picked James up at the airport.

"Fine, no delays, no problems, *Suikerbossie*," he assured her.

"I'm going to take Jamboree," she said. "The 55 is a parking lot already, I can't imagine what the 91 would be like!"

"How are you doing?" he asked.

"Better now that you're here!" she said. "It's been a long week."

"Well, we'll soon be moved and then I'll be home almost every night," he promised.

"There's not much travel with this job, then?" she asked. She was concerned because some of James's previous jobs had involved a lot of travel. She accepted that it was part of the job, but it did not make it any more palatable.

"Not much," he agreed. "The only trip I've taken so far has been that one quick flight to Washington, but that was only a day trip. I suppose there might be some times that I have to stay overnight somewhere, but that hasn't come up yet."

"Yet," she commented. "How cold was it in Utah?"

"There was a cold front that came through in the morning and dumped snow on the Wasatch Front, but it is only just below freezing, so not too bad," he replied.

"Is the house well heated?" she asked.

"Yes, I've checked it and there are two furnaces, one for each floor," he explained.

"So not as cold as Wisconsin then?" she asked.

"Not unless you go to the top of the mountains," he laughed. "It's nowhere near as bad as Wisconsin."

As they worked their way through the stop-and-go traffic of Southern California, James gave Katrina an account of his week and the issues that had arisen. She wanted to know about the different people on his team and was pleased to hear that he had hired Bill Evans. She was friends with Bill's wife, Amanda, and she was happy to hear that there would be at least one person that she knew in Utah. She wanted to know when Bill and Amanda would be moving to Utah, and James thought that it would probably be towards the end of January. It all depended on when they could find a house. Katrina said that she would call Amanda in the morning and talk to her. Then James said that that was enough work stuff for the next few days, it was now time to think about themselves and their respective families.

"Do you have your Christmas shopping done?" James asked.
"What Christmas shopping?" she asked. "Are you expecting to get something?"
"I don't need anything," he laughed. "I've got you for the next few days. I don't need anything else."
"More to the point," she then said. "What did you get me?"
"I thought you said that you didn't want anything?" he protested.
"What I say and what you need to do are two different things!" she laughed. "I expect to see something under the tree on Christmas morning!"
"Well, I suppose I could slip out tomorrow early and find something at K-Mart," he suggested. "But they're probably all sold out by now, so it will have to be whatever is left over."

"Your mom called today," Katrina said, changing the subject. "She wanted to know when we were moving and what the new address would be."
"I suppose we'll have to call them either tomorrow night or early Sunday morning," he commented. "We need to call your folks as well. Are they going anywhere for Christmas?"
"My dad called to tell me that they're spending Christmas in Botswana with Will and family," she replied, referring to James's brother Will.
"There are days I envy them," he said. "Botswana has an appeal."
"I'm still a little surprised that Will and Bridget left their jobs in Jo'burg and moved to Botswana," she said. "I'm sure they're not getting as much money there as they were in South Africa."
"I don't know," he said. "They seem to enjoy their safari business a lot more than they did their jobs in Jo'burg. Maybe there's something to be said for less money but more fun."

"I wonder how the girls are doing?" she said. "I can't believe they're already thirteen and ten?"

"They do grow up fast," he noted.

"Do you think Francesca is enjoying school in Italy?" she asked.

"Well, I suppose it's a bit like you going to boarding school, but she's staying with family," he replied. "She's almost exactly the same age as Valeria, and from what we've heard from Alex and Vincenzo, they get on well."

"Do you think Will and Bridget will also send Alessandra when she's old enough?" she asked.

"I would think so, she can go to school with Vittorio, he's the same age," he replied. "Will did tell me that they opened up a new international school in Gabs this year, but that costs more than sending the girls to live with Alex."

"Do you think they picked up much Setswana?" he asked.

"My guess is that Alessandra will have picked up more than Francesca because she's being home-schooled and must be spending a lot of time with the Botswana staff," he thought. "Setswana would be an interesting language to know; the girls will be able to talk about others without much chance of being overheard and understood."

"Except, of course, in Botswana," she laughed. "And picking up Italian won't hurt either."

The development where James and Katrina lived was festooned with Christmas lights. It looked as if the whole area had gone overboard that year. Katrina told James that Villa Park had had its boat parade around the streets, and it had now become quite an attraction. There was something endearing about a community that was just a little offbeat, and having a boat parade by towing decked-out boats around the streets was more than a little unusual. It was a counterpoint to the Newport Harbor boat parade, which was also quite an event, but it was boats being piloted around the harbour showing off their lights. Katrina had not put lights up on their house, but James promised that he would at least put a strand or two of lights around the front porch.

"I can't remember, does the new house have a bath big enough for two?" Katrina asked later as she and James were soaking in their bathtub together.

"It does," he assured her. "It's one of those old-fashioned looking baths with claw feet."

"Oh yes," she said. "I remember it now. "It's set against some windows overlooking the valley with a view out across the lake."

"What's the plan for tomorrow?" he asked.

"I've got nothing special planned," she said. "We've been invited to a couple of houses for drinks in the evening, so you can get your shopping done in the morning if you need to."

"I don't need to," he admitted. "I brought you back a Molly Mormon dress from Utah, so that you'll fit in when we move there."

"A what?" she asked.

"The LDS Church asks that its members dress modestly, whatever that means, so the general trend for women's fashion is big hair and long, somewhat shapeless dresses that come down to mid calf at least," he explained. "Some of the more bizarre breakaway sects of Mormonism carry it to the extreme, and they call those Pioneer dresses."

"But why Molly Mormon?" she asked, intrigued.

"I was told that the ultra keen members, those that do everything that they're supposed to, are often known as Molly Mormons, particularly the younger ones," he explained.

"Well, I don't think I'll be turning into a Molly Mormon any time soon," she commented. "I like my wine in the bath with my *ou man* and I don't quite see myself in a dowdy thing like you're describing!"

"Ah, *Suikerbossie*, with what you're wearing right now, you could never be called dowdy," he said appreciatively.

On Christmas Eve, James put up some strings of lights around the porch and wrapped his gift that he had bought the last time he had been in California. He had not bought her a Molly Mormon dress but a new kitchen gadget. Katrina liked kitchen gadgets, and this was a Cuisinart food processor. He found a suitable cardboard box that was a different shape from the one the processor came in and disguised his package. He also wrapped a couple of books he had bought for her.

Those he did not try and disguise, but simply wrapped them up and added nice bows.

Katrina and James did not stay out late on Christmas Eve, but excused themselves with the necessity to call overseas. Their first call was to Botswana and James's brother Will. Bridget answered the phone with "*Dumela*," the standard Setswana greeting.

"Howzit, Bridget?" James asked. "Merry Christmas!"

"Oh, James, Merry Christmas, just wait until I get the rest of the family, is Katrina there?" she asked.

"I'm here," Katrina assured her.

"Your folks are here with us," Bridget told her. "Your Dad's been telling us all about your family and the Botswana connection."

"Oh, you mean all about *Oom* Jan," Katrina laughed. "How are you, Bridg?"

"I'm fine, we've got everyone here, Francesca's back from school in Italy and Valeria and Vittorio came with her. Alessandra is bugging your Dad, wanting him to take her and Vittorio into the bush again. Your mom just wants to cook, which is fine with me, and Will is talking about changing the location of our safari outfit," was the rather long answer to what Katrina had thought was a simple question.

"It sounds like chaos," Katrina laughed. "How have the rains been?"

"Good," Bridget said. "The bush is looking good right now. Some of the roads have been difficult, but nothing really bad. We got bogged down a couple of times, but nothing too bad, unlike James, neither of us has managed to stall a *bakkie* crossing a river! Here's your Dad, he wants to say hi."

"*Liefling, hou gaan dit?*" he asked.

"I'm fine, Dad, and you?" she replied.

"What you forget the *Taal?*" he asked.

"No," she laughed. "What's it like in the madhouse of Will and Bridget?"

"It's only *baie aangenaam man*, I'm telling you, I really like the little one, Alessandra, she reminds me of you when you were that age," he replied.

"What do you think of Valeria?" she asked.

"Man, there's one jacked-up *meisie*," he replied, impressed by the cousin from Italy. "I went shooting with her today and she's better than me, and then she was driving the *bakkie* too."

"It sounds like fun," Katrina sighed a little wistfully. "How are you and Mom doing?"

"Just *baie aangenaam man*," he assured her. "We have some good Hannepoort this year. I was going to send you some, but it's hard to ship, so Will and I drank it all."

"I hope you both got a good *babbelas* from it," she laughed. "It would serve you right for drinking my Hannepoort!"

"Here's Valeria, wants to say howzit, *tot siens liefling*," he said as he handed over the phone.

"*Tia* Katrina, *come stai?*" Valeria asked.

"*Bene, grazie e tu?*" Katrina replied.

"When are you coming to see us?" Valeria asked.

"One day, I promise," Katrina said. "How are your Mom and Dad?"

"They're fine, I think they've gone for a shady week somewhere while we're here," Valeria confided.

"A shady week?" Katrina asked.

"You know, when they get all lovey-dovey," Valeria explained. "You and Uncle James must know what I'm talking about! Hold on, here's Francesca."

"*Dumela Mma*," Francesca greeted her. "*Hou gaan dit?*"

"*Goed dankie*," Katrina assured her. "How's school?"

"It's only *baie aangenaam man*, I go with Valeria and we're in all the same classes, we're going to a Liceo Scientifico because Valeria wants to be a pilot," Francesca replied. "I think that might be fun, so we're trying to persuade Uncle Vincenzo to get us flying lessons!"

"Is Alessandra around?" Katrina asked.

"I'll get her to stop beating up Vittorio and drag her to the phone," Francesca said. Katrina heard her in the background yelling for her sister, and then she heard the footsteps as she came running to the phone.

"*Tannie* Katrina, your Dad took us into the bush yesterday and we saw a lion!" she said.

"Was Vittorio with you?" Katrina asked.

"Yes, he wanted to know if it was going to eat us," Alessandra explained. "But, I told him not to be silly, I told him that it's the lady lions that do all the killing and the men are just lazy ones that come later and take all the food."

"Male lions do kill Alessandra," Katrina reminded her.

"Yes, I know that, but Vittorio's only a boy, even if he is quite acceptable, and he needs to learn that we really rule," Alessandra commented. By this time, Katrina was having a hard time not laughing and asked if her mother was available. She heard a clunk as Alessandra put the phone down on the table, then she heard her run off into the kitchen calling for *ouma, ouma* Englebrecht, then her mother picked up the phone.

"So, how are you, dear?" she asked.

"I'm fine, Mom, how are you doing in that madhouse?" Katrina asked.

"It makes a change," her mother laughed. "It's hard to keep up with the conversation sometimes, the two girls switch into Italian, then Will and Bridget speak in Afrikaans to your Dad and the small one, Alessandra, *praat* Setswana!"

"How are you and Dad doing?" Katrina asked.

"Well enough," her mother said. "The farm is fine and we've had good rain, the new grapes have taken well. Help is hard to find. There have been a lot more bombs and explosions this year, some even in the Cape."

"Any near you?" Katrina asked.

"Not yet," her mother assured her. "There was one in Cape Town and one in Stellenbosch. But it's good that the deal with South West is now done, and the boys will be coming home from Angola and South West, and the Cubans will be leaving."

"How long before there's a change in government in South Africa?" Katrina asked.

"I don't know, there are the *verkrampte* Nationalists who say they will die with their boots on, but it will come," her mother said. "Anyway, how's it with you?"

"We're moving in the New Year," Katrina reminded her mother.

"I know, how is everything? Did you sell the house? What's your new house like? Is it cold in Utah?" her mother asked.

"The move is all organised," Katrina began. "We've sold this house and the new one is up on a hill looking towards the lake, with the mountains behind. James said that it snowed yesterday before he came home, but it does not get as cold as Wisconsin."

"I must go, dear," her mother interrupted. "Bridget needs help in the kitchen, and it's a *gemors* that I need to go and sort out. *Tot siens liefling.*"

"Well, they sound as if they're having fun," James commented. He had been listening in on an extension and had heard all. "Who shall we call next?"

"Let's give Alex and Vincenzo a bell and ask them about this shady week that they're having," Katrina suggested. The phone rang in Italy, and James's sister Alex answered, "*Pronta.*"

"Alex, hi, it's Katrina."

"Katrina, we were just talking about you and James. I was telling Vincenzo about my trip to Zambia and your wedding," Alex said. "How is everything with you?"

"We're fine," Katrina assured her. "We understand from Valeria that you and Vincé are having a shady week while the kids are in Botswana."

"A shady week?" Alex asked.

"That's what she said," Katrina assured her. "She said that's when you and Vincé would get all lovey-dovey."

Alex laughed and called to Vincenzo, and Katrina heard her in the background explaining to him about their week. "Katrina," Alex came back on the line. "Are you still there?"

"Still here, Alex," Katrina promised. "We're just listening in!"

"We, does that mean that James is there too?" Alex asked.

"I'm here, Alex," James said. "So, what are you and Vincé doing for your shady week?"

"We're going skiing on Boxing Day," Alex replied. "Vincé has some time off, the villains have taken a holiday, so we'll get a week or so to ourselves in the Alps."

"Don't break anything," James told her. Then he continued, "When are you coming out here to see us?"

"Some day," Alex promised. "I've promised the *bambini* a trip to Disney Land."

"You do remember that we're moving?" James reminded her.

"Yes, but Utah's a lot closer to California than Italy," Alex laughed. "We thought we might come and see you in the summer and then drive down to LA and go to Disney Land, what do you think?"

"I think that would be wonderful," James said, and Katrina chimed in with her agreement. "Would you bring Francesca with you?"

"That's up to Will and Bridget," Alex said. "But if they wanted to send the two girls to us for the summer, we'd bring them."

"Think about it," Katrina urged.

"We will," Alex promised. Have a happy Christmas, you two and don't freeze in Utah."

"Happy Christmas, Alex and *Buon Natale* to Vincé," Katrina and James chorused.

"I suppose we should now call my folks," James said after they had hung up the telephone. "I wonder if we should leave it till later, or should we get it over with?"

"That's up to you," Katrina said. "It's only you that has a problem with talking to your folks, I do alright with them."

"Maybe it's best to get it over with," James thought. "I'll do it now so that we have a clear day tomorrow." He rang the number and his father answered. "21784." James had forgotten that it was common in England for people to answer the telephone with the number.

"Merry Christmas, Dad," he said. "How are you both?"

"Oh, James, Merry Christmas, we were just thinking about you. What time is it out there?"

"It's just gone midnight," James told him. "So it's Christmas now."

"You're up late! We're both fine, but there's no one here, all the family are off by themselves, and we're here, just the two of us," his father complained.

"Well, you'll have some time to spend together then, just the two of you," James suggested. "Do you have a white Christmas?"

"No, it's just cold and damp," his father commented. "I suppose it's sunny and warm out there in California?"

135

"Actually, no, it's been raining, which is good because it cleans out the air, but we'll get our share of snow soon when we go to Utah," James told him.

"Here's your mother," his father announced.

"James, happy Christmas, how are you, and is Katrina there?" she asked.

"I'm here," Katrina assured her. "I'm just listening in."

"Are you all ready for your big move?"

"Yes," Katrina told her. "We'll actually pack and move right after the New Year, and James and I are driving north to Utah."

"Well, drive carefully. What will you do if there's snow?"

"We'll be fine," James assured her. "We've had plenty of experience driving in snow in Wisconsin."

"Have you heard from Will and Alex?" James's mother wanted to know.

"We've just called them both," James told her.

"Oh, and you left us until last," she commented. James looked at Katrina and grinned and mouthed "guilt trip". But to his mother, he replied. "Well, the time change to you is least, so it made sense to call Will first, then Alex, then you."

"Oh, I see," his mother said, not seeing at all. Obviously, she was not convinced and was put out about being last on the list for calls. "Well, I suppose it's late there in California, and I should let you go to bed. Have a happy Christmas and remember to come and see us one day."

"We will, bye Mom," James assured her, then he hung up and laughed. "She'll never change," he commented to Katrina. "Remember how miffed she was when your folks got the see this house before she did?"

"Oh yes, I remember that," Katrina said. "All the little 'poor me' asides that we got."

"Well, at least she's warmed up to you a little," James commented. "Do you remember what she was like when you first met her? She made all those *verkrampte* comments about acceptable even if you weren't wholly white."

"I remember," she said. "But, you're right, she's mellowed a lot. Well, I'm off to bed. Are you coming?"

*   *   *

136

"Are you ready?" Isabella asked Colleen. "If we're going skiing, we need to go!"

"I'm ready," Colleen replied. "Snowbasin?"

"Of course, do you want to drive or shall I?" Isabella asked.

"I think I'll drive," Colleen said. "We don't need any speeding tickets!"

"What do you mean, me get a speeding ticket?" Isabella laughed.

"I sometimes think that you're related to Ayrton Senna," Colleen said.

"He drives much faster than I do," Isabella lamented. "But then if I could ever get to drive a Formula 1 car, I bet I could get it to go *mais rapido!*"

Later, when they were on the slopes at Snowbasin, Colleen saw a familiar figure. It was Bernard, and he was there with a young blonde girl. At first, she was not sure whether or not she had been spotted, but at the bottom of the slope, Bernard came over to say hello.

"Hi, Colleen, this is Melanie. Melanie, this is Colleen, one of our backroom research staff. She digs out the dirt on people," he joked.

"Hi Melanie, Bernard, this is Isabella," she said, making the introductions.

"Do you ski a lot?" Melanie asked. "I've just started and I'm not very good."

"Colleen's really good," Bernard told her. Don't ever try and race her down a slope and don't put money on it, you'll lose."

As they skied away, Isabella commented to Colleen, "Where did he pick up that jail bait?"

"I think Bernard's just lonely," Colleen replied. "I think he's a fairly good reporter, but I think he's found it difficult settling in Utah."

"Where's he from?" Isabella asked.

"Pennsylvania," Colleen replied. "He has family here in Utah, but he doesn't seem to have too much to do with them."

"I'm hungry!" Isabella announced. "Where shall we eat?"

"Let's go and see what we can find open in Ogden," Colleen suggested.

"Will there be much open?" Isabella wondered. "It is Christmas Day."

"If nowhere else, there's always the Ogden Marriott," Colleen thought.

For his part, Bernard wondered who Isabella might be and decided that she must be a friend, a good-looking friend at that. For the moment, though he had Melanie to entertain. She was a college senior on a skiing vacation in Utah from New York, and he had met her in the bar at one of the resorts at Alta and had convinced her that the skiing was better in Snowbasin. His real reason for picking Snowbasin over Alta was that he had a season pass to Snowbasin and additional passes that he had been given after he had given the facility a good review in the paper. Melanie was not quite the beginner she claimed to be; she was every bit as good as he was, but not quite up to the level of Colleen.

*   *   *

The day after Boxing Day, a British traditional holiday that falls on the day after Christmas, James flew back to Utah. On the flight north, he thought about the holiday and was pleased that Katrina had been delighted with her Cuisinart and she had even experimented with it a few times on Christmas Day and Boxing Day. She had given him a new amplifier to go with his hi-fi system, and he had only been asked to turn down the volume once. He would have to see where in the new house he would set up his music system and what the acoustics were like.

James drove out to the plant in the snow. The plant was quiet. There were crews working, but it was at a minimum staffing level. There was a meeting that James had scheduled to review the restart of the mixers. Simon Wilmott led the meeting and went through the various steps that had been taken. George Wheelwright showed them data from the tests that he had conducted on the circularity of the bowls and the arcs that the blades described. He also produced data on the perpendicularity of the mix axes. One of the other engineers then went through the metering devices and the gauges and showed photographs of lock wires on all nuts and grounding straps on all unconnected pieces of machinery. With that and the experiments, simulated conditions and what ifs, they could find no reason not to start with the afternoon shift that day. James looked for agreement from all around the table and asked if anyone had any data or other empirical evidence as to why they should not go back into production. He asked the question several times and in different ways, trying to make it clear that this was not a situation where agreement was expected just because he wanted to get started. If there really was something they had not considered, he wanted to know, and if there was actual data that suggested that they not start, then he would not. In the end, the only holdout was the Air Force, which tried to hide behind their brief to oversee only contractual items. James asked Captain Melling if he was in accord or not, and Melling waffled. James had some sympathy for him; he was being asked to buy off on the company's actions with the knowledge that they actually did not know what had caused the incident. Melling knew that Ridings's career was essentially over, and he did not want his to be over, too. In the end, the weight of the evidence convinced him that all precautions had been taken and that all probable, likely, possible and even unlikely events had been considered and evaluated. James gave the final go-ahead, and Simon left to give instructions to the mix crews and to actually witness the first mix himself.

James then checked the work schedule and drove out to one of the control bunkers that was in use. The crew there was engaged in tool removal from a cast motor.

"Hi, guys," James said as he went into the control bunker. "How's everything?"

"Fine, Mr. Martin," one of the crew assured him. "We've got the core popped and it's coming out nicely, just like a bad tooth."

"No issues then?" James asked.

"No, everything looks good from here," he was assured by Cody, the team lead.

"How well did you guys know Michael Miller?" James asked.

"Not real well," Cody replied for the team. "I thought he was a bit of a goat roper."

"Really," James temporised. He would have to ask Heather about the connotations of being described as a goat roper.

"Yes, he was always looking for information, but he didn't seem to really know anything," Cody elaborated. "I asked him a couple of times for help with a process, and he put me off."

"Yeah, but he had really had a foxy babe for a wife," one of the others interrupted.

"Really?" James asked.

"Yeah, my kids were up in the mountains behind the Huntsville Reservoir last summer, and they came across Michael Miller and his wife in a mountain meadow. They sneaked up on them, and my oldest took some good pictures! I had to confiscate them, because they were quite unsuitable for the kids!" Randy said.

"You just mean you wanted them for yourself," Cody accused.

"Oh my heck yes," Randy agreed. "Better than Playboy! There's no way I'd let the Bishop get a look at them."

"You've still got those pictures, Randy?" Cody asked.

"Oh my heck yes," Randy assured him. "She's the pin-up on the back of my locker door. Wait five and I'll get it."

"You're right," James agreed with them when he was shown the photograph. "She's a looker, alright! Was she Jewish?"

"No, I don't think so," Cody said. "They went to the same Stake House that I do. Why?"

"This pendant she's wearing, it's a Star of David," James explained.

"You noticed that?" Cody asked, looking at James sideways. "I've never seen that before."

"That's because you've always focused on the boobs!" Randy laughed.

"She's got this great tan," Cody pointed out. "She must have really worked at that."

James did not think so. He thought it was natural colouring. There were no tan lines where a watch might be or any bikini lines. Katrina had the same type of skin colour, and he had long ago learned that it was all natural. He remembered with some wistfulness the first time he had remarked on her colouring. They had been driving in Zambia, and she was wearing shorts and had put her feet up on the dashboard, and he had asked her if the rest of her was the same colour. He had found out later that it truly was. So, he was pretty sure that Mrs. Miller was naturally dark. That might mean something, or it might mean nothing. The Millers were becoming more of a mystery. Michael Miller was not who he had claimed to be, and now his wife was caught on camera dressed quite immodestly and wearing a Star of David. Of course, she might just like the pendant, and it might have absolutely no significance.

"Did Miller spend much time out in the plant?" James asked.

"You know, I saw him a few times in the hills above the mix buildings," Cody replied.

"You're right," Randy agreed. "You remember that one day when he looked like he had been rooting around like a pig?"

"He was just weird," Cody said. "I asked him about that, and he said he was interested in the bushes and flowers."

"Where exactly was he rooting around?" James asked.

"Up here," Cody said, pointing to a map on the wall. "We're in this bunker, B234, and this is M385, the mix building that went up; he was here behind the building up on this slope. It's thick up there, lots of sage and other brush. I took a look up there one day, but couldn't see what there was to be excited about."

"I see," James commented. Then he made a note of where it was that Cody was pointing to and wrote down the approximate coordinates from the plant grid.

"There, it's all out nice and clean," Randy announced. "Scuse us, Mr. Martin, we'll need to go up the casting building and stow the core so that we can change tools and pull the fins."

"Okay, thanks, guys," James said as they all left the bunker. He waited a while until he saw them on the monitor as they entered the casting building and wished that the closed-circuit cameras had sound. He was curious as to what they might be discussing. As he thought about it more, he thought that it really would be a good idea to have sound as well as video, because it might be useful to hear what was going on as well as watch it.

James went back to his office and then opened up the office that Isabella was using in her cataloguing of the paperwork they had found in Michael Miller's desk and filing cabinet. She had pasted the plant map on the wall and the posters that Miller had had in his work area. James looked at them and found on the map the approximate location that Cody had pointed to, but was at a loss to see why anyone would go there. He stared at the posters and wondered if there was anything significant about a picture of the city of Truro and a country house by the name of Bourton Grange. He noticed the Ian Allan book on the desk and looked up Bourton Grange. It was in the book with the wheel arrangement of 4-6-0. He already knew that the City of Truro would be in the book with a wheel arrangement of 4-4-0, it being a unique locomotive unlike others named after cities. He remembered an item from *"The Andromeda Strain"* by Michael Crichton and wondered what 460 and 440 would be in binary. He sat and made the conversion and finished up with two longer numbers, all ones and zeros. Then he looked again at the plant plan and tested the numbers as northings and eastings. One way did not fit, but the other way put him in the same general area as the one that Cody had indicated. Of course, it could all be just a coincidence, and numbers could be made to fit almost any circumstance, but to him, it warranted further investigation. As he thought about it, James wondered if he was just trying to find something suspicious about Michael Miller. The only thing he was fairly certain of was that the Michael Miller who had been killed was not who he claimed to be. Perhaps he was finding things to suit his own view of the world, and it was difficult to believe that if the posters were part of a coded message that it was that simple.

There was too much snow on the ground and it was coming down too heavily for an expedition that day, so James just made some notes for himself and went back to reviewing the rest of the material that Isabella had catalogued. She had arranged everything, and it was an almost complete dossier on how to build the Sagitta motor. As James leafed through the material, he was alarmed to find a small handwritten reference in one corner of a drawing that actually said Sagitta, followed by a question mark. As the drawings were clearly marked Auriga Type B, he wondered where Miller had heard the name Sagitta.

James then locked up the office and went for a wander around the rest of the plant. He found the odd little groups of people working and was greeted warmly by each of them. It was a good opportunity to get to know some of the workers. He found a couple of foremen having coffee in a break room and spent some time with them. They were fairly disparaging about the previous regime and were full of positive comments about Simon Wilmott. "At least he knows what the processes are and what might happen if we need to change a process," one of them commented. Simon had also tightened up the disciplines of change control, which was actually appreciated by the foremen because now there was a set of fixed processes to work to and no one would come in and tell them to do differently, unless they had a signed change package, something that had been lax before and which had led to operations being done differently by different crews.

After a couple more days of work at the plant, James was ready to go back to California for the New Year and the move. Katrina met him at the Orange County airport. There were still a few things that needed doing around the house before they left and handed over the keys to the realtor. Katrina had a list of items that she gave to James, and he quickly looked through it and planned out what he was going to do first. Katrina had already been through the pantry and pared down to a minimum the amount of food she had stored there, and it was only non-perishables that remained in any quantity. They could be moved along with the household goods. So they would be eating out for the next couple of days.

*   *   *

On New Year's Eve, Bernard sat glued to the television to watch the Playoff game between the Chicago Bears and the Philadelphia Eagles. He had his own money riding on the game now, and he was most anxious to see the results. He had been smart enough with Bill Ridings not to give any kind of points spread, just a basic prediction of a win by the Bears. The game turned out to be bizarre. During the second quarter, a dense fog rolled in, and it was hard to see what was going on. Bernard supposed that the players could see better than he could, but he wondered what it was like on the field when both teams essentially gave up on long passes and took to running the ball. The television coverage was only marginal because the cameras just could not penetrate the gloom, and it was only the referee announcing the gains and the yards that gave him any sense of what was happening. It was tense because the Eagles seemed to have the ball a lot, but fortunately for Bernard, they did not seem to be able to actually get it into the end zone and score. Twice, they had touchdowns nullified by penalties; all in all, it was not a good day for them. Bernard was immensely relieved

143

at the final whistle and the score of 20 to 12 in favour of the Bears. Now the Bears would face the San Francisco 49ers in the Conference Championship, but he had little doubt about the outcome of that game; in his opinion, the 49ers would take it easily.

Bernard could now face the colonel with some level of confidence. He would hand over the winnings and take the opportunity in the euphoria that would inevitably follow to pose his questions again. He doubted whether the answers would be any different; he had just exhausted the colonel's knowledge and possibly his tolerance for harassment. After their last meeting, he had been genuinely concerned that the man might actually crack, and if he did, it was possible that he could be running from a maniac armed with an M-16 rifle. He thought that the best course of action now was to focus more on the LST people and see if any of them would be willing to talk. It was always possible, in his mind at least, that the company was hiding something from the Air Force.

*   *   *

The movers arrived at eight in the morning on January 2nd and started packing. James and Katrina had been through this process a few times before, so knew to generally stay out of the way. By four in the afternoon, everything was gone, and they swept out the house and waited for the realtor to stop by and collect the keys. With the keys gone, they then started on their drive north. Unfortunately, it was the beginning of the rush hour and traffic was heavy, so the going was slow. However, once past the bottleneck on the 91 freeway and out past Chino, they were able to make better time on the I-15. James suggested that they stop for the night in Victorville or Barstow, and Katrina decided on Barstow. It was just after seven when they stopped for the night. The early part of the drive had been really slow and had added to the time it would normally take. The next day was a long day, but there was little traffic and no delays. They crossed Nevada and the small corner of Arizona before entering Utah up the Virgin River Canyon to St. George, where they stopped for lunch. After that, it was the climb out of St. George and north. They stopped for the night in Nephi, which meant that they had a fairly short drive the next day to Ogden.

James and Katrina arrived at their new house in Ogden on Wednesday, after a brief detour to the airport at Salt Lake City to pick up James's car, to find the moving van parked outside. The driver told them that he had only been there about thirty minutes and that the unloading crew was due to arrive imminently. James unlocked the house, and when the crew arrived, he and Katrina directed loads into the various rooms. They had decided to do the unpacking themselves. When the moving company crews unpacked, things tended to be just put away somewhere and finding them afterwards was sometimes a challenge. They had learned over the years that it was better to do it themselves and then have the company come and collect the boxes and packing materials later.

The utilities to the house had been transferred to the Martins, so they had electricity, gas, water and a telephone. James called the plant and talked to Heather, then Simon. Although there were issues, there were none that demanded immediate attention, and some he delegated to Simon to handle. While the crew was unloading the truck, James told Katrina about his experiences with the water. The other utilities had been simple to transfer; he had simply called the various companies and made the necessary arrangements, but when it came to water, he discovered that it was different. He had been directed to a house in Uintah, and there he had met with one of the directors of the local water company and learned that the supply to that part of the town was actually managed by a private water company, and they would have to buy a share in the company to get water. Fortunately, the price of the share was not outrageous, so he had paid and was assured that water would flow!

*   *   *

Bernard Rasmussen met with Bill Ridings in Ogden late on Wednesday afternoon and handed over the satchel now stuffed with money. "Here you are, Bill," he said. "All present and accounted for."

"Do I need to count it?" Bill asked.

"You probably should so that you can be sure I didn't cheat you," Bernard advised. "But, I wouldn't do it here, too public, and there are at least four guys from the Ogden IRS office sitting over there in that corner."

"How do you know?" Bill asked.

"I've skied with them," Bernard explained.

"What are they like?" Bill wanted to know.

"Just your typical government bureaucrats," Bernard laughed. "They're more concerned with their department budgets and what it means to their salaries and pensions than anything else. But they do get bonuses for screwing the likes of us out of money, so be careful with that satchel!"

"You bet I'll be careful," Bill assured him. "And I will count it when I'm at home. You know, I thought for a while they were going to call the game on New Year's Eve."

"So did I," Bernard agreed. "When all that fog rolled in, I thought we were screwed."

"You would have been had you been wrong about the result or if the game had been called," Bill said. "I meant what I said about coming after you with an M-16!"

"Okay, okay," Bernard tried to mollify him. "Any news about the incident? Do you know what happened yet?"

"I'm feeling generous today," Bill said. "So, I'll answer your questions, and the answer is still no. We've tried all kinds of experiments and tests, and we can't figure out why. And before you ask, I checked on that other thing you asked about, and no one I know has ever heard of this Auriga Type B thing. You must have misheard or have been imagining things."

"Okay, subject closed," Bernard promised. "What's next for you?"

"I go to Kirtland on Friday and get my review and chewing out, and my new assignment," Bill replied.

"Do you know where yet?" Bernard asked.

"Actually, yes," Bill said. "I've got a friend who sees all the assignments, and he gave me a heads up that I'll be going to Dover in Delaware and switching commands to the trash haulers."

"Excuse me, trash hauliers?" Bernard asked.

"Military airlift," Bill explained. "And as it's a flying Command, I'm really low on the totem pole as a non-pilot and may just resign my commission and use this to buy a pizza restaurant. At least in Dover, there are plenty of guys who'll buy pizza!"

"You won't get discharged then?" Bernard asked.

"No, there'll be no dishonourable, if they were even thinking of that, there would have already been a hearing," Bill explained. "No, I'm just tainted now with the fuck up of the LST guys."

"Well, what's in that bag will go a long way to helping you buy that pizza franchise or restaurant," Bernard assured him. "How will you get it by the IRS?"

"I've been thinking about that, and I have a scheme," Bill grinned.

"I don't want to know!" Bernard protested, throwing his hands up.

"I'm out of here," Bill announced. "Do yourself a favour and never try and contact me or talk to me again."

"Don't worry, I won't," Bernard promised.

"And if you've got any brains at all, don't try and pull this kind of stunt on the guy who will take over from me," Bill advised.

"Do you know who that will be?" Bernard asked.

"Yes, a new light colonel who's out to prove to the world just what a clever dick he really is," Bill replied. "His name's Craig Robinson and he's on a fast track, so will probably come in, throw his weight around and then leave in eighteen months for his next posting. I won't see you again, ever, and I can't say that it's been a pleasure doing business with you, so I'm off."

Bernard watched as he left the club and wondered if he should commit the ultimate act of betrayal and bad faith and tell the IRS people about the colonel and his recent gambling winnings. He decided against it, only because it was likely to lead back to him, and he would be investigated as well for unreported income. That he did not want, because they would probably go back in time and audit prior years, something he did not wish to happen. So, he left it and watched Bill drive off. Now he had to decide whether to continue to pursue this story, if there actually was a story, or drop it altogether and find another story to work on.

A strange call

On Monday, January 9th, a more normal routine for James resumed. He had taken trips into the plant the previous week but had kept short hours so that he could help Katrina sort things out around the house. He had not always done that and had decided that on this move, he would try and be more supportive. He had not been in the office long when he received a call from the AFPRO office asking if he could join them for a change in command ceremony. James went to their offices and there was greeted by Bill Ridings, who was dressed in his best uniform. Bill introduced James to Major General Williams, the head of the command that directed the AFPRO offices. Most of the others James knew, except a new lieutenant colonel whom General Williams introduced as Craig Robinson, Bill's replacement. James watched fascinated as the change in command ceremony was conducted and decided that it really was a little like a changing of the guard that he had seen while a student in London. After the ceremony, Williams wanted to talk to James and let him know that the Air Force was not happy with the fact that there had been an incident. Then Robinson wanted to get his two cents worth in and told James that he wanted the operation to run smoothly like a cookie-cutter operation churning out missiles as if on a bakery production line. James listened to all this, then asked what Robinson's background was. The General obliged and gave James a quick résumé of Robinson's career. As James listened, it was all procurement, acquisition and a little program management, which probably meant overseeing someone else. He was not a combat or line officer and had not been in an explosives factory before. James saw him as another bureaucrat who was probably skilled at passing the buck and managing his own career, but who would not be followed into the breach by anyone, mainly because he would not be leading any charges into the breach; he would more likely be waiting outside to assign blame when the forlorn hope attack failed.

James thanked the Air Force for their invitation and returned to his office to find Lieutenant Commander Reinsch waiting for him.

"Ah, James just back from the plane jockeys, I see," she kidded. "Though I doubt many of them can actually fly a plane?"

"Can you?" he asked.

"Yes, checked out on S-3, E-2C, C-130 and P-3," she replied, then she added. "I've flown F-18s and even an F-14 once, but they don't like us near fighters or attack planes."

"Why aren't you on a carrier then instead of being here?" he asked.

"No women on carriers, yet," she said.

"But, what about land-based Naval Air Stations?" he asked.

"I've flown my share, but this was a promotional posting, and if I do well, then I can pick my next posting," she explained.

"So, what may I do for you?" James asked.

"I need an update on where we are with the new mixer so that I can report back to the admiral. I also want to know how the restart went," she replied.

"We have a review meeting at one," James suggested. "We'll be going over the results of the restart of the mix and cast process, and we'll also get an update on the progress of the new mixer."

"That's fine," she thought. "I'll call the information in tomorrow. Any surprises?"

"Not that we can find," James told her. "The mixers we put back into service are producing better than before, probably because we're doing a better job of monitoring the process and the motors we have cast look good. We'll know for sure when we run them through the CT machine, but for now, all looks good."

After Lieutenant Commander Reinsch had gone, Heather came in to tell James that Bill Evans had arrived. She had been helping him and had introduced him around to those whom he had not met and had found office space for him, and had sent him on a plant tour with Simon Wilmott. Heather also told him that Isabella wanted to see him. James asked her to let Isabella know that he was available and to let him know when Bill Evans came back to the offices.

"Isabella, what's up?" James asked.

"I've finished cataloguing everything that Miller had in his desk, file cabinet and locker," she replied.

"Any conclusions?" he asked.

"It's a very comprehensive set of documents and drawings for the Auriga Type B missile," she said. "The only thing I could not find was a precise recipe for the propellant mix itself."

"I'm pleased to hear that, I think," James said. "I hope Miller never got his hand on it, which is good because it's classified. But, I suppose there's always a chance that he found it and stored it somewhere else."

"But, if he has the mix instructions, could he not work out the recipe?" she asked.

"If he watched the mix and noted the amounts of each ingredient as it was added," James thought. "Do you think that's what he might have been doing?"

"I don't know," she admitted. "I don't suppose any of us will really know."

"The stuff on the walls," James changed the subject. "Did you put it back up just as he had had it in his office area?"

"Yes," she confirmed. "I've no idea if it has any significance, but thought it best, so I put the posters back up on the wall in the same arrangement as he had them. He seemed to have had this thing about old English country houses and cities."

"So, what's next for you?" James asked.

"That's up to you," she replied. "Robert Warner told me that I'm assigned to you until further notice."

"How are you on regular HR stuff?" he asked.

"I know all the systems and benefit packages; in fact, I wrote some of the stuff. I've dealt with people before and done my share of hiring and firing," she replied.

"How are you with the hourly folks?" he asked.

"I've never had any problems," she said. "I grew up being the boss of picking crews on the plantation and work gangs in the distillery, so I've met my share of people, good and bad, drunk and sober."

"What would you think if I offered you the HR slot here?" he asked.

"What, take over Gene's position?" she asked. She then looked around to see if the door was closed and if anyone could hear them or not.

"Yes," James confirmed. "I'm not happy with Gene and have agreement from Robert Warner and Ken Butler to make the change if I wish to.

Ken has another job he wants Gene to take that is probably better suited to his personality."

"It's a bit of a commute," Isabella thought. "But, I'll work it out. Perhaps I can find people from Ogden to carpool with and only drive myself north from Kaysville."

"So, will you take the job?" James asked, looking for confirmation.

"Oh, yes, *muito obrigada*, thanks, I won't disappoint you," she promised. "I was just gathering my thoughts and planning logistics."

"Okay, I'll get onto Ken and make the arrangements," James said. "I'll have an announcement for you to look at later. Would it be okay if we dated it tomorrow and made the appointment effective as of then?"

"Oh, that would be fine," she said. "Thank you."

After Isabella had gone, James looked at his organisation chart and circled the next position he wanted to change. He was less than happy with the Quality Manager and wanted someone else in that job. He had looked at the existing Quality structure and had seen no one that he wanted to elevate to the manager position, and he had found no likely candidates in the engineering of programs offices. Manufacturing needed all the talent it had to stay in place, so he needed to go outside. Ken had been running blind advertisements for him, and it was now time to interview candidates and see who had applied. It was, of course, possible that none of the potential candidates would be suitable, and he might have to resort to a headhunter. James called Ken Butler and told him that he had made his decision about Isabella and Gene Bonds, and Ken said that he would drive out that afternoon to talk to Gene. Because Ken had another assignment for Gene, it meant that James was not going to be stuck with the severance costs for Gene, which he was happy about. He also thought that Gene might be happier because he lived in Bountiful, and it was quite a commute for him to the plant every day.

The afternoon review of mix and cast operations was lengthy, mainly because they had to explain a lot to Craig Robinson. Robinson had wanted to know who Lieutenant Commander Reinsch was and why she was there, and had actually left the meeting for a few minutes to confer with his command. Whatever the answer was that he had been given, he came back in with a different attitude and was all smiles and cooperation, a condition that probably was belied by his true feelings. As James had told the lieutenant commander earlier, the results, to date, of the mix and cast operations were very encouraging. It was almost as though they had started from scratch, but without the need to go through a whole qualification process. Simon had shaken up the crews and had made some re-assignments, and was happier with the way things were. The new mixer was on schedule. Delivery had been promised on March 9th, and Baker Perkins was holding to that date. The site had been completely cleared of debris, and a new pit had been cast, and steel was being delivered that week to begin construction of the new building. The temporary structure that James had insisted on was paying for itself every day. Work was able to continue no matter what the weather, and the heating installed had prevented any freezing issues. Plumbing and electrical work was lined up and contracted, and Simon was confident that they would have a building to put the new mixer into.

The next hour of the meeting was a wrangle about the number and type of mixes that would be necessary to qualify the mixer. James pointed out that the process was qualified, and all they were checking was to see that the operational characteristics of the new mixer were the same as the other mixers. Robinson wanted a much broader qualification process. James finally told him that what he was looking for was a complete qualification of the propellant and mix systems, something that was not called for. Robinson called for a break and went out to call his command structure for advice. Lieutenant Commander Reinsch also called her command structure and told them what was happening. Some time later, Robinson returned and told the assembled team that his command structure had consulted with BMO and BMO's advice was to qualify the mixer as additional capacity and not capability. That was in concert with James's plan, so Robinson saved face by instructing the company to follow BMO's plan for qualification. Judging by the lieutenant commander's very private, quick smirk, James knew that her Command had issued instructions and that they had been passed on through BMO to Robinson.

While this had been happening, Ken Butler had arrived at the plant. After James had given the news to Gene Bonds, he turned him over to Ken. Gene was not happy, but faced with the option of severance and outplacement, had taken the alternative that Ken had offered. Ken then met with Isabella and told her what he was expecting from her, and went through an announcement with her that the company planned to release the next day. All they needed now was James's approval of the notice, and Ken would be on his way back to Salt Lake City.

Snow started to fall heavily, and by the time James and the other managers left the plant, it was accumulating on the hillsides quickly. Simon had had the plant maintenance crews plough the road to the gate and then on to the freeway on-ramp. Once on the freeway, the going was quite good; the State Highway Department had had its ploughs out early, and they were keeping ahead of the accumulation, but James guessed as he drove home that by the morning, there would be snow on the road. At his new house, the last few hundred feet up the slope was a challenge, and he considered himself fortunate that he did not have to walk the last few steps to the house. Katrina was waiting for him, anxious because of the falling snow and relieved when he arrived.

James had invited Bill Evans to dinner, and he arrived shortly after with his wife, Amanda. Amanda and Katrina immediately went off to discuss houses, house hunting and other things, leaving James and Bill to discuss the weather or business. Both Katrina and Amanda were delighted that they would now have someone in the town whom they actually knew. Making friends in new places was something they had both done, but when they looked back at all the places they had lived, the conclusion was that they had made many acquaintances and a few very close friends. Those friends stayed friends no matter where they might be in the country.

*   *   *

When Isabella got home, she was excited to tell Colleen her news. It was not every day that one received a promotion!
"Colleen, guess what?" she blurted out as she came into the house.

"I know," Colleen grinned as she waved a piece of paper at Isabella. "We just got this over the wire service before I left the office. You got promoted!"

"Yes, isn't it great!" Isabella enthused. "It'll be such fun and look good on my CV," she added, referring to her curriculum vitae or résumé.

"What about the commute?" Colleen asked, concerned about the amount of time that Isabella was going to have to spend on the road.

"I found three car pools in Ogden, so I thought I would drive to Ogden, then car pool the rest of the way," Isabella explained. "I'll give each of them a try before I decide which one, and I'll check to see who is the most flexible in terms of hours."

"Do we need to get you a new car with Four Wheel Drive?" Colleen asked. "I want you to be safe."

"Maybe," Isabella agreed. "Perhaps this weekend we'll look at Jeeps and things and see what there is and how much."

"How was the drive home today?" Colleen wanted to know. "It looked like it was coming down pretty good to the north."

"It was," Isabella agreed. "The plant had made a good job of access to the freeway, and then I followed James Martin to Ogden. South of Ogden, there has been enough traffic to keep the roads clear. How was your drive home?"

"It was a little slushy on the side streets," Colleen recalled. "And getting to the office tomorrow will be a challenge if they don't plough the secondary roads."

"How was your day apart from that?" Isabella asked.

"Well, I didn't get promoted," Colleen laughed. "But it was good enough; I've just about got all the data on Bangerter's Pumps, so the reporter can now write up the story. I just wish I had a better source for aerial photographs so I could get a feel for the extent of the flood plain they are using and if it's affecting anything around it."

"With all this new snow, do you think we could sneak off tomorrow and go skiing?" Colleen asked a little later, after Isabella had divested herself of overcoat, hat, boots and scarf.

"I'd love to, but I don't think it would be the right thing to do on my first day of my new job," Isabella laughed. "But, if we get enough, maybe we can go to the Tetons this weekend?"

"That sounds like a great idea," Colleen agreed. "I'll see if I can get us a place at one of the lodges on the basis of a story for the paper."

"I wonder how many of the management at the plant won't show tomorrow," Isabella pondered.

"I would think that at least one or two would have new snowitis," Colleen said. "I'll bet that we'll be short a few tomorrow and His Holiness the editor will tear his hair!"

"I didn't think he had enough hair to pull?" Isabella commented, puzzled.

"Figure of speech, figure of speech, my dear," Colleen said. "So what are you making for dinner? It's your week, you know."

"I know, we're going to have Vatapá de Frango," Isabella informed her.

"What's that?" Colleen asked.

"Chicken Vatapá, it's chicken done with onions, cayenne peppers, tomatoes, shrimp, peanuts, cashews and coconut milk plus a few other things," Isabella explained. "I'll serve it with Brazilian rice."

*   *   *

Bernard Rasmussen looked out of the window of his hotel in Washington and tried to plan out his campaign for the next day. He had a meeting with an aide to one of the Utah congressional delegation, and he was hoping for a miracle. His attempts to wring information out of Colonel Ridings had been fruitless because he simply had nothing to tell. But Bernard was still convinced that there was something to the Auriga Type B label, and he was going to test the waters with a different approach. He had thought about using the contacts that Colleen had with the delegation, but had decided that she might hear of it, get cold feet and tell the delegation to put him off, so he was trying his own approach. He had contacted some of his reporter friends and asked who was the most arrogant of the congressional aides. He also wanted to know if that aide would respond badly to the idea of not knowing about something that he thought his congressman ought to know. The friend who had provided him the name of the aide had laughed about the 'most arrogant' comment and had pointed out to Bernard that the whole of the Congress was full of people whose arrogance was only matched by their ignorance. Bernard asked him what he meant, and his

155

friend explained that whatever altruistic notions the politicians might have when they were elected evaporated as soon as they were seated and started to think about being re-elected. The staffers and aides trafficked in information because information and access to it were power, and power meant the ability to direct and allocate monies to one's home district, which was the surest way to get re-elected. Bernard thought that this was rather cynical, but had to admit that the more he thought about it, the more true it sounded.

*   *   *

James dug his driveway out and drove to work. The drive did take longer than usual. It seemed that the going was fine until about Brigham City, then there was a patch of heavy snow that had only been partially cleared, and the freeway was down to one lane in each direction. The access to the plant was clear. The plant maintenance people had done a good job and had even shovelled some of the walkways around the buildings. Of James's team, only two called in with excuses. Ron Hilliard, the financial wizard, was quite straightforward and said that he was taking a personal day to go skiing, and Ben Loyola, the Quality Manager, called in with a lame excuse about the snow blocking his driveway. Heather was listening and shook her head. She whispered to James that Loyola lived near her and the street had been ploughed. James sympathised with Loyola, but suggested that the next time he might be more straightforward and request a day off to go skiing. Ben apologised and promised that he would do that the next time.

James had started through his reports when the telephone rang. He noticed that it was the line that had been transferred from Michael Miller.
"Hello," he answered.
"Hello, I'm looking for Samuel," a female voice responded.
"I'm sorry, I'm new here and don't know all the people," James temporised. "But, I've not come across a Samuel. May I help you?"
"Samuel gave us this number in case we really had to contact him," the voice explained. "He told us only to use it in a real emergency."

156

"And you have an emergency?" James asked.

"Yes, we're desperately in need of a cantor for this evening," the voice explained.

"I'm sorry, a what?" James asked.

"A cantor," the voice repeated. "I'm Rebecca Rosenberg with Temple Beth Shalom. All this snow has caused havoc with our usual people; we need a cantor for tonight. We have used Samuel Levin in the past; he has such a nice voice, and we were hoping he would be available tonight."

"I'm sorry," James repeated. "I don't know of anyone by that name here. Would you hold a few minutes while I ask someone else?"

"Of course," Rebecca said.

James put the call on hold and called Isabella, and asked her to quickly do a search of personnel records for a Samuel Levin. As he expected, she was back in only a few minutes with the answer: no, Samuel Levin, either now or in the past five years. James punched the line button on the telephone and spoke to Rebecca Rosenberg.

"Ms. Rosenberg, I'm sorry, but our Personnel Department has no record of a Samuel Levin. I'm afraid that you may have the wrong number," he explained.

"Oh, well, I need a cantor for tonight. I was sure that that was the number he gave me with specific instructions about only using it in dire emergencies," she complained.

"I can appreciate that," he sympathised. "But we have no Samuel Levin here."

"Where am I going to get another cantor at this late hour?" she asked, James hoped semi-rhetorically.

"I'm afraid I'm quite unable to suggest any alternatives. Have you tried other congregations?" he asked.

"Yes, I've tried them all," she complained. "But, no luck, which is why I used the number that Samuel had given me. I think this is a dire emergency."

"I understand," James sympathised. "But, I'm sorry we don't appear to have anyone here by that name; the number he gave you must be incorrect."

157

"Well, thank you for your help; I'm sorry I didn't get your name," Rebecca asked.

"I'm sorry, ma'am, I didn't give you my name," James said. "I'm sorry we could not be more help; good day."

He had only just hung up the telephone when Isabella was at the door.

"Who's Samuel Levin?" she asked.

"No idea," James lied.

"Why did you ask me about him?" she asked.

"There was a call looking for him," James explained. "I'm new enough that I don't know everyone, so needed to check so that I could redirect the call if he was here somewhere."

"Oh," she said, and James thought that she looked quite disappointed.

"So, how's the new job?" he asked her, changing the subject.

"Fine, I'm finding my way around and have had meetings with all your managers, and we have some work to do," she replied. "I'm concerned with the general skill level in the plant and wonder if all the people can read, write and do arithmetic to the standard we need."

"What do you suggest?" he asked.

"We can run an assessment," she suggested. "But, I'd need everyone in the plant to do it, including you, if I am to get the results I want and protect us from future litigation if we have to terminate anyone who does not make the grade."

"What do we do if people don't make the grade?" he asked.

"We set up courses with the local colleges and give people a timetable, you have three, six, months, whatever, to make the grade, or we have to let you go," she thought.

"Okay, sounds good to me," James agreed. "But make sure that you have the education and training set up ahead of the testing so that you can immediately offer support to anyone who does not meet the standards."

"Okay," she promised. "I'll start contacting the schools and colleges now. Thanks."

*   *   *

In Washington, Bernard Rasmussen sat in the dining room of the Marriott and waited for his contact. He nursed his drink and ran over in his mind what his approach would be. His reporter friend had set up the meet at noon, so one of them was probably going to pay for lunch, and Bernard guessed that it would be him. Finally, a few minutes after noon, the person seating guests brought a man over and told Bernard that his guest had arrived.

"Hi, Bernard Rasmussen," he said, introducing himself.

"Tyler Harrison."

"Thank you for meeting with me," Bernard continued. "Can I get you something?"

"I'll just have a Coke, thanks," Tyler replied. "So, what's this about?"

Obviously, there was no beating about the bush for Tyler, so Bernard decided to plunge right in.

"What do you know about a secret government missile program called Auriga Type B?" he asked.

"Auriga Type B, never heard of it," Tyler replied quite honestly. Bernard read that honesty and confusion in the man's face; he might work in Washington at the centre of the universe and power, but he would make a poor gambler.

"Auriga Type B," Bernard repeated. "It's a secret missile being built in Utah at great expense, and the Air Force is trying to cover it up. I asked the local Air Force lieutenant colonel, but he is clueless and has no idea about anything."

"Why would the Air Force confirm or deny anything? How do you know this Auriga Type B program is connected to Utah?" Tyler asked.

"I have my sources," Bernard said.

"What do you expect me to do?" Tyler asked.

"I only want confirmation that Auriga Type B exists and why the Air Force would want to hide it," Bernard said.

"You just said a mouthful, friend," Tyler stated. "If this Auriga Type B program exists and is secret, then it's secret for a reason, and you should not be advertising its existence, and I would be breaking the law in revealing it to you."

"I realise that secret programs do exist," Bernard allowed, not believing for a minute that the aide would not leak the information to him if it

159

served the purpose of his Congressman. "But if they are operated with a risk to the local population, can that be permitted?"

"What do you mean risk to the local population?" Tyler asked.

"The LST accident where thirteen people died is what I'm talking about," Bernard explained.

"I read about that," Tyler said. "Pity about the people who died. Do you know what caused it?"

"I don't think anyone does," Bernard said. "All my efforts to talk to the company and the Air Force have met with stonewalling."

"That's typical of the Air Force and of anyone in the Pentagon. They think the world will end if they don't have their little secrets and the slush funds to pay for them," Tyler said a little bitterly. He had recently been excluded from a briefing given to his Congressman and had only heard snippets after the fact. He was waiting for the Congressman to be in a more expansive mood, and then he would draw out of him the essentials of the briefing, and he was confident that the Congressman would tell him all, even though he was supposed to keep it to himself.

"Do you think Congressman Wheelwright knows of this program?" Bernard asked.

"Don't know, couldn't say if I did," Tyler brushed off the question. "You know you've wasted your time in coming here, I don't know anything about your Auriga Type B, and if I did, I wouldn't be sitting here talking about it with you."

"I understand," Bernard said a little ruefully. "It was a shot I had to take."

"You reporters," Tyler laughed. "You seem to think the world owes you explanations about everything."

"Don't the people have a right to know?" Bernard asked, trotting out one of the most hackneyed lines in journalism.

"The people," Tyler snorted. "The people are so gullible they'll believe whatever half-truths you write for that paper of yours and even a good portion of the downright fiction."

"We only write what we can document and verify," Bernard protested.

"Spare me," Tyler said. "I pulled some of your items before I came today, and you enjoy raking people through the mud."

"Is it any different from the lines that are fed to the people from here in Washington?" Bernard asked.

"Why should I talk to you and not someone from the Post or the Times?" Tyler asked. "Yours is just a second-rate local rag; at least the Post and the Times enjoy status here on the East Coast and are widely read across the country."

"We don't have their circulation or cachet," Bernard admitted. "But I see this as a local issue and want to protect the citizens of Tremonton, Howell and Snowville, most of whom voted your way in the last election."

"What did that amount to, a thousand votes?" Tyler sneered. "Look, Bernard, I can't help you, and I've a meeting to go to."

"If you do learn of anything, will you call me?" Bernard asked.

"I doubt it, except to lean on you for your source," Tyler said. "I don't plan to waste any time on this."

After Tyler had gone, Bernard ordered lunch and thought about their conversation. He had not expected any great response from the aide, but no matter what Tyler had told him, he knew that he would be talking to the Congressman about the name and if there was anything there or not. So, as far as he was concerned, he had succeeded in his visit. He had dropped the pebble in the pond, and now he would wait and see where the ripples went and how soon a ripple bounced back towards him. For his part, Tyler went back to his office and immediately went to see Congressman Wheelwright, who knew nothing about any program called Auriga Type B, but who determined to find out. He had been stonewalled by the Air Force on secret stealth programs and was after their blood. Any way he could find to discomfort and embarrass them, he would. So, Bernard had succeeded, and the pebble had been well and truly dropped, and the ripples were already forming and spreading out.

*   *   *

Bill Evans came to see James with a plan for reorganising the Matériel function. James looked through the plans briefly and then told Bill to proceed. Bill wanted to bring in some experts to provide MRP training to his staff. He told James that they did not need any fancy computer program to manage things, but they did need the basic disciplines.

There was just not enough discipline in the whole manufacturing process. Simon Wilmott was making changes in the field of operations, and he needed the support of a good master schedule and the knowledge that what it told him was valid and informative. James asked Bill to work with Isabella and set up a program, and then to let him know what the cost would be. Bill's comment was that if past history was anything to go by, they would more than cover any costs in the first year following the start of the process.

Simon Wilmott joined them and detailed the operational changes he had made. He was focused on doing things right the first time, which meant reviewing the documents that described how to make things and deciding if it was possible to actually achieve any useful result. James had seen before where instructions had been written by people who obviously had never tried to follow them, because failure caused by following the instructions rigidly was not uncommon. Simon's team had already identified several processes where it was just not possible to make the parts using the instructions as written. That had driven the operations people to make their own changes, which they had done, and that did not always lead to good results. With the review of the procedures, Simon had already managed to reduce the number of defective or questionable parts and was now working on the time it took to make things. He was confident that they would see a significant change in operational results within a few months.

Craig Robinson arrived next, and James quickly went through with him the essence of the matters that he had been reviewing with Simon and Bill. Craig was pleased with the results and noted that any improvements that they made in yield and process times looked good on his reviews as well. He suggested that he and James set up a schedule of plant tours so that he could become more familiar with all aspects of the process. James was happy to oblige and promised plant tours to visit all areas. Craig asked if they had any further information on the incident, and the consensus was no. Simon went through the steps in the mixing process and explained what might go wrong at each particular step, but he always came back to the same hypothesis: blade-to-bowl contact; the problem they were still having was understanding how and why that may have happened. He also had no explanation for the number of people unless there was something that the two shifts wanted to discuss and review, and had invited Miller, as an engineer, to join them. The problem with that was that Miller was not one of the mixing process engineers, so it was all still a mystery.

After Robinson, Simon, and Bill had left, Lieutenant Commander Reinsch came to visit.
"What did the plane jockey want?" she asked.
"He just wanted to schedule some plant tours," James explained.
"He seems brighter than the last one," she commented.
"I'm sure he's just fine," James reassured her.
"I wish we knew just what actually happened out there," she said. "It bothers me a little that we have to be back in production, but we really don't know what went on."
"It worries me as well," James admitted. "But you've seen all the test and experimental data, there's nothing obvious out there."
"We need to be in Washington on Friday," she told him. "We need to brief the admiral on progress in the investigation and on the restart of the mix and cast processes."
"Is Robert Warner coming?" James asked.
"I checked and he won't be coming, it'll be just you," she replied.
"Okay, Lieutenant Commander, I'll be ready," James promised.
"It's Josephine," she reminded him. "Look, you didn't cause this incident; you've just inherited the cleanup. The admiral doesn't hold you responsible; in fact, he was most concerned that the company would just find someone else from inside and, as he put it, use the same monkeys in the tree on different branches."
"Well, I hope his confidence won't be misplaced," James said. "I'll make some plane reservations. When's the meeting?"
"Thirteen hundred hours, Friday, same room as before," she said. "I'll be going a day early to pre-brief everyone, so I'll see you there."

After the lieutenant commander had gone, James called Robert Warner and confirmed that the briefing was on and that he was going alone. Robert had another engagement that he could not break, so was unable to go. He also told James that he was confident that he would be able to handle the briefing on his own. They then discussed James's next personnel change, that of Quality Manager. The blind advertisements had turned up some candidates, and Ken Butler had whittled those down to two. If neither of those were suitable, then it was back to square one and a search firm. James asked Ken when he could see the two candidates, and Ken told him that the following week was good for all, and he also suggested that the interviews be in Salt Lake City and not at the plant. There was no need to create rumours and gossip any more than was necessary.

James went home and told Katrina that he had a meeting in Washington that Friday and asked her if she wanted to go, and they would make a weekend of it. Katrina thought that sounded like fun, so James called Delta and made reservations for two on the Thursday afternoon flight to Washington. He would use Friday morning to prepare for the meeting and then the evening of Friday, all day Saturday and Sunday morning was theirs to do what they would like. Katrina had plans to visit the Vietnam monument and the National Cathedral, so she was happy.

They had just sat down to dinner when there was a knock at their front door. James answered it, and two men were standing there.
"Good evening," one of them said. "I'm Elder Rasmussen, and this is Elder Thomas. We wanted to welcome you to the neighbourhood and invite you to join us at the Stake House."
"Thanks for the invite," James replied. "But, we're not members of the Church."
"Perhaps, we could leave this Testament with you," Elder Thomas suggested. "We did not realise you were in the middle of dinner. We just want you to know that even though you are not members of our congregation, you and Mrs. Martin may call upon us at any time if you need help, either spiritually or practically."
"I appreciate that," James replied. "You seem to be well informed."
"It's a small town," Elder Rasmussen commented. "And, it's not every day that the new boss of the LST plant moves in. We're sorry to have disturbed your dinner. Perhaps we will see you in the town at some time."

After they had left, James reported his conversation to Katrina, who pointed out that any one of a number of people could have told the church members who they were. The realtor, the movers or the utilities people were the most likely candidates, but she was betting on the realtor.

"It's a bit like living in Zambia again," she said. "It's a small town, and we can expect people will be curious."

"So no sunbathing outside in your birthday suit," James kidded. "If you do it will be all over town by the end of the day!"

"This is hardly birthday suit weather," Katrina laughed. "More like survival suit weather! What did they give you?"

"The Book of Mormon," he said, showing the blue volume to her. "We can add it to our collection of religious tomes to gather dust and stay unread except for days when some crossword clue comes up that calls for answers that we don't have ready to hand."

*   *   *

On Friday at twelve forty five James presented himself at the entrance to the Pentagon. After they had verified his identity, he was asked to wait for his escort. James did not have the appropriate badge that allowed him to roam the halls of the Pentagon at will. Josephine Reinsch came to collect him and led him to the appropriate room, where they waited with all the other players for the admiral.

"Gentlemen and lady," the admiral greeted everyone as he entered the room. "Mr Simonds, have all those present been identified and vouched for?"

"Yes, Admiral," Lieutenant Simonds confirmed. "I have identified all present, and they are all on the list."

"Thank you," the admiral said. "Now, Mr. Martin, I understand there has been a leak?"

"Sir, to my knowledge, the only leak has been a statement made by a member of our integration contractor's audit team," James replied. "Apparently, he made that statement within the hearing of a reporter who mentioned it to his researcher, who then asked our Human

Resources Manager. She is unaware of the program and denied all knowledge of it."

"That's my understanding as well," the admiral confirmed. "But apparently this reporter tried to wheedle it out of the AFPRO light colonel, and failing that, had his researcher call a staffer here in DC. Now he has approached another Congressional aide. That aide went to Congressman Wheelwright, who is now asking questions, fortunately of the Air Force and not us, pissed because he's not on the need-to-know list. I'm not happy, gentlemen, that someone connected with this program had the stupidity to mention it in a public place. It cannot be too much longer before the Air Force caves under the Congressional questioning and bounces the query back to us."

"Sir," a civilian that James did not know, but whom he suspected was with the offending contractor. "We have taken steps with the person in question."

"Maybe, but now General Williams has Congressman Wheelwright asking him questions in hearings, and he doesn't like it, and I don't like it," the admiral thundered, striking the table with the flat of his hand. "So far, General Williams has been a great barrier, but we cannot expect him to dissemble forever, and eventually he is going to have to admit that he's covering for us. That can't happen! I expect you all to know when to shut the fuck up and stay off the booze!"

"Yes, sir," was the general response of all in the room.

"What do we do about this reporter?" the admiral asked.

"Can we get the FBI to lean on him?" a captain suggested.

"Why, what's he done, he's only asked a couple of people some simple questions?" the admiral said. "We can't have the FBI leaning all over people just because they ask questions; if we did that, then half the population would be visited by the Fibbies."

"Could we feed him some red herrings and have him go off and look into something else?" another civilian suggested. James was no expert, but he decided that he was with the CIA.

"I'll leave that to you guys," the admiral agreed. "You're the experts."

"Now, back to the program, how's it going, James?" the admiral asked.

"Sir, we have restarted the remaining mixers and are mixing and casting segments," James reported.

"So, I understand. You've also made people changes. How's that working out?"

"Very well, Sir," James confirmed. "We made several changes in the Operations Management group and are seeing results in lower defect rates, fewer Material Review Boards and faster cycle times. It really pays to do it right the first time. I have provided Lieutenant Commander Reinsch with all the data."

"It's actually Commander Reinsch now," James was informed. "Do you still need the new mixer?"

"I could actually make the schedule without it, if we continue to make the improvements that we have seen to date," James said. "But, if we have any issues at all with the other mixers, then I would be faced with a severe constraint. The new mixer will allow us to properly take down each of the other mixers in turn and do appropriate maintenance on them."

"Okay, what about cases, nozzles, igniters, etc.?"

"I have here a production schedule that shows each major component and its status," James said as he produced a roll of paper that was a chart of all the major pieces and where they stood in terms of completion. The chart went out six months and James explained that they had the same chart that went out for a year and a more basic set of data that went out three years.

"Is this chart valid? How often is it updated?" the admiral asked.

"We have daily production meetings and a weekly master schedule meeting," James explained. "If necessary, we make adjustments on a weekly or monthly basis."

"How are you husbanding our materials?" the admiral asked, grinning.

"Sir, I have recruited a Matériel Manager and he is restructuring the group that is acquisition, production planning and scheduling and warehousing, receiving and shipping," James explained.

"Okay, what about Jerry's concern about differences between the CAT scan images and the film images?"

"We have done parallel imaging, film and CAT, and our conclusion is that the film shows all the motors to be well within spec limits and well within family, but that the CAT imaging gives us more detail, and we are seeing a level of detail not available to us before," James explained.

"Jerry?" the admiral asked, turning to Jerry White, the civilian who had asked about the issue at the first meeting James had attended.

"That is consistent with our understanding," Jerry confirmed. "And it's consistent with experience at the other producers of solids."

The brigadier general, whom James had seen before and who he had learned was Brigadier General Howard from BMO, then spoke up, "These operational changes that you've made and the improvements you say that you are seeing in defect rate reduction, do they also apply to our Auriga Program?"

"Yes, General," James confirmed. "We have made improvements to operational discipline plant-wide and are seeing the same reductions in all areas."

"Does that mean I'll get a lower price?" the general asked.

"I'm sorry, general, but our contracts are fixed price and we have just moved them out of the red and into the black, and if we continue as we are going, we will make a modest return," James explained.

"Well, perhaps when we come to negotiate the follow-on, we'll be less generous," the general commented. "You contractors are all alike, all take and no give."

James let that remark go and decided that it would be politic to just ignore it. General Howard either had an intense dislike for all contractors and suppliers, or he had had a bad experience, and his attitudes were now coloured by that experience. To James, the general did not fit his image of a general. This one was lean, almost cadaverous and wore glasses that he perched on his nose. He looked for all the world like a Latin teacher James had had when he was at school. The admiral then threw the meeting open to the floor and asked for any other questions. For the next hour, James fielded questions on anything from the calendering process for the rubber insulation to tape laying for nozzles, from case winding to curing and tool removal and from ammonium perchlorate agglomeration to HMX grinding in the fluid energy mill. Finally, there was a lull, and the questions stopped, and the admiral stepped in to take control of things again.

"Is there anything else for Mr. Martin?" the admiral asked. "No, in that case, Mr. Simonds will see you out. Thank you for coming. We will see you in a month."

"Thank you, Sir," said James and then he followed Lieutenant Simonds out of the room and down the corridor towards the building exit. James noted that as he left, so did the BMO general. Apparently, whatever else the Navy had to discuss, it did not involve the Air Force, which was not surprising, as the only reason the Air Force was included in the Sagitta briefings of LST was that they were the vehicle to wash the contract through. On their way out of the building, James met Costanza Albertini in the escort of a civilian with a Pentagon badge.

"James," Costanza said. "What are you doing here? How's it going?"

"I was just delivering some briefings on my programs," James replied. "What brings you here?"

"Shipping stuff around the world," Costanza replied. "We contract with the Services to move stuff occasionally."

"Are you staying here in DC?" James asked.

"Yes, I'm at the Marriott on Pennsylvania Avenue, and you, are you going back to Utah tonight?"

"No, I'm here for the weekend with my wife," James replied. "We're also staying at the Marriott."

"Maybe we could get together for dinner?" Costanza asked.

"Great," James agreed. "We'll be in the bar of the Marriott when you get out of here."

"Okay, see you probably around six then, *ciao*," Costanza said, setting up the meeting.

"*Ciao ciao, ci vediamo presto*," James said, saying that he would see him soon.

"I didn't know you spoke Italian," Lieutenant Simonds commented after Costanza had gone. "Who's he?"

"Costanza Albertini," James explained. "He runs the shipping subsidiary of Waterway Chemicals, the parent company of LST." But privately, James was wondering why Costanza was there again when he was there, and was there a connection? Although there had been no obvious signs of recognition between the lieutenant and Costanza, James was sure that they knew one another.

When James got back to the Marriott, Katrina had just returned. She had been to the National Cathedral and was comparing it to cathedrals she had seen in England and, in her mind, placing the newness of the Washington structure on the old English buildings to imagine what they looked like when new.

"*Suikerbossie*, how was your day?" James asked.

"It was only *baie aangenaam man*," she said. "I had a great time, I could wander at my own pace and not have to worry about you pacing around behind me and muttering about old buildings!"

"Who me?" James asked in all apparent innocence

"Yes, you," she laughed. "I've lived with you too long *ou maat*. How was your day?"

"Well enough," James admitted. "I met the guy who runs the shipping company for Waterway Chemicals, and he asked us if we would like to have dinner together."

"What's he like?" Katrina asked.

"Of definite Italian origin, but I suspect a citizen today. He spends his time between Livorno and Houston," James explained. "He knows the village where Alex and Vincé live. He's staying here and will meet us in the bar later."

"I need to bathe and change, then if we're going to meet someone for dinner, I look a right scruff," she said. "What time is it?"

"It's just after three," James replied. "We've got plenty of time."

"Plenty of time for what?" she asked.

"Time enough to bathe," he replied.

"Is that all?" she asked. "I thought you had other things on your mind!"

"Of course," James admitted. "For you, I've always got time."

"You're only saying that because you're mentally undressing me," she laughed.

"If this weren't such a public place, it wouldn't be mental undressing," he boasted.

"Well, come on then, let's go to our room and see how well you do at undressing," she invited.

Suspicions confirmed

When James and Katrina went back downstairs, they found Costanza in the bar. He waved to them, and the man he had been talking to excused himself and left. James was sure that he had been one of the civilians in the briefings that he had seen earlier.

"Costanza," James greeted him. "This is my wife Katrina."

"*Piacere,*" Costanza said. "I understand from James that you have family in Italy?"

"Yes, James's sister and her family live in the hills above Viareggio," she replied.

"I know the area well," Costanza said. "I have a villa in Quattro Venti in the hills above Pisa."

"Have you lived there long?" Katrina asked.

"My family has lived there a long time," he replied. "I now divide my time between Italy and Houston."

"James tells me that you run the shipping company of Waterway. What do you ship?" she asked.

"We have two fleets," he explained. "One is large bulk carriers and some oil tankers, the other is small commercial freighters that carry general cargo."

"So you ship for Waterway?" she asked.

"Occasionally," he admitted. "As I am sure you know, oil and chemicals are traded freely, so we carry some for Waterway, but more often we carry for another buyer."

"What sort of stuff do you carry in the other fleet?" she asked.

"General cargo mainly, anything from small amounts of fertiliser to equipment for construction, supplies for coastal cities, foodstuffs like coffee, cacao or tobacco and cars and household goods, anything that is not containerised. The ships are all about fifteen hundred to two thousand tons gross, so are much smaller than the large bulk carriers we use for oil and chemicals. But, they have the advantage that they can go to places that cannot take a large vessel, and they can all self-load and unload," he explained. "So, we do a lot of coastal shipping in and around the Med and down the coasts of Africa, both east and west."

"Are your ships safe?" she asked.

"Yes, our record is good; we have had no spills or major losses. My greatest fear is piracy," he explained.

"Piracy?" she asked.

"Yes, the Molucca Straits and I think the next problem area will be the Horn of Africa, now that there are more problems in Somalia," he elaborated.

"Are your ships armed?" she asked.

"Most countries do not like you to enter their ports with weapons on board, so we have found a way to put people on and off when the boats are transiting risky zones," he replied.

"Does that work?" she asked.

"It does in the Moluccas," he said. "The pirates are becoming more sophisticated and know enough to leave us alone."

"Have your ships ever fired upon any pirates?" she asked.

"We would never engage in an exchange of gunfire," he said in mock horror. "But, enough of rusty old boats. Shall we go in to eat?"

Over dinner, Costanza told them a little about his life in Italy. He had children, one of whom was attending a Liceo Classico and the other a Liceo Scientifico, both part of the traditional Italian education system. The Liceo Classico focused mainly on Latin, Greek, philosophy and other subjects, whereas the Liceo Scientifico focused on mathematics, physics and chemistry with a smattering of the other subjects. He also had them enrolled in additional English classes, because he wanted them to maintain the fluency they had acquired in the US and knew from his own experience that high school classes just did not achieve that. He had joined Waterway Chemicals through the shipping company and had worked his way up until they had been moved to Houston, where they had lived for eight years, long enough to get citizenship and for the children to gain a good grounding in English. His family ran a bakery and café in Pisa, and that kept them busy. He had decided early in his life that he would find something to do other than work in the family bakery; the hours were just terrible, and he left that to his brother and sister. He extended an invitation for them to visit him at his villa and even promised to take them sailing on the Mediterranean.

For their part, James and Katrina shared their somewhat torturous path from Zambia to the current assignment in Utah. Costanza was curious about how James had managed to adapt to different industries and how Katrina had adapted to living in the different cities and states they had moved to. James told Costanza about his brother Will and the safari business in Botswana, and about his sister Alex and her family in Italy. Although they told Costanza that Alex and Vincé lived near Viareggio, they did not elaborate upon the job that Vincé did or where he worked. Katrina told Costanza what little she knew about her father's foray into grape growing and the wine industry in South Africa. Costanza actually knew quite a lot about that business but was not that familiar with the Hanepoort grape or the sweet dessert wine that was made from it. He finally decided that it was probably very like the Vin Santo that he was familiar with. Both James and Katrina had sampled and liked different Vin Santo wines when they had visited Alex and Vincé in the past. They knew that Vin Santo is a classic Tuscan favorite, particularly when served with *cantucci*, or traditional almond cookies.

After dinner, Katrina commented to James that it had been funny to watch him and Costanza both dancing around, asking each other any questions about what they had both been doing at the Pentagon that day. James told her that he had not wanted to put Costanza in the position of having to dissemble about what he had been doing that day, so just kept the conversation to much safer general subjects. James did wonder if he should ask Vincé if he had ever come across Costanza, but decided to leave that avenue alone for now.

Back in Utah on Monday, James sat through his regular review meetings, then called Robert Warner to brief him on the meeting. Robert was happy to leave future meetings to James and was not surprised when James told him about the BMO general and the complaint about pricing. Robert's comment was that the Air Force was replete with officers, all of whom had to find some way to justify their position and existence, and that the particular general they were talking about was a good example of incompetence finding its way to the top. He only hoped that by the time the selection process came for additional stars that reason would set in and that the general would be topped out. Robert compared the Navy and Air Force approaches and said that he preferred dealing with the Navy because at least they knew what they were talking about. Most of them had been in the ballistic program office of the Navy for years, so knew all the issues and problems that had gone before. In contrast, the Air Force was always moving people around, and many of the officers they dealt with knew less about missiles than James did.

James had just finished talking to Robert when Commander Reinsch arrived at his door.

"James, got a minute?" she asked.

"Of course," he replied. "What's up?"

"The admiral asked me to check if you or anyone here had been approached by that reporter to ask about Sagitta, either as Sagitta or as Auriga Type B."

"Not as far as I'm aware," he said. "I know that everyone here doesn't love me, but I think I would hear if a reporter had been asking around. What do they plan to do about the reporter? Who is he, by the way?"

"His name is Bernard Rasmussen and he works for the Salt Lake City Star," she explained. "We understand that he's been trying for some time to put a story together about the incident, even to the extent of setting up our good Colonel Ridings for attempted blackmail."

"What was that?" James asked.

"My sources tell me that Rasmussen was playing the numbers on football games and set up Ridings to take a big loss. Apparently, the guy likes to gamble, and he got suckered into a losing bet that put him at risk with less-than-savoury characters. Fortunately, Ridings really didn't know anything, so Rasmussen let him off, but Ridings did walk away with some loot, which the IRS is now looking into," she explained. "His Command has been informed, and he may get some counselling about his gambling habits, after he's made his deal with the IRS."

"Did this all come up last week?" he asked. "How do you know all this?"

"After you had gone and the plane jockeys had all gone, the shit hit the fan," she moaned. "Ridings has been under surveillance for some time as a security risk because his gambling habit was documented. The Air

Force in its infinite wisdom did nothing as usual, 'Our officers would never do that', right, bunch of useless uniforms that would run at the first sign of any real action."

"You don't seem to like your brothers in blue," James commented.

"There are some that are fine," she admitted. "In fact, they have some pretty gutsy fly boys who are as good as it gets, but it's an officer-heavy service that is outdated and becoming more so with UAVs. Why send a man up when the plane can be piloted remotely?"

"Wouldn't that also apply to naval aviation?" he asked, thinking that unmanned autonomous vehicles, or UAVs, could be used by either service.

"Of course," she agreed. "It's probably the only way I'll get to see air-to-air engagements. When and if they develop air-to-air capability in a UAV."

"So, what do we do now?" he asked.

"Nothing," she instructed. "Just be aware, James. No talking to reporters, and this conversation has the same classification as the Sagitta program, so nothing said to anyone, except me, not even Robert Warner."

*   *   *

Bernard Rasmussen left his favourite diner after a hearty breakfast of pancakes. Before he got to his car, two men in Air Force camouflage fatigues fell in on either side of him.

"Just walk with us a little way," one of them said.

"Who are you guys? What do you want?" Bernard asked.

"Just walk with us," the other repeated. "Our officer would like a word."

They walked over to a pick-up that had Air Force markings, and there stood a man dressed in similar camouflage fatigues but with the insignia of a major, unlike the escorts who were sergeants.

"What's this all about?" Bernard demanded. "You can't just shanghai people off the street, I have rights!"

"Do those rights include blackmail and espionage?" the major asked.

"What do you mean, I haven't blackmailed anyone and spy, spy for whom?" Bernard demanded to know.

"Don't play the innocent," the major told him. "Right about now, your pal Ridings is singing his heart out to the IRS and the FBI, hoping to get off an espionage charge. He'll hang you out to dry. Who are you actually working for?"

"You guys are crazy," Bernard protested. "Look, I'll just yell and people will come over to see what's going on, and then you'll have to explain that you're harassing a citizen and a reporter, protected by the First Amendment!"

"Go ahead, yell," the major invited. Bernard opened his mouth to yell, and all that came out was a quiet little squeak, probably as a result of the wind being knocked completely out of him by a blow that he did not see coming and that had been delivered from less than a foot away. The people he was dealing with obviously had capabilities that he had not expected. When he was able to breathe again, he gasped out, "What do you guys want?"

"We just want your cooperation," the major asked. "Is that too hard?"

"I don't know anything," Bernard protested.

"Then why did you try and blackmail an Air Force officer?" the major asked.

"I didn't blackmail anyone!" Bernard protested again, more desperately this time.

"But you tried, and that's the problem we're having," the major said. "Bernard, I may call you Bernard? Good, we just want you to go on being a good little reporter and focus on the environment or something equally important."

"I can do that," Bernard promised, planning all the while to check up on these Air Force people. He had noted the name on the major's uniform as Richards, and he had made another mental note of the number of the pick-up.

"Yes, but can we trust you, Bernard?" the major asked. "You could just be lying to us."

"Why would I lie?" Bernard protested.

"Because you're a reporter and reporters lie," the major sneered. "Give a reporter any information and he'll twist it and turn it so that the story that comes out is unrecognisable."

"I would never do that," Bernard promised.

"We'll be watching you, Bernard," the major promised. "We know where you live and where you eat, so just back off any approaches to any more Air Force people, *capisce!*"

That said, the Air Force people left, and Bernard was happy to see them go. He waited until they were out of sight, then found a pay phone and called his contact at Hill Air Force Base and asked for information on Major Richards. His contact was back in about three minutes with his report.

"Major Elizabeth Richards, 32, single, scheduled for redeployment to Hickham Air Force Base in Hawaii."

"But that can't be," Bernard protested. "You must have another Major Richards, tall, about thirty-five, black, well built, well spoken. What about this pick-up truck?" Bernard read out the numbers he recalled and waited.

"I doubt that you saw that vehicle," he was told. "That's the number for a line refuelling truck."

"Okay, well, thanks all the same, sorry to bother you," Bernard apologised, then hung up.

Bernard digested this information this then stood back to really think. Obviously, the people who had talked to him were not with the Air Force, unless of course they came from a different base. But then again, they had made it so easy to check on their lack of bona fides that he began to get concerned. He was being given a message by someone, and that someone was probably not the Air Force. He concluded that it must have something to do with his conversation with the Congressional aide the week before. Perhaps he should lie low for a while and not make waves. He had no real family in Utah, no steady current girlfriend and the editor would be happy to see the back of him, so his disappearance would not be noticed for a while. He went to his office, genuinely concerned and wondered if his phone was tapped and his house bugged. But perhaps he thought to himself that he was just being paranoid. These things happened in the movies, not in real life.

As he drove back to his office, Bernard wondered what had driven the approach by whoever they were. He speculated that they were actually part of the Air Force but had disguised their ranks and names so that if he reported the harassment, it would go nowhere. That made sense to him, and in fact, the more he thought about it, the more he decided that it was actually a ploy by Ridings to make sure that he did not continue his approaches to anyone in the Air Force. That explanation made the most sense to him. He decided to change his approach and drop the line of enquiry he had been following and focus more on the incident itself and the potential causes. That would mean trying to pry information out of people who worked at the plant, but that might be more profitable than trying to work with the Air Force.

At the newspaper office, Bernard went first to see Colleen.
"Hi, Colleen, don't ask questions, but just deep six anything you have in the way of notes, memos, files or anything that might relate to the incident at LST," he said.
"Why?" she asked.
"Don't ask," he repeated. "Let's just say that it has become not exactly the topic of the week, and I need to find another story to think about."
"Okay," she agreed. "Are you in trouble?"
"Nothing I can't handle," he said. "I'm just trying to simplify my life."
That done, he went back to his office and wondered what, if anything, he should do about declaring his gambling winnings to the IRS. If Ridings was under investigation, he had no doubt that the IRS would come knocking at his door sooner rather than later. Fortunately, he had the cash to pay whatever taxes and penalties might be levied, but there was always the chance that they might go back and audit previous years.

*   *   *

James left his office and went out to the mixer control bunker. He checked in at the bunker and talked to the foreman, Ed Clark. James needed help getting to the location where Michael Miller had been seen. Ed checked with his crews and told James to take the pick-up truck parked outside. It had Four Wheel Drive and should be quite capable of negotiating the steep track in the hills behind the mix buildings. James drove slowly up until he came to a spot where he could turn around, then he parked and looked about him. It took a few minutes to orient himself and find the approximate location of the site that he had marked on the site plan in the office. Then it was just a matter of rooting around. James was beginning to think that he had been leading himself astray when he kicked something hard and hollow. He cleared away the snow and the underbrush and found two aluminium suitcases, both covered in green and khaki canvas. He struggled with them both got them back to the truck, and loaded. Then he kicked the brush back over the area, and the disturbed area disappeared beneath of covering of sagebrush.

Back at the control bunker, James transferred the suitcases to the trunk of his car and then went in to talk to Ed.

"Hi, Mr. Martin," Ed greeted him when he went back into the bunker. "You find anything?"

James was pretty certain that he had been observed with the closed-circuit television cameras, so saw no point in denying the obvious.

"Hi, Ed. Yes, I did. I am taking it back to my office for a better look."

"Do you need any help?" Ed offered.

"I don't think so," James temporised. "But, there is one thing you can do for me."

"Just name it!"

"I know you're in the Guard," James commented. "So I want you to treat this like any other operation. I would rather the whole world did not know that I went up there and found something."

"You can rely on me, Mr Martin. Here's the tape from the camera that followed you up the hill, and mum's the word," Ed promised. "Do you think there was something fishy about that guy Miller?"

"Do you?" James asked, turning the question back onto Ed.

"Yeah, I do," Ed confirmed. "The other guys did too, and they were going to have a meeting and confront him when the accident happened."

"What do you mean confront?" James asked.

"Well, there was twelve of them, if you get my meaning, and Charlie Dawson and Bernard Carson, the two foremen who died, were going to present information to him that said that he was not who he said he was."

"Who else have you told about this?" James asked.

"No one," Ed confessed. "I was beginning to think that I had been imagining all this, and the guys were wrong. But you keep prodding into things, and I think you have suspicions as well."

"You never thought to tell anyone else?" James asked again.

"I'm not one who runs around telling people everything," Ed commented. "All I knew was little bits that I had heard, and there was nothing concrete."

"Is there anything else that you want to tell me now?" James asked.

"Not that I can think of, but if you have questions, I'll do my level best to answer them," Ed promised. "Charlie and Bernard were my friends, and I'd really like to know what happened."

"What do you think happened?" James asked.

"I think there was blade-to-bowl contact," Ed stated. "I think that was caused by something falling into the mixer. That suggests to me that the inspection port on the top of the feed mechanism was open, but does not tell me what was dropped in or who dropped what."

"You don't think any of the feed or metering devices broke and fell in?" James asked.

"No, I've looked at them all and can't figure that. No, something was dropped in through the open port. What I want to know is who, Miller or one of my guys."

"If Charlie and Bernard wanted to confront Miller, why not do it in his office or in the cafeteria?" James asked. "It seems a little out of the way to do it in a mix building."

"It's hard to hear shouts and screams from those mix buildings," Ed commented, looking at the ceiling. "I always figured that confront also meant a little persuasion."

"Remind me never to get invited to a mix building," James laughed.

"No, you're fine, Mr Martin. You've done more for us on the line than the last boss did in five years. You care and are interested, even though you ask all kinds of difficult questions."

"Okay, Ed. If I have any bright ideas or questions, I may get back to you to try and jog your memory of things that might have happened over the past few months," James said. "I'll see you around, Ed."

James decided to wait until most of the people had left in the afternoon before transferring the suitcases from his car to the room with the other

Michael Miller information. It took him a while because the cases were quite heavy, and he spent some time looking for a dolly to make the move easier. He would have spent less time if he had moved one case at a time and just dealt with the weight. He resisted the temptation to open the cases that evening and left them until the morning. He had no idea what he might find and did not wish to constrain himself for time.

At home that evening, Katrina had news. His brother Will had been thinking of changing the location of their safari business, and he had settled on two possibilities: the Kalahari Gemsbok National Park in Botswana and the Kafue National Park in Zambia. The two locations were quite different. The Kalahari Gemsbok Park was desert and was located in the southwest corner of Botswana, adjoining the South African border. The Kafue National Park was about 100 miles west of Lusaka, the capital of Zambia, and included quite a variety of habitats, including riverine around the Kafue River itself. In both cases, it was a question of negotiating with the government and arriving at some sort of deal that would be advantageous for both. Access to either park was not the easiest, perhaps, the Kafue park being slightly easier to get to because it would be a relatively easy drive from Lusaka, and there were international flights into Lusaka from Europe and South Africa.

"Would you like to go one day?" he asked.

"Just tell me when, and my bags are packed!" she laughed. "I'm always ready for a trip to the bush."

"Do you remember our last trip into the bush?" he asked.

"Oh yes! That was when you chased me around the sausage tree."

"With what you were wearing, or not wearing, are you surprised?"

"What do you mean, not wearing?"

"As I recall, you had on a hat and nothing else."

"Well, it certainly got your attention," she laughed. "I don't recall running very fast."

"It wouldn't have mattered," he boasted. "I would have caught you and had my way with you."

"You think so?"

"I'll show you," he promised.

"Just wait there a minute," she told him. "I think I have that hat somewhere. I'll be right back." When she reappeared, she was wearing the hat and nothing else, and James felt the same overwhelming desire for her that he always did. She led him on a short dance around the room and into the next room before allowing herself to be trapped in a corner.

"Why, *meneer, wat doen jy?*" she asked.

"*Ho voglia di te!*" he replied, switching languages.

"*Andiamo a letto,*" she surrendered. Then she led him upstairs to the bedroom and the delights that lay there.

* * *

Bernard Rasmussen drove north into the top end of the Cache Valley of Utah and into Logan, which was not far from Smithfield, where he had learned that most of the people who had lost their lives in the incident had lived. He was in no hurry and was prepared to hang around all day if necessary to find the best avenue of approach. Logan was not large, as cities go. It had a population of about fifty thousand people and was dominated by a university. Bernard found a diner and settled in to eat lightly and wait. His patience was rewarded by a group that sat near him. As far as he could judge from their conversation, they were all from the nearby Utah State University and were all political science majors engaged in deep philosophical discussions about the defence industry.

Bernard excused himself to them and apologised for his interruption. "I was interested in your discussion."

"What are your views?" one girl asked him.

"I think the defence industry has driven our Congress to wars that we did not need or want, and that they will do so again," he commented.

"That's right," one of the other girls agreed. "The big companies all just want to sell more weapons because they don't know how to make anything else."

"And what use is it all?" Bernard asked. "I'm Bernard, by the way."

"I'm Twyla," the first speaker said. "And this is Heather, Kaylee and Rylee," she added, going around the table in order. "And to answer your question, none, look at the LST plant. They make who knows what, and is it useful, or will their products just sit in silos and rot away?"

"Why, what do they make?" Bernard asked.

"According to my sister's boyfriend, they make rockets that go to the Air Force, but the things they make can just as easily be made by Thiokol or Hercules. Why do we need so many companies all building the same things?"

"Didn't LST have some kind of problem?" Bernard asked.

"Yes, thirteen people from here or near here died needlessly," Twyla announced.

"What happened?" Bernard asked.

"What I heard was that they were having some kind of meeting and then the mixer thingie blew up," Heather replied.

"Yes, and it was an unusual meeting because normally there would have only been four or five people there," Twyla agreed.

"Wasn't there some sort of question about the engineer?" Kaylee asked.

"Yes, there was this new guy, Miller, and he didn't fit in somehow, and they were having a meeting to resolve that," Heather explained.

"Resolve how?" Bernard asked.

"I think to let him know that he was not welcome," Rylee replied.

"Why was he not a good member of the Church?" Bernard joked.

"I heard that he was a regular Peter Priesthood," Heather laughed.

"I think he was just a little too good to be real," Twyla said. "It was almost like he was acting the part and going overboard."

"His wife was pretty, though," Kaylee commented.

"Too much so," Twyla agreed. "I caught my Ralph eyeing her more than once."

"I don't think she was a true member of the Church," Heather commented. "I saw her once rolling her eyes when the Bishop was talking."

"We've all done that," Kaylee said. "Bishop Romney can go on a little sometimes."

"Yes, but there was something else about her," Heather added. "I think that you were right about him and that she was the same, too good to be real. My brother and his friends saw her once in the mountains frolicking with her husband in the woods. He took some pictures, and my dad took them off him. He said that they were too much and that he should not be looking at those kinds of pictures."

"Why, what were they?" Bernard asked.

"Nude pics," Heather whispered. "They were in the woods in the nude!"

"Where is she now?" Bernard wanted to know. He thought it might be nice to get a look at this person who had so offended the standards of the Church.

"She left right after the accident," Twyla replied. "It was kinda weird, really, one minute she was all Molly Mormon and the next minute she had just disappeared. The Relief Society had offered to help her, but she just vanished."

"No funeral or memorial service for Miller?" Bernard wondered.

"As I understand it, there was not much left to bury," Kaylee commented.

"Ooh, that's gross," two of the other said in unison.

"Yes, but it's true," Kaylee confirmed. "It seems as if she got the news from the company, then left."

"Is LST still making the same things that it did before the accident?" Bernard asked.

"I believe so," Twyla confirmed. "They were stopped for a while when they did their investigation, and then this new guy came in and held things up some more to check, and now they are back in production."

"Who's the new guy?" Bernard asked.

"Some guy from California," Twyla reported. "Apparently, he's not a member, so we don't know much about him."

Bernard interpreted "not a member" as meaning that the new guy, whom he knew to be James Martin, was not a member of the LDS Church.

"So will they have another accident?" Bernard asked.

"Who knows?" Heather replied. "It seems like all the rocket companies have something once in a while. It's not that safe a job, that's why they're way out there in the desert."

"Except for Hercules," Twyla interrupted.

"Yes, except for Hercules," agreed Rylee. "It's real close to Magma, and if anything ever happened there, oh my heck, there would be problems."

"Do you think we need these weapons?" Bernard asked.

"We need to be able to defend ourselves," Kaylee commented. "But as far as I know, the only thing you can do with those things is attack."

"Yes, but that's what deterrence is all about," Rylee added. "If we didn't have all this stuff, people could threaten us."

"We need to help them find the Lord," Twyla said. "And then we wouldn't have the need of them."

"That may be a tall order," Bernard commented. He had also noticed that Rylee and Kaylee had rolled their eyes at each other on Twyla's pronouncement and had apparently had this conversation before.

"Twyla's going to go on a Mission," Rylee said to Bernard. "Maybe she can reduce the threat a little."

"Rylee Anderson!" Twyla started.

"She was only pulling your leg," Kaylee interrupted. "You know we're all behind you on this."

"I must go," Bernard excused himself. "I have some appointments in Ogden that I have to keep. It's been interesting talking to you all, and Twyla, good luck on your Mission."

Bernard left. He decided that he did not want to be in the middle of a cat fight, and it certainly looked as if it could head that way. But he had learned something. There was obviously something about Michael Miller that had antagonised the hourly workers, and it might be a clue to what actually happened in the incident. It was difficult for him to imagine what might be the circumstances that would cause anyone to actually initiate an incident, but perhaps something went wrong, and it was all unintentional. He recalled that Ridings had said that the new guy, Martin, had raised the possibility of someone dropping something into the mixer, either accidentally or purposely.

*   *   *

James waited all day before returning to the cases he had found in the hills behind the mixer control building. There was a break in the afternoon with no meetings and nothing else scheduled, so he told Heather that he was going out in the plant for a while and could be reached with his in-plant pager. He went to his car and retrieved a small toolbox box then let himself into the secure room. He spent some time looking at the cases. They were in good condition, just dirty and covered with the cloth that made them difficult to see in the brush.

They were locked, and he wondered if they might be booby trapped with something, anything from explosives to the packets of dye that banks used. A little apprehensive, now he spent some time tapping the cases before committing to opening them. They had found a bunch of keys among the possessions of Michael Miller, and James tried likely-looking ones to see if they might work. One did, so he unlocked the cases. Hoping that he was just being overcautious, James rigged some line onto the latches on one case, then retired behind some large filing cabinets. He jerked on the line and heard the latches go and the case pop open. There was no explosion, no hiss of gas or anything else that he could detect, so he came out from hiding and looked.

The case was pull of papers. They were arranged in bundles, and each bundle was labelled, some marked Secret and some Top Secret. James sorted the bundles out and then addressed the second case. Telling himself he was being paranoid, he went through the same procedure when he opened that case. As with the first, there was no unpleasant surprise, but better to be safe. This case was also stacked with papers, but with room to add more. They were also removed and arranged on the table. James leafed through them and found a small folder entitled *Sagitta Project*, and it contained a listing of companies and products. On the list, he noted Bath Iron Works as the shipyard listed under *Hull Modifications*. That made sense. Bath Iron Works was a famous shipyard well known for building naval vessels, including the FFG-7 frigates and was now building the first of the DDG-51 destroyers. They would have the Navy contacts for this kind of work and probably even had a dock where it could be done discreetly and away from prying eyes. As James thought about it, it seemed to him that the hull modification was the process most likely to be observed. Everything else could be done inside buildings where access could be controlled. Modifying a hull without being seen would be quite a challenge, as he was sure that the Soviets would have satellite cameras trained on the yard.

The list also included Waterway Chemicals Shipping Company as *Source of vessels*, various and sundry and other companies for different components, the Escape Systems Division of Waterway Chemicals for *Gas generators and inflators* and a company called JWA in England listed under *Flotation collars and aids*. James found LST towards the bottom of the list and noticed a set of notations. It seemed from the notations that the LST documents had yet to be added to the file, but otherwise it was fairly complete.

James spent some time leafing through the various bundles until he found a system schematic, and then the whole concept became clear and was truly bizarre. The basic plan was to modify the hulls of small freighters by creating large indentations in the underwater part of the hulls and fitting them with doors. That obviously cut down on the cargo space, even more so because the interior of the hull was modified to disguise the change in shape. The doors were activated by hydraulic cylinders, and there were clamps attached to the doors. It looked as if there were smaller doors to flood the interior of the hull modification, which made sense if the doors were to be opened at sea. The doors opened like the doors on a Gull Wing Mercedes-Benz. In the clamps were canisters, which, judging by the drawings, were made largely of fibreglass. It looked as if the clamps were designed to open and essentially drop the canisters when the doors were fully opened.

Inside each canister was a launch tube with a Sagitta missile. The canisters were also equipped with little pop-out thrusters, so presumably there would be some mechanism to control positioning to a limited extent. The rest was fairly obvious. There were flotation collars to stop the canister from falling to the bottom of the ocean, and there were gas generators to eject the missile. James noticed some more flotation devices and assumed they would be activated when the ejection generator was fired to balance the loads. There was a cable reel and motor to pay the cable in and out and attached to the cable was something that looked like a small buoy. There was also something that he guessed would be a sea anchor that would deploy, presumably to limit drift. James guessed that both the buoy and the sea anchor would be deployed when the canister was separated from the ship.

There was a compartment that housed batteries, and there were several that were labelled as to function, from communications to buoy control to thrusters. There was also an electronics package separate from the missile that he guessed was how it was commanded to fire. Something else also now made sense. Every missile they shipped had a range safety package installed to allow for self-destruction in case something went wrong. That, according to his rocket guys, was unusual. Normally, test birds had the range safety package, but war shots had none. All kinds of questions came to mind. He tried to imagine what the mess would be if the range safety package were triggered underwater. There would be fire, explosion and a blob of molten stuff afterwards. Collecting that would be hazardous if there was a warhead attached, because it would be highly radioactive.

James picked up the schematic again and looked at it more closely. He was gratified to see that there were actually safety systems built in. There was a sonar detector that was linked to the winch that was used to pay in and out the cable that held the buoy. He supposed that if a boat approached, then the cable would be winched in, pulling the buoy under and out of harm's way. The buoy had a number of antennas, which he presumed would be for communication with the command and control system, wherever that might be. Satellites made all this possible. He also noticed some pressure sensors that were linked to the range safety destruct system. It looked as if any change in pressure, caused by a depth change, probably greater than some band the designers had programmed in, would cause the device to self-destruct. That could be a nasty shock for anyone who snagged one of these canisters and tried to bring it to the surface for a better look. It also answered one of his own questions: what happened if it sank? It looked as if sinking would also trigger the self-destruct mechanism through the pressure sensor package, but in this case, increased pressure. As he had noted earlier, the resulting fire and explosion would cause a nasty environmental problem, but he doubted if the people who had conceived of this system were particularly concerned about the environmental impact.

There was another set of schematics that detailed a recovery vessel. The vessel was constructed with watertight compartments around a hull that opened to the bottom. As James interpreted this, the hull clamshell doors could be opened and an object floated up into the hull, then the doors would be closed and the space pumped out. He looked again at the flotation packages and found one that would bring the canister to the surface lying longitudinally; that would allow a recovery team to float the missile up into the hull, without it being observed. The hull space was covered with top doors that could be opened. He assumed that there must be a mechanism to disable the pressure switches that triggered the range safety package and allow the canister to be recovered. The notes on the vessel schematics indicated that there were two such vessels, both stationed on the East Coast. Given this mode of recovery, James did wonder why it was also not used as the deployment method. All the vessel had to do was sail into an area, open the bottom doors and let the canister fall out. The flotation packages would take care of arresting the sinking and establish neutral buoyancy that would let the canister hang in the water. It seemed to him that this would be a less risky approach than putting systems on quasi-merchant vessels.

If the CIA was determined to use merchant vessels, then the Waterway Chemicals fleet of small freighters would make the perfect vehicle for deployment. But who would captain the vessels, and how would they know when and where to release their loads? How could the captains be trusted not to reveal what they were carrying? That suggested more government involvement in the selection of crews and officers. But then, perhaps only the captain knew what they carried. This explained why Costanza Albertini was at the Pentagon each time he had a briefing; Costanza must also have a briefing. That surprised him. He thought that the Pentagon would have separated the briefings to be sure that he and Costanza did not meet and begin to compare notes. Thinking about it further, James was surprised that he had not seen Walter Green of the Escape Systems Division; there were enough packages on the system that used the Escape Systems inflators and gas generators. Perhaps his briefing times were different and timed so that they would not meet.

James thought back to his first briefing with the Navy and the comments that Robert Warner had made afterwards. Robert had told him that he thought that several of the people in the room had been CIA. That made James more than a little uneasy. Perhaps the captains

189

were actually in the pay of the CIA as well as Waterway Chemicals. He could see how this system worked and how an innocent-looking freighter could steam into an area, deposit its deadly cargo and then depart. He did wonder at what depth the canisters would float and how drift would affect them. Although the small thrusters that were fitted would afford some degree of position control, if the canisters were in a sea lane or in any kind of strait, their ability to maintain position would be limited. He presumed that whoever had thought up this system had taken all that into account. It was a very frightening scenario.

That led him to the next question. Who did Michael Miller work for? He guessed a government, and he went through the usual suspects, the Russians and the Chinese, but his bet was the Israelis, based on his call from the Temple south of Salt Lake City. For them, it would be perfect. They could ring their neighbours by using the Mediterranean, the Red Sea, the Black Sea and the Arabian Gulf and make a first strike that no one would see coming. That did not bear thinking about. In many ways, it was a weapon that would scare the Russians even more than the Midgetman, the SICBM that he was competing against with the Auriga Type A. The Midgetman was going to be based on mobile launchers, essentially big trucks that would drive around the country in times of crisis. The Russians could hardly be thrilled about that, and they would be even less impressed if they knew about the Sagitta program and its basing mode. Perhaps it was all just a ploy to apply pressure in the ongoing Strategic Arms Reduction talks.

Now James had a real quandary. To whom should he report this find? As he found Secret and Top Secret documents, he clearly needed to do something, and quickly. The local Air Force contingent was out because they were not read into the project. Of the Navy people that he dealt with, at least one of them might be a confederate of Miller, so that was risky. Going to Robert Warner might have the same risk. Finally, he decided that perhaps the best course of action was to talk to someone from the FBI. They were the ones that were supposed to deal with domestic espionage, which is what this had to be.

James re-packed the suitcases and then checked to see if they might fit in one of the secure cabinets. They did not, so he re-locked the cases and then went looking for a shipping container, or something in which he could stow the cases and secure them. He had thought about just changing the combination of the secure room, but Commander Reinsch also had the number, and she might ask why it had been changed. The better plan was to move everything related to his find to a quiet location that he could lock and that would be unlikely to be visited for a while, until at least he had placed the documents into other hands. He found a steel container in shipping that fitted the bill. It had been used to ship materials in and was about to be discarded. That was perfect. He called Ed Clark and told him that he needed help with his operation. Ed agreed to move the box for him to a storage building where they kept forgings. James had been in there a couple of times and knew that the building was opened once a month to retrieve forgings and that he had three weeks before the next withdrawal. That ought to give him enough time to manage the transfer of the material to better hands.

With the cases safely locked away and with a new and different padlock on the storage building, James went home. He started to look carefully at the other cars coming and going on the road and wondered if any of them might be those of confederates of Michael Miller. He had not noticed anyone out of the ordinary lingering near the plant, but there was always the possibility that it was under surveillance from the hills. Under the pretext of checking on plant security, James went to see his Head of Security, Ruben Wheelwright, and asked him how secure the perimeter was. Ruben admitted that he had not given that much thought lately after the furore that had followed the incident had died down. He told James that he would have two of the guards walk the perimeter the next day, weather permitting and look for signs of fencing issues or possible unauthorised access. James asked him to extend the sweep by driving up the various jeep trails that led into the hills around the plant and let him know what could be seen from them.

The Road to Paradise

Bernard Rasmussen decided that perhaps it was time to concentrate his research on Michael Miller. He was the odd one out in the event and had generated some degree of antipathy among the mix crews. He searched the obituary notices and employment announcements and came up with very little. All he really found was that Miller was a graduate of Penn State. He had no contacts there but decided to call the placement office anyway. By calling himself a prospective employer, he was able to confirm that Michael Miller had graduated from Penn State with a degree in chemical engineering, and he had been placed at a small anodising firm in Pittsburgh. He called them and got confirmation that Miller had worked there, but then had left, and they did not know where he had gone. The only forwarding address they had was the Penn State Placement Office. Bernard called back there and got the next part of the story, the move to Utah and a job with LST. None of that told him any more than he already knew.

His next tack was to consider the marriage. The obituary notice had mentioned a wife, so it seemed logical to assume that Miller had married in the period between graduation and moving to Utah. Searching marriage records could take time, especially as he did not know in which state Miller had been married. Supposing it could have been Pennsylvania, he called newspapers in Pittsburgh, State College and Philadelphia and asked for searches on marriage announcements. That might take some time, so he was content to wait and focus in the meanwhile on other stories. There was plenty to do, and the editor had already told him to drop the LST story and get back to work.

*   *   *

James stopped on his way to work at the Flying J gas station on the north side of Ogden and found the payphone. He called the FBI office in Salt Lake City. He identified himself and then asked to speak to an agent.

"Assistant Agent in Charge Booth, how may I help you?"

"I have some information that I would like to pass on to you," James replied.

"Why don't you just come into the office in Salt Lake and tell us what you have?" Agent Booth suggested.

"I have some concerns," James countered. "I would rather meet somewhere where access is less observable."

"Okay, what do you have in mind?"

"Are you familiar with the road to Paradise that goes out behind Ogden past the Huntsville Reservoir?" James asked.

"Yes, I know where that is," Agent Booth agreed.

"There is a shooting range just off the road about eight miles from the reservoir. I'll be there at ten on Saturday morning," James suggested.

"Fine, I'll be there," Agent Booth agreed.

James hung up, and now he was committed. If he did not show up for the meeting, they might call him to ask why, which might get complicated if they called either the Corporate Office in Salt Lake City or the switchboard at the plant.

At the plant, after the morning production and staff meetings, Ruben Wheelwright asked to see James. He had had his people walk the perimeter fence and was ready to report.

"Hi, Ruben," James greeted him. "How are things?"

"I've had my people walk the perimeter, and a couple of things concern me," Ruben replied.

"Okay, what did they find?" James asked.

"First, they are out of condition, so I need to introduce an exercise program, which may take away a little from the crew size that is active. Second, I was thinking that I need to check on the Fire Department and see how out of shape they are," Ruben started.

"Okay, why don't you work with Isabella and get something set up for fitness training. I don't think you'll need any more bodies. Let's get some cameras on the back gates so we don't actually have to man them," James suggested.

"Okay, that was going to be my suggestion," Ruben agreed. "The other thing we found was that someone has been up the jeep trail that leads off Magpie Canyon."

"Really, when?" James asked.

"A couple of times, by the look of it, there are two different sets of tyre tracks and two sets of boot prints, both made a while back. Someone was up there keeping an eye on the place," Ruben explained.

"What can you see from up there?" James wanted to know.

"It's about the highest point around, and you can see most of the plant, except for some of the side canyons where some of the mix and cast buildings are," Ruben replied.

"Let's get a camera on one of the buildings and point it at that spot," James suggested.

"I was thinking of that," Ruben agreed. "I'd also like to put an infra camera there as well to see if anyone comes at night."

"Good idea," James agreed. "When you do that, put the cameras inside some form of cupola, so that they're not obvious. Do we have a jeep trail around the perimeter fence?"

"No, it's not feasible," Ruben explained. "There are a few spots where you just could not put a road. I'll just have my people walk the fence at least once a week. It'll be good for them, and they might see something that they would miss from the comfort of a truck cab."

"Okay, Ruben," James agreed. "Let's get the cameras installed ASAP, and let me know how you plan to aim them and how you will review the footage. When your guys walked the fence, did they find any fence breaks?"

"No. There were no holes or obvious recent repairs, just a couple of spots where the deer have been coming over. They also found a couple of badger setts, and we may have to take action with one of them because it basically makes a hole under the fence," Ruben reported. "It looks like the badgers are out of hibernation early this year."

"See if you can fix the hole, without upsetting the badgers," James asked. "We don't want the DNR people after us!"

"Right," Ruben laughed. "I'll get right on things."

*   *   *

Katrina was concerned about James. He had been strangely withdrawn and quiet. She wondered what was happening and called Isabella to ask if everything was going well at the plant. Isabella assured her that it was.

Katrina then asked her if she would like to join her and James for dinner that night. Isabella was delighted but asked if she could bring her partner. That was fine with Katrina.

When James got home that night, he seemed much more relaxed. She told him that she had invited Isabella to dinner and that she was bringing her partner. That led to great speculation; speculation that was proven wrong when Isabella arrived with Colleen. Katrina met them at the door, and Isabella introduced herself and Colleen. James was interested to know what Colleen did for a living, and she explained that she was just a lowly researcher at the newspaper. Over dinner, conversation went back and forth, and Isabella and Katrina shared stories about what it was like to be an immigrant. Katrina and James had had an advantage over Isabella because they at least spoke English as a native tongue, even if they had had to adapt their vocabulary a little to make themselves understood at times. James told of some entertaining incidents where the differences between American and English English caused confusion, and then he told them that if you threw in the South African English, things became even more confused. After dinner, Katrina asked Isabella about Brazil and where she was from.

"My family has a plantation in the interior of São Paulo Province," she replied.
"Were your family originally from Portugal?" James asked.
"A long time ago," Isabella replied. "But they went to Angola first. My great-great-grandfather went there with his wife in the 1850s and 1860s. Sometime in the mid-1860s, he went on a trading expedition and never returned. My great-great-grandmother Maria never knew what happened to him."
"What did they do in Angola?" Katrina asked.
"I'm not really sure," Isabella admitted. "He apparently was some kind of trader, probably in ivory and other commodities."
"What was his name?" Katrina asked.
"Francisco Roberto Oliveira da Silva," Isabella intoned.
"When did he disappear?" Katrina asked.
"I think about 1866," Isabella replied. "Why?"

"My great-great-grandfather was in Angola then and had a run-in with a da Silva," Katrina replied.

"What kind of run-in?" Isabella asked.

"Let me get something and I'll explain," Katrina promised. She left the room, and James took the opportunity to refresh drinks. When Katrina came back, she had an old leather-bound journal and a pocket watch.

"This is the journal of Jan Englebrecht, my great-great-grandfather," she explained. "He describes several encounters with a Francisco da Silva."

"What kind of encounters?" Isabella asked.

"Well, that da Silva was a trader in ivory, but it wasn't elephant ivory, it was black ivory," Katrina replied. "He was a slave trader."

"I often wondered," Isabella admitted. "There were odd stories in the family about the activities of Francisco."

"Your Francisco da Silva and my Francisco da Silva have to be the same person," Katrina decided. "Let's see, yes, here it is. The one that *Oom* Jan ran into was Francisco Roberto Oliveira da Silva. What's the chance that there were two people in Angola with that exact name that both died in 1866?"

"So what happened in these encounters?" Colleen asked.

"In the last one in March of 1866, there was a battle, and everyone was killed except *Oom* Jan and my great-grandfather Koos. Your great-great-grandfather was killed in the battle," Katrina explained.

"Oh," Isabella said. "How do you know?"

"Because *Oom* Jan wrote about the battle in his journal," Katrina explained. "He lost his wife and daughter in the same battle and the rest of the Bushman band that he was with."

"Who killed him, your great-great-grandfather?" Isabella asked.

"No, actually, it was Katrina, the sister of my great-grandfather, as I said, she died in the battle along with her mother," Katrina explained.

"Wow, who'd have thought!" Colleen said.

"There is something I'd like to give you," Katrina offered. "This is a watch that *Oom* Jan took from the body of da Silva."

Isabella took the watch and opened it, and looked at the image inside. "This could be my great aunt Maria," she gasped. "The likeness is incredible."

"*Oom* Jan wondered who it was," Katrina said. "Apparently, he thought that it was either a wife or a girlfriend."

"Thank you," Isabella said. "This is such a treasure. I never thought I would have any likeness to great-great-grandmother Maria."

"Wow, this is weird," Colleen said. "I can't get over the coincidence that after so many years, descendants of these two men would meet in Utah of all places!"

"When James first told me that you were working there and that you were from Brazil, I did wonder," Katrina said. "But you're right, this is really remarkable."

"I must call my parents this weekend and tell them," Isabella said. "They'll be really interested."

"Just as long as they don't declare a vendetta against Katrina," James laughed.

"Oh no, there are enough skeletons in the closet of the da Silvas that we don't need to add more by vendettas," Isabella agreed.

"How did your great-great-grandmother survive in Brazil?" James asked.

"Apparently, she arrived in Brazil with her son and with some money. She bought a small plantation, her son eventually took it over and added to it, and it grew until it is what we have today," Isabella explained.

"She never remarried then?" Colleen asked.

"No, never," Isabella said. "The story I heard was that she always thought that Francisco would come from Angola to join her."

"Look at the time, we'd better be going, Bella," Colleen said. "It is snowing a little, and we need to get back to Kaysville."

"Thank you so much for the dinner and this," Isabella said, hugging the watch to herself. "I hope one day you can visit Brazil and meet the rest of my family."

After Isabella and Colleen had gone, Katrina asked James if he knew they were partners in the gay sense. James shook his head and said that he had no idea. His only concern was the fact that Colleen worked for a newspaper. He realised that he would have to trust Isabella, but just did not like the idea of any of his people too close to the press. His experience with reporters was that they seemed to get things more wrong than right, and if given any quotes, they inevitably turned them into something quite different. With the investigation into the incident still open and no definitive conclusion it would be easy for a reporter to draw the wrong conclusions and write material that was inaccurate and presented a completely erroneous view of the incident.

"It has to be difficult for them in Utah," she commented. "Let's face it; this place is pretty well male-dominated."

"I'll bet lesbianism isn't exactly on the Mormon bill of fare," James commented.

"Has she said anything at work?" Katrina asked.

"Not a thing," he replied. "I'm sure that no one there has even an inkling."

"Does it bother you that she's gay?" she asked.

"Not anywhere near as much as the fact that Colleen works for a newspaper," he said.

"Well. I wish them well," Katrina said. "I'd heard that Brazilian women were some of the most beautiful, and having met Isabella, I can see why people would say that. I wonder what, apart from Portuguese, is in her heritage?"

"You mean like you?" James asked. "A touch of the tar brush!"

"I'll tar brush you," she said. "But, yes, you know what I mean. Any time you mix races, you seem to get good results."

*   *   *

On Saturday morning, James drove out to the firing range. It was cold, clear and sunny. There was no one else at the range, so he had it to himself. The range sat at the bottom of a hill. To the north, the road wound up and over the hills to Avon and then Paradise. To the east, the direction in which he would be shooting, the ground rose up at the end of the range into the hills. There were a number of concrete shooting stands in place, but no other amenities. He had bought himself a new rifle in Ogden and wanted to try it out. He walked out onto the range and set up a cardboard box with a target taped to it, and then set about destroying it. Katrina had taught him well, and he still was able to get his shots into a tight grouping. While he was shooting, a car pulled up, and James quickly glanced at it and saw two men, dressed like Mormon Missionaries, get out. They waited until he had finished and safed his gun, then came over to talk to him. He noted that they had the badges worn by the Mormon Missionaries and read their names as Elder Booth and Elder Goodsell.

"Good morning," Elder Booth said. "Can we talk to you about the teachings of the Lord this cold morning?"

"I'm not a member of the Church," James replied. "May I offer you some coffee, or something else hot?"

"Hot chocolate would be wonderful, if you have some," Booth replied. "You are James Martin, I presume?"

"In the flesh," James agreed. "And you are?"

"Assistant Agent in Charge Booth, and this is Special Agent Goodsell," Booth identified himself and showed James his identification by opening a Book of Mormon and allowing James to read the badge without it being exposed to any observer.

"Isn't it a little unusual for you to be handling field contacts?" James asked.

"Yes, but when the GM of one of our rocket factories calls, we take that seriously," Booth agreed.

"Am I keeping you from Church business?" James asked.

"No, not at all," Booth assured him. "This was a good way to stay under the radar. Anyone who happens upon us will presume that we are here to bring you the testament."

"You're a little older than most of the young missionaries I see around," James remarked.

"True, but then there are senior members in charge of Mission Houses, and we could pass for them," Booth assured him.

"Okay, here's some hot chocolate, let me tell you my story," James began.

He then went through the incident, the investigation, the discovery of the cache of documents in Miller's office and then the discovery of the two suitcases. He described where he had found them and what was inside. He also mentioned the Star of David pendant that had been seen on Mrs. Miller and the strange telephone call that he had received looking for Samuel Levin. They were most interested to learn how he knew where to look for the suitcases and if there was any other correspondence among the documents that had been found in Miller's desk. James told them that there was a letter that looked like an itinerary addressed to Geoffrey Miller, the cousin in England, whose only known address was an accommodation address in Paddington in London. Then they wanted to know where the suitcases were. James told them that they could take them then and there. Goodsell spent some time looking around, looking for anyone who might be observing them and then reversed their car close to James's and quickly transferred the cases. James told them that the other papers they had found in Miller's office were still at the plant and that he would find a pretext to have them boxed up and sent to storage, by which he meant the FBI.

"So, it looks as if you were shooting fairly well there," Booth commented.
"I just bought this new rifle," James told him. "I wanted to see what it would shoot like."
"You always shoot over open sights?" Goodsell asked.
"I like to," James replied. "But I have used a scope."
"Do you mind if we try?" Booth asked.
"Not at all," James agreed. "Let me set up a new target."
They all walked over to where James had placed his original cardboard box and taped a new target to it, and then placed another box next to it, also with a target.

Booth shot first, and James saw that he was actually pretty good. His groups were tight, better than his own. Goodsell shot next, and it was clear that Goodsell was an expert. Whereas James had thought he had shot a good group, Goodsell put all five rounds in the space of a half dollar. In fact, with the size of the holes the bullets made, it was difficult to tell how close the shots all were. All that James could say for certain was that they had made a nice hole in the cardboard. While Goodsell was shooting, Booth asked James a few more questions.
"Why did you come to us and not go to your own management or the AFPRO office on site or the Navy?" he asked
"I guess I just didn't know who to trust," James began. "Look, I was only read into the part of the program that deals with missile segments, I knew nothing about the stack up or the basing mode, certainly nothing about the deployment, although Robert Warner has his suspicions, based on gas generators."

"What do you mean, who to trust?" Booth asked.

"Whoever put that pile of documents and information together must have collected it over time or had confederates collect it for him. So, that suggests a wider net and also suggests someone inside to tell them where to go, because I would not have known about the containers, the ship modifications or any of the other parts of this program," James explained.

"That makes sense, so what are you thinking, another Pollard?" Booth asked.

"Something like that," James agreed. "It seems to me that this is a concerted effort. The problem is, who's he spying for?"

"That's a good question," Booth agreed. "You're presuming he is spying, which I would tend to agree with. But, you're right, who for? It doesn't pay to speculate; we need something more tangible. Maybe we'll get lucky if we check on the other companies listed here, and we'll also follow up, trying to trace the mysterious missing cousin in London."

"Where did you learn to shoot?" Goodsell asked James. Goodsell had collected the targets and had them laid out to look at.

"My wife taught me," James replied.

"Where?" Booth asked.

"In Zambia," James replied. "I was working there when we met, and she was much more comfortable in the bush than I was, and she decided that I needed to learn how to shoot."

"Well, she did a good job," Goodsell commented.

"What about you?" James asked.

"Marine Corps sniper school," Goodsell admitted.

"How are you with a handgun?" Booth asked.

"I don't know," James confessed. "I've never tried."

"Try this," Booth suggested and gave James a semi-automatic pistol. "It's not my service weapon, so feel free to blast away." He showed James how the magazine fitted and where the safety was, and how to cock the pistol. James tried it for weight and then found the sights and aimed down the range. It kicked differently to the rifle, and two hands were definitely better than one, but he achieved creditable results. Goodsell then handed him a revolver and told him to try that. James surprised himself and managed to shoot a fairly tight group. Then he was shown up by the experts, and he watched in awe as Booth and Goodsell blasted away at targets, putting their bullets through the smallest of circles.

"Do you think that's enough to satisfy any casual watcher?" Booth asked the others.

"I think so, Boss," Goodsell agreed. "We're out here on this range and we've shot the heck out of a couple of cardboard boxes, just two city boys having fun."

"What next?" James asked.

"We'll take all this stuff back to the office and probably pass it on to Washington, then it's up to the people in the Hoover Building to decide what to do," Booth replied. "If we need to contact you again, how do you wish to manage that? I presume you've got reservations about going through the plant phone system?"

"Why don't you call me at home, from a pay phone and suggest we go shooting again?"

"Good idea, James," Booth agreed. "We'll be in touch and probably see you out here in the future. When you came out here this morning, were there any cars behind you or in front of you on the road?"

"No, after I got off the 84 at Mountain Green and came over Trapper's Loop, there wasn't another car in sight," James assured them.

"If you notice anyone following you out here, if we meet again, park over there facing away from the range, we'll abort the contact and try again another time," Booth instructed.

"That sounds very much like something out of a le Carré novel," James laughed.

"Maybe, but better to be safe," Goodsell said.

"Okay then, James, we'll see you," Booth said, then they both got into their car and left. James stayed for a while and fired off a few more clips of ammunition, watching the road between shots to see if there were any cars. None appeared, so finally he packed up and went home.

When he arrived home, Katrina met him at the door and immediately saw that he was more relaxed. Something had been lifted from his shoulders.

"Are you cold?" she asked. "You've been out all morning, and it's chilly out there."

"A little," he admitted. "I could use a hot bath, then I'll warm up."

"I'll run it for us," she offered. A little later, when they were both sitting in the bath, James told her in general terms what had been bothering him over the past few days. He omitted details but told her enough that she understood his concern. She was pleased that he had gone to the FBI; at least now it was in other hands, and they could do the investigating.

"Who else at the plant knows about this?" she asked.

"I've no idea," he admitted. "It's possible that there's someone out there who was working with Miller, but my sense is not. If there had been, I would have expected them to try and claim the personal effects of Miller by now."

"So, no one has tried to claim his stuff?" she asked.

"Not a soul," he confirmed. "I would have thought some family member, or someone claiming to be a family member, would have shown up by now. The company had sent a notice to the address provided for Geoffrey Miller in London, but so far no response."

"Well, maybe they will, then you can tell the FBI who and when and let them follow them and see where it leads," she suggested. "If you think this Miller *ou* was a spy, who was he spying for?"

"My bet, the Israelis," he stated. "We are all conditioned to think that the big bad wolf of the Soviet Union is who we need to look out for, but I bet there are Brit, French, Japanese, Chinese, South African and Israeli spies all working here in the US."

"Why would the Israelis want to spy on something that the Congress will probably give them anyway?" she wondered.

"I don't think we've ever given them any ballistic missile technology," he replied. "I think it's one of those areas that the US just does not want to share with anyone, except perhaps the Brits, who have a special agreement with the US."

"That makes sense," she agreed. "Anyway, enough of spies, unless you want me to be Mata Hari, dressed only in a bra and some jewellery?"

"That sounds like fun," he agreed. "Why only the bra and jewellery?"

"Because apparently Mata Hari was concerned that she had small boobs and she was embarrassed by them, so kept them covered," she explained.

"Where did you learn that?" he asked.

"I must have read it somewhere," she thought.

"Well, maybe we'll just leave the bra and jewellery," he suggested.

"Come on then *ou man*," she invited. "Are you going to wait there all day?"

*   *   *

Bernard Rasmussen collected his mail and found a packet from a newspaper in State College and one from Pittsburgh. They both contained marriage announcements that had appeared in the respective papers. In the State College paper, there were six Michael Millers over a two-year period that would fit his window of enquiry. In the Pittsburgh paper, there were twelve, so he had eighteen leads to run down. Reading through the announcements, he was able to cull out twelve immediately. Nothing about them fit his situation; the college was wrong, the degree was wrong, age was wrong, or the announcements included details of jobs in other parts of the country. That left six to run down, five from Pittsburgh and one from State College. He decided to enlist Colleen on Monday and get her to find out all she could about the remaining six Michael Millers and then see what the paper in Philadelphia might yield.

Colleen was at that moment shopping for a new ski jacket at REI in Salt Lake. She and Isabella had taken the day off from skiing. Isabella had all new equipment from the Lewis company, but her size was wrong for Colleen, and she was uncomfortable asking her sponsor for clothing not for herself.

"What do you think, Bella?" Colleen asked. She was modelling a North Face jacket.

"Is it comfortable? Can you move well?" Isabella asked.

"It feels fine. How warm will I get in this?" Colleen asked the salesman.

"It depends whether you're skiing or just sitting in the lodge," he replied.

"She'll take you down any slope any time," Isabella said to the salesman. "What do you think, Colleen?"

"I'll take it," Colleen said impulsively. "I had enough of trying on jackets, what I need is a cup of coffee!"

Over coffee, she and Isabella talked about the bombshell that Katrina had dropped on them earlier in the week. Isabella had called her family and told them all about it, and now they wanted to see the watch and the picture inside the case. She had taken a photograph of the watch and the picture and had mailed them that morning to Brazil so that they could see for themselves, and her brother was now trying to check in Portugal for the antecedents of Francisco da Silva.

"What do you think about your family being in the slave trade business?" Colleen asked her.

"It was the time," Isabella replied. "I suppose that at that time people did all kinds of things. From what I've read, people went from Portugal to either Angola or Mozambique, ran small farms or traded for ivory, white and black, and then tried to make enough money to move to Brazil to a really big estate. I suppose that's what my great-great-grandmother did. Whether or not she knew about the slave trading, I've no idea."

"She must have known, surely," Colleen protested.

"I think so, yes. But that was then, and it's not the same now, except in East Africa, where it still goes on with Arab slave traders," Isabella commented. "I certainly don't have the Middle Class American guilt over such things. I don't traffic in slaves, except of course I am looking to enslave you!"

"I'm already enslaved!" Colleen laughed.

"Let's go home," Isabella suggested. "And we'll see just how much of a slave you are."

"Okay," Colleen agreed. "But only if I drive, you drive too fast in this snow!"

"No, I don't," Isabella protested, laughing. "Anyway, that's no way for a slave girl to talk. You may drive me home, James and don't spare the horses!"

*   *   *

Assistant Agent in Charge Sean Booth called Washington on Monday morning and talked to Deputy Director Adams.

"George, hi, it's Sean, I've just had a strange meeting with a guy from one of the local rocket factories," he began.

"Hi Sean, tell me," George instructed. Sean then went through his earlier call from James and his subsequent meeting at the shooting range on Saturday morning. He described the contents of the suitcases. He had spent all Saturday afternoon and evening and all day Sunday going through the documents and carefully stacking them in appropriate piles. He had handled them as evidence and asked George whether they could get James Martin's fingerprints from either the INS or DOD databases, or whether they should get an independent set, so that they could eliminate Martin from the list of those who had handled the documents. George thought about it and then instructed Sean to contact James and get their own set of fingerprints. If they went to the DOD and the Fort Holabird people of the Defense Investigative Service, that might alert a potential agent inside the Navy, so better to be safe. There was also no point in alerting the INS. The Immigration and Naturalization Service people were paranoid enough without throwing up any flags that might cause them to look at Martin's citizenship. Sean also told George about the supposed cousin in London and the accommodation address in Paddington. George thought that he would get someone from the Embassy to check there on the pretext of informing Geoffrey Miller about his cousin's death.

"What do you think about this guy James Martin?" George asked.

"I've checked what we can about him, and he seems sound enough. He's had an interesting career, from mining copper in Africa, to mining and construction machinery in Wisconsin, then aerospace components and systems in California," Sean enumerated.

"Perfect cover for a spook," George laughed. "You'd better check him out carefully just to be on the safe side. Who knows, he could have been running the operation and then come to us when it looked like it was going to blow up, just to protect himself."

"I'll do that," Sean agreed. "Do you want this stuff shipped back there?"

"I don't think so," George said. "I'd rather we left it all with you. Just keep it away from any DOD people that come in and from the spooks at Foggy Bottom. They're in this somewhere, and they could have another mole; they've had them before. Remember Howard and Pelton, okay, I'll agree Pelton was NSA and not CIA. We're going to keep this strictly to ourselves until we're ready to bring in the Justice lawyers and let them present the case."

"The real question is, if there is a mole inside the Navy, who's he working for?" Sean asked.

"That's a good one," George agreed. "We can get so hung up on the Soviets that we tend to forget that there are others out there that are also spying on us. Your man Martin was hinting at the Israelis?"

"Yes, I think he put together a couple of small data points and drew his own conclusions. But, of course, that might all be a coincidence, and he may be barking up the wrong tree altogether," Sean agreed.

"Well, I'm inclined to believe he could be right," George stated. "But, there's a huge problem with Congress. The Jewish lobby has Congress in the palm of its hand, and it'll be hard to pin anything on them. So, sit on things and don't talk to anyone, not DOD, not CIA and certainly not anyone from any of the Congressional offices. Those guys would sell their souls for another dollar or two from any of the lobbyists to buy some more votes."

"One thing is for sure," Sean noted. "There'll be a network, because one guy could not have put all this stuff together."

"I agree," said George. "We'll need the list of all the contractors and subs that you found among the documents, then we'll have to go and quietly check each one. Don't fax it, send Goodsell with it tonight, and we'll go to work on it from here."

"Okay, I'll do that, and as for the documents, we'll sit on them. There's another thing that may be related," Sean added.

"What's that?" George asked.

"There's a local reporter, Bernard Rasmussen, who you may recall tried to set up the LST AFPRO light Colonel Ridings in a blackmail operation based on the guy's gambling habit. Rasmussen was looking for information on the LST incident, and he thought he'd get it through the back door. As it transpired, the colonel knew no more about the incident than anyone else. But they both finished up with some money, and now the colonel is being counselled for his gambling habit and will be quietly moved aside. There was an incident recently with some ersatz Air Force Major Richards who roughed up Rasmussen a little and told him to lay off the Air Force," Sean explained.

"Why ersatz major?" George asked.

"Because Major Richards is short and is on her way to Hawaii, and the guy that roughed up Rasmussen was big and male," Sean explained.

"So, what does Rasmussen know?" George asked.

"I don't think very much," Sean commented. "But I think he's looking into Michael Miller, the same Michael Miller in whose office Martin found all the documents. He requested newspaper reports on marriages of any Michael Miller in Pennsylvania over a two-year period."

"Is there any reason to deduce anything from that?" George asked.

"Not yet, but I'll keep an eye on it, and perhaps you could have the Philadelphia and Pittsburgh field offices check out Michael Millers," Sean requested.

"Okay, we'll do that, you keep on this Martin guy and see what else you can learn," George instructed.

After Sean had hung up, George then called Art Rowe, an Assistant Secretary of the Navy. "Art, hi, it's George, I have something you are really going to want to hear, can we meet?"

"Sure, George, the usual place at three?"

"I'll be there," George confirmed. At three, the two met in one of the side galleries of the National Gallery of Art.

"Art, thanks for coming," George said. "We have some information on the latest espionage sally by our supposed allies from Tel Aviv," he told him. He then went on to report his conversation with his agent and the materials that James had found.

"So, we have a leak either on the Hill by one of our elected pols or one of their minions, or within the Pentagon, is what you're telling me?" Art asked, looking for confirmation.

"Whoever it is provided them a complete list of all the contractors working on different elements of Sagitta, as I understand it, giving them enough information to be able to build it themselves without having to do any engineering," George confirmed.

"Why, we'll probably give them it anyway?" Art wondered.

"Unlikely," George disagreed. "We've never given them any ballistic missile technology."

"There's always a first time," Art commented.

"Perhaps," George agreed. "They know how to push the envelope and then yank on the chains of all the weasels in Congress who will do whatever they ask."

"Now now, George," Art cautioned. "We mustn't talk about our valuable Middle East ally that way."

"Why not," George asked. "What do we get from them, apart from grief?"

"Well, certainly not oil," Art joked. "I'll go to work on things here, get me whatever you can on this situation."

*   *   *

Bernard Rasmussen called Colleen and asked her if she would help him dig up whatever information she could find on Michael Miller.

"Why, what are you up to now?" she asked.

"Look, he's dead," Bernard complained. "There's nothing I can do to him. All I want to know is what you can find out about him."

"What have you done so far?" she asked.

"I got hold of some newspaper records of marriages in Pennsylvania and culled out six Michael Millers that I would like to learn more about," he said.

"Why only marriages?" she asked. "And why Pennsylvania?"

"Because the obituary said that he was a graduate of Penn State and was from Pennsylvania and was survived by his wife, Roberta, no other family mentioned," he explained. "We've already confirmed he went to Penn State and have followed the leads they gave us, both of which led nowhere. So, I'm looking for the marriage of one Michael Miller to Roberta, last name unknown, so that perhaps we can trace her and ask why she bailed out so quickly."

"Anything else?" she asked.

"Yes, I was talking to some girls in Idaho that knew Miller at the local Stake House, and they weren't the most complimentary."

"So, based on the stories of some teenagers, you now want to build a story?" she asked.

"Look, will you help me or not?" he asked.

"Okay, I'll dig up what I can about Michael Miller," she promised. "What about the others that died in the same incident?"

"According to my teenagers, he's the only one that did not fit and was the odd man out, and there was some kind of tension between him and the rest of the crews," Bernard explained.

"Well, he was the new engineer, wasn't he?" she asked. "If they were not doing things properly and an engineer was on their case, then sure, they wouldn't like him. But, that's hardly the basis for any story."

"I agree, but there's something about this guy that just doesn't ring true. Why did his wife just disappear after the accident? Why is there almost nothing about the guy anywhere? The obituary was about the shortest piece I've ever seen on a dead guy. Why, what's to hide?" he asked himself because Colleen had already left and gone back to her office.

*   *   *

The following Tuesday, the audit team from California announced that it was done and was ready to give an out brief to the management of the Division. James called them together, and then they waited for the audit team to deliver their message.

"We want to thank the management and staff of LST for the cooperation we've been shown during this audit," Scott McIntosh said. Scott had replaced the unfortunate Bob Blake, who had been recalled after his opening salvo when the audit began. "We have here a report that we will deliver to you containing our findings."

"Thank you," was all James could think of saying. They had not seen any of the findings and had no way of knowing just what the auditors would report. He suspected that whatever they might have said as the audit proceeded that in the end they would behave as typical auditors and find fault wherever they could to justify the time and money that they had spent.

"We have noted a total of eighty-one gigs that we would like to see corrective action on," Scott continued. "Those gigs have been itemised in this summary and range from advisory to requiring action."

"I see," James said. "We will review and respond."

"We don't want you to think that this was in any way a witch hunt," Scott said. "We are focused on the safety of the people at this plant and the proper execution of the programs." What that meant to James was that they had nitpicked things and were mainly concerned with being seen to do their jobs as tough auditors.

"As I said," James repeated. "We will review the report and respond."

"When can we expect your written response?" Scott asked. James was tempted to answer that they would get his response when he was good and ready, but that probably would not go down too well. Instead, he temporised.

"We will review the findings and give you a first response within the week that will include a definitive date for a final response," he told them. "I am sure you will understand that there may be items that we will wish to investigate thoroughly before we commit to any course of action."

"We will stay in touch," Scott promised. "We do not want this to drag on indefinitely and want to close out all the corrective action requests as soon as possible."

"Thank you for your time, gentlemen," James told them. "I think now we need to review these findings, and if we have any questions or need for clarification, we will be in touch."

After the audit team had gone, James let Simon and the other managers rant for a while. He agreed with them that the majority of what they were skimming through in terms of findings were already covered by action plans they had put in place following the incident. It was as though the audit team had ignored the corrective actions already in place and was considering the status of things before the incident. In most cases, their suggested course of action was in fact what was already in the action plans. Of the eighty-one gigs that were listed, he found two that were of use. They were suggestions regarding the procedures to be followed in the event of evacuations. The balance, as Simon had pointed out, was just filler to make it look as if they had done something to justify their time. James was also disappointed in Scott McIntosh. He had replaced Bob Blake because Blake had approached the audit with enough aggression that it was clear that nothing useful would come of the audit, and now McIntosh had done just the same,

211

but with a little more finesse. He had come across as very reasonable and accommodating, but had written the report exactly as Blake would have done.

The next audit outbrief was on Thursday, and it was the UOSH team. Kim Wheelwright asked to meet with James and gave him a quick overview of their report.

"We're happy to say that we found no items that warrant citation," Kim stated. "The changes that you have instituted make us very comfortable that the safety and health of the employees here is in good hands."

"Thank you," James said.

"That being said," Kim continued. "There are some issues I need to discuss with my management."

"Such as?" James prompted.

"Well, based on the changes that you have made, it would suggest that if we had conducted an audit six months ago, then there would have been conditions that would have warranted citation," Kim explained.

"Why would that be a problem now? That has to be in the realm of speculation," James asked.

"I am inclined to agree," Kim said. "But, I need to clear it with my management and ensure that they do not wish to retrospectively levy penalties on past practices."

"I'm sure you'll appreciate that the Company would have to challenge that?" James suggested.

"Yes, I realise that, if only because any post-dated citation could be used by lawyers to argue that unsafe practices existed and contributed to the fatalities," Kim agreed. "Even though the areas where we found the most change that could be construed as warranting citation actually had nothing to do with the incident."

"So, what do you propose?" James asked.

"Let me talk to my management," Kim said. "My position will be that we found a plant that meets and exceeds all standards, and that is what we should be judging. What may or may not have been the case in the past is of interest but difficult to build cases upon."

"I understand," James said. "I'll wait to hear from you."

"Okay, James," Kim said. "We're out of here, and we may come back for a quick audit in about six months, but I would be surprised if that turns up anything."

Investigation revisited

Two weeks after James had met with the FBI, he received a call from Agent Booth. They arranged to meet at the shooting range on the following Saturday morning. Booth had called early in the morning and had just caught James before he left for the plant. James wondered what he wanted and if they had made any progress that they would share with him. He considered it more likely that Booth just wanted to check on some detail that he had overlooked.

At the plant, he went through the usual meetings, and then Allan Black and Simon Wilmott wanted to see him.

"What's up?" James asked.

"We've an update on the investigation," Allan replied. "We took your suggestions about the debris field and the rest and have created some models which are interesting."

"Any conclusions?" James asked.

"I hesitate to say conclusions," Allan demurred. "But, there are strong inferences that we can draw."

"We mapped all the debris," Simon added. "And then we went back and calculated the energy required to project all the items the distance they actually travelled."

"We then looked at several scenarios with the mixer," Allan interjected. "Lid off, lid on, lid locked, lid locked with inspection port open."

"That led us to conclude that the lid was on but the inspection port was likely open at the time of the explosion," Simon commented.

"Right, so then we found the piece of the top with the inspection port; we did need the help of the Baker Perkins guy for that, to help us identify it," Allan explained. "An examination of the inspection port and its mounting shows indications of ablation through the port and no damage to the hinge pin or locking hasp. That leads us to a definite conclusion that the port was open at the time of the explosion."

"Good work," James commented.

"Wait, there's more," Allan said. "We then found and examined the remains of the blades, and we found on one of the pieces indentations.

We matched those indentations to the adjustment screw on the monkey wrench that is part of the mixer tool set."

"Ah, I see," James said. "Any chance that that would have happened during the explosion?"

"No, the toolset is far from the mixer, and the trajectories of all the other tools take them the other way to the blade pieces," Allan explained.

"So the inference is that the monkey wrench was dropped into the mixer?" James asked, looking for confirmation.

"Yes, and there's more," Simon added. "Just after the incident, the Air Force helped a lot, and they got a team from the Tripler Army Hospital in Hawaii to come over. They are the experts at body identification. They provided the coroner with a lot of help, not only in identifying parts but explaining the damage. I guess to them it was like looking at the effects of a bomb. We checked with the coroner's office and asked them if they noticed anything peculiar about the remains that we found."

"And?" James prompted.

"Apparently, skulls survive intact best of all body parts," Simon explained. "And the coroner told us that it was odd that all the skulls showed evidence of the heat and shock wave fronts hitting them from behind."

"So, the inference is that they were all leaving?" James asked.

"That's my conclusion," Simon agreed. "I think they saw the monkey wrench go in and then tried to get the hell out of there as fast as they could."

"If we infer that the wrench was dropped in through the port, can we infer by whom?" James asked.

"I've thought about that too," Allan said. "It seems to me that whoever dropped the wrench in was standing on the platform and had the furthest to go to get out, so would have probably been impacted the most by the blast."

"So, whose remains are the most damaged?" James asked.

"They were all pretty bad," Simon replied. "But, according to the coroner, the two that showed most blast damage were Michael Miller and Charlie Dawson. There was pretty much nothing left of them, except small body parts that took a while to find. We must have had cadaver dogs here for a week, just turning up bits. Pretty gruesome, really."

"How do we know it was them?" James asked.

"In order to identify the remains and return them to the correct families, the Trippler guys did a bunch of DNA checking. The only one they could not do that for was Miller, because there are no relatives close or on file. With the others, there are enough brothers, sisters, sons, daughters, fathers and mothers that they were able to positively ID them all, with the odd man out being by elimination, Miller," Simon explained.

"So, your inference is that they were on the platform?" James asked.

"Yes," Allan confirmed. "That just leaves us with the real question: what the heck was Miller doing out there, and why were there two mix crews there?"

"Was Miller perhaps showing them something about the mix cycle?" James asked.

"Highly unlikely," Allan said. "He was not one of the mix team, and he really didn't know much about the mixers or the mix cycles. So we're left with one probable cause and one unsolved mystery."

"How do we know it was actually Miller?" James asked.

"Well, the CCTV tapes show the various people going into the building, and Miller was among them. No one left before the incident, so it's reasonable to assume that Miller was there," Simon explained.

"Great work, guys," James praised them. "Now we need a presentation to the whole investigation team. I would lay it out with evidence, give conclusions and inferences and make the distinction. Be prepared to defend your calculations and conclusions."

"We can do that," Allan stated confidently. "I feel much better now about restarting the mixers. There seems to be no evidence at all that anything broke or went wrong with the mixer itself."

"What changes have we made to the lanyarding of tools?" James asked.

"We've put lanyards on all tools that did not already have them, and we've also put the tools in a locked cabinet. The cabinet is keyed so that it has to be locked to withdraw the key, and that key is required as part of the mix control panel," Simon explained.

"There's no way we can fix the cabinet so that all the tools have to be present to lock it?" James asked.

"Maybe we could fit magnetic switches at each shadow board location and then run electrical circuits to an electronic lock, but that would take time, and I'm not sure if it would even work," Simon replied.

"Okay, look into that, but in the meantime, what can we do?" James asked.

"We just have to make sure the guys understand the issues and the need to keep foreign objects out of the mixers," Simon commented.

"So, if we maintain operational discipline, we should be better protected?" James asked.

"Yes, if!" Simon agreed.

Later that day, James convened a meeting of the full investigation team and Allan and Simon, together with members of the teams, went through the analysis again. This time, there were a lot more questions. Although the Air Force is by nature a very technical service, not all officers are engineers, so it took a little while to explain some of the concepts that were obvious to the engineers in the room, but not obvious to the non-engineers. All the challenges thrown up by the technical members of the investigation team were answered, and at the end of the meeting, the consensus was that the cause of the explosion had been determined, but that the underlying cause, the presence of the monkey wrench, was still an unanswered question. As James summed it up, the explosion was physics, the cause was management in some way, either failure to do something or failure to recognise a circumstance that could lead to problems. That, it was concluded, was a remark that would be un-minuted. The view of the corporate members of the team was that the company lawyers would cringe at such a comment and would be afraid of liability lawsuits. That said, there was general agreement about the sentiment, and the Air Force members then wanted a review of operational practices so that they could be reassured that the "management issue" had been addressed.

James called Robert Warner and told him that he was sending a copy of the investigative work that Allan and Simon had presented. He also told him that they were no further in trying to understand why the incident occurred. They now believed there was enough evidence to say how it had happened, but the why was still a why. Robert told him that some things stay mysteries forever, and they probably would never really find out. He was, like Allan, happier about the restart of the mixers now that they knew how the incident had occurred. Preventing a recurrence would now be up to James and his management team. James then asked Robert how much he should disclose at the Pentagon briefing that was scheduled for Friday of that week. Robert told him to give them the conclusions without the analysis. They would have already received reports from both Craig Robinson and Josephine Reinsch, so James was not going to tell them anything new. It would just be politic to disclose all they knew so that the admiral would continue to trust them. James agreed, hung up and then called to ask Simon to give him an executive summary that he could leave at the Pentagon, if required.

*　　*　　*

Colleen called Bernard and told him that she had the results of her search into the mystery of Michael Miller. She had been through each of the marriage announcements that Bernard had given her for Pittsburg and State College, and she had also checked those for Philadelphia. Not satisfied with that, she went back and checked all those that Bernard had culled before. The result of all her searching was nothing. None of the Michael Millers married in Pennsylvania during that two-year period matched the Miller who worked at LST. Widening her search, Colleen had also checked New York, Ohio, West Virginia, Maryland, Delaware and New Jersey. She was now satisfied that if Michael Miller had married Roberta, last name unknown, then it was further afield than they had presumed, or at a different time.
"So, what do you think, Colleen?" Bernard asked. "What's the deal with this guy Miller?"
"Well, I suppose that there's always the chance that we're just looking at too short a time frame," she suggested.
"I'd wondered that too," Bernard admitted. "But, I've also got this sneaking suspicion that all is not what it appears with Mr. Miller."
"Why do you say that?" Colleen asked.

"Well, according to my teenagers, he was a real Peter Priesthood and very active in the Church, but I've done some asking around in the Mormon community in State College, and no one has ever heard of him," he explained.

"Maybe he just got converted while he was in Pittsburgh," she suggested. "You know that those who are converted are often more gung-ho than those born to it."

"Agreed, so here's your next challenge: track him back through the Church and see if you can't find something on him that way," he instructed.

"There were twelve others who died in the accident," Colleen thought. "The Air Force guy told us that was way more than usual, but that he knew of nothing unusual going on, so why all the people and why twelve?"

"Twelve good men and true?" Bernard asked, almost of himself. "No, that couldn't be."

"What do you mean?" she asked.

"Twelve good men and true, a jury," he explained. "But if a jury, a jury for what? Look, why don't you go to Pittsburgh for a couple of days and see if you can't find someone to talk to who worked with him when he was with this plating company, or whatever it was? Maybe you can learn something."

"Are you going to pay for that?" she asked.

"The paper will pay," he promised airily.

"Perhaps," she agreed. "But, perhaps not, our Lord and Master has already told you to dump this non-story and get back to work. How are you going to get this one by him? If you really want me to go, it will be on your signature. I'm going to draw enough against your account for a plane ticket and living expenses so that I'm not out a lot of money if our Lord and Master decides not to reimburse me!"

"Okay, fine, fill out a form for a draw and I'll sign it," he said. "God, Colleen, you can fuss about stuff at times."

Later that day, Colleen told Isabella about her trip to Pittsburgh. She was not that excited to go, but it was part of her job and she had drawn enough money to cover all her expenses, so would not have to use her own money. She was leaving the next day and would be back in about a week, so she gave Isabella a schedule with flights and hotels listed. Isabella told Colleen that she would be telling James about the trip, and Colleen understood. Colleen had come to the decision earlier that her relationship with Isabella was more important than the newspaper job, so she would disclose to Isabella all that she was doing, but would not disclose to Bernard the fact that she was passing the information to someone inside LST. She had agonised about this but had finally come to terms with the notion and was now at peace with herself. They talked about what she might discover in Pittsburgh, and Isabella was then faced with her own dilemma. Colleen was being open with her; should she not be open with Colleen and tell her that she and James were already certain that the Michael Miller who died in the incident was probably not the Michael Miller who had graduated from Penn State? What they did not know was when the substitution had occurred, before or after the company in Pittsburgh. She finally decided that she would wait and see what, if anything, Colleen unearthed in Pittsburgh and then make her decision about whether or not to reveal what she already knew or suspected.

*   *   *

Isabella asked to see James after the morning staff meeting the next day and told him that the newspaper was continuing to investigate Michael Miller.

"What do you think they'll discover?" he asked.

"Knowing Colleen, if there's anything to find, she'll find it," she said. "She's a really good researcher."

"So, what do we do if she finds out what we already suspect, that our Michael Miller may not be Michael Miller at all, but someone else?"

"I think we cross that bridge when we come to it," she thought.

"We'll do that," he agreed. "But, I may do some preparatory work with our customers in case this all blows up in our faces. I'll also take care of briefing Robert Warner."

"When do I tell Colleen that we already suspect Miller was not all he claimed to be?" she asked.

"I think wait until she comes back from Pittsburgh, then if she finds out something, tell her that I had briefed you on my suspicions and had told you to keep it to yourself, deflect any issues back onto me," he said. "I presume your relationship with Colleen is important to you?"

"Yes, and I thank you for understanding," she said. "It's difficult here in Utah, as you can imagine. How did you know?"

"My wife told me," he replied. "After you had been to dinner, she told me."

James called Robert Warner and gave him the bare bones of what he knew, the fact that Michael Miller did not quite check out and that a reporter was now nosing around. Robert Warner was concerned about the reporter, but as James pointed out, there was little they could actually do. James suggested that they let the Navy know and let them handle it. Robert liked that idea and told James to ask for some time with the admiral the next time he was in Washington and give him a private briefing. James agreed and suggested that he set that up through Commander Reinsch.

Later that day, James called Josephine Reinsch and asked to see her. He then gave her the same facts that he had given Robert Warner. She was quite concerned and promised to get James some time with the admiral. James was concerned that the circle of people who now knew that not all was not what it seemed with Michael Miller was getting too large and would soon become uncontrollable. He was a believer in the notion that the risk of leak increased as the square of the number of people who knew. Josephine left to talk to Washington and said that she would let James know about a meeting with the admiral.

At home that evening, James shared his concerns with Katrina. He asked her whether or not she had seen any odd cars lingering in their neighbourhood.

"It depends on what you mean by odd?" she laughed. "There were some high school kids lurking outside the house of the girl up the street, but I think they were just trying to get her attention."

"Nothing else odd?" he asked.

"No, some delivery vans, but they actually did drop off packages," she replied.

"Have you heard any odd clicks on the telephone?" he asked.

"Why, do you think it might be tapped?" she asked.

"Not really," he thought. "Maybe I'm getting just a little paranoid."

"You're probably right to be wary," she commented. "If Miller was a spy, then he may have had help, and they may be looking for the stuff that you found."

"I'm glad now that I handed it over to the FBI," he said. "So, enough about my day, how was your day?"

"Interesting," she said. "I signed up at a gym for aerobics classes and some weight training."

"Why was that interesting?" he asked.

"Well, there was an odd mix of Mormon wives and others. The two groups really didn't mix that much except for a couple who obviously knew each other and got on well," she explained.

"Who is the instructor?" he asked.

"A peppy early thirties brunette, called Brenda," she said. "It's her business; she rents the studio and has a weight area, some machines and a larger free area where she does aerobics."

"Is she a Mormon?" he asked.

"I don't think so," she said. "I heard her talking to one of the other ladies about going to the booze store, so unless she's a really *verligte* Mormon, she's more than likely like us, a Gentile!"

"So, what's your exercise program?" he asked.

"I'm going to go three times a week, and she's set up a weight program and an aerobic program," she replied. "I started after I signed up today, and I feel better for it. I had been missing the routine that I started in California. We need to make sure that you get some exercise, too. Sitting all day in the car and the office won't keep you fit and trim."

"I've been trying to take a walk at lunch time," he said. "But that rather depends on the weather. If it's too cold, then it's not a good idea, and if it's snowing, I definitely won't be out in it."

"Well, we need to be sure that you do something," she persisted. "I want you to stay the hunk that I fell for and married in Zambia."

"I'll work on it," he promised, then he changed the subject. "What did you wear to the gym today?"

"You remember the outfits I bought in California?!" she asked. "The bright red leotards and the silver tights?"

"What do the Mormon aunties think about them?" he asked.

"I think they've already identified me as a scarlet woman, but one of them whispered to the others that I was Mrs. Martin and that sent them scurrying off into a corner," she said. "I suppose that as their society appears, from the outside at least, to be so male and status dominated, and that who you are is driven by what your husband does, then because you're a Bwana at LST, they'll give me some leeway."

"So, do you feel like a scarlet woman?" he asked.

"Not really," she thought. "I think I'm just normal and everyone else who is different."

"I'd agree with that," he laughed

Later that night, Katrina told James that she had also bought some new underwear. Then she told him what she had heard at the exercise class that losing weight, getting more exercise and changing one's underwear were usually indicators of extramarital activities. James had not heard that one but supposed that it was possible. He asked if she thought that likely of any of the women at the exercise studio, and Katrina told him that she had her suspicions about one lady who was very quiet and just stayed in the background, but was very determined.

*   *   *

Colleen landed at the Pittsburgh airport, rented a car and drove to a Holiday Inn in the university area of the city. She then went exploring and found the anodising company on a side street that led to the river, just upstream of the McKees Rocks Bridge. She was a little concerned that it was hardly the best part of Pittsburgh, but then it was in an industrial area, and that was to be expected. She decided that a direct approach might be the best and went to the company and asked to see the Personnel Manager or Human Resource Manager, telling the receptionist that she was looking for background on Michael Miller. Mrs Pam Willis came out from the depths of the company and introduced herself as the Human Resource Manager. Colleen explained her mission as trying to gain some background on the people who had died in the LST incident. Pam remembered Michael Miller and was sorry to hear that he had died.

"Was he married at the time he worked here?" Colleen asked.

223

"No, he was a strange white boy, he was single and a bit of a loner, and I don't think he had any serious relationship," Pam replied.

"No one by the name of Roberta?" Colleen asked.

"No, not that I recall," was the answer.

"Was he religious, perhaps, a Mormon?" Colleen asked.

"Not him," Pam laughed. "He would hit the bar down the street with some of the guys from the line and would pound down boiler makers with the best."

"Do you have a picture of him?" Colleen asked.

"Well, that's the funny thing," Pam said. "When I heard you were interested in Michael Miller, I went to pull his file, and it seems to have been misfiled somewhere. Will you be in town long, because if I can find it, I'll be happy to get you a copy of his company picture?"

"I'll be here for a few days," Colleen said. "I'm staying at the Holiday Inn in the university area."

"Why don't I call you if I find anything?" Pam promised; then she hailed a man who was leaving the plant. "Hey, Riley, this lady is trying to find out something about Michael Miller. Maybe you can help her?"

"Sure thing, Ms Pam," Riley promised. "I'm going for a drink, do you feel safe enough to join me?"

Colleen looked at Pam, who nodded very slightly, and then she accepted Riley's invitation. They left the building, and he suggested that she follow him to the bar. At the bar, he ordered a boiler maker and she asked for a Budweiser, then he shooed away all the other men who had clustered around like moths to a candle, and they sat at a small table in a corner.

"Michael," he started. "Now, there was one strange white boy."

"How do you mean strange?" she asked. She was curious now because Pam had said exactly the same thing.

"It was almost like he was two people," he explained. "When he started here, he would come with us to Kowalski's, then after about a year, he stopped coming and went all quiet like."

"How do you mean quiet?" she asked.

"Almost like he had been told by someone to stay away from us, and not talk to anyone," he explained. "We asked him what was up, and he just told us that he had a greater mission now. I figured he'd found God or something or a girl."

"Did he ever mention anyone?" she asked.

"Nope, never did. Never saw him with anyone. Wondered if he was queer, but never saw him with any guy either," he replied.

"He never mentioned anyone called Roberta?" she asked.

"Why, did he get married?" Riley asked.

"When he was in Utah, he was married to a Roberta," she confirmed. "But I don't know when or where he got married."

"Well, fancy, he did get married," Riley wondered, almost to himself. "What did she look like?"

"According to people who knew them, she was really good looking," she told him.

"Good looking, like a six, an eight?" he asked.

"I understand more like nine or ten," she said.

"Well, I'll be," he exclaimed. "I didn't think that white boy had it in him. I wonder where he met her?"

"We don't know," Colleen admitted. "In fact, we're finding it hard to get anything on Michael."

"I know he went to Penn State," Riley said.

"Yes, we've confirmed that," she agreed. "And Penn State told us that he came here, but that's it. After he left here and came to Utah, there was very little. In Utah, he was a very staunch member of the Mormon Church."

"Well, there you go," he said. "He found some hot Mormon chick, got converted and married and went off to make babies."

"They had no children," Colleen told him.

"But I thought that that was almost a requirement," he laughed.

"Almost," she agreed. "But for them, maybe they couldn't, because they had none."

"And you say she was like a nine or ten?" he asked, seeking confirmation.

"What I've been told, yes," she confirmed.

"I knew we should have taken that boy out and gotten him laid," Riley said. "We always wondered if he ever had, you know, maybe he just didn't know how!"

225

"Mormon girls are not known for not knowing how," Colleen remarked dryly. "If he didn't know how, I'm sure she would have shown him."

"Are you Mormon?" he asked.

"No, never have been," she said.

"How's it living in Utah with all those Mormons?"

"It's difficult sometimes," she admitted. "I get asked a lot why I don't have a husband and six kids. I usually tell them that I'm gay and that makes them run a mile."

"I suppose it would," he agreed.

"Is there a Mormon church around here anywhere?" she asked.

"Don't know?" he admitted. "Hey, Kowalski, where's the Mormon church in Pittsburgh?"

"It's the other side of downtown," someone in the bar interjected. "It's near the university."

"There you go, Riley," Kowalski said. "Ask and ye shall find out! Are you being converted over there in the corner? I thought the missionary kids were all guys and travelled and hunted in pairs?"

"No, she's not trying to convert me," Riley laughed. "You remember Michael Miller, who used to come in here with us?"

"Yeah, I remember him, white kid, about six feet, could drink like a fish," Kowalski remembered."

"Well, he died in an accident in Utah, and this lady's trying to find his family," Riley explained. "It's as good an answer as any," he added in an aside to Colleen.

"Poor bastard," Kowalski commented. "What, did the Mormons get him?"

"No, some accident in a rocket factory," Riley explained.

"Sorry to hear that," Kowalski said. "Not a good way to go."

"So, maybe that's your answer," Riley said, turning back to Colleen. "I know Michael was taking some extra classes at the university; he said something about an MBA. The Mormon church is close to the university, so he found his hot chick there and nature took its course."

"I suppose that's possible," she agreed. "Maybe I'll check it out tomorrow. I'd better get back to my hotel and check in with the office."

"I'll walk you to your car," he said. "Some of these guys can be real jerks at times."

"Pam said that if she found anything, she'd let me know," Colleen said. "She will," he promised. "Ms Pam is the best. If there's anything she can do for you, she will. She knows where to get a hold of you?"

"Yes, I told her which hotel I was staying at," she confirmed. "Thank you for the beer and the time. I appreciate you talking to me."

"You did me the favour, honey," he laughed. "Those guys are not going to be able to get over the fact that I brought a white ten to the bar!"

"Well, thank you, Mr Riley," she said, blushing. "That's most kind of you."

Colleen drove back to the Holiday Inn and called Bernard Rasmussen in Utah. She told him what she had learned and what her next plan of action was. Later that evening, she called Isabella and told her about her day in Pittsburgh. She told her that the Mormon church in Pittsburgh was going to be her next stop, but that she really did not expect to learn much. Isabella was worried about Colleen driving around Pittsburgh until Colleen pointed out that it was no worse than her driving around São Paulo. Isabella reluctantly agreed, but told her to be careful and lock the car doors. She laughed when Colleen told her about her conversation with Riley and the part about fending off Mormon men with the comment that she was gay. If only Riley knew, Isabella joked.

The next day, Colleen found the Mormon church, which incidentally was quite close to her hotel, and discovered that it had a Family History Centre. That was useful because non-members are welcome to use the Centres, and they are usually staffed by knowledgeable people. She went in and told the ladies there that she was doing some studies at the university and had taken the time to try and find out a little more about her family. She gave them the name of Miller and wanted to know what Millers there might be in town. She invented a father and grandfather and brought the grandfather over from Germany just after World War II. They found all kinds of records for her, and then she asked them if a distant cousin, Michael Miller, had been a member of their congregation. That led to a great discussion between the ladies. They told her that there had been a Michael Miller, but that he had left and gone to Utah. He and his wife, Roberta, had arrived one day from Washington and had done good works in the community. Colleen asked where Michael had worked, and none of them knew. They all assumed that he worked in the city somewhere. One of them hushed the others for a moment and called the Bishop. He told her that Michael Miller had told him that he worked for the Government and that what he did was on a need-to-know basis. The Bishop had understood that and had warned everyone else off.

Pam called her about lunchtime and said that, based on Colleen's conversation with Riley, she had decided to do a little more digging and had talked to others in the plant. Colleen took notes while Pam talked on the telephone. Apparently, Michael had been going to the university and had been studying towards an MBA. The company had been giving him time off for his studies and had been funding his fees. So, they were a little less than impressed when he said that he was leaving. Pam did say that after Michael had been at the university for about six months, he began to change. He became more withdrawn, almost as if he were trying to decide something momentous. She did not know what, but one day, one of the plant people, Reggie, had seen him in a café with two men, dressed like government agents or Mormon missionaries, white shirts, ties, suits, etc., and a girl. The girl, he reported, was a knockout and would turn heads in any restaurant or bar. They seemed to be trying to persuade Michael of something, particularly the girl who was coming on to him in a very strong way. The one thing that Reggie had noted was that one of the men was a dead ringer for Michael. He could have passed for Michael easily, particularly if you only knew him casually. When Reggie had asked Michael about the girl the next day, Michael had brushed him off with a comment about old friends.

Colleen dutifully reported back to Bernard what she had learned. Bernard asked her to check marriages in Washington, DC and the State of Washington. They both assumed that Washington, DC, was the likely place meant by the ladies at the Mormon church, but it was always possible that they may have been wrong, and it was the state. The government job was an enigma, unless of course, it had been just a ploy to throw casual enquirers off the scent. Colleen asked Bernard to find out from his teenagers if any of them had a picture of Roberta Miller. If she could get a picture quickly, she would show it to Reggie and ask him if it was the same woman. If they could not get a picture quickly, then she would get one upon her return to Utah and send it to Pam and ask Pam to show it to Reggie.

*   *   *

Isabella reported to James the next day what Colleen had learned in Pittsburgh.

"So, what did we learn new?" James asked her.

"Perhaps something new," she replied. "We don't know for sure, but it looks as if he may have been recruited in Pittsburgh."

"It certainly sounds plausible," he said.

"Maybe," she thought. "And perhaps he was being literal when he said he worked in a government job. He just didn't say which government."

"So, we're left with the real question," he said. "If the switch occurred in Pittsburgh, what, if anything, happened to the Michael Miller who graduated from Penn State?"

"What are you going to tell the Navy on Friday?" she asked.

"I'm not sure yet," he admitted. "I'll have to tell them something, maybe I'll just tell them that Bernard Rasmussen is still investigating and leave it up to them."

"What are we going to do with the stuff from Miller's desk and locker?" she asked.

"Why don't you box it up, and I'll find a good, secure place to store it," he suggested. Privately, he was pleased that Isabella had raised the issue because he could store it in the most secure place he could think of, the FBI.

"Fine, I'll have it ready for you when you leave tomorrow for your trip to Washington," she promised. "I was assuming that you were going to store it off-site, so that we can keep casual searchers from digging through it. And, I presume, you'll want that secure room back again."

"Thanks, that would be perfect," he said. "I'll take it with me, and I have just the place in mind to store it."

Pentagon briefing

When James was getting ready to leave the office to drive to Salt Lake City and then catch a plane to Washington, Isabella told him that she had all the materials from Michael Miller's office packed and ready to go. They loaded it all into James's car, and he left. In Tremonton, he stopped and found a pay phone and called Sean Booth.

"Hi Sean," he said. "Are you available to meet this afternoon?"

"Hi yourself," Sean said. "I can be free, when and where?"

"I'm driving to the airport now, so how about the Redwood exit off the 215 at one thirty?" James suggested.

"Fine, I'll be there," Sean promised.

Sean was at the exit as promised, and James pulled off and parked behind him. There was no one else around, and no cars had been on the section of the I-215 highway since James had left the I-15, so he felt reasonably sure that he had not been followed. He asked Sean if he was being paranoid, and Sean told him no, it was a reasonable precaution, and if he had seen any cars displaying an unusual interest in James, he would have driven off. He also told James that he had had a spotter at the intersection of the I-15 and the I-215 and that he had seen nothing that looked like a tail.

"So, what's up?" Sean asked.

"I have the balance of Michael Miller's papers from his desk and locker," James replied. "It's possible still that someone may come forward to claim it as next of kin or that the company may want to review things, so I'd appreciate it if the material did not leave Utah and that I could have access to it if needed."

"We can do that," Sean promised. "We would be most interested if anyone did come forward to claim it and would actually ask you to surrender it, suitably redacted or modified, of course, so that we could get some kind of line on Miller's associates."

"Are we still on for Saturday morning?" James asked. "Do we need to meet again?"

"If you don't mind," said Sean. "We actually need to get a new set of prints from you so that we can eliminate you from others who have handled the documents you found."

"Don't you have my prints on file?" James asked.

"They are in the DOD and INS databases," Sean agreed. "But if we request them, that may signal someone that we're looking at you, and we'd rather not send that signal just now, so we're going to do it the old-fashioned way with cards and ink, and then we'll have a set that we can use to eliminate you."

"Okay, I'll be there," James promised. "I'd better be going, I've a plane to catch."

By the time James got to Washington and his hotel, it was ten thirty in the evening, and he just wanted a bath and bed. As he was walking through the lobby, he saw Costanza Albertini, who waved and beckoned him over.

"Buy you a beer, James?" he asked.

"Just one, then I'm going to bed," James agreed. "What's up in the big wide world of shipping?"

"Not much, we just placed an order for a new bulk carrier, and we've been debating what to call it," Costanza replied.

"I thought the fleet was all named after small Italian towns?" James asked.

"You've been doing your homework," Costanza laughed. "Yes, you are correct, but now we have the debate, Pietrasanta or Torre del Lago. Which do you think?"

"I think Torre del Lago sounds a little too much like Torrey Canyon," James commented.

"Do you think people will still remember that disaster?" Costanza asked.

"I think people who are avid tree huggers will hear Torre and equate it to Torrey, and all they will think is bad," James commented.

"Madonna, you are right," Costanza said. "I had not thought of the Torrey Canyon, Pietrasanta, it is."

"Happy to be of service," James laughed. "Now, I'm going to bed. Will I see you at the Pentagon again tomorrow?"

"Perhaps," Costanza said. "I have a new contract with them for shipping to the logistics centre at Camp Darby between Pisa and Livorno, so must discuss that with them."

In his room, James called Katrina and told her that he had arrived safely with no delays and no problems. She had news for him. Will had finally decided on their new location. They had received a concession from the Government of Zambia to operate inside the Kafue National Park and to put a lodge there. They were building a small lodge and putting up Habitents for guests. They had found a number of local Zambian guides and were working to be ready for business when the dry season came. They were going to continue homeschooling Alessandra until she was old enough to go off to Italy to school with her sister. Meanwhile, she was learning the safari business and becoming quite a reasonable tracker. They had had to take a couple of sponsors to help with the finances, and Bridget was concerned that they find a way to quickly buy their sponsors out so that they would be independent.

"So, when are we going to Zambia?" James asked.

"Not soon enough!" she laughed. "Maybe you could get some time off this summer, and we could go towards the end of the dry season?"

"I'll see what I can do," he promised. "How much are Will and Bridget charging?"

"I'll find out," she said. "I'm thinking what you're thinking, we should go as paying guests, at least until they get themselves established."

"Okay, *Suikerbossie*, I'll see you tomorrow night when I get home, love you," he said.

"Love you too, honey, I can't wait until tomorrow," she said, then hung up. James thought about his brother for a while and wondered, not for the first time, if he would not be happier earning less but being in a more pleasant place doing something that was fun and interesting. The only downside to running a safari business was having to deal with people and their egos and idiosyncrasies. He was sure that quite a number of those who could afford African safaris fancied themselves as experts on the bush, or else were so ignorant they just had no clue what was going on around them, but had enough money that they thought they could buy anything, including the experience of a lifetime. For now, at least, he decided to leave that business to Will and focus on his job at hand.

James presented himself at the Pentagon the next day, at ten in the morning. Commander Reinsch had arranged a private briefing with the admiral, prior to the regularly scheduled briefing at one that afternoon.

"So, James, what do you have to tell me?" the admiral asked.

"I have here a presentation that indicated to us that the cause of the explosion was definitely blade-to-bowl contact occasioned by a foreign object," James stated.

"I gather from Commander Reinsch that we're talking about a monkey wrench," the admiral noted. "As you Brits would say, a spanner in the works!"

"Yes, Sir," James agreed. "We've also narrowed down the people who most likely may have introduced the wrench into the mixer as being Michael Miller, the engineer and Charlie Dawson, a foreman."

"This is the same Miller that the reporter guy is asking about?"

"Yes, Admiral," James confirmed. "In fact, we have information that he is still looking into the background of Michael Miller and has had a researcher in Pittsburgh checking on the guy."

"Bastard reporters," the admiral grunted. "Okay, James, what do you know about this program?"

"We supply a Sagitta missile to you as an Auriga Type B, to distinguish it from the Air Force version, the Type A, which is less energetic and has a different propellant mix," James replied.

"That's all?" the admiral asked. "You've not been read into anything else?"

"No, Sir," James confirmed. "I have speculated on the basing mode, and I know that Robert Warner has similarly speculated."

"Well, keep your speculations to yourself," the admiral warned. "If this reporter guy approaches you, the missiles go to our brothers in blue, and what they do with them is not your affair!"

"Of course, Sir," James agreed.

"Anything else?"

"I think the reporter may have tried to see within the plant from the surrounding hills," James told him.

"Did he get onto the site?"

"We don't believe so," James told him. "The evidence is that someone, probably him, approached the fence at the highest point on the hills to the south, which would give them a commanding view of the site. We have put cameras on buildings that will give us good shots of the hills and have used infrared and visible light cameras."

"Okay, keep me informed if anyone tries to get on site," the admiral instructed. "What are you going to brief the team on this afternoon?"

"I will, in general terms, discuss the findings of our ongoing investigations," James told him. "And I will also present an update on the new mixer building."

"Okay, sounds good," the admiral agreed. "Keep this stuff about the reporter between us, and let me know if there are any developments. Now what is this about poor findings in your recent audit?"

"Admiral," James began. "The Sunnyvale audit team issued eighty-one gigs, most of which were already addressed in our own correction action plans. There were two items that I am considering that dealt with evacuation procedures. There were two items that my propellant chemists told me that if we follow the recommendations of the audit team, we would create an environment that is significantly worse than it is today, and which would be, in fact, patently unsafe. It seems that none of the audit team had qualifications or expertise in propellant chemistry, and they fell into a common trap."

"That's the conclusion I had also reached," the admiral commented. "Lucky for you, Commander Reinsch has been keeping me fully briefed on what's going on out there."

*   *   *

Bernard Rasmussen raced north to Logan in the hopes of trying to find his teenage sources. He was in luck and saw Heather. She recognised him and waved.

"Heather, hi," Bernard said. "I was wondering if you had any pictures of Roberta Miller?"

"What sort of pictures?" she asked a little suspiciously.

"I'm just looking for a headshot to see if someone recognises her," he promised.

"I don't," she said. "But if you get a copy of the Church News insert in the Deseret News in the last week of November of last year, there was a picture of her in a candid shot. I remember her being cross about it because she said no one had asked her permission to print it."

"Thanks, Heather," Bernard said. "You've been a great help."

He sped back to Salt Lake City and found back issues of the Church News in the library. Thumbing through them, he came across what he assumed must be the picture; it was the only picture in the issues of November and December that had pictures of anyone he would regard as more than a six, so it must be her. The reports had been right; she was a looker. Bernard copied the picture, then found a fax machine and sent a copy to Colleen at her hotel. Colleen happened to be in her room preparing to check out and return to Utah, so she took the picture to Pam and Reggie was summoned.

"Yeah, that's her," Reggie agreed.

"You're sure?" both Pam and Colleen asked.

"Absolutely, positively sure," he said. "I wouldn't get that wrong."

"Thanks, Reggie," Colleen said. "You've been a great help. Maybe now we can find the family of Michael Miller."

"Well, good luck with that," Reggie said. "You've got to wonder who the honkies were who were with her. They had the look of Feds or maybe Mormon Missionaries, you know, all clean cut, short hair do's, conservative clothes, ties, the whole nine yards."

"Did you see any badges?" Colleen asked. "You know the badges that the Mormons wear that say Elder Smith or whatever."

"Can't say that I did," Reggie admitted. "But then I wasn't looking at them, you know."

"We understand," said Pam. "Thanks for your help, Reggie."

"Thanks a lot, Pam," Colleen told her. "If you're ever in Salt Lake City, call me and I'll buy you lunch at least."

"I'll do that," Pam promised. "Have a good trip back."

From the airport, Colleen called in and talked to Bernard and gave him the news. But what did the news tell them? Michael Miller had turned up in Utah with his wife, Roberta, and they now had a witness who had seen them together before they came to Utah. According to the records of the anodising company in Pittsburgh, Michael was single, so did he get married before he moved to Utah? In fact, did he get married at all? When was one ever asked to produce a marriage certificate? That was a good question and one to which they had no answers.

Colleen also called Isabella, mainly to tell her that she was on her way home, but also with the news that there was a picture of Roberta Miller available. Isabella called the Salt Lake City office of the company and got one of the secretaries there to go to the library and get a copy of the picture. As Bernard had found there was little mistaking which picture it should be, and Isabella soon had a copy, albeit a black and white faxed picture, of the mysterious Roberta. She had to agree with all the reports; this woman would turn heads; it was no wonder that the photographer from the Church News had snapped her picture.

*   *   *

James made his presentation to the assembled masses in the briefing that afternoon. When he came to the details of who they considered most likely to have dropped the wrench into the mixer, he tried to see if anyone reacted at all. He was disappointed. But, then he reasoned, anyone engaged in espionage would have the ability to control their emotions and not betray themselves; their very life might depend upon it. He had taken six copies of the material with him, a number he guessed would be insufficient, but he had not thought that literally everyone in the room would ask for a copy. In the end, the admiral solved the problem by instructing his aide to see to it that enough copies were made for general distribution.

"Now, tell us about your progress on the new mixer," the admiral then instructed.
"We're ready for the delivery of the mixer, which is still scheduled for March 25th," James told them. "We've installed most of the ancillary equipment that we can that will not interfere with the installation of the mixer body."
"Do you have a qual plan for the new mixer?" one of the civilians asked.

"Yes, we do," James confirmed. "The local AFPRO office is on board now, and we will be ready to start turning blades in inert propellant about two weeks after installation and live about two weeks after that."

"Okay, what about the nozzle on stage two?" another man asked. "We don't want another SICBM on our hands where we have to rely on the Frogs for technology!"

"We have a similar nozzle on the second stage, both for the Auriga Type A and Type B, or Sagitta," James explained. "But, we plan to use a carbon/phenolic rather than a carbon/carbon design."

"What's the weight penalty?" the questioner asked.

"If the Admiral wishes us to release that data, I will do so," James stated. "But, suffice it to say that it is not appreciable."

"Could you have done a carbon/carbon version?" the questioner asked.

"Yes, but I believe that in the early PDR and the CDR, it was concluded that the nozzle would be a carbon/phenolic," James replied. Although he had not been there when they had had the Preliminary Design Reviews and the Critical Design Review, he had been through the reports and had also received briefings from Allan and Simon.

"That's correct, John," another man spoke up. "We went through the PDR and CDR with both versions and, although there is a slight weight penalty, we directed the carbon/phenolic variant."

"Okay, I guess," John grumbled. "I would have liked to have seen a carbon/carbon nozzle on this bird."

"Actually, there are two," James interrupted. "One on the third stage, and one on the boost vehicle."

"How are they made, woven technology, needled preforms, or 3D billets?" John asked.

"We would rather you not discuss it," one of the Navy officers instructed.

"Really, could I get a look at their manufacture sometime then?" John asked rather peevishly.

"That's up to the Admiral," James said, deflecting the question.

"I think we'll just wait a while, John, until we've flown a few birds, then we can start visiting the plant," the admiral instructed. "I don't want the place crawling with sightseers and drawing any attention to the program."

"Okay, I know I'm new to the program, so bear with me," John continued. "What about burn times on the various stages?"

"The first stage is designed to burn out in about 40 seconds, the second in about 44 seconds, the third a little longer," the admiral replied. "Mr Simonds, please get John a briefing package on the program and make sure it has the appropriate tech specs in it."

"Aye, Sir."

"What are you doing about the flotation collar inflator issues?" John asked.

"This briefing is about the Sagitta motor stages one, two and three," the admiral interrupted. "All other subjects should be addressed in the next session."

"Is there any way to reduce the cure time?" one of the other civilians asked.

"The cure time of what?" James asked.

"The first stage motor," the questioner elaborated. "I want to see if we can't speed up the whole process of making these things."

"Not really," James replied. "The binding agents have a certain rate of polymerisation, and changing the ratios to accelerate that rate would be problematic at this stage because it would be outside the data set that we have for complete polymerisation and the gas generated by the exothermic reaction and the relationship of that to voids and other defects."

"Oh," the questioner said. "I'd not thought of that." Neither had James until that moment, but it was a long answer that sounded good.

"What do you mean by exothermic?" a civilian asked.

"That means that heat is generated by the reaction," James explained. He privately wondered who the questioner was. It was surprising to him that among this group of fairly technical people, there was one who did not know the term exothermic. In James's mind, that made him CIA.

"Do you always get this exothermic reaction?" the questioner continued.

"Yes," James replied. "It's basic chemistry and happens with most types of glue mixes. Try mixing up a large amount of epoxy in a plastic container one day and see if the heat of the reaction doesn't melt through the bottom."

"I'll try that," the questioner said, grinning. "Maybe I'll get my kid to do it and then wow him with my knowledge of exothermic reactions."

"There is one other item," the admiral announced. "When any of you send audit teams out to your contractors, I expect useful constructive comments, not gigs for the sake of gigs. And if you have no expertise in particular matters or processes, do not make recommendations that you know nothing about. I'm not thrilled and delighted with the quality of the audit recently conducted at LST quite frankly, I have a mind to tell LST not to respond to any of the gigs issued. But that would defeat the purpose of the audit process, so James, make your report to the auditors and let me see a copy."

"Yes, Admiral," was all James could say. He hoped that the admiral had not made enemies for him among the people from Sunnyvale, but it was nothing he could address at the moment.

"Anything else?" the admiral asked. "No, well then we'll see you next time, James, have a good weekend."

James was glad to leave and hurried off to catch his plane back to Salt Lake City. He did not see Costanza waiting, but there were plenty of side offices where he could be. He called Katrina from the airport and told her when to expect him home. The flight back to Salt Lake City was long but uneventful. When James landed in Salt Lake City and was walking down the concourse to leave, he saw Colleen, who had just arrived from Pittsburgh.

"Hi, James," she greeted him. "Where are you coming from?"

"I had a meeting in Washington," he told her. "Not very exciting, but necessary. What about you?"

"Pittsburgh," she told him. "You may hear from Isabella, but I went to check out your Michael Miller.

"Did you learn anything?" he asked.

"Not much," she admitted. "But it did seem that he changed while he was there, almost like he got religion or something."

"How do you mean?" he asked.

"Well, one minute he's this hard-drinking guy that will go to the local bar with guys from the plant, the next minute he's a loner, withdrawn and distracted," she explained. "Then there was Roberta, who was a real looker, so maybe he met her, got converted to the LDS Church and then moved to Utah to be closer to God."

"Well, I suppose that's a possibility," he admitted. "Love will make you do different things."

"True enough," she agreed. "But where did she go after the accident?"

"That I don't know," he said. "It's almost as though she dropped off the face of the earth. Weird for a spouse to just vanish."

"I agree," she said. "You've had no communication from her at all?"

"No," he said. "If you manage to track her down, let us know and we'll return the few personal items of Miller's that we still have at the plant."

"I'll do that," she promised.

"Well, have a good weekend and say hi to Isabella for me," James told her as they parted, each to their own car and way home.

The drive back to Ogden from Salt Lake City was slowed by the fog and light snow that was falling. There was not enough snow to make any appreciable accumulation on the road, likely, but there was fog, and James was more than a little concerned about the other road users, many of whom he concluded must have X-ray vision because they were tearing along at speeds that he thought grossly unsafe given the visibility. When he did finally arrive home, James found a strange car in his driveway. Puzzled, he let himself into the house to be greeted not only by Katrina but also by his sister Alexandra and brother-in-law Vincenzo.

"James," Katrina said. "Isn't this a lovely surprise?"

"Hi Alex, Vincé," James said. "We didn't expect you."

"Vincé had some business in Washington, so we decided to pay you a visit," Alex explained.

"Well, I hope it's just not for tonight, then gone tomorrow," James laughed.

"No, we've got a week, if you can put up with us for that long?" Alex asked.

"Stay as long as you like and you can," James said. "You know that our house is yours. What have you done with the children?"

"*Nonna* Bernini is staying with them," Alex told them. "We'll have to repair the damage when we get back and reintroduce discipline into the house again."

"Is there much snow?" Vincenzo asked.

"There's plenty, do you fancy a day out tomorrow skiing?" James asked.

"If that would be possible," Vincenzo confirmed.

"Well, you know we don't ski, but if you don't mind going with my Human Resources Manager, I think you might have a good day," James suggested. "Are you up for skiing as well, Alex?"

"No, I want to stay and gossip with Katrina," she said.

James called Isabella at home and, after apologising for calling her, asked her if she would be skiing the next day. When she said yes, James told her that he had a visitor who had expressed a desire to go skiing, and would she take him to Snowbasin. She asked whether or not his visitor could ski, and James assured her that she would find him quite expert. She agreed, and they arranged a time for Isabella and Colleen to collect Vincenzo the next day. That done, Katrina wanted to hear all about the family in Italy, and the conversation continued through drinks and then dinner. After dinner, James was clearing up the dishes, and Vincenzo joined him.

"Perhaps in the next few days we may find some time to discuss something privately?" he asked.

"Of course," James agreed. "Anything wrong?"

"No, but I need your expertise, and I need to talk to you. May we find a place that will be difficult to overhear and to observe?" he asked.

"Of course," James agreed. "May I ask what we will talk about?"

Vincenzo just shook his head, and James left it at that. Obviously, he had something on his mind, and for whatever reason, he felt that James might be able to help him. Well, James was happy to do that; he was family.

The next day, after James had seen Vincenzo off on his skiing trip with Isabella and Colleen, he excused himself and drove to the shooting range on the road to Paradise. He parked and set up his target, and shot a few rounds from his rifle. It was cold, and he was trying out some new gloves to see if they could be worn while shooting, or if they would be too large and interfere with the trigger guard. A car pulled in next to his, and Agent Booth got out. This time he was dressed in jeans, plaid shirt and jacket and boots.

"Hi, James," he greeted. "How are you today?"

"Cold," James replied. "I hope your print ink is still mobile at these temperatures."

"It's in the car with the print card, so if you want to get that done quickly, we can finish here," Booth suggested.

While Agent Booth was busy rolling James's fingers across the card, he asked if James had looked through all the materials he had given them, and, if he had, what did he think of it all?

"I think it's quite a bizarre scheme," James told him. "I think that if the Russians ever get wind of it, they'll see it as a first-strike weapon and freak out."

"I'm rather inclined to agree with you," Booth said. "Who else at your plant knows anything about this?"

"There are people who know all about the missile segments," James told him. "They also know that both variants that we make go to the Air Force, but there are quite a few who are not dumb enough to believe the Air Force would have any use for the Type B variant because it's too much like a Navy missile."

"Does anyone know how they will be based?" Booth asked.

"No," James confirmed. "The closest I've heard is from Robert Warner, who thinks they are going on to disused oil rigs or platforms in the ocean."

"Have you heard anything more about Michael Miller?" Booth wanted to know.

"Bernard Rasmussen had his researcher in Pittsburgh this last week, and she's chasing his history there," James told him. "She may be getting close to working out that the apparent personality change that the anodising plant people observed may not be quite as simple as that, but I don't think she's thought about a different person completely yet.

"Keep me informed, if you will," Booth requested. "How are you shooting today?"

"It's bloody cold and my fingers are not working right," James complained. "I've got these new gloves, but I'm not sure that they're doing me any good."

"I understand you have guests?" Booth asked.

"Yes, my sister and her husband are here for a week," James confirmed. "Why do you ask?"

"We like to keep track of foreign officials when they are in our area," Booth told him. "Where is your brother-in-law today?"

"Skiing," James told him. "It seems that's really all he wanted to do today. He said he'd been on business somewhere and wanted a few days to himself."

"Where did he go skiing?" Booth asked.

"I fixed him up with my HR manager, and they've gone to Snowbasin," James replied. "I think he'll enjoy the skiing there, there's not much else to do!"

"You're right about that," Booth laughed. "Oh well, I suppose I should get back to Salt Lake and start eliminating you from the list of people who had handled all those documents. I'll see you!"

*　　*　　*

At Snowbasin, Colleen and Isabella were both struggling to keep up with Vincenzo. Isabella had taken James's assurances with a rather large pinch of salt and was now regretting it. The women found that they just could not keep up with Vincenzo or match his skill in downhill skiing. They both wanted to know where he had learned to ski and had he ever competed. Vincenzo just laughed the questions off and tried to explain, in poorer English than he actually spoke, that it was all the product of a misspent youth. They saw Bernard Rasmussen from a distance with a new skiing partner. Someone about the same age as the last one they had seen him with, but a better skier, in fact, quite a bit better than Bernard. He did not see them, so Colleen was happy not to have to explain who Vincenzo was.

They finally took a break and went into Ogden and found coffee at the Marriott. Colleen then began to tell Isabella all about her trip to Pittsburgh. Vincenzo feigned lack of interest but actually took it all in. Colleen did directly address him once, and that was to show him the picture of Roberta Miller. Had Colleen been a master of reading body language, she would have seen the smallest signs that indicated that Vincenzo recognised the person in the picture. He did confirm for her that she was quite the looker and asked what the interest was. Colleen quickly then told him that her husband, Michael, had been killed in an

243

accident at the LST plant, but that immediately after the incident, Roberta had disappeared, not even waiting for whatever remains might be found, or to collect the personal belongings of her husband. That, Vincenzo agreed, was unusual in the extreme and most peculiar.

*   *   *

When Isabella and Colleen delivered Vincenzo back to James and Katrina, they had forgiven him for skiing much better than they could and even were at the point of asking if he would give them a lesson or two. James intervened on that note and laughingly told them that he was there on vacation, not to give lessons to young ladies, something confirmed by Katrina and Alex. Isabella told James that she would see him on Monday, and they left.

"She works for you?" Alex asked.

"Yes, she's my Human Resources person," he confirmed.

"She's really beautiful," Alex commented.

"And very gay," Katrina added. "Colleen's her partner."

"They seem quite devoted," Vincenzo added. "I don't think she's after James."

"If you say so," Alex reluctantly agreed. "But you have to admit, there will be people who will speculate."

"You've been living too long in backwards Italy," James joked.

"Backwards, what is this backwards?" Vincenzo said as if he were incensed.

"It's the place where men think they run things, but really the women do, only they don't let the men know so that they can all continue living in their own dreams," Katrina explained.

"Ah, I see," Vincenzo laughed. "Well, I am thirsty from all the skiing, do you have any wine in this forwards house of yours, ours is so backwards we had to build a special room to keep it all?"

About two hours before sunset, Vincenzo asked James if he would like to take a walk. He asked Alex and Katrina if they wanted to go, but both women said no, they just wanted to spend more time talking about other things. James drove down the hill to the Weber River, where there were vacant areas and trails that ran close to the river. It was

244

unlikely that anyone would overhear them there, particularly with the running water, and it was a pleasant enough place to walk among the trees.

"*James, lo conosci quest'uomo?*" Vincenzo asked. He showed James a small group of photographs and asked if James knew who it was.

"*Be', non posso dire che lo conosco,*" James temporised, denying that he actually knew the man, but he did explain that a man answering to that description was known to them and was killed in the incident. He also told him that he had reason to believe that he might also go by the name of Samuel Levin. "*Ma, quell'uomo, Michael Miller, a quanto fare fu ucciso in un incidente nell'impianto propulsore LST l'anno scorso. Ho anche motivo di credere che si chiamasse Samuel Levin, perché?*"

"*Perché, abbiamo seguito le sue tracce per tre anni e poi le abbiamo perse quando arrivò qui,*" Vincenzo explained to James that they had been following him for three years, but that he had dropped off their radar screens when he moved to Utah.

"*Chi é lui?*" James asked, seeking to find out who he was.

"*Crediamo sia Avi Ben David,*" Vincenzo explained, naming the man, then he went on to say that he worked for the Israeli Secret Service, better known as Mossad. "*É un agente operativo del Mossad. Come fai a sapere che é morto?*" he continued, looking for an explanation that confirmed the man's death.

"*É stato visto sulla CCTV entrare nel fabbricato e nessuno ne uscí più,*" James explained that the man had been identified from CCTV tapes as entering the building, and they knew that no one came out. "*In aggiunta, abbiamo fatto un test del DNA sui cadaveri ed li abbiamo identificati tutti tranne uno, che abbiamo dedotto essere Miller, o come si chiamava.*" James explained about the DNA testing that had been done and the elimination of all except one, whom they all had assumed was Miller.

"*Conosci questa donna?*" Vincenzo then asked, showing James some photographs of a woman.

"*Credevamo fosse Roberta Miller, la moglie di Michael Miller,*" he replied, explaining to Vincenzo that they knew the woman as Roberta, wife of Michael. "*Chi é lei?*" James now wanted to know who she really was.

"Lei é Ruth Avraham, un altro agente del Mossad," Vincenzo explained that Roberta was in fact Ruth Avraham, another Mossad agent, then asked James if he knew where she was. *"Sai dove si trova?"*

"No, é sparita subito dopo l'incidente," James explained that she had just vanished after the incident.

"Sai nulla riguardo il programma Sagitta?" Vincenzo asked, curious to see how much James knew about his missile program.

"Più quello che dovrei," James admitted to knowing more than he was officially cleared to know, then he told Vincenzo about the documents he had given the FBI, which were, in essence, everything needed to build the system. *"Ho recentemente consegnato tutto il materiale che avevo all'FBI. All'interno c'erano tutte le informazioni necessarie per la costruzione e lo sviluppo dell'intero sistema."*

"A chi mi devo risolvere nell'FBI?" Vincenzo asked, looking for guidance as to whom to talk to.

"L'agente assistente in carico Booth," James told him. *"Posso organizzarti un incontrato."*

"Si grazie," Vincenzo confirmed, wishing to meet with Booth. "What do you really know about this Sagitta program?" he asked again. James noted the switch to English and was secretly very relieved; he had been struggling with the conversation. James's Italian was passable, but he spoke it so infrequently that it did not flow naturally, and he found it hard work doing the mental translations. He knew that if he were to use the language more then it would come more naturally, but that was unlikely any time in the near or foreseeable future. His sister Alex had become completely bilingual, and she would chatter away in whichever language was being used at the time.

"I know it's a missile program that we deliver the segments to the Air Force," James replied.

"That is true," Vincenzo agreed. "But you and I both know that they are not the customer. Your Navy buys them through the Air Force, and the CIA deploys them."

"How do you know?" James asked, dumbfounded.

"It is my job to know what affects my country," Vincenzo said. "Let me tell you how we discovered this program." He then told James a story about one of his informers working in the Livorno docks who had noticed a man who seemed very interested in certain boats, all belonging to Waterway Chemicals. They had watched him and seen him diving below the boats and wondered what it was he had been looking for or at. Vincenzo had organised a customs search one day of one of the boats and had himself dived below it while the captain and crew were busy with the customs people. What he had discovered alarmed him. He found the modifications to the hull and recognised the modifications as large doors. His report from the customs people was that the boat was clean and there was no contraband. Thinking that it was a clever smuggling technique, they began to keep a close eye on all the Waterway Chemicals vessels and soon discovered that only six of the coastal fleet had had the modifications.

Then they had had a break, one of the boats had hit the quay, and the subsequent furore had attracted attention. He had seen the captain go down in diving gear to inspect the hull, and he had done likewise during another arranged customs search. From the photographs that he took and the samples that he had scraped from the hull, his analysts had presented several scenarios. None of which was attractive. They had then turned their attention back to the man who had first drawn their interest. They finally identified him as an agent of Mossad, which made them focus on the possibility that this was a scheme to smuggle weapons. It was unlikely that the Mossad would waste its time on common smuggling. A careful break-in at the man's apartment and an even more careful bugging of the apartment and his phones had disclosed much more, including contacts. They had quietly and patiently followed up on all the contacts and had pieced together the rest of the story. They knew that the program was a system to deploy nuclear weapons in the ocean and guessed that the CIA would probably like to use them against all manner of enemies, real and perceived. What they did not like was the fact that the boats were docking in Livorno, on Italian soil, without any by your leave from the Americans. That rankled. It was from the Mossad agent that they learned the name of the program and the location of several agents in the US and one in the United Kingdom, all dedicated to obtaining the details of the program. They were run by the control in London, the mysterious Geoffrey Miller, and they tried to put tails on him, which was not as easy as it was in Italy, particularly as they had not involved the British SIS, the Secret Intelligence Service.

James asked him if they suspected Costanza Albertini of being complicit in the Mossad operation, and was gratified when Vincenzo told him, no. In their view, Costanza was just doing his job. They were not thrilled by the idea that an Italian, even one with US citizenship, would not have told them about this scheme, but they were prepared to make certain allowances. When James had taken the job with LST, it was the perfect opportunity to visit Utah and see if they could discover more and, perhaps, even find the last two Mossad agents that they had been looking for. The apparent death of Michael Miller and the disappearance of Roberta Miller complicated that. So they had decided that it was time to involve the FBI. Vincenzo did not like to do so because he felt that the Americans relied too much on technology and could themselves be undone by that reliance, they also talked too much and told too many people, including their politicians who could be guaranteed to leak the information if they felt it was to their advantage against a political opponent, or if they felt it enhanced their image as a man in the know. He regarded the Americans as generally lacking in subtlety and as being heavy-handed. He also had guessed that the Mossad must have someone inside the Navy or the CIA, and did not want to tip his hand. So both the CIA and the Navy were out, and that left the FBI. He had actually contacted the Deputy Director of the FBI, whom he knew from past associations, and the Deputy Director had authorised his contact with the local agent. All this was a lot for James to absorb, and he was quite glad when Vincenzo told him that it was time to go home and eat. *"Adesso però si é fatta l'ora di andare a casa per pranzo."*

Over dinner, the family talked about the new venture that Will and Bridget were about to embark on. They had a successful safari business in Botswana with return clients, so it was a little surprising that they would be thinking of a change.

"You don't suppose they're being thrown out like the Owens's?" Alex asked.

"I doubt it," James thought. "They haven't written any books that could be interpreted as criticising the government."

"Maybe they just fancy a change," Katrina suggested. "The northern part of the Kafue Park has got to be a little different to Chobe, so a new experience and a new opportunity."

"Will you visit them?" James asked of Alexandra and Vincenzo.

"Of course," Alex replied. "It gets Vincé away from the office and from his phone for a while, and it's safe there."

"I suppose safe means that lions are a lot less dangerous than criminals," James laughed.

"They may wish to eat you," Vincenzo said. "But, you know that and you know that there is no malice in them, just hunger."

"Katrina is safe from lions," James stated.

"Why?" Alex asked.

"Her ancestors from Botswana had a relationship with lions," he told her. "Apparently, her great-great-grandmother Motshaba was comfortable with lions."

"Only those of the resident pride," Katrina interrupted. "The same thing did not exist with other prides."

"We heard about that from Valeria and Vittorio when they came back after Christmas," Alex told them. "Your dad had told them the whole story, about *Oom* Jan trekking north to make his fortune, losing everything and then being taken in by the Bushmen."

"I'm just not sure where the fortune that he did get from the diamonds he finally went back south with actually went," Katrina laughed. "We certainly didn't seem to have any of it when I was growing up!"

"What's the plan for the rest of the week?" James asked, bringing things back to the present.

"Well, tomorrow I thought we might take a drive to Hardware Ranch and see the elk," Katrina suggested. "I heard about it from one of the ladies at the gym and would like to go."

"That sounds like fun," Alex agreed.

"I would like to see the Golden Spike," Vincenzo said. "And then perhaps Alex and I will drive to Yellowstone Park."

"Why don't you get James to meet at the Golden Spike on Monday?" Alex suggested, signalling that she did not want to go.

"Yes, why not?" Katrina agreed. "His factory is not that far from Promontory."

"I'll do that," James agreed. "I can take a little longer lunch break and meet you there."

"Do you want me to arrange something for Yellowstone?" Katrina asked.

"That would be great," Alex said. "Is the park even open at this time of the year?"

"Some of it," Katrina told her. "I think that the only road that is open year-round is at the very north of the park, and it runs through to Cooke City, but there are snowmobile tours in the park, and I'll find out tomorrow if we can get you on one of those."

"That would be fun!" Alex agreed.

"I need to pop out for a couple of minutes for some more wine," James said. "I'll be back in about ten minutes."

He left and went to a pay phone and called the number he had been given for Agent Booth. James told him that his visitor had some information regarding their mysterious Michael Miller, and he was prepared to share it with the FBI. James and Booth arranged a time and place for a meeting, and James returned home with the extra wine that he had bought at the State Liquor Store in town. He wrote out the directions for Vincenzo, noting the time of the meeting west of the Golden Spike Memorial on one of the rights of way that could be driven on. They would meet by the sign that commemorated ten miles of track laid in one day.

Test flight

Bernard Rasmussen arrived at his office in time to answer the telephone. He had heard it ringing from the hallway and had hurried the last few steps so as not to miss the call.

"Bernard Rasmussen, this is Tyler Harrison. We met in DC a short while ago."

"Yes, I remember clearly," Bernard agreed, recalling the arrogant staffer of Congressman Wheelwright and his brush-off. "What may I do for you?"

"It's probably more what we can do for you, but maybe you can help us too," Tyler told him. He sounded sincere on the telephone, but Bernard had long ago learned that all politicians and their minions were very skilled at sounding sincere. "We would like you to come to DC and meet with the Congressman," Tyler continued. "It's about that matter we discussed before; there may be something of interest there after all."

"Okay, I could be in DC on Wednesday, would that suit?" Bernard agreed.

"Let me check the Congressman's schedule quickly," Tyler said. "Let's see, no hearings scheduled and it doesn't look as if they'll be any votes of consequence needing his attendance on the floor, so yes, Wednesday would be good, let's say ten at the Washington Monument."

"I'll be there," Bernard told him. After Harrison had hung up, Bernard wondered what had caused this change of heart and what they might be able to tell him about the mysterious Auriga Type B program, for he assumed that was what they were prepared to talk about. But, given that Wheelwright was a politician, it might all just be a ploy to garner some good press and thereby more votes.

Bernard checked with the editor, who was actually quite positive about the idea of an interview with the august Congressman. The editor gave Bernard some insights into what he might also ask the Congressman, apart from any discussions about the military and their programs. The editor was interested in support for the Winter Olympic Games and wanted to see if the Congressman was for or against. Bernard then called Colleen and asked her to prepare for him a background package that gave him as much information about the Congressman as she could find. He was particularly looking for those small items that others might not have immediately discovered and which might give him an edge when talking to the Congressman. The editor did point out to Bernard that politicians did nothing without an agenda and that it might be difficult at first to work out what that agenda was. He cautioned him against agreeing to do anything without giving it some serious thought, and if at all possible, not to agree to anything without calling him first. He accepted that that might not be possible, but as a basis for operating, it was probably good sense. Bernard thanked him for the opportunity and went off to make his reservations.

Colleen did her research and gave the materials to Bernard, then she left the office and walked to a coffee shop. From there, she called Isabella and told her that Bernard was on his way to Washington to see one or more Congressional aides about some program that LST had a contract for. Isabella went to James and passed the information on.

∗   ∗   ∗

James drove from his factory to the Golden Spike Memorial, a drive of about thirty-five miles which took him just over forty minutes. Traffic on the road was non-existent, and neither the Utah Highway Patrol nor the County Sheriffs spent much time in this remote part of the state. It was cold, hovering just around the freezing mark, but it was dry, no snow, no ice or sleet, so the roads were dry and clear with little risk of slipping and sliding. He was at the appointed place early, so spent a little time looking around. The old rights of way of the competing railroads that had both pushed hard to meet were evident, and it was on one of them that he was now parked, right next to the sign that commemorated the laying of ten miles of track in one day. That was much better than the five and a half miles in one day laid in Central Africa on the line from Victoria Falls to Broken Hill. James supposed that the impetus to try and lay ten miles in one day was probably driven by the sheer idea of it and by the railroad companies vying to see who could go the furthest before a halt was called and the lines were judged to have met. That was why there were two rail beds. The companies

252

overshot one another in their bids to go the furthest and thereby grab the most land. He had no idea who had finally decided upon the meeting place, but it could have been anywhere in the approximately ten miles or so of parallel tracks. The act of Congress might say the Promontory Point, but who actually decided where?

It was a good place to meet. It was open and exposed enough that anyone coming would be seen while they were some distance away. The dirt roads meant that any vehicle approaching would leave the telltale dust cloud behind it. To the south of the sign, the ground dropped away over the county road and then a gulley, where on good days a small stream might flow, then up to the low hills that formed the backbone of the Promontory Peninsula. To the north, there was a small hill, and to the east and west, there was a valley formed over time by the stream, which was probably why the railroad took the path it was on. It was a good way through the hills in the area. The hills were covered in low grass lightly covered with snow, so that only the taller grass heads poked through the white blanket, giving the whole area a sort of light brown to white hue. There were some low bushes, also dusted with snow and very few trees, and those only where there was likely to be water. It was chilly; the wind was coming from the south and blowing across the lake and then the hills, bringing with it traces of salt from the lake and infrequent moisture from the snow in the south. James had listened to the weather forecast in the morning, and although light snow had been predicted for Salt Lake City, none had been forecast for the northern part of the state, and it was quite clear, with good visibility all around.

James saw Vincenzo arrive first, cautiously navigating Katrina's Jeep along the dirt road that paralleled both rights of way. Then, almost immediately afterwards, they saw another vehicle, and it was an old Chevrolet Blazer with both Agent Booth and Agent Goodsell. James was pleased to see that they had eschewed the standard government-issue plain four-door sedan that they would have normally used. That would have been festooned with antennas and would have been as obvious as a red flag in these hills. They had gone with something that would attract a lot less attention. The Blazer was old enough that rust was showing here and there, the tires were oversized, and the suspension had been raised a little. It had, what the Australians would call, a Roo Bar on the front and spare wheels on the roof and on the back door. The Blazer even had gun racks, complete with shotguns and rifles, arranged down the sides of the back of the vehicle, making it look even more authentic. They had dressed sensibly against the cold and looked for all intents and purposes like a couple of duck hunters gone astray.

James made the introductions, then he and Goodsell walked along the Central Pacific right of way towards the east and then up onto one of the hills to the north, while Vincenzo and Sean Booth walked the other way, to the west. Goodsell had binoculars with him and started making a careful survey of the hills around and the approaches. Although the Central Pacific right of way was used as a vehicular tour route for visitors to the Golden Spike, it was one-way and entry was from the west, so visitors would have to pass them on the dirt road before doubling back onto the tour route. The chances that anyone could happen upon them unobserved were remote.

"Whose Blazer is that?" James asked.

"It's mine," Goodsell told him. "I use it for hunting, I normally go out a few times a year, both for elk and deer and for birds."

"Are we alone?" James asked him.

"Are far as it is possible to tell, yes, we are unobserved, but a good sniper would be hidden from our view," Goodsell replied. "Even if we are observed, we can be seen but not heard, and that's probably all that matters right now."

"If you were watching us, where would you hide?" James asked.

"To your left, five degrees about five hundred meters that knoll, just to the right of it, to your right, twenty degrees about three hundred meters that whitish rock just below it and a couple of other places would make good stands," Goodsell reported. "At least that's where I would have set up."

"Were you successful?" James asked.

"I'm here," Goodsell joked. "But, yes, I was successful. The Marines taught us well, and my dad had a friend in Scotland who introduced me to a ghillie on some laird's estate, and he taught me the rest."

"Are we safe here?" James asked.

"From a good sniper, no," Goodsell said, which was hardly reassuring for James. "A good sniper will make a five-hundred-meter shot, but I don't think our suspects are out there lurking, not unless our phones are tapped or our office is bugged. I assume you used a payphone to call Sean and set this up?"

"Yes, I try and use a different one each time I call him," James said. "I'm having to drive a little further afield now, I've used all the phones close to home."

"Well, it's a good precaution," Goodsell agreed. "I'm curious as to why you ask if we are being observed?"

"Someone has been near the perimeter of my factory," James told him. "They, and it could have been two different people at different times, or the same person twice, were set up on a hill to the south overlooking the plant and with a pretty good view of the plant. That was a little while ago, and they do not appear to have been back. I now have my security people walk the fence every day looking for evidence of someone trying to get in."

"You've checked the access to this place?" Goodsell asked.

"Yes, it's a jeep trail and we've been up and it certainly hasn't been used lately," James replied.

"Well, most likely it was some reporter trying to get pictures for a story right around the time you had your accident," Goodsell thought.

"Do you fancy some coffee?" James asked.

"That would be great, do you have some here?" Goodsell asked.

"That's why I've been lugging this bag with me," James laughed. "It's got coffee, food and other life essentials." He sat on a convenient rock and poured the coffee, and they sat and drank, watching the hills around and the approaches.

"What do you think they're talking about?" James wondered after about ten minutes of silent watching.

"I doubt it's the weather," Goodsell laughed. "But, I'm sure you know what the conversation is about."

"Just the basics," James admitted. "That's why I called Sean and set up this meeting."

"Well, it looks like they've about finished, we'd better get back to the cars" Goodsell commented. "Did you bring enough for all of us? It's cold here in the wind, and I'll bet they could use something warm by now."

"I've got more in the car," James told him.

"Sean will drink coffee today, it's cold enough that he won't care about any taboos," Goodsell said. "Will your friend drink this coffee?"

"He'll probably make some rude remark about it being weak American-style dishwater, but I'm used to that and make allowances." James laughed.

"Well, James," Sean Booth said as they rejoined them. "You've done us a great service, or should I say that Vincenzo has, he's answered some questions that we had and pointed us in the right direction. Is that hot chocolate?"

"Coffee is all I have, I'm afraid," James apologised.

"It's hot, it'll be fine," Sean agreed.

"What's next?" James asked.

"We've got Vincenzo to agree to stop by our offices in Washington next week, after he's risked life and limb on some crazy snowmobile outing in Yellowstone," Sean replied.

"I promised Alex, so matters of state must wait," joked Vincenzo.

"Seriously, we've got some work to do before we meet again, so too early would not be productive," Sean said. "As I said, Vincenzo has given us much to think about and to follow up on; we're going to be busy."

"What he means is that I'm going to be busy," Goodsell commented wryly.

"Well, we must be getting back," Sean said. "Thanks a lot, Vincenzo and I'll see you next week in DC. Thanks for the coffee, James. I'll see you around sometime."

"Oh, one more thing before you go," James added. "Our reporter Bernard Rasmussen has a meeting on Wednesday with Congressman Wheelwright, who apparently is now prepared to give him some information about this program. They are set to meet at the Washington Monument at ten."

After they had gone, James and Vincenzo sat on the hood of Katrina's Jeep and drank their coffee.

"This is a nice place," Vincenzo said. "A little cold and exposed, but peaceful, not many people."

"We like it here," James confirmed. "If we skied, it would probably be even better. Did Katrina manage to set something up for you in Yellowstone?"

"Yes, we drive tomorrow to the Teton Park in Wyoming, and then they take us to a place called Flagg Ranch, and we go on snowmobiles from there. So we will be back on Friday," Vincenzo explained.

"Do you have enough warm clothes?" James asked.

"The snowmobile company has said that they have the outside clothes and we have enough for underneath," Vincenzo confirmed. "But, I may stop in Ogden and buy some new boots for myself and for Alex, cold feet are bad. I remember when I was training in Sardegna, how cold the mountains were and how cold my feet were. I do not wish that to happen again."

"What did you think of Agent Booth?" James asked.

"I think he is a competent agent," Vincenzo allowed. "He is honest and admits to what he does not know. I sense that he is determined and will react poorly when he learns that his investigation will be killed by your Congress."

"What do you mean?" James asked.

"Most of us outside the United States see your Congress as supporting Israel to the point of the absurd. Any investigation which points to the government of Israel will be stopped by one of your Congressmen or Senators," Vincenzo explained. Unfortunately, James could believe that. Although there had been odd cases in the past of Israeli spies being prosecuted in the US, he believed that those cases were few and far between, and he was sure that there was much more that went on that was just never disclosed or that was quietly hushed up. He was sure that it had to be frustrating for agencies like the FBI and the CIA to chase down the spies, only to have some arrogant member of Congress tell them to leave it alone. He was also sure that there had to be some that would not bow to the pressure of the Israeli and Jewish lobbies, but they might actually be hard to find. He recalled his father saying once that the US had some peculiar guilt about Israel and the Jewish people in general, perhaps related to their belated actions in the Second World War, or rather their inaction prior to the war when the rise of Nazi

Germany was in full roar. His father believed that the problems in the Middle East were unlikely to be solved within his lifetime, or for that matter, within James's lifetime, and that the Israelis were as big a problem as the PLO or any of the other Palestinian groups. There seemed to be an intransigence that just went with coming from that part of the world.

"So, I suppose I should get back to the factory," James told Vincenzo. "I'll see you later when I get home."

"Okay, James, drive safely, *ci vediamo presto*," Vincenzo bid him farewell.

When James got back to the factory, there was a message from Isabella that she wanted to see him. James called her, and she told him that the two candidates for the Quality Manager position had arrived and had been interviewed by the rest of the team. She had also sent them on plant tours with Simon Wilmott, and she had one of them back in her office. If James was available, she asked if he could conduct his interviews within the next hour or so. As this was the last of his management team that he really wanted to change, James told her to send the first one up. Isabella arrived a few minutes later with the first candidate. She asked him to wait a couple of minutes, then came in to give James a brief review of the man's work history. It was all classic aerospace business, with much of it Department of Defense related. James asked her what she thought, and she told him that he would be acceptable. He rather thought that was damning with faint praise and asked her what she meant.

"He's all by the book and sticking to the quality manual," she explained. "He recoiled at the idea of certifying the manufacturing people to buy off their own work; his exact words were, 'We're the last line of defence against poor work getting out', not exactly what I think we're looking for."

James smiled at the "we" but accepted it as an indication that she truly did understand how they were trying to change the business. "Okay," he thanked her. "Why don't you show him in, and I'll call you when I'm done."

Isabella brought in the candidate and introduced him. "This is Mark Wheeler. Mark, this is James Martin, the VP and General Manager of this operation."

"Thanks, Isabella, won't you have a seat, Mark?" James offered. "You found us then?"

"There was no problem," Mark assured him. "The directions that Ken Butler gave me were perfect."

"So, tell me a little about yourself," James suggested. Mark then launched into a five-minute résumé of his career, which had essentially started with a degree in manufacturing technology, whatever that was, and then successive postings in quality department-related jobs. As Isabella had said, he was a very much by-the-book man and apparently more concerned with the systems of reporting quality issues than getting to the root cause of problems and finding lasting solutions. He was more of a policeman-type of quality manager. James then asked him a series of questions that dealt more with how he related to people. They were in a fairly remote and isolated facility, and escapes like going out for lunch somewhere were not feasible, unless one counted the diner in Tremonton. So, the ability to work in close proximity with the rest of the management team was essential. James also wanted managers that he could rotate into different slots, and having a specialist quality type was constraining, particularly as Mark made it clear that he had no interest in the manufacturing or safety positions. When James gave Mark the opportunity to ask questions, they all dealt with the mechanics of the Quality System that the Missile Systems Division used.

"Why do you think that's important?" James asked him.

"A well-structured system is essential to catch defects and bring the problem back to the man who caused it," Mark answered.

"What do you do with a process that just isn't capable?" James asked.

"Then we have to apply even more rigid inspection and test criteria to see that nothing escapes," Mark opined. Obviously, he would add test after test before trying to resolve the fundamental issue.

"What do you do if the parts are routinely out of spec, but we always accept them?" James asked.

"Well then, we would have to question the specification and find out why our process does not meet it," Mark answered.

"Do you think you could work out here in this wilderness after the hustle and bustle of LA?" James asked.

"Well, at least the workers all speak English and we won't have problems with a Hispanic workforce," Mark commented. "I am having real problems where I am now with so many Mexicans, they never seem to get anything right and don't understand the simplest of instructions."

"I see," James said. "Well, I think that's all I need for now, Mark. Thank you for coming all this way to see us." He then called Isabella and asked her if she would come up and collect Mark. When she arrived, he said his goodbyes to Mark, then, as they were leaving quietly, said to Isabella, "*Cá entre nós, ele é un chato.*"

Mark looked at them both and said, "Excuse me, I didn't catch that."

"It was nothing," James assured him, but he did catch Isabella almost exploding with laughter and struggling very hard to keep a straight face.

Isabella was back in about ten minutes with the second candidate. "Lisa Bennett, this is James Martin, our GM and VP. James, Lisa has been on a tour with Simon and has seen everyone else, so you're the last. When you are finished, please call me and I'll come up to collect her."

"Lisa, please have a seat. How was the tour?" he asked.

"It was fascinating," she replied. "I've worked in a foundry and this has some aspects of that, but it also has elements of a bakery and a yacht builder."

"What kind of foundry did you work in?" he asked.

"We cast mainly brass, but we occasionally did some special jobs with bronze, and we even cast a church bell once," she told him. "I was the foundry metallurgist, and it was my job to work out the moulds, gates and risers and to figure out how to quench to get the right properties."

"It sounds interesting," James thought. "Why would you leave?"

"We've just been bought by a much larger company, and they have started consolidating operations into their main facility in New Jersey, and my prediction is that the foundry will close within a year," she said. "I've no real desire to relocate to New Jersey, if they were to actually offer me the chance."

"Your operation is in LA," James remarked, reading from the résumé that Isabella had given him. "As you can see, this place is a little remote compared to LA. Do you think you could adjust to that?"

260

"My husband, George, is a gunsmith, and this would be heaven for him," she replied. "George has built up a clientele over the years, and it really doesn't matter where we live. For myself, an escape from the 91 freeway would be a relief."

"What do you see as your role here?" he asked.

"In a perfect world, I would eliminate my job by qualifying the processes, tools, equipment and operational procedures, but I don't see customers going for that just yet, even if Boeing does have some programs that essentially do that," she replied. "If we can engineer the processes properly and the tools and equipment used for the processes, we should be able to get a Six Sigma plant in a reasonable time frame."

"And you don't think we're there yet?" he asked.

"I'm afraid not," she commented. "I asked Simon about process capability, and he gave me numbers that tell me that you have a ways to go."

"Do you think you could work with these guys?" he asked.

"I think so," she replied. "When I did my first degree in metallurgy at MIT, women were not exactly common in the classes, so I learned to hold my own."

"You said your first degree," James remarked. "Ah, I see you also got an MBA. Did that help?"

"In some ways, yes," she confirmed. "But in other ways, no. Many of the MBA class saw business as just finding ways to manipulate money and finances, and many of them had no clue about how to actually get anything done, except when it came to negotiating financial deals."

"How do you think you would work with the Air Force?" he asked.

"You appreciate, I'm sure, that we have our customers who buy the products and another customer who just wants to be sure that we follow all his rules."

"I don't think that would be an issue. I've worked with DCAS before on some Government jobs we did, and some of them were okay, and some were just idiots. Not that I ever told them that. They just had no clue about the technical details I gave them," she replied, describing her contacts with the Defense Contract Administration Services people.

"You mentioned that this plant has some of the aspects of a bakery. Have you worked in a bakery?" he asked.

"I did a couple of summer internships at a bakery," she told him. "The mixers we used there look very similar to the ones you have here."

"Did you have any problems with them?" he asked.

"Never with the mixers," she said. "But sometimes with the ingredient addition. There were times when we added too much or too little of something, and the breads came out wrong. Scrapping a 600-gallon load of dough costs a load of dough!" she laughed.

"Are there any questions that I may answer for you?" he asked.

"This business is dependant upon the military," she began. "What happens if things change and you lose contracts or peace breaks out? Can the rockets you make be used to launch satellites?"

"I'll answer the last question first. Not really, the rockets that we build take off quickly and the launch loads are probably too high for most satellites; they typically need something not quite so hot. As for peace breaking out, I'm sure that you will appreciate that there are no guarantees," he replied. "If either peace breaks out or the Air Force cancels our contacts, we would do our best to help people find new jobs, and I'm sure that the management team that we're building would have no problems at all."

"Yes, I got that sense from Simon Wilmott," she agreed. "He thinks that you have done a lot for this operation, even in the short time that you've been here."

"I'm pleased to hear that," James laughed. "Let's hope we never have to put it to the test. Is there anything else to would like to ask?"

"No," she said. "I think I have a pretty clear idea of what you need and how I could help."

"Thank you for coming out here. I'll have Isabella escort you out, and you'll be hearing from us shortly," he told her. James then called Isabella to come and collect Lisa.

After Lisa had departed, James asked Isabella for the feedback from all those who had interviewed both candidates. The only vote for Mark Wheeler came from Ron Hilliard, his finance man; in some ways, that did not surprise him. Ron was very conservative, and the idea of another woman in the management team probably bothered him. He also would be much more comfortable with someone who placed their absolute faith in systems and procedures than with someone who could blithely say that the best thing they could do was eliminate their own job. He would have to look a little more closely at Ron, but the thought of making another change to his management team at this time did not exactly bring joy and delight. With the voting in and with his own leanings, he told Isabella to go ahead and make an offer to Lisa.

*   *   *

On Wednesday, Bernard Rasmussen made his way to the Washington Monument and was there by nine. He was early, but he wanted to see who came and went before his appointed meeting time. At least it was warmer than Utah. There was a slight breeze from the south that was beginning to freshen, and the temperatures were up in the low sixties. There was also the threat of light rain, which he could feel in the wind. Bernard had arrived the night before and had stayed close by. The downside to that was that the hotel was expensive. He could have stayed further out, but that would have meant a taxi ride in, and he preferred to walk.

At the appointed time, Bernard saw Tyler Harrison walking down the Mall towards him. With him was an older man, whom he recognised from newspaper articles as the Congressman, and a young woman. They crossed the road, and Tyler spotted Bernard.
"Hi, Bernard," he said. "Good to see you again." Something that Bernard did not believe in the least.
"Tyler," Bernard greeted him.
"Bernard, meet Congressman Wheelwright and Susan Watson," Tyler said, making the introductions.
"Bernard, good to see you," the Congressman said. "I heard from Tyler that you were concerned about something, so I looked into it a little and came up against the classic DOD stone wall. So, I did an end-around and recruited the aid of my good friend Senator Baker, who is the ranking minority senator on the Senate Select Committee for Intelligence. Susan is one of her aides, and I'm going to leave you in Susan's good hands. Thank you for coming in and drawing this to our attention." On that note, he left, and Tyler lingered long enough to

263

whisper to Bernard, "Don't contact me ever again!" Bernard was a little put out. The Congressman had suggested the meeting, and he had really wanted to ask him about the Winter Olympics, not only to satisfy his editor, but because he had a personal interest. To be introduced to someone and then dismissed was, in his view, quite rude.

Susan watched the Congressman and Harrison walk away, then motioned for Bernard to follow her.

"The Senator has misgivings about this program," she told him. "We are told by our friends from Annapolis that this particular system will be used as a decoy. Apparently, the heat signature, or whatever they call it, closely resembles that of our submarine-launched missiles, and the idea is that one of these launched will confuse our Soviet friends as to the whereabouts of our submarines."

"Should you have told me that?" Bernard asked.

"Told you what?" she asked. "I've just asked you to have lunch with me."

"I see," Bernard said. "Does lunch include more than just an appetiser?"

"The menu offers several courses," she said. "I would suggest that you try the fish, it's good this time of year. The boys in black shoes have some kind of plan to get them to suitable locations, and then satellite links will allow the President to control the launch."

"Fish sounds good," he agreed. "Why would you recommend the fish to me? I would have thought that there are better-known papers to wrap this up in than our little paper."

"That's true," she agreed. "But if we use the other mass circulation rags, then there is always the chance that they will want to confirm things with their normal contacts, and there is the chance that the location of the fishing grounds will get back to the sharks that patrol these waters."

Bernard was a little unsure how to take this last bit of circumlocution, but he assumed it to mean that his paper was small enough and with no base of contacts in Washington, therefore unlikely to talk to anyone else, it also probably meant that Susan and her sponsor, the good Senator, were protecting their backs.

"If I were to fish in these waters, how would I go about it?" he asked.

"Our suggestion is that you review the package you now have in your pocket, and I'm sure you can find someone in DOD to name as a source," she told him. Bernard felt in his pockets, and in the left one, there was a slim envelope. How and when she had put it there, he had no idea. He began to wonder what other talents she might have and decided that it would be safer not to find out.

"Is there coffee and dessert on the menu?" he asked.

"Coffee at least," she promised. "They serve quite good coffee at the Marriott on Pennsylvania Avenue. Would you walk there with me?"

"Of course," Bernard agreed. "If I need to, how can I contact you again?"

"You do not," she told him. "If there is anything that I or the Senator wish to communicate with you, we know where to find you. Oh, and by the way, I believe that it is possible that you may have some financial issues that you would rather not have our friends who scrutinise such things look too closely at. If you cooperate with us, that will not be an issue."

"I see," Bernard said. "I'm sure that you will not find me indiscreet in any way. But, what if some other agency wished to ask me where I obtained such an interesting story?"

"You can always hide behind the First Amendment that you reporters are so happy to quote," she commented. "Now I'll take that tape recorder you have in your pocket, thank you."

"What tape recorder?" he tried to dissemble.

"The one I'm going to take from you if you do not give it to me," she told him. "Trust me, you would not enjoy the experience." Bernard handed over the tape recorder, then was stunned when she said, "And the other one." How she knew he had two recorders, he had no idea, but he was now in no mood to provoke anything, so meekly handed over the second machine. She disassembled both, took the tapes, batteries and stripped out the recording heads, then threw the rest into a garbage can. "Don't do that again," she cautioned. "Next time, if there is a next time, I will not be so nice."

Bernard believed her. They had now arrived at the Marriott, and she asked Bernard to order her some coffee while she made a quick trip to the bathroom. Bernard dutifully ordered coffee and sat back and waited for her to join him. After ten minutes, he finally realised that she was not going to be joining him. He had been watching the entrance to the

265

bathrooms and had not seen her come out. So he concluded that she must have changed her appearance and slipped by him. He tried to think of all the women whom he had seen come from that general direction. There had been the elderly grey-haired lady, the two younger professional-looking types, two others that looked as if they were tourists and one that he had taken for a member of the oldest profession. He had absolutely no idea which one might have been Susan Watson, if indeed that was her name, something that he was now prepared to bet money on, which was more misdirection. Bernard drank his coffee, then left and returned to his hotel with the envelope almost burning a hole in his pocket.

He also had not seen the observation team that had shadowed him since he had arrived in Washington. The FBI team had been active and had photographs, video and sound recordings of his conversations with Tyler, Wheelwright and Watson. Unlike him, they had followed Susan Watson, both in and out of the ladies' room, and she was now under surveillance. George Adams had debated having both Tyler and Watson picked up, but he was content at the moment to have them watched. He was not altogether surprised by the fact that Senator Baker was leaking information; she was seriously irritated with the Navy and was known to be looking for some way to make their lives as miserable as she could. The fact that it might involve National Security was interesting to her, but not an overriding consideration. In George's mind, she was typical of the arrogant Senators that he had to deal with, who, once elected, forgot that they worked for the People and focused their attentions on personal aggrandisement and reelection. She thought that she was safe hiding behind the idea of an anonymous source and had used Susan before for such missions. Susan was not officially on her staff, but was funded through a separate account she had carefully built up with campaign funds. George knew all this and decided that he would keep a much closer eye on the activities of Ms Susan Watson, or Jennifer Black, as she was known to the FBI.

In the privacy of his hotel room, Bernard opened the envelope and removed the papers inside. Looking at them, he could see that they had been censored, then copied, then trimmed. The trimming had removed all the page numbers, headings, classification notes and any indication of where they might have come from. He held them to the light and looked for watermarks, and all that told him was that he was looking at commonly available paper used in copying machines. He scanned quickly through the pages, then settled down to read them. What he had in his hands was a briefing paper that described how the Auriga Type B system had been conceived as a decoy. He noted that they focused on the system itself and not the method of deployment. The system was described as having an inert warhead, whatever that meant. The decoy was meant to confuse the Soviets in time of conflict by deceiving them as to the location of the missile submarines. The item that was conspicuously missing was the method of deployment. The missiles did not seem to him to be the kind of things one just carted around and hoped people did not see, so how did they propose to get them to the places they were to be used from?

On the face of it Bernard thought that it sounded like a good idea, except for the glaring omission of transportation. Then he began to wonder why the Senator had misgivings. Perhaps it was the transportation scheme, perhaps it was just politics, and the funding for this program was money that she would have rather seen spent on something else, preferably in her own state. That made sense to him. But, then again, perhaps it was just a ploy to force the Soviets to the negotiating table for arms reduction talks. Perhaps that made even more sense and was where he came in. If he published this story, the Soviets would get hold of it and, no matter how many denials there were from the government, they would believe it. It might actually make a difference. He put the papers back in the envelope and tried to think what to do next. Finally, he decided just to mail them to himself. So, he went to the lobby of the hotel, begged a stamp from the front desk, then walked down the road to a Post Office and mailed the envelope to himself at the newspaper office in Utah.

The balance of Wednesday and all of Thursday, Bernard spent seeing the sights in Washington. He had never spent much time there and took the opportunity while he could. He had called his editor and told him that they had no quote for the Winter Olympics, but that he might have a story. He was reluctant to discuss it on the telephone. He also told him that he had some materials that they would need to review and discuss before they went further, but those materials would not be available immediately. He also wanted some time to think about what their storyline might be. He promised to be back in the office on Monday morning early and told the editor that he was flying back on Friday afternoon after he had visited the National Air and Space Museum at the Smithsonian. He wanted to get a look at whatever rockets and missiles they might have on display, particularly the Navy systems.

*   *   *

Before James left the office on Wednesday afternoon, Commander Reinsch came to see him.

"James," she began. "You need to be at Vandenberg Air Force Base on Friday morning at oh six hundred. Stay at the Best Western in Lompoc and I'll pick you up there at oh five hundred."

"Okay," James agreed. "What are we going to see?"

"We're going to witness a test flight, which will be announced at oh six hundred hours Pacific Standard Time tomorrow morning. The announcement is coupled with our notification to the Soviets that we are conducting a test, so that no idiot decides that we've completely lost our minds and started World War III. Twenty-four hours' notice is agreed upon by both parties, so as soon as we announce, they will be scrambling to get their surveillance vessels in the right place," she explained. "You cannot disclose to anyone here the purpose of your trip, nor should you tell your wife. Fly to LA and drive; that way, you are not disclosing your destination. Call the hotel directly and make your own reservation there."

"Okay," James agreed again. "Do I need to take anything?"

"Take some warm clothes," she suggested. "It could be cool out there at that time of the morning. Okay, James, I'll see you Friday morning early."

Before James called Delta and made his airline reservations, he got a call from Robert Warner, who wanted to know if he would need a ride to

Southern California the next day, as he was going. He told James that he had business in Oxnard and would be flying there in the company plane. James immediately put two and two together and concluded that Robert was also going to the test flight. He confirmed with Robert the departure time and then asked if he had a return time. Robert suggested that his business should be concluded by noon so that they would be back in the late afternoon. James then called the hotel and ensured that he had a room, then he went home and told Katrina that he had to go out of town for a couple of days, but was not permitted to tell her where. He told her he would call her when he arrived and let her know what he could. She understood but was curious. She then told him that Alex and Vincenzo had called her from the Tetons and that they were having a great time. They would be back on Friday, which prompted her to ask James when he would be back, and he was able to tell her late afternoon on Friday.

At eight the following morning, James met Robert at the FBO they used, and they took off for Oxnard. Robert told James that he had a meeting with Abex in Oxnard, and he was welcome to tag along. That sounded interesting as Abex made hydraulic pumps, motors and other devices. Neither mentioned their second destination, which amused James because he was sure that the pilots had worked out why they were going. There had been two test flights before of the Auriga Type B system, and the arrangements had been the same then as now.

Late that afternoon, James drove Robert to Lompoc, and there they found the hotel and also Commander Reinsch. James also saw a couple of the people that he recognised from the Air Force, including Craig Robinson and the BMO general, Frederick Howard. They were all trying hard to be inconspicuous, but it was difficult; anyone looking at them would have pegged them as members of the armed forces. James wondered if the Soviets had the hotels in and around Lompoc and Santa Maria staked out for unusual activity, but he concluded that that would probably be a waste of time, because there was always something going on at the Vandenberg Air Force Base. He called Katrina that evening and was able to tell her where he was and what he was doing there. They were now well inside the twenty-four notification period for the Soviets, so he was giving nothing away.

At the appointed hour of oh five hundred, James and Robert met Commander Reinsch, and she drove them to the Air Force base. It was quite chilly, and she was concerned about a weather front coming through that looked as if it would change the wind direction from the north, where it was then, to the south, where it was predicted to be later in the day. Still, no high gusts were predicted and only a slight cloud build-up, so all in all, a good day for a launch. The sun would not be up until almost eight, so the launch would be quite visible in the early morning darkness. At the gate, they had to identify themselves to the guard and then again to another guard as they approached the launch area. Commander Reinsch drove them to an observation bunker where they had a good view of the launch facility. She gave them each headphones which were tied to the launch control facility. Soon, they were joined by Craig Robinson and Brigadier General Frederick Howard from BMO.

"Glad you could join our test flight," the general said. "This will be Colonel Robinson's first launch. Have you been to any before, Mr Martin?"

"Yes, I was invited to a Peacekeeper launch a couple of years ago," James replied. "It was very spectacular."

"I trust this will go off well, then gentlemen," the general said, addressing himself to Robert and James. "And, Commander, I'm pleased to welcome you to our test flight. Are you here to see how things are really done?"

"Thank you for the invitation, General," Commander Reinsch replied. "It's always good to be able to learn new and interesting things. I'm sure that your launch will have much to teach us."

James listened to this interchange and smiled to himself. It was clearly for the benefit of Craig Robinson and others in the bunker, because both General Howard and Commander Reinsch knew that the program was really a Navy program, and she was there to see that all was managed properly. Any slackness on the part of the Air Force would be reported up the command chain and would descend upon the heads of the Air Force test group.

"Where is this missile going?" James asked.

"Kwajalein," General Howard answered him.

"This is a test flight of the Auriga Type B System. We have five minutes to launch," a voice announced over the intercoms. "All personnel should be in secure zones."

"Well, young James, will your missile work?" the general asked.

"I sincerely hope so," James replied.

"It's a clear morning anyway," the general commented. "We should be able to see stage one burnout and separation, and stage two ignition. Is there any coffee anywhere?"

"I'll get some," Craig Robinson said. He went to the back of the observation bunker, where there was a coffee urn and Styrofoam cups. The coffee was not bad, considering it was not yet six in the morning.

"One minute to launch," the voice announced.

"So, what will you do if it fails?" the general asked.

"That rather depends on what failure may occur," James replied.

"Thirty seconds to launch," the voice announced.

"Any minute now," Robert said. "Here's hoping!"

"Ten, nine, eight, seven, six, five, four, three, two, one, zero, fire, gas generator ignition successful, bird ejection successful, first stage ignition successful, fuck away!" the voice concluded.

James and the others watched as the missile was hurled skyward by the gas generators in the canister, then it ignited and shot into the early morning sky. James counted to himself, and at almost forty, the flame died out, and then there was a new burst of flame as the second stage ignited.

"First stage burnout, stage separation successful, second stage ignition successful," the voice intoned.

Now they had to wait another forty or so seconds, and then the voice again intoned its message. "Second stage burnout, stage separation successful, third stage ignition successful."

"So far so good," the general commented. A little over a minute later, they had their next bulletin. "Third stage burnout, stage separation successful, boost stage ignition successful."

Now the wait was longer as the payload, or warhead, in this case a dummy warhead, continued on its way in the outer atmosphere until they got the message that confirmed reentry body separation. Then

271

there was a short wait until it reentered the atmosphere and plunged back to earth towards the Kwajalein atoll. The voice had one final announcement for them. "Splash down of the payload within the target area at fourteen seventeen Zulu."

"Well, congratulations," General Howard said to all. "I'm delighted with this test and trust that the Auriga Type A test scheduled soon will go as well. Colonel, Commander, gentlemen, I'm afraid I must leave you; we have much data to review. I will contact you if there are any anomalies that you should be aware of." On that note, he left, as did most of the others in the bunker, finally leaving only the Utah contingent of Robert, James, Josephine and Craig. "Well. I'm going back to the hotel for some breakfast," Craig announced. "Do you guys want to join me?"

"Thank you, we will," Robert accepted. "We'll be right behind you."

"Well, that was a success," Josephine said as she drove Robert and James back to Lompoc. "The next test will be off Cape Canaveral and will be more complex. I'll find out if you'll be able to come to that one."

"Do you have a date for the test?" James asked.

"Tentatively, we have it set for the end of March, but that may change when we get the data from this flight. We'll want to look closely at the telemetry and see if there were any anomalies before we commit to the next test," she replied.

"You have the stages, though?" James asked.

"Oh, yes, we have a stacked bird ready to go," she confirmed. "We're just making sure that we know what's happening before we fire it off."

"How much longer will you be with us?" Robert asked.

"I'm afraid for you, there's no end in sight," she laughed. "The admiral has assigned me to this program and wants me on site."

"How do you square that with the AFPRO guys?" James asked.

"Fortunately, I don't have to," she commented. "That's all done way above my pay grade. The one time Ridings whined, he got shut down pretty fast."

"What's he doing now?" Robert asked.

"I'm not really sure," she admitted. "I thought he was going to some trash hauler post, but he doesn't seem to have reported yet. So, I don't know what's going on."

"You know we hired a new quality person?" James asked.

"So I heard. Lisa Bennett, right?" she asked, looking for confirmation on the name.

"That's right," James said. "She has a different background and I think will be able to shake those guys up a little."

"What is this, the petticoat revolution?" Josephine asked. "First, Isabella da Silva, now Lisa Bennett, you must be really making some of the more Neanderthal types quake in their boots. What's next?"

"I've nothing planned," James told her. "Maybe the next step would be my job?"

"Not just yet," Robert interrupted. "You've got too much to do just now without throwing me a real curve ball."

"Okay, here we are," she announced. "Let's see what our friendly Air Force weenie has to say about today's test flight."

"That was really great!" Craig said when the rest joined him at a table for breakfast. They had just sat down when a couple of people, who were laden down with sophisticated video cameras and recorders, came up to them and asked what they had seen at six thirty in the morning. Craig explained that there had been a rocket test from the Vandenberg Air Force Base, which allowed the one to collect five dollars from the other, with a "See, I told you so!" thrown in. Then the same man added, "If we jump on it, we can sell the tape for news at six!"

After they had gone and breakfast had been ordered, Craig asked. "Have you ever seen any launches before?"

"I have seen a few," Robert replied. "And you heard James tell us earlier that he had been to a Peacekeeper launch, what about you, Commander?"

"I've been on the barge when we test flew C4 birds," she told them. "It's interesting to watch them come out of the water and then light off."

"If you launch from the East Coast, where is the target area?" James asked.

"In the south Atlantic," was all that she would say. "So Colonel, how are you finding your new assignment?"

"It's very focused on the technical," he commented. "It would be easy to get overwhelmed by all the terminology, but what I'm focused on is getting the production down to be a cookie-cutter operation that just hums along."

"Where were you before?" James asked.

"I had an administrative post at Kirtland at CMD Headquarters," Craig explained. "This is my first independent command. This is also the first place I've worked where the product can do real damage if anything goes wrong."

"Occupational hazard," Robert commented. "It's not uncommon in chemical factories of all types. We've had the odd incident in Houston at one of our facilities there. Did you ever run into anything risky when you worked down a mine, James?"

"There was risk," James agreed. "One of my friends was killed in an accident underground."

"What about the rocket fuels, though? Aren't they even more hazardous?" Craig asked.

"Well, we used explosives underground that had a nitroglycerine base, and we used a lot of ANFO, both underground and in the surface mines. I always thought that the biggest problem was the headaches you got from the nitroglycerine until your body adjusted to it," James replied.

"I've had a powder headache," Josephine added. "Not nice."

"Do either of you want to ride back with us to Utah?" Robert offered. "We have the plane in Oxnard, and it will leave as soon as we get there." Both officers looked at each other and obviously were thinking about the possible ramifications of accepting this offer. These were the days of the "Straight Arrow" program that was specifically aimed at preventing the suggestion of collusion, bribery or whatever other influence might be sold or brought to bear. In the end, they both declined and said that they had to go off and report in to their respective Commands. James thought that part of the reason they both declined was that there were two of them. If it had only been Craig or Josephine, they might have had an acceptance of the offer of a ride. But the two officers did not know each other well enough to trust the other. Neither wanted the other to run to their respective Commands and whine about the other accepting something that could be considered as an incentive of some kind. Rides on company planes could only be accepted if they had prior written approval, preferably in triplicate, from their respective Commands.

James drove back to Oxnard and called Katrina from the FBO while Robert talked to the pilots.

"Hi, *Suikerbossie*," he greeted her. "I'll be home by about two. We're all done here and can come home."

"Great, did everything go well?" she asked.

"As far as they know, perfectly," he told her. "There might even be a small note on one of the evening news programs, because I saw some guys earlier and they were trying to find out what they had seen at six thirty this morning and then they said they were going to try and sell a tape they had, which must have been a long shot of the launch, to a TV station for the nightly news."

"Well, drive carefully back to Oxnard and from Salt Lake City," she cautioned; then she told him what to expect in terms of weather conditions. "There's no snow today, but it was cold last night, it got down to seven degrees!"

"Wow, bloody cold," James agreed. "I'll be careful, see you soon."

Next steps

On the plane back to Utah, Bernard sat and fumed. The papers he had been given proved that Bill Ridings had been a better gambler than he ever suspected. It stood to reason that Ridings knew about this Auriga Type B and also knew of Navy involvement. That explained the comment he had once heard about Canoe U guys and the meeting that Ridings had to leave to attend. He also suspected that, however much Ridings may have disliked the idea of being reassigned and whatever his feelings were towards his replacement, he had probably told his successor that he was being pursued for information on the various programs. That meant that any approach that he now made to the new man in charge would be met with great suspicion. He would have yelled aloud in disgust if he could, but the plane was fairly full. On the plus side, the one flight attendant had already been back to him twice to ask if he needed anything more and was openly flirting with him, so perhaps the trip and flight would not be altogether wasted.

Back in Salt Lake City, Bernard drove home, with the flight attendant's phone number in his pocket, and contemplated his next step. He needed to talk to the editor and see how they would construct a story that would grab them headlines and not land them in hot water, Susan's dig about hiding behind the First Amendment notwithstanding. He put together a list of things he wanted Colleen to research, but first, he would show her the documents and show her that far from blackmailing Ridings, he had been taken for a ride by Ridings. That should mollify her somewhat. He really needed her to work on his story. He had discovered that she was by far the best researcher that they had, and now that he had some material to work with, he wanted the best.

His trip to the Air and Space Museum had been instructive, but he was now even more confused about the missing element of his briefing paper, the deployment of these so-called decoys. All the missiles he looked at, even some of those that went onto planes, were larger than he thought, and the idea of quietly slipping into some out-of-the-way place with one of those things under one's arm was a non-starter. To convince the Soviets that they were looking at the exhaust from a large Navy rocket suggested a reasonable sized rocket, even as a decoy. Too small and even he could guess that the heat signature, or whatever it was that Susan had talked about, would just not be big enough. He was sure that the Soviets had satellites that could pick up such exhaust plumes and identify them for what they were. All of this kept bringing him back to the same point: the missile must be fairly big, and moving it around could not be done with a pickup truck. The Navy had to have a plan, and he wondered just what it could be.

*   *   *

James had been home for about an hour when Alex and Vincenzo returned from their expedition to the wilds of Yellowstone.
"So, how was it?" James asked.
"Cold," Alex said. "My feet were cold, but it was spectacular and I would go again."
"What now?" he asked.
"We have to leave on Sunday," Vincenzo said. "I have a meeting on Monday in Washington and we return to Italy on Tuesday."
"When will you be back?" Katrina asked.
"I'm not sure," Vincenzo said. "We are definitely still planning a trip this summer to bring the children and see some of Utah, but also to go to Disneyland."
"What would you like to do tomorrow?" Katrina asked.
"Perhaps we could go skiing again?" Vincenzo asked.
"That's fine, *amore*," Alex agreed. "I'll come with you this time. I'm not sure I like James's plan of you skiing with his young ladies, they might get ideas!"
"Will you come?" Vincenzo asked of Katrina and James.
"We'll come with you to Snowbasin," Katrina promised. "James and I can wait in the lodge for you."
"You won't be bored?" Alex asked, concerned.
"No," Katrina promised. "James and I need to get a little time to ourselves with no telephones or other distractions."

"Do you ever manage to get Vincenzo away from work?" James asked Alex.

"Only if I take him somewhere where they can't find him," she laughed. "It's a challenge, but it comes with the job."

"I'm thinking we should go sometime to visit Will and Bridget," Vincenzo said. "I am sure that communications there in the wilds of Zambia will be difficult."

"Not if you have a satellite phone," James told him.

"Yes, but we cannot afford those luxuries," Vincenzo laughed. "We are not the CIA with all the latest technological tools."

"Don't you have a deputy?" Katrina asked.

"Yes, I do," Vincenzo confirmed. "He is very capable, but my boss seems to think that he still must send everything through my office."

"Maybe he doesn't trust your deputy?" Katrina suggested.

"No, it is more of a cultural issue, the chain of command and the status of the people he will talk to," Vincenzo explained.

"Well, for tomorrow at least, they won't be able to contact you," James told him. "There is not much phone service at Snowbasin."

*   *   *

On Monday morning, Bernard took his materials first to the editor, and they discussed for over an hour what possible approach they might use for a story. Then Bernard asked Colleen to come to his office, where he showed her the materials and told her about his trip to Washington.

"So, this guy Ridings played you?" she asked, amused.

"It certainly looks like it," he agreed. "And I thought I had read the guy really well. Maybe I'm not as good a poker player as I thought I was."

"So, what now?" she asked.

"I'd like you to see what you can find out about decoys," he asked. "If you can find out anywhere how good the Soviet satellite systems are for detecting launches, and if they can figure out how big the thing is that is being launched. We need to be able to guess the size of this Auriga Type B that LST is building, and then how they would transport it and how the Navy would use it."

"That's quite a challenge," she commented. "I don't suppose that's the kind of thing they talk about much."

No, I agree," he said. "But there must be something out there, even if it's only speculation."

"Okay, I'll try," she promised. "I'll start with Av Week." The publication she was referring to was Aviation Week and Space Technology, sometimes also called by the less respectful Aviation Leak. It being suspected in many quarters that the publication was sometimes used as a vehicle to disseminate information or, when deemed desirable, disinformation.

"That's a start," he agreed. "Whatever you need, just let me know."

"I will," she promised. "What if I need to travel?"

"No problem," he said. "Just let me know ahead of time where you're going and what the costs are likely to be."

"How much time do I have?" she asked.

"We've no real deadline," he told her. "As far as we can tell, no one else is onto or after this story."

"You called this decoy thing the Auriga Type B," she said. "I suppose that means there is a Type A?"

"I guess so," he agreed. "I suppose the easiest thing for the Navy to do would be to take another rocket and adapt it to their purposes."

"Well, if that's so," she said. "We can make a pretty good guess already as to size, because the Auriga program is a competitor to the Midgetman program, and it's reasonable to assume that Auriga is in fact Auriga Type A."

"So, how big is the Midgetman?" he asked.

"If I remember correctly, it is a rocket with one warhead and the rocket itself is about four feet across," she said.

"Do you know how long it is?" he asked.

"Not off hand," she admitted. "But I'll dig up the details and get whatever I can."

"So what's your plan?" he asked.

"Just off the top of my head, I was thinking of going to the Av Week offices to see if I can find someone to talk to me about Soviet satellite capability," she suggested.

"Sounds good," he agreed.

"There are also a couple of books that I might want to buy," she added. "They're put out by Jane's, the guys that publish the guides to all kinds of things, including aircraft and missiles."

"Go ahead," he agreed. "You know that won't be a problem."

"They're expensive," she warned him.

"How much?" he asked.

"I would guess somewhere between five hundred and a thousand dollars each," she told him. "I'll find out exactly how much, but it's going to be somewhere in the region."

"Are they worth it?" he asked. Although the price shook him a little, he realised that they were specialised works and that they generally would not make the mass market lists. Although there were probably copies in the reference archives of each major aerospace company, foreign and domestic, that still did not add up to production runs in the many thousands.

"They're kind of the Bible in the industry," she told him. "It's also possible that there might be one on satellites that will include the Soviet satellites."

"Okay, go ahead and buy whatever you need, but stick them in the paper's reference library."

"Do you trust this Susan Watson and Senator Baker?" she asked.

"As far as I could throw them," he laughed. "But, it's the only lead I have that is supposedly solid, so we must follow it up."

Colleen left Bernard and returned to her office. She made reservations to go to Washington to see the Aviation Week people, and then she left the office and went to the agency they used for books and periodicals and ordered the Jane's books and the last twelve months of issues of Aviation Week. While she was at it, she placed an order for a subscription to Aviation Week for the coming year; that done, she called Isabella.

"Bella, you're not going to believe this," she told her.

"What?"

"I've been given an assignment to check into the Auriga Missile that you guys make. Apparently, Bernard was slipped a document by an aide to some Senator, and it describes an Auriga Type B missile as a decoy that will be used to confuse the Soviets," she explained.

"What's a decoy?" Isabella asked.

"Something to use to distract or lure your prey or opponent into doing the wrong thing or following the wrong direction," Colleen explained.

"Oh, a *chamariz*," Isabella said, understanding. "And you say that we make this Auriga Type B?"

"Yes, it's not the regular Auriga that you have a contract with the Air Force for; this one is for the Navy," Colleen explained. "Bernard showed me a piece of paper that explained the whole thing."

"Oh," Isabella said, understanding. That at least explained the constant presence of Commander Reinsch. "And you say that Bernard got this information from the office of a Senator?"

"So he told me," Colleen confirmed. "Or at least this woman, Susan Watson, was introduced to him by a Congressman as representing Senator Baker."

"So what is your assignment?" Isabella asked.

"I'm supposed to find out all I can about decoys and this system," Colleen explained. "I'm going to Washington to the offices of Aviation Week to see if they have someone there who knows about this stuff."

"When are you leaving?" Isabella asked.

"I'll go tomorrow and try and be back on Friday," Colleen promised.

"Okay," Isabella said. "Let's talk about it tonight. Ciao, babe."

"Ciao ciao Bella."

*   *   *

When Colleen hung up, Isabella made a beeline for James's office. He was in, but had Commander Reinsch with him. Isabella knocked, and James motioned her to come in.

"What's up?" he asked.

"I just got a call from a friend who told me that Bernard Rasmussen had been slipped some information by a Senator's aide that describes an Auriga Type B missile as being a decoy that will be used by the Navy," she announced. That got their attention.

"What else did the aide say?" James asked.

"I don't know," Isabella admitted. "All I know is that Bernard had some paper that explained the program."

"Is Ms. Da Silva a citizen?" Commander Reinsch asked.

"Isabella is a citizen and has proven to me to be worthy of our trust," James promised.

"Well, Isabella," Commander Reinsch began. "We will have to look into the information that this Bernard Rasmussen has, but I am sure that you will discuss this with no one else except for James and me."

"My contact also knows what the document says," Isabella warned them.

"You're right, of course," James said. "We cannot control what goes on outside the company. Do you know what they plan to do next?"

"A researcher is going to Washington to talk to the people at Aviation Week, and then I suppose it will depend upon what they find out," she replied.

"Do you think it would be possible to get a copy of this paper?" asked Commander Reinsch.

"I think that may be difficult," James replied for Isabella. "I don't want to put Isabella in a difficult situation."

"Is there another way?" Commander Reinsch asked.

"Perhaps," James told her. "Let me work on it and I'll see what I can come up with."

"Okay, I'll give you a few days," she agreed. "Isabella, did your friend say which Senator?"

"I think it was Senator Baker," Isabella replied. "The information was actually passed on by a woman by the name of Susan Watson."

"That makes some sense," Commander Reinsch commented. "Senator Baker is in a position to know everything, and she's also not our biggest fan at the moment. We failed to award a contract to one of her major donors and constituents recently, so she's not happy."

"Do you need me any more?" Isabella asked.

"No, I'll call you later," James told her. "As the Commander said, please do not share this information with anyone else."

"Don't worry, I can keep secrets," she promised. After she had gone, Commander Reinsch told James that she was going to talk to her admiral and pass on this news. What he would do with it, she had no idea.

James was thinking of calling Sean Booth when Heather appeared at his door and told him that he needed to report to the nurse's office for a drug test. The system they had was that a computer drew names at random and then when called, the individual had a maximum time to get to the nurse's station for the drug screen test. Taking too long to get to the station negated the test, and it was re-run at a later date. James approved of the system. It had meant that people had been called out of meetings at odd times, but for the system to work effectively, it had to be random and cover everyone in the plant, including himself. The need for drug testing was absolute. It was not just a question of killing oneself; there were always others involved, and drug usage around explosives was definitely not good. Their testing protocols had passed all the State tests for intrusion into personal lives, etc, and it was regarded as a model. They had had one or two complaints, but it had been pointed out to the complainers that they had agreed to the testing when they signed on. It paid to read the fine print!

As James was leaving the clinic, he was hailed by Craig Robinson. "James, I want to do a walk-around inspection. Are you coming?" "Sure," James agreed. Spies aside, there was still a factory to run and product to be made. He went back to the clinic and called Heather to let her know where he was and where he would be going for the next hour or two. Craig wanted to start in the nozzle wrapping area, so they went to that building. James was not concerned about the safety issues and other things that Craig might look at. Simon had done a good job as the operations head and had changed the whole emphasis to the shop floor workers. Now they recognised that the fundamental responsibility of keeping the place clean and tidy rested upon them, but they also knew that if they wanted anything changed or improved, it would be done. That had not always been the case, so corners had been cut and housekeeping had been less than desirable.

Craig walked through the area and found little to comment upon. He then told James the reason for his inspection. His general and the general from BMO had both said that they wanted a tour and had told him to set it up for the following week. That news just filled James with delight. Air Force generals were used to having people run after them and answer to their beck and call. Having two on the site at the same time was going to be interesting, particularly as the customer, a mere Brigadier General, was outranked by the contracts overseer, a Major General. He actually felt a little sorry for Craig, because it was Craig who was going to have to collect them from whatever airfield they flew into, and it was Craig who was going to have to walk the line between trying to control the visit and acquiescing to their demands. He asked Craig what was required in the way of presentations and what kind of plant tour they might expect. Craig suggested that James start with a quick program review and then talk about the incident and the subsequent changes to the management and the results they were seeing. James agreed and, in his mind, already had such a presentation formulated.

When James drove home that evening, he stopped at a truck stop in Ogden, not the Flying J; he had already used that one and did not wish to create a pattern of behaviour. He called Sean Booth.

"Sean, hi, it's James. We have an issue with Bernard Rasmussen and information passed to him by an aide to Senator Baker."

"Hi James, thanks for the call. We actually knew about the contact but not what was passed," Sean commented.

"Apparently, it's a document that describes the Auriga Type B missile as a Navy decoy rocket used to emulate a Trident launch," James explained. "I don't have a copy, but the Navy would really like to see it. Can you get it?"

"We could never be party to such an action," Sean protested. "I could get the other information you had already asked for. Would Thursday be soon enough?"

"Thanks," James said. "I'd forgotten about that."

"Is there anything else?" Sean asked.

"Sooner or later, we're going to have to tell someone in the Navy about the other stuff," James replied.

"That's already been done at a high level by my Deputy Director," Sean assured him. "Let's leave things as they are and let the elephants waltz."

"If you say so," James agreed. "You also need to know that Bernard is sending a researcher to Washington to see what she can learn about the Auriga program from people like Av Week."

"I expected that," Sean said. "Don't worry. Whatever the researcher comes up with is likely to be in the public domain, or else easily found."

*   *   *

Colleen found her way to the Aviation Week office in Washington and asked to talk to a staff writer who dealt with US and Soviet missile technology. The gatekeeper wanted to know why and who she worked for. Colleen produced her press credentials as working for the Salt Lake City Star. She was finally granted admission and directed to the office of Larry Skilling.

"Good morning, Ms Richards, what did you want to see me about?"

"Good morning, Mr Skilling," Colleen replied. "I'm working on a story for our paper that covers one of our local rocket builders."

"Which one, Hercules, Thiokol or LST?" Larry asked.

"LST," Colleen said. "We're interested in their Auriga program."

"Ah, yes," he said. "It's a competitor system to the Midgetman, a sort of system on the cheap."

"I'm sorry, what do you mean by system on the cheap?" she asked.

"Well, the rocket itself is probably about the same size and performance as the Midgetman, so it would cost about the same, given similar production rates," he told her. "But the basing mode is different."

"What do you mean, basing mode?" she asked.

"Well, the Midgetman is construed as a mobile system and the method of transport and launch is with a special vehicle called the Hard Mobile Launcher," he explained. "The idea is that in time of war, the vehicles will travel around the country and make more difficult targets, unlike the silos that will be used for the Peacekeeper missile."

"I know Midgetman is a Thiokol and others project. What's different about the LST?" she asked.

"Well, their prime contractor is looking to do it on the cheap," he said. "They are planning to use essentially off-the-shelf equipment and rely on the fact that they can move around quick enough to avoid detection. They are also working on the philosophy that it's a one-time use system, fully expendable, so no fancy armour systems, ploughs or all the other gadgets that the Hard Mobile Launcher has."

"What do you mean by off-the-shelf equipment?" she asked.

"They're planning to use Caterpillar off-highway trucks with special trailers," he replied.

"And those would be cheaper?" she asked.

"A lot cheaper," he assured her.

"Would the Russians be able to track them?" she asked.

"Well, as they're based at particular Air Force bases, it would be pretty easy to track them when they leave to be deployed," he said.

"So what's the big difference between the two systems?" she asked.

"It's a difference in philosophy," he started to explain. "The Midegtman goes on this Hard Mobile Launcher that is supposed to be able to withstand some level of nuclear blast and the radiation that follows. The Auriga system dismisses all that and is based on a much wider dispersion pattern in the event of hostilities, banking on the fact that they will get the missiles away before they're blown off the face of the earth."

"Would the Hard Mobile Launcher withstand a direct hit?" she asked.

"Not a chance," he laughed. "I suppose they've calculated how far away from ground zero they would need to be to survive and be able to launch, but it's got to be quite a ways."

"Does the Navy have any of the Midgetman sort of missiles?" she asked.

"No, they're not much use to them," he replied. "They only carry a single warhead, and it would be a waste of space on a submarine to fill a launch tube with a missile that only had one warhead as opposed to one with ten."

"Do the Russians have similar systems?" she asked.

"Oh yes," he confirmed. "They have put great emphasis on mobility with their land-based rocket forces; it's one of the reasons we are looking at mobile systems. There is the Midgetman, and the Air Force is looking at putting Peacekeepers on special trains."

"I heard a story that we are also looking at missiles to be decoys," she said. "Could that be true?"

"Well, it's known that we put decoy warheads on some missiles to confuse the Soviets, so I suppose it's possible that we might have a decoy launch as well," he thought. "But it would be an expensive decoy as it would have to be a genuine rocket to fool the surveillance satellites."

"Could the LST Auriga be a decoy?" she asked.

"I've not heard that one," he said. "It seems unlikely to me that the Air Force would spend the money for something that's a decoy. The silos for the Peacekeeper are all identified, and I'm sure the Russians know where they all are, so pretending to launch from them would not make any sense, and the Midgetman and Auriga programs are mobile anyway, making them a little more difficult to pre-target."

"The launcher truck thing you mentioned, could any of them be decoys?" she asked.

"I suppose so," he thought. "They're cheap enough that if you just stuck an inert slug on board, it would look like a missile truck and drive about the same, so I suppose you could send out a bunch of them and have the Russians wonder which was which."

"What about the Navy?" she asked. "Could they use a decoy?"

"I suppose that might make some sense," he thought. "If you could fool the Russians into thinking you had a submarine where one wasn't, it might make it safer for the others. But how would you deploy such a system and launch it?"

"Could it be done?" she asked.

"What have you heard?" he asked, curious now that Colleen had shown her hand and revealed what her real interest was.

"Nothing really," she said. "Someone mentioned to one of our reporters that part of the LST system, the Auriga Type B, was for the Navy and that it might be used as a decoy."

"That would be interesting if we could confirm it," he said. "The real question is, how to confirm it? Are you in a big hurry?" he asked.

"No, I've got all day," she said.

"Let's go and have some lunch, and I'll get someone to join us, and we'll see if we can learn anything," he suggested.

Larry called a couple of numbers, and then he and Colleen left the building and went to a quiet hole-in-the-wall diner in Alexandria. They were joined there by another man, whom Larry simply introduced as Dean. They first agreed that everything said or discussed would be off the record and that each would be forthcoming in their answers. For the next two hours, they fenced back and forth with Larry asking most of the questions and Dean either answering or avoiding, apparently at random. Colleen had time to observe, and she noted that when Larry asked about the Auriga Type B, Dean's eyes narrowed very briefly, then when he heard the rest of the question, he visibly relaxed. That confused Colleen. To her, it was clear that he had heard of or knew about the Auriga Type B. That had caused him concern, and she had seen the reaction. But when he heard it linked with decoys, he had not reacted at all; in fact, the opposite. To her, that meant that they were only partially on the right track. The Auriga Type B existed, but not necessarily as the decoys that Bernard had been led to believe. All that did was deepen the mystery.

Dean then started asking his own questions, and Colleen was put in the hot seat. He particularly wanted to know where Bernard had gotten his information, and Colleen finally decided to throw caution and discretion to the wind and told them both about the meeting with Susan Watson, arranged by Congressman Wheelwright and his aide, Tyler. Larry then commented that he was not sure that he was going to pursue the story because he had heard of Susan Watson and the fact that she did under-the-table jobs for Senator Baker. He did not relish the thought of crossing swords with the Senator, who was known to be vindictive and petty. Dean made no comment, other than to say that the Senator was not exactly bosom buddies with any of the Services. The fact that she had leaked a document was no great surprise, but the motivation behind the leak was difficult to understand. He speculated that she might be trying to influence the upcoming START, Strategic Arms Reduction Treaty, talks and establish herself as a power player in international affairs, thus rounding out her portfolio for when she made a run for President. Dean and Larry then debated the pros and cons of Senator Baker as President, which was of some interest to Colleen but not enough to hold her attention completely. She was more interested in the reactions that Dean had had to the words Auriga Type B and decoy.

Dean finally told them that he had to leave and reminded Colleen that everything they had discussed and that she had heard was off the record. He cautioned her that if any of his comments turned up in print, then any sources she might have had in Washington would dry up, because he would make it his business to shut her and her newspaper down. He gave no such caution to Larry, so Colleen assumed that they must have a working arrangement already. After Dean had gone, Larry asked her, "Any the wiser?"

"Not really," she admitted. "It did seem to me that Dean had heard of the program, but I'm not convinced that it is as advertised."

"Well, for what it's worth, I'd drop it," he told her. "Senator Baker is not one to be trifled with, and unless she's got some weird agenda and actually wants you to publish, then I'd leave it alone."

"How would we know if she really does want it printed?" she asked.

"Susan Watson knows where to find you guys and, trust me, you'd hear from her," he told her. "But if you can avoid her, do so. She's a nasty piece of work."

"In what way?" she asked.

"Just believe me when I tell you, don't piss her off," he cautioned.

"Why, what can she do?" she asked. "We're protected by the First Amendment."

"Dream on," he told her. "First Amendment rights don't bother her; you'd probably have all sorts of subtle things happen, like tax audits, harassment on the highway by strange unmarked cars, who knows. Just believe me when I tell you, don't piss her off."

"But they can't do that," she protested. "This is the US, and we have a constitution that provides protections."

"You'll find when you've lived here in Fantasy Land for as long as I have, that there's one set of rules for you and me and a completely different set for them, the jerks we elect to Congress," he told her. "It's one of the greatest disappointments for me. I had always thought that the Government could be trusted and was filled with people with our best interests at heart."

"That's a pretty cynical view of things," she remarked.

"I suppose so," he agreed. "Maybe I've been here too long. Look, I have to get back," he continued. "I hope we were of some use to you and enjoy the rest of your stay here."

*   *   *

When Dean got back to the Pentagon, he went straight to the office of Admiral Keene, where, because of his own status, he was given an immediate audience.

"John, you've got a problem," he announced.

"What do you mean, Dean, what problem and why?"

"I've just had a session with Larry Skilling from Av Week and a lady researcher from a Utah paper," Dean explained. "She was following up on information leaked to one of their reporters by Senator Baker's office."

"What information?" John asked.

"Essentially, it bills your Sagitta program as a decoy," Dean explained.

"A what?" John asked.

"A decoy," Dean repeated. "I'm not sure whose bullshit story that is, but it's going to get reporters sniffing around the program, or at least the Auriga program."

"Can we rely on the Air Force to stonewall?" John asked.

"It depends on what's in it for them," Dean thought. "If they think they can screw you and get more funding for their own programs, then they won't hesitate to have their own regrettable leaks and drop you in it."

"You said this leak bills Sagitta as a decoy. Was there anything about deployment?" John asked.

"Not that I could gather," Dean assured him. "But that might not last too long if some of the other Committees get it into their heads to start asking questions, or too many reporters start playing their sources among the staffers."

"You're right there," John agreed. "We can rely on the staffers to leak like fucking sieves if it suits them. Okay, Dean, I'd better make it clear at the next progress review that there may be problems."

"How long do you think we'll be able to keep this under wraps?" Dean asked.

"I'm hoping a while yet," John said. "The Air Force was very successful in keeping the F-117 under wraps for quite a while."

"True, but LST is not a Skunk Works," Dean said. "And we can't fly missiles within the bounds of Nevada for testing."

"The Sovs have to have some idea what we're up to," John thought. "When we test fly a bird, the exhaust signature has got to look too much like a Navy bird for them to believe it's a competitor to the Midgetman."

"You could be right," Dean agreed. "But, I just like the idea of having something handy near those nations that are or will become dickheads. North Korea may not warrant a stand-off Trident boat, but a couple of Sagittas could take out Pyongyang."

"I'd better run this up the flagpole, Dean and let Art know what's going on," John said. "Thanks for letting me know."

*   *   *

James sat through the morning production meetings and was satisfied with progress. Simon had done an excellent job, and they were now winding rocket cases in about half the time it used to take. They also had the nozzle fabrication down to a reasonable time. Propellant mix and cast were more governed by mix times, so it was more difficult to reduce the time it took, except that they had knocked out most of the dead time between individual mixes and pours. Bill had put some systems in place for material management, but he was just getting started. He gave a briefing at the meeting and showed them all where there was about $25 million in cash to be realised fairly quickly. That got everyone's attention. James then warned them all again about the impending visit by the Air Force brass. Simon assured him that the plant would stand up to any scrutiny or inspection. James asked Tom Cameron, the Air Force program manager, if there were any issues outstanding that might cause concern, and he was assured that they were up to date on all their reports and corrective actions that the Air Force had imposed.

After the meeting, Isabella told James that she had been talking to Lisa Bennett, and Lisa had accepted their offer and would be starting work on the 1st of March. Lisa's husband was staying behind until their house sold, but Isabella already had the company purchase package option set up in case their sale did not go well. Isabella was also working with Lisa and George to help them find the right community in which to live and had set them up with realtors. George was excited about moving to Utah and had already enquired about shooting ranges. Isabella had been able to tell him of at least one that she was aware of, the one that James used on the road to Paradise. Isabella then nagged James about completing the performance reviews for his staff. It was not a task that James enjoyed, even though it was required and even necessary for salary reviews. He did comment to her that he had been surprised by his program manager group. They were all performing better than he had hoped. His only remaining concern was his financial manager, Ron Hilliard, who to him seemed a little trapped in the sixties. He would have to work with Hilliard to get him to be a real contributing member of the team and not just a passive reporter of past history. Before she left, James asked Isabella if she could join them for dinner that evening. He had had his instructions from Katrina and was tasked to invite her and Bill, and Amanda Evans. He had seen Bill earlier, so had passed on that invitation already. Isabella thanked him and said that she would be there.

Meetings done for the day, James had just wandered off to talk to people in the cafeteria when he was paged by Heather. He found a telephone and called.

"James, there's a Geoffrey Miller on hold here; he says he needs to talk to you," she told him.

"I'll be right there," James promised. It took him about three minutes to get to the office, and Heather handed him the telephone. "Hello," he said. "How may I help you?"

"Hello," a very British-sounding voice said. "This is Geoffrey Miller. My cousin Michael Miller used to work there, and I've just been informed by the American Embassy here in London that he died in an accident there at your factory. The chaps from the embassy were very kind, and they gave me your number and suggested that I call you."

"Mr. Miller, thank you for calling," James said. "We've been trying to contact you for a while. I'm sorry it has taken this long to get this bad news."

"I understand," Geoffrey said. "I've been out of the country and only returned yesterday to a blizzard of mail and a message from your embassy."

"How may we be of service?" James asked.

"Well, I really was not that close to Michael, but I am his only family. What happened to his remains?" Geoffrey asked.

"I'm not sure how to put this," James said. "I'm afraid the explosion was severe enough that all we were able to do was create memorials to those who died."

"Ah, I see," Geoffrey said. "That must have been quite unpleasant for you chaps."

"I was not here at the time of the incident," James explained. "But, yes, you are right; it was not their best day."

"So I was wondering if you have any of his personal belongings there," Geoffrey asked.

"As a matter of fact, we do," James told him. "Do you happen to know the whereabouts of his wife, Roberta?"

"No, I'm afraid not," Geoffrey said. "You have not been able to contact her?"

"No," James admitted. "She left the State immediately after the incident, and all efforts to contact her have failed."

"Well, Bobby has always been a little bit of a loner, and she has not contacted me at all," Geoffrey remarked.

"We would prefer to hand over the belongings we have to his wife," James told him. "But as we seem unable to contact her, I would be happy to hand them over to you."

"Look, I've got a skiing trip planned to Colorado this weekend and am leaving tomorrow. I was looking at the map, and Utah is close, so why don't I drive up and see you chaps there?" Geoffrey suggested.

"That would be fine," James agreed. "If you prefer, we can meet in our Salt Lake City office; that way, you do not have to drive out into the wilderness."

"No, no, I'll come out there. It would be interesting to see where Michael worked," Geoffrey said.

"Do you need help with accommodations while you are in Utah?" James asked.

"That's very kind of you, but I've taken a shufti at the map and some guide books, and it looks like Ogden would be about a 460-mile drive from Aspen and would be a good place to stay," Geoffrey said. "I'll make my own arrangements for hotels. Would it be convenient if I arrived at your factory on Wednesday of next week?"

"That would be fine," James assured him. "If you tell me at which hotel you will stay, I will leave directions at the front desk for you."

"Excellent, look, I'll be staying at the Marriott there in Ogden. I plan to arrive on Tuesday afternoon, weather and road conditions permitting, so could be at your factory any time on Wednesday," Geoffrey replied.

"Why don't we set a time for ten on Wednesday?" James suggested. "It should take you no more than an hour and a half to drive from Ogden, so that will give you time for breakfast without having to get up at the crack of dawn."

"Excellent," Geoffrey said again. "May I call this number next week if I run into delays on the road or get trapped by a snowstorm?"

"Of course," James reassured him. "Just let us know if there is any way in which we can help you."

"Excellent," Geoffrey said yet again. It seemed to James that this was a favourite expression; then Geoffrey continued. "I look forward to seeing you chaps next week. Thanks a million, bye."

After Geoffrey had hung up, Heather looked at James and asked him if all Brits sounded like that. He was able to assure her that a certain class of people did, but that he suspected that much of the accent was actually contrived. It just did not sound quite right to him; it was just too British and, although a good caricature of Britishness, just a little too much. He told her that Geoffrey Miller would be arriving the following week to collect the belongings of Michael Miller, and they should be prepared to serve him lunch. Now he had to retrieve the items they had found in the desk and locker of Michael Miller so that he could, in fact, hand them over.

The next call was from Craig Robinson to let them know that the visit by the generals was now set for the following Tuesday. He was scheduled to pick up his general at 08:00 at Hill Air Force Base and then they were going to wait for the BMO general who would be flying in from the Mountain Home Air Force Base and expected to be at Hill by 08:28. So Craig told James to expect the party, he plus the generals and however many aides and flag lieutenants they might have with them, at about ten. James told Craig that he had put together a dog and pony show that had him for fifteen minutes, followed by Tom Cameron, who would quickly brief the Air Force programs, after which Simon Wilmott would talk about the plant in general and then John Edwards, safety matters and a pre-tour briefing, after which they could take the tour. He suggested the inert areas first, then the live areas, starting with a Class 1.3 mixer, used for the true Air Force program, as opposed to the Class 1.1 mixers used for the Navy program and then going to a casting building. Craig agreed and asked if they could add the Computed Tomography building as the technology was impressive and they could see the final result of the manufacturing process.

After work, James stopped at a truck stop in Brigham City and called Sean Booth.

"Sean. Hi, it's James."

"What's up?" Sean asked.

"Geoffrey Miller," James replied.

"Oh, has he surfaced?" Sean wanted to know.

"Yes, and he'll be here next Wednesday at the plant to take possession of Michael Miller's personal stuff," James explained. "When can I collect it?"

"How about this weekend?" Sean asked.

"That would be fine," James agreed. "Where?"

"Locomotive Springs airfield," Sean told him.

"Where?" James asked again.

"You take 84 to Snowville, exit at Snowville, go into town and take the road west, parallel to the freeway. At the first left, follow the road around under the freeway, then you're on Locomotive Springs Road, follow it for twenty miles roughly southwest and then bear left for another six-tenths of a mile, I'll be there," Sean told him. "It's an abandoned grass strip airfield west of the Golden Spike. You'll find it."

"Okay," James agreed. "Why all the way out there?"

"One of my agents told me that it was a good place, hard to sneak up on unobserved. And I'll have company on Saturday," Sean warned him. "And we don't want to be seen. The range on the Paradise road is too public."

"Who's coming?" James asked.

"My boss from Washington," Sean told him. "My guess is he'll be coming out for the next week or so, maybe even with someone from the Navy. I told you they'd been talking."

"Just don't make it all too obvious," James warned him. "We don't want a convention out there."

"Don't worry, James," Sean assured him. "We know what we're doing."

"Maybe," James said. "Just don't attract too much attention! If you're bringing some big shot, they'll probably want to get out there by helicopter, in which case we should just put a sign up."

"There'll be no helicopters, James, relax, we'll manage things," Sean tried again to reassure him.

"Have you finished with your analysis of the papers and other items?" James asked.

"We've photographed them, X-rayed them, Xeroxed them, scanned them, taken infrared and ultraviolet pictures of them, exposed them to just about every form of electromagnetic radiation you can think of, we've also dusted them for fingerprints, swept them for microdots, bugs, and I do mean insects, seeds, you name it. If there's anything to be learned from these documents, we've gotten just about all there is to get," Sean explained.

"I'll have a couple of standard file boxes for all the stuff," James told him. "What about the posters?"

"I'll have them rolled up and ready for you as well," Sean promised.

"And the choo choo train book, you Brits and your trains!"

"Okay, Sean, I'll see you Saturday at say ten?" James suggested.

"That's fine. Are you planning to call your man in Italy, or do you want me to do that?" Sean asked.

"As you've met and have contacts, and I don't know if my phone may be monitored, why don't you make the contact? It would be more secure?" James suggested.

"Okay, I'll do that," Sean promised.

*   *   *

Bernard Rasmussen listened to Colleen's account of her day and then sat back to think. It seemed even now that nothing was straightforward. He had been wrong about Ridings; he had been warned off the Air Force by some goons, and now it looked as if he were being led astray by a Senator's aide. To him, it all spelt one thing, conspiracy! That LST made rockets was undeniable, but the issue seemed to be, who did they make them for? They had a contract with the Air Force for the Auriga program, which was a matter of public record, but what other contracts did they have? From Colleen's description of the man, Dean's reaction, Auriga Type B was real, but the decoy story might just be that, a decoy. Then there was the question in his mind: was this mysterious Auriga

Type B program in any way related to the incident at the factory and the deaths of the people there? Perhaps it was a new and highly experimental system that was new enough that it just had bugs that needed to be worked out. He even doubted now that the Navy was involved. The idea of the Navy firing off decoy rockets was fanciful, and he had been given nothing that explained just how that would be done. It would seem illogical to fire them from a submarine because then they would not be decoys luring some adversary away from the submarine. If they were launched from a surface vessel, the vessel itself would be plainly visible, so it would hardly be taken seriously as a decoy. Launching them from land was equally as implausible because it would be apparent that it was a land launch so nothing to do with submarines. His best guess was that it was all misdirection on the part of the Air Force.

The more he thought about his contact with Susan Watson, the more doubts he had about the validity of the document she had provided him. It was just some papers with no headings, no dates and no classifications, and he was certain that anything having to do with ballistic missiles would be at least Secret. He went to the reference section of the paper and searched for anything relating to Senator Baker. What he found was a history of antipathy towards the armed services and the Navy in particular. All her speeches and votes in the past few years had been opposed to any military spending, and she was consistent in her criticism of all matters military. Bernard decided that she was definitely a peace and love type. He then thought about her motivation in passing the so-called information to him about the Auriga program and decided, rightly or wrongly, that it was disinformation designed to prompt investigations and digging by reporters that would probably produce nothing of substance, but which would distract and occupy the Navy. As far as he was concerned, he was being led up the garden path by a vindictive Senator who was trying to use his supposed natural curiosity and, sad to say, typical drive of a reporter to get a story no matter what the cost, in order to further her own agenda. Well, while he had no compunction in using whatever means he could to generate his own stories, he was damned if he was going to be used by a Senator for her own ends.

He went back to his notes and the material that Colleen had given him before. When the Air Force was developing the Minuteman rocket, they had had failure after failure on the launch pads until finally it worked. Perhaps that was the situation now; LST was working on something really new and risky. The question was, was there a story there? He knew that for any real advances to be made in any technology, there were always failures before successes, but the public's squeamishness about losses, either of life and limb, or of money, had made the Congress question any failure, so perhaps LST was covering up a failure so as not to be scrutinised by some Congressional sub-committee. He decided that that would be his story, "Unconfirmed rumours and unidentified sources at the Pentagon hint at daring new experimental rocket technology at LST!" That sounded good. He could develop the whole story around the Auriga Type B program and weave in the deaths as a consequence of rash and precipitous actions by a management looking to be the "firstest" with the "mostest" and damn the consequences. That should sell well and even be good for follow-ups, as the major East Coast papers jumped on the bandwagon.

With this idea in mind, Bernard started laying out his story and even typed up a couple of draft versions. He would share those with his editor the next day or so and then hone them until they felt that it had the right mix of truth, speculation and out-and-out fiction. He did not want to go too far and come across as a cheap Utah version of the National Enquirer, but felt they could use the materials he had been given to develop the story around. The usual reticence to speak of both the Air Force and LST would play nicely into his hands. He was certain that neither would want to actually make any statements that confirmed or denied anything, so he had a nice bare canvas to work with.

He called Colleen at the hotel in Washington and told her to come home. He was sure that they would get nothing more substantive than they already had, so her being there was a waste. She was thrilled at not having to stay longer and told Bernard that she would be back in the office the next day, either around lunchtime or early afternoon, depending on what flights she could get. Colleen called Isabella and told her that she was coming home early, her assignment over. The fact that it had ended inconclusively was of no matter; she was done with it. She had made contact with Larry and would keep in contact. Who knew when that might be of use in the future?

Locomotive Springs

James spent the next couple of days focused on the plant and the impending visit by the Air Force brass. Craig was concerned enough that he actually wanted daily tours of the factory, particularly the areas that were on the visit route. James tolerated this but told Craig that it really was not necessary and that Simon really did have things in hand. Craig was not to be deterred and told James that his next promotion largely depended on how well he managed things at LST.

Commander Reinsch told James and Craig that on the visit day, she had a meeting with some Navy people at the Hercules plant at Bacchus West and would not be back until after the Air Force brass had been and gone. That made Craig a little happier. He no longer had to worry about whether or not to include her in the briefings and the tour, even though she had already assured him that she would stay out of sight and not get involved in any way.

By Friday afternoon, James was ready to leave and take some time away from the plant. However, he was not totally free of the company. He and Katrina had decided to host a gathering of the management team at their house, and he was expected home to help set up, but Katrina had enlisted the help of Amanda Evans, and between them, they had everything just about done before he got home. That was a great relief. The first to arrive that evening were Simon Wilmott and his wife Janet. They lived fairly close and had actually debated walking up the hill, rather than driving, but it was still cold enough that that meant heavier boots or shoes and overcoats. The next to arrive were Lisa and George Bennett. Although not yet officially part of the team, James thought it would be a good opportunity for Lisa to meet the rest in a more social setting. He had arranged for her and George to be flown up for the week end and Lisa would stay on to sign on March 1st while George went back to California to settle their affairs. Things quietened a little when Isabella arrived with Colleen, but that awkwardness was soon past. James had watched his team members closely to see who reacted to the relationship between Isabella and Colleen and noticed that there was generally better acceptance among his staff than with their spouses, with the exception of Ron Hilliard. Ron, he decided, was living in the sixties, not the swinging sixties, but the sixties of the large corporations and the politics of management advancement made famous by the book The Pyramid Climbers by Vance Packard.

Later in the evening, James asked Bill if he could borrow his truck the next day. He rather suspected that the road out to Locomotive Springs might be a dirt or gravel road, and he did not really want to take the company car. Bill was happy to let James take his truck and suggested that he just leave it with him because Amanda had arrived with her own car earlier when she came to help Katrina with setting up the party. James did note that two of his managers, Allan Black and Bernard Zaun, did not drink, and he learned that they were members of the Mormon Church. He got a short lecture on the evils of alcohol and other vices from Agnes Black until Allan rescued him. There was no such issue with Cynthia Zaun, who told James in a quiet moment in the kitchen that Agnes had converted to the Church, and as she put it, there were none so pure as the purified.

Isabella had come armed with *cachaça* and the other ingredients to make *caipirinhas*, which she did to the delight of everyone. However, she limited them to one each, pointing out that it would be really easy to overindulge on the *caipirinhas* as they tasted so good. Even so, she was kept busy because she served eighteen drinks in all, and each she made individually. By the time everyone had left and all had been cleaned up, James and Katrina were ready to drop, but both agreed that the evening had been a success. Melding the old management team with the new members was an ongoing challenge, and James was trying to find every way he could to make that happen.

"So, what do you think?" James asked Katrina when they were in the bath.
"I like this team," she said. "A couple of the wives are a bit full of themselves."
"Who?" he asked.

"Well, Agnes Black kept on at me about families and children until I was rescued by Cynthia Zaun," she said. "Courtney Hilliard is a bit of a pain, too. She kept telling me how Ron was the saviour of the division because he kept you guys all on the straight and narrow."

"What did you think of our newest member to be, Lisa?" he asked.

"She's great, but I'm not sure how the Mormons are going to take her," she commented. "I like her husband, too. He'll go down well here; he'll fit right in with the hunting, shooting, fishing group."

"Did Amanda have any comments?" he asked.

"Yes, she told me that Elizabeth Cameron and Barbara Macintosh were both rather overwhelmed by being asked to the boss's house," she replied. "I gather that the past regime was a little more rigid in hierarchy, and they didn't mix much."

"Any comments about Isabella and Colleen?" he asked.

"I heard a few whispers in the corners," she told him. "Mostly from Agnes and Courtney."

"I suppose it will be public knowledge now," he commented. "With this many people probably guessing if not knowing, it seems to me that it would be hard to keep it quiet."

"Maybe," she said. "But I think most will just leave it alone, and the two that have the problem won't want to discuss it because they can't deal with it; besides, they are still enough in awe of you that they'll be afraid that you'll fire their husbands if they make too much noise."

"What do you mean awe?" he asked.

"I overheard a couple of conversations," she told him. "Most of them think that you're capable of firing anyone for the slightest reason, and they can't quite work out what you know and what you don't know. You have this habit of asking questions that often leaves people wondering why you asked it and what you actually know."

"I thought I was being nice to these guys," he protested.

"You are dear," she reassured him. "But, you have to admit that you have a reputation that follows you around. There are a lot of people who think you come across as this supercilious Brit who is the expert in put-downs and who makes people nervous."

"Ah, well, as long as they all don't leave and drop all the work into my lap," he laughed.

"They won't do that," she promised him. "Most of them actually like you. I can't imagine why."

"It's because I'm just a likeable sort of person, *Suikerbossie*," he told her. "Now, can we get out of this bath and go to bed?"

Saturday morning was cold and clear with bright sunshine. James drove out on the I-84 to Snowville and then found the Locomotive Springs Road. Sean had been right, the road ran almost directly south west and, with the exception of two or three small detours around things, ran straight for almost the whole twenty miles. James knew that he had to be getting close when he crossed the old railroad grade, and it was not much longer before he made his veer to the left and then found the old airfield. There was really nothing left of the field except the fact that the two grass strips that had been the runways were evident. He had been there about ten minutes when the Chevrolet Blazer that he recognised as belonging to Tom Goodsell approached from the east, probably from the road leading from the Golden Spike. Tom had Sean Booth with him.

"Hi Sean, Tom," James greeted them. "Are you alone?"

"Yes, the elephants are taking the route I gave you," Sean explained. "We thought we'd come a little early and check the place out."

"From what Tom told me, we'd never know if there were observers," James commented.

"That would be true but for the fact that my people have been here since yesterday," Sean agreed. "Any of them have anything to report?" he asked Tom.

"No, boss," Tom told him. "I've checked in with all of them, and I've got a rundown on all traffic in the area over the past day. No drop-offs, no lingering, no apparent undue interest."

"Okay, we'll take that as low risk then," Sean commented.

"You mean there could still be someone out there?" James asked.

"It's possible," Sean agreed. "We gave you enough notice that if my line is tapped, a good sniper would have been out here three days ago and set up concealed where we'd never find him. That's why we prefer to give rendezvous points as close to the meet as possible, then we will have already pre-positioned our own people, and anyone else would risk detection trying to get here and set up."

"Boss, they're here," Goodsell told them. It was a few minutes before they saw the Chevy Suburban that bounced over the old airfield towards where they were parked. It was a Chevy Suburban that had seen better days, which was good because it did not look like a standard-issue Government vehicle. James was surprised to see Admiral Keene.

"James Martin," the admiral said. "Until they told me why I was coming all the way out here into the wilderness, I had not expected to see you until our next review."

"Good morning, Admiral," James greeted him. "I did not pick the place, Agent Booth made that selection."

"James, this is Deputy Director George Adams of the FBI and Assistant Secretary of the Navy, Arthur Rowe. Gentlemen, this is James Martin, the guy who has been giving us all heartburn," Sean announced.

"James, hi, Sean has briefed us and we've been through all the material you recovered. Is there anything else you can tell us?" George Adams asked.

"If Sean has briefed you, then no," James told them. "The only new information is that Geoffrey Miller called earlier in the week and will be here next Wednesday to pick up the personal belongings of Michael Miller."

"That's why we're here," Art Rowe said. "We want George and his people to pick this guy up."

"What about the contact in the Pentagon?" James asked.

"What do you mean?" Art countered.

"Well, the documents I found represented an almost complete set of drawings and manufacturing details of how to make the Sagitta system. The program is limited access, and I was only briefed by the admiral's team on the missile segments, nothing else, so had no knowledge of the basing mode until I found the cases. That suggests to me someone close to the program who had access to a listing of all the contractors," James explained.

"I presume that's why you did not come to me when you found this stuff?" Admiral Keene asked.

"Yes, Admiral," James agreed. "I suspected a leak, and that meant someone in your office or close to it, so I had no idea who to trust. So I went to the local FBI office, and as they had never heard of the program, I concluded that they were a good risk for me."

"That makes sense," Admiral Keene agreed. "But I have to tell you I was royally pissed when I first heard that you'd found this stuff and gone to the FBI and not come to me."

"He made the right decision, Bill. He was right to suspect, because he had no way of knowing who might be the leak. Why don't you go through everything again for my benefit?" Art asked. "I'd like to hear it from you."

For the next hour, James told his story and answered questions. He covered the investigation at the plant and his growing belief that some of the people at the plant had discovered that not all was as it should be with Michael Miller and had taken it upon themselves to do something about it. He also discussed the review of the items from the desk and locker of Michael Miller, the discrepancy with the limp, the telephone call from Rebecca Rosenberg and so on. George wanted to know how much James knew about the investigations of Bernard Rasmussen. James told him what he had been told by Isabella. Then they wanted to hear what Vincenzo had said. Sean was able to add to that with a review of his meeting near the Golden Spike. Eventually, George looked at Art and said, "He checks out Art."

James looked at them both, and George provided the answer. "We had to be sure that this was not just some ploy by you to cover your own tracks. We've checked you out quite thoroughly. You've had quite an interesting life."

"Have you identified the leak within the Pentagon?" James asked.

"Ah, well, we can't actually tell you that," George apologised. "I'm sure that you'll understand."

"What do I do about Geoffrey Miller?" James asked.

"Have him out to the plant, give him these boxes of stuff and let us do the rest," George instructed. "When is he due to see you?"

"At ten on Wednesday morning," James replied. "He says that he's driving from Aspen and will arrive on Tuesday."

"You said, 'he says' as though you don't quite believe him?" George commented.

"Just a feeling," James told them. "Because Vincenzo told me who he really is, I was listening closely. He's got the Brit bit down very well and, no disrespect intended, any of you would be completely convinced that he is a Brit, but he's not, and I could tell that he isn't. I also thought that his whole pitch about driving up from Aspen was a little too well done. I think he will fly to Salt Lake City and drive from there. I think he will arrive at least by Monday, if not sooner and will check out the place. If he is expecting more in the way of papers than we give him, he'll either ask if we have the rest or he'll figure it's still hidden. My guess is that Michael Miller had a backup plan and told him where to find the stuff in case of problems, so he'll go looking."

"Anything else?" George asked, amused.

"Yes, if I were Michael Miller, I would have had an alternate hiding place and would have found a way to let Geoffrey know where that was. So, when we don't give Geoffrey the two cases, he'll first check out the location on the plant, if he's not already done that, then he'll go looking for the alternate. And, if you want my best guess, the alternate site will be somewhere near, in or around the temple that Michael Miller used to go to as Cantor Levin. If he doesn't find the cases at either place, he'll assume we know and find a way to disappear. Can you actually track him if he wants to disappear?"

"Is there a way that you can check whether or not he gains access to inside your perimeter without him knowing?" George asked.

"I think so," James told them. "I have cameras pointed at the best places to gain access, both visible light and infrared. I also have the perimeter walked by my guards every day. I know a good tracker can remove evidence of tracks, but there will be something. I'll get his picture for you when he's in the plant. I'll also get his fingerprints and footprints."

"Are you sure you checked this guy out, George?" Art asked. "It sounds to me like he works for the SIS."

"No, I already called them," George said. "Neither of the agencies claims him."

"Who are we talking about?" Admiral Keene asked.

"SIS, the Brits, often referred to as MI5 or MI6," George replied.

"Do the Brits have a line on Geoffrey Miller?" Art asked.

"They lost him," George told him. "My bet is he's in country already, maybe came in using another ID, and he'll assume Geoffrey Miller again when he sees James on Wednesday."

"If he doesn't get what he wants on Wednesday, will he come after me?" James asked.

"That's a good question," George admitted. "We don't know much about this guy, but the Mossad play by their own rules, and my guess is he'll want to know what happened to his information."

"So you're saying he will come after me?" James asked. "This is all starting to sound a little fanciful. Why would the Deputy Director of the FBI be talking to me? It's all a little like a novel, and a second-rate novel at that, like someone indulging in flights of fancy."

"There is nothing fanciful about espionage," George said.

"I had always thought that the real spy problem was with the Russians and the Chinese," James commented.

"True, but there are probably as many Japanese, French, British and Israeli spies," George said. "Their motivations are different. With the Japanese, it's all about industrial espionage; with the rest, it's trying to find out what we won't share with them. They recruit people locally and go to work."

"What motivates citizens to spy on their own country?" James asked.

"Idealism, think Philby, Burgess, Maclean and Blunt, then there's blackmail, think Profumo, there's always money, and then there's vengeance for wrongs real and perceived," George enumerated. "You should recognise those names as notorious Brit spies from the fifties and sixties."

"I do indeed," James admitted. "I also know where Mandy Rice-Davies's house was, and we lived close enough to Clivedon to get all the local colour on that story. So, have you identified the Pentagon source?"

"Do you have anywhere you can go for the next couple of days?" George asked, ignoring James's question.

"Look, we just moved to Utah a couple of months ago," James replied. "We only know a few people casually, the family I have is spread to hell and gone, and we're rather short on options. Why don't you people pick him up after he leaves the plant on Wednesday?"

"Because we really want his source inside Bill's organisation," Art said.

"We could probably place an agent in your house," George offered.

"Who, Goodsell or Sean?" James asked.

"I'm afraid not," George told him. "It would have to be one of the other agents from the office."

307

"How do I know I can trust them?" James asked.

"Can your brother-in-law get here quick enough to stay with you?" Sean asked.

"I've no idea," James admitted.

"Call him," Sean said, thrusting a satellite phone into James's hands.

James called the number in Italy, and Alex answered the phone.

"*Pronta.*"

"Hi Alex, is Vincé there?" he asked.

"No, he's on his way to you. He left yesterday; he should be there by now. Are you okay?" she asked.

"I'm fine," he told her. "Are you okay?"

"Yes, I know he's on an operation," she told him. "Because I've seen at least three of his agents here, so I'm fine. Just be careful and don't let him talk you into anything. And make sure he doesn't do anything stupid."

"Okay, Alex," James agreed. "I have to go, I'll call you later."

"Apparently, he's already on his way and may in fact be at my house already," James told Sean.

"What was that about?" Admiral Keene asked.

"Our friend Mr. Martin has important connections in another Service," George explained. "Sean just suggested a professional babysitter."

"When can I tell my boss about all this?" James asked.

"We'll take care of that," George assured him. "We'll have him come to the office on Monday and run through everything with him. Don't worry, we'll tell him that you were operating under strict instructions from Agent Booth not to discuss it with anyone."

"Is there anything else?" James asked.

"No, we have to go and try to work on the Pentagon contact," George told him. "I would be obliged if you and Sean would wait for a while before you leave. It might also be better if you took a different route back."

After the elephants, as Sean called them, had gone, James looked at Sean and asked him, "Now what?"

"We set up some monitoring around your plant," Sean replied. "We're also working the airports and rental car agencies to see if we can find Miller before he gets here."

"Do they know who the Pentagon contact is?" James asked.

"I believe they've narrowed it down to three possibles," Sean replied. "More than that, I either am unable to tell you or cannot tell you."

"What if the confederate comes after me?" James asked. "I need to know who I'm looking for."

"I'll talk to George," Sean promised. "But I can't guarantee that he'll let me tell you."

"That's just great," James complained. "Now I know what it feels like to be the goat staked out for the tiger."

"You'll be safe enough with Vincenzo," Sean assured him.

"You set that up, didn't you?" James accused him.

"Yes, after we talked, I stayed in touch and then when Geoffrey Miller surfaced, I got George to agree that he should come over here," Sean explained.

"I guessed something when my sister told me that he was already on his way here," James said.

"Do you have a gun apart from the rifle I saw you with?" Sean asked.

"No," James simply said.

"Okay, well, we can help there," Sean promised. With that, Tom opened his Blazer and took out several guns. "Here's a couple of 9mm pistols and two shotguns. Here's the ammunition for them. I figured that you'd give one of each to your brother-in-law, because I doubt that he's brought his own gun, and you'd take one, and maybe your wife would take one."

"Thanks, Sean," James said. "Hopefully, we won't have to use them."

"Let's hope so," Sean agreed. "If we hear anything before Wednesday, we'll let you know. If you see anything strange in your neighbourhood, let me know. We're going back through Rosette past the Grouse Creek Mountains to Montello, Nevada and then back to Salt Lake, so we'll be heading west; you pick which way you want to go home."

"Okay, Sean, I'll be in touch," James promised.

James waited until they had gone, and then he drove home. He took the most direct route that led him past the Golden Spike Memorial and then through Corinne to the freeway. When he arrived home, there was a strange car in the driveway. A little apprehensive that Geoffrey Miller might already be there, he cautiously opened the door and relaxed when he heard Katrina and Vincenzo laughing in the kitchen.

"*Suikerbossie*, I'm home," he called.

"James, look who's here again!" she said.

"*Ciao*, James," Vincenzo said. "We'd better tell Katrina what's going on."

James agreed and told Katrina where he had been and what might be happening in the next few days. She knew that something was wrong; James had told her some of what he had been doing and what he had found. She was concerned about their safety, but Vincenzo assured her that they had nothing to worry about. James then produced his arsenal. "Ah, the Beretta 9mm I see," said Vincenzo. "The American-made model, adequate but not up to the standard of the Italian original. These I like," he said, indicating the shotguns. "Mossburg, pump action, pistol grip with the short barrel, perfect gun for urban use around the house. You have ammunition?"

"Right here," James replied. He produced the boxes that Tom Goodsell had given him, and Vincenzo showed them both how to load each weapon. He suggested that they keep one of the shotguns in their bedroom and the other in the kitchen. He would take the handguns. As he explained to them, shooting anything under extreme stress was difficult at best, and their best chance of hitting anything was to use the shotguns. Vincenzo then asked if there was somewhere he could park his car that was nearby but not at their house. James called Simon, and he was happy to let them park it in his driveway.

For the next day, James stayed on edge, unable to really relax. Even with Vincenzo camped out in the basement and making his forays in the evenings, it was still difficult not to be concerned. James was amazed at Vincenzo. He watched him leave the house one day by the walk-out basement access, and then he disappeared into the scrub oak and was gone. Try as he might, he could not follow Vincenzo's progress through the scrub.

By Monday, it was almost a relief to go to the office and address pressing issues. After his regular morning meetings, he asked Isabella and Ruben Wheelwright to stay behind.

"I've asked you both to stay because Geoffrey Miller, the cousin of Michael Miller, will be coming to collect his personal belongings," he told them. "What you didn't know, Ruben, is that we don't believe that Michael Miller was, in fact, his name. We believe he assumed the identity of Michael and was here for the purposes of espionage."

That got their attention. "Spying for who?" Ruben asked.

"That I'm not sure of," James fibbed. "But we did find some documents that he had collected and stored on the site. They were here," he continued, pointing to a point on the plant map that was pinned to his wall. "I believe that Geoffrey, or whatever his real name is, is coming expecting to find those documents. That will mean that he will try and cross the fence and go to this location. I believe that Michael sent a coded message to Geoffrey telling him where the stuff was."

"Okay, so what do you want me to do, bust him when he crosses the fence?" Ruben asked.

"No, what I want is pictures of him, fingerprints and footprints," James explained. "Do you have any really good hunters and trackers in your security group, Ruben?"

"I do, but the best two on the site are Ed Clark from Production and Zan Wilson in Quality," Ruben admitted.

"Borrow them for the next couple of days, until Friday, unless I call them off sooner. Have them carefully walk the fence and look for evidence of anyone trying to gain access. Do you think they could find that even if the guy tries to erase his tracks?"

"Yes," Ruben stated quite confidently. "Ed was an Army Ranger, and Zan is just this great tracker; he guides in the Wind Rivers and has never failed to bring his clients to a successful hunt."

"Please keep in mind that he may already be in the area and watching the site, so don't make your patrols too obvious, try and stage them so that they look like routine perimeter checks," James cautioned Ruben.

"No problem, James," Ruben promised him. "We'll be careful. Of course, if there is anything obvious, we would have to investigate to stay legitimate."

"Agreed," James said. "For footprints, I was thinking of laying down tacky mats by the visitor conference room and having you pull them up and change them a couple of times," he suggested.

"I could do that," Ruben agreed. "Why don't you call me from the conference room and bawl me out about not changing them?"

"Okay, I'll do that," James agreed. "Isabella, use my office as a place to photograph him from. You'll have a clear shot of the parking lot and the approach to the main entrance"

"Why don't we just use the surveillance cameras that are by the front entrance?" Ruben asked.

"We need high-resolution stills, so let's use one of the plant cameras that takes good still pictures," James suggested.

"How will I know who it is if there is more than one visitor?" she asked.

"Start taking pictures of anyone in the parking lot or near the main entrance from about nine," he told her. "After he's been, we can cull out anyone else. I'll also leave it to you to have papers for him to sign and something to drink so that we can get his prints for the FBI."

"Oh, are they in on this?" Ruben asked.

"Yes, they're meeting with Robert Warner now," James told them.

At ten am sharp on Tuesday, Craig Robinson arrived with the two generals and their aides, one for Major General Williams and two for Brigadier General Howard. Both generals had been there before, so they knew the procedures about fire prevention, and General Howard surrendered a lighter at the reception desk. It would be returned to him when he left the facility. James had seen them arrive, so he met them at the door and escorted them to the conference room.

"Colonel Robinson tells us that he has approved many changes since the incident," General Williams stated. "We are here to review those changes and see for ourselves that this factory is run in a safe and effective manner."

"General," James started. "We have a review prepared that details those changes, and we have a plant visit organised that I believe will validate the changes."

"I'm not interested in presentations," General Williams said. "I think we'll learn much more if we just make an inspection of the plant."

"Where would you like to start?" James asked.

"What was on your prepared visit?" the general asked. James went through the proposed tour and indicated buildings on the plant layout map that he had.

"We can skip all that," the general said. "We want to go here and here and here to start with," he added, pointing to various different buildings at random.

"Very good," James agreed. "I must caution you that in this building, there is no activity; it is a storage building for live segments, and there is a stage one Auriga section there, but there is no activity."

"Just take us where I have indicated," the general said. "Then we'll pick some more buildings if I think it's needed. I don't want to go to any buildings that you've neatly laid out for a tour."

"Very well," James agreed. "We will need hard hats, legostats, lab coats, and I will need all pockets to be emptied before we proceed to this building," he added, pointing to the mixer building that General Williams had indicated. "My secretary has secure storage facilities where you may leave your personal items."

"Not necessary," General Williams countered. "Lieutenant Black, you will stay in this room and secure all personal items that we will leave."

"Very well," James said. "If you are ready, we may begin." He led the way out of the building to a parked van and asked them to board, and then he introduced Simon Wilmott.

"How far is it to each of these buildings?" General Howard asked.

"About two miles to the first, then another mile back to the second and a further mile in the opposite direction for the third," James replied.

"Why is it all spread out so much?" Lieutenant Hill, one of the aides that General Howard had brought, asked.

"We have rules that are known as the Quantity/Distance rules," James explained. "The rules dictate how far apart each building must be, depending on what is stored or located there. The idea is to reduce the amount of explosives in a given area."

"Well, let's get on with it then," General Williams said, clearly impatient to be off. "I've got better things to do with my day than stand around and listen to idle chatter."

Simon drove to the storage bunker and led the group to the door. James had his keys with him and opened the door. Inside the building, on a shipping cradle, was a finished Auriga Stage 1 segment ready to go.

"Why is this thing here and not delivered?" General Williams asked.

"General Howard's staff has asked us to store several segments here until such time as they wish to use them," James explained.

"Good enough, I suppose," the general muttered. "Let's get on then. To the next building," he commanded, pointing down the road.

James turned the lights back off and locked the doors, and they left. The next building was the mixer building, but first, they stopped at the control bunker.

"Why are we stopping here? I distinctly said that building," General Williams complained.

"We are here to check in at the control bunker so that they will know we are in the building and not activate any systems that might pose a risk to us," James explained. "And, I need to empty my pockets."

"You said risk, what risk?" Lieutenant Hill asked.

"The mix ingredients in this building include a nitroglycerine and nitrocellulose mix, HMX, ammonium perchlorate and aluminium powder. The high explosives should be treated with respect, and there is always an element of risk," James explained.

"Lieutenant Hill is new to my Command," General Howard explained. "This is his first trip to any rocket factory."

"Enough of that, let's be going," General Williams commanded. James caught the eye of General Howard, who just lightly shrugged and rolled his eyes very slightly. Simon drove them to the mix building and left the van parked with the keys in it. He led the way into the building and pointed out all the aspects of the mixer and the ingredient addition systems.

"Wasn't it a building like this that blew up?" General Williams wanted to know.

"Yes," James replied. "It was identical to this. The only changes we have made are to the measuring and addition systems to ensure that no items may break off or otherwise fall into the mix."

"So, what actually happened in that incident?" General Williams asked.

"We have demonstrated that the explosion was a result of blade-to-bowl contact involving a foreign object," James replied. "There are marks on the remnants of the blades that are consistent with a monkey wrench. What we are unable to state with certainty is how the wrench came to be introduced into the mixer and why there were so many people there at that time."

"You sound like a damned lawyer," General Williams complained. "I want to know what happened!"

314

"General, there are no data that allow us to definitively state that we know what happened. We have some data, and we have experimented and have achieved results consistent with the incident," James tried to explain.

"There you go with that data stuff again," the general complained. "That's the problem with all you engineers, you want everything to be black and white."

"General, we are satisfied that LST has resolved the issue and has identified the cause," General Howard interrupted. "The fact that we are not stating things as fact is because we do not know them to be fact, but we are satisfied that the data fits the circumstances and explains the incident."

"Damned engineers," General Williams said again. "Okay, let's go to the next building."

Simon drove them back to the bunker, where James collected his belongings and signed them out. The next stop was case winding, and they were able to watch Auriga Stage 1 and Stage 2 cases being wound. James sensed that General Williams was satisfied that all was well and that safety and cleanliness standards were more than met, but he also got the sense that he was disappointed, almost as if he had come wanting to find fault and complain. Well, he would be in for a big disappointment.

"Well, I'm done; do you want to see any more Howard?" General Williams asked, then continued without giving General Howard a chance to respond, "We've checked three buildings selected randomly and I'm satisfied with their condition. Colonel, you've done an excellent job here. I knew it was just a case of putting the right man in the job and you would soon lick these people into shape. I've got another meeting at Hill, so I think we're all done here."

A suggestion like that had really only one answer, and General Howard agreed. As they drove back to the office to collect their belongings, he told James that Lieutenant Hill would be staying on for a couple of days to learn more about the process. James told him that that would be fine and that they would give him a basic course in rocket-making. Craig told James that he would take the generals back to Hill Air Force Base and that he would be back at the plant the next day. He quietly apologised for his general and gave him the excuse that he had been passed over for his third star and was a little bitter.

After they had all gone, Simon came to see James.

"What the hell was all that about?" he asked.

"According to Craig, he's pissed because he can't put up his third star, so he's looking to make shit run downhill and in his mind we're lower than whale shit," James told him. "Maybe the guy is also just a jerk, and we're just seeing his natural personality, which probably explains why he didn't get his third star, even the Air Force uses common sense at times."

"Giving the credit to Robinson seems to me a bit of a stretch," Simon commented.

"A stretch?" James said. "It's downright bullshit, and he knows it. Craig Robinson is an okay guy, but he knows no more how to run a factory than he does fly to the moon."

"What shall I do with this Hill guy?" Simon asked.

"Run him through the safety class and make sure he understands that he has to pass to be let loose in the factory, then assign him to the ops foremen and let him see each process," James suggested.

"Okay, James," he agreed. "There are days when I'm glad it's you, not me, in that chair!"

Simon left, and then Heather came in to tell him that Robert Warner had called and wanted to talk to him. James called the Salt Lake City office. "James," Robert started. "I had an interesting meeting yesterday. It seems you've been holding out on me. I was more than a little annoyed until it was made clear to me what was going on. Do you need any help? Are you okay out there? I'm not sure I'm really happy with this cloak and dagger stuff."

"I'm sorry that I was not able to tell you immediately," James apologised. "I wasn't sure just what to do and who to go to. I'm not that keen about all this stuff myself and will be glad when they make their move and end it all."

"Well, just remember that if you need anything, call. I'm on the side of the good guys!" Robert assured him.

After lunch, Ruben Wheelwright came to see James. He had with him Zan Wilson and Ed Clark.

"James, it looks like your guy has already been," he said. "Tell him what you found, Zan."

"Well, Mr Martin, Ed and I did a fence walk, and there was evidence of an entry above the mixers. We investigated and found evidence that someone had penetrated the fence, then worked their way down to this point," Zan said. He was indicating a point on the plant map that was almost exactly where James had found the cases. "He had been pretty clever about backtracking and removing signs, but I followed him all the way in and back to the fence, then to a vehicle. The vehicle had been parked off the jeep trail that is near there. I would judge that he had been here on Saturday and had made his entry with the sun at his back, which would have confused the cameras. He's not the first guy to have been up there. Someone was there a few months ago; the same vehicle tracks show up a couple of times, but he did not penetrate the fence. Looking at the vehicle tracks, wheelbase and track where our recent visitor turned around, I would say that our man was driving a Ford Bronco or Ranger; the guy before used a longer wheelbase, larger pickup."

"We reviewed the footage from the security cameras, and as Zan said, right when the sun comes over that mountain, you can't see anything," Ruben confirmed.

"Thanks," James told them. "How do you know it was Saturday, Zan?"

"There were other tracks that crossed his," he explained. "After John Doe had been, there were three deer, then another two, then a bobcat, and I saw him yesterday, and finally the first three deer again. One of them has a misshapen hoof, so is easy to track. Judging by the age of the deer sign, he was definitely here on Saturday."

"Could you get a usable footprint cast?" James asked.

"We got one," Zan told him. "I followed the Bronco down the hill, and he stopped and took a quick trip into the brush, probably for a pee by the look of it, but he didn't do such a good job of erasing his tracks. I'll have the cast to you tomorrow when I've cleaned it up a little."

"That's great," James told them. "Anything else?"

"Yes, there are three pairs of guys set up as observers or something on different peaks around the plant," Ed said. "Unfortunately for them, the area above the mixers is dead ground from their stands."

"I knew that there would be observers," James told them. "They're with the FBI, but it's a shame that they wouldn't be able to see anything and that they probably were placed too late to see our guy."

"Should we keep checking on that area?" Ruben asked.

"Please," James asked. "Until I let you know that it's no longer necessary, and I know I can rely on you not to repeat any of this to anyone."

"It looks like Charlie and Bernard were right after all," Ed said. "They figured that that guy Michael Miller was a spy, and everything you're asking tells me you do too."

"It looks like it to me," James admitted. "But, I'll leave it to the FBI to get all the evidence and decide whether he was or not."

"You might want these then for the FBI," Ed said. He gave James the pictures of Roberta Miller that Cody had shown him before.

"Thanks, Ed," James said.

"Okay, we'll get back to it then," Ruben promise. "We're going to fix the cameras so that sunrises don't blind them, and I'll have a look at sunsets as well. Okay, guys, let's leave Mr Martin to his pile of paper here." Ruben indicated a pile of papers that had built up on James's desk and which now required attention. It would keep James busy until almost six, by which time he was ready to call it a day and go home.

James made a short detour on his way home and called and gave Sean the news that someone, probably Geoffrey, had already been on the site before he had placed his surveillance teams and had checked the location where the cases had been found. He told him that he had used a Ford Bronco or Ranger, or something very close. He also told Sean that his three teams had been spotted by his people. That did not please Sean at all. For his part, Sean told James that Geoffrey Miller had checked in on Friday at one of the ski resorts in Aspen, but that he seemed to have dropped out of sight. James supposed that that meant that the FBI surveillance team had lost him; that was hardly happy news. Closer to home, James stopped at the Marriott in Ogden and dropped off the directions to the plant that he had promised to leave for

Geoffrey. He asked at the desk if Geoffrey had checked in and was told that they had heard from him and that he expected to be there within the hour.

James arrived home and found Katrina in the kitchen. She was busy making dinner and was happy to see him.

"Where's Vincenzo?" he asked.

"Behind you," she said.

"Oh, hi Vincenzo, I didn't see you," he said.

"You were not supposed to," Vincenzo said. "I was just checking to see that you were alone and that no one followed you up here."

"So, is everything okay?" James asked.

"Everything is good," Vincenzo told him. "There have been no cars in this area today, except for the people next door and those who live at the end of the cul-de-sac."

"How was your day?" Katrina asked.

"Oh, frustrating," James told her. "The one Air Force general that came was a real *does*, but fortunately did not stay long."

"I'm sorry," she told him. "Fancy a beer?"

"Absolutely," he said. "My people also found that someone has been onto the site, they told me on Saturday."

"So, Mr. Miller is already here," Vincenzo commented. "It would make sense. I would be early to see how the place was and what else I could learn."

"When's he coming tomorrow?" Katrina asked.

"We set an appointment at ten," James replied. "Booth and his people are supposed to keep him under surveillance afterwards, but it would be hard to do that and not be noticed. There's no traffic on our road except to the plant, and once he gets to the freeway, they'd have to be pretty clever to pick him up without being seen. Traffic isn't exactly heavy on that road. I'm assuming they'll have an observer on the hills and have him radio someone waiting by the Howell off-ramp. That would mean six miles, so say six minutes. He could really screw them up and go north so that anyone coming south from the Howell off-ramp would have to do a one-eighty at our off-ramp, and that may be a little obvious. Still, it's Booth's problem and I'm sure he's thought it all out."

Geoffrey Miller

James drove to the plant the next day and laid out his plan of action. He placed the boxes of papers and other personal items on the table in the conference room. Isabella had produced an inventory of all the items with a signature block for Geoffrey Miller to acknowledge receipt. Where they had removed items, she noted that with a short explanation for the removal. James was willing to bet that there were no fingerprints on the duplicate copies of the lists that she had lain out; he had seen her earlier with some latex gloves, so he guessed that she had loaded the printer and removed the documents while gloved. He noted that Ruben had placed tacky mats at the entrance to the conference room, and so that they would not attract attention, had placed them by all the doors visible in the building. There were cups and saucers and glasses on a tray, and he presumed that coffee would be brought just before ten and, perhaps, water and or soft drinks. As far as he could tell, they had staged everything as well as they could.

After the regular morning meetings, Commander Reinsch came to see him to ask about progress on the new mixer. Delivery of the new mixer had been promised for March 25th, but Baker Perkins had done the impossible, and the mixer was actually on its way. The truck had left the factory that morning and was expected in Utah by the following Monday. They would be ready for it and have a crane ready to place the mixer and then re-install the roof of the building. Simon was going to organise a crew to remove the roof over the weekend so that they could easily drop it in. All James hoped was that they did not get a late-season snowstorm, which would delay everything.

"So, what else have you got on today?" Commander Reinsch asked. "I saw you carrying stuff into the conference room."

"Geoffrey Miller, the cousin of Michael Miller, one of the guys killed in the incident last year, is stopping by today to collect his personal things," he told her. "I was making sure that we had everything that we could give him."

"What can't you give him?" she asked.

"There were some process sheets that we had to pull out," he told her. "They are company propriety and should not be taken out of the plant. Other than that, everything we found in his desk and his locker we'll give him, including the hard hat and coveralls, presuming he wants them. He may just tell us to keep them; what use could he have for them?"

"When's he due here?" she asked.

"He'll be here at ten, I don't suppose it'll take more than an hour at the most," he replied. "You're dressed up today, what's the occasion?"

"I have to go to a meeting later," she told him. "And I was told that it was dress blues, no khaki and no fatigues for anyone."

"Did you hear about our visit yesterday?" he asked.

"It sounded like just the kind of visit I would want to avoid," she laughed. "I'm no great fan of much of the Air Force, but Williams sounds as if he's difficult."

"It was interesting," he told her. "I think he thought he could catch us napping if he randomly picked buildings that he wanted to go to."

"He probably would have been right six months ago," she said. "I think you've done a good job here."

"I've not really done anything, except point the right people in the right direction and let them loose," he said. "Anyone could have done the same."

"Perhaps," she disagreed. "But my reports still show that you have the credit for the changes."

"Thank you for that," he said. "But, it's not necessary."

"What's with the tacky mats?" she asked.

"We've been getting odd stuff tracked in," he explained. "We haven't found any live material yet, but as a precaution, I've decided that we'll now use mats in this building and then add them to the burn pit when they lose their tackiness."

"Good idea," she agreed. "It'll certainly help keep the offices cleaner."

"My only concern is how they will function when it's wet or snows out," he commented. "I'm pretty sure that the adhesive was not formulated to work wet."

"What if you installed some drying mats before the tacky mats?" she suggested. "You'd have to burn them as well, but that might work."

"Good idea, I'll talk to John Edwards about it," he replied. He appreciated her input. She was likely to know what would give his customers a good impression.

"Well, I'll leave you to your stack of paper," she said. "If you could get some pictures of the new mixer being installed, they would go down well at the next briefing at the Pentagon."

"I'll arrange that," he promised.

*   *   *

"Sean, this is Frank. Subject has left hotel and is proceeding north on 15 in a maroon Mercury Sable with Utah plates," an agent reported in.

"Fine, Frank, pick him up as far as Brigham City, then break off," Sean instructed. "Let us know when you're near Brigham."

"Sean, this is John. Subject checked out and is not coming back. I've been over the room, but nothing of interest yet," the next agent reported.

"Okay, John, keep looking," Sean instructed. There was a wait until Frank called in again to say that they were nearing the Brigham City exit and that he was pulling off he also told them that the car they were following was the only maroon Mercury Sable he had seen all morning, so should be easy to pick up..

"Okay, Frank, make your car switch and rejoin the freeway," Sean instructed. "Heather, pick him up now and follow to the 15/84 split, take off north on 15."

"Roger that," Heather acknowledged. "I have him," she reported. The next report was to say that they were nearing the split of the freeways and that Heather was breaking off to take the I-15 north, away from Geoffrey Miller.

"Bill, you should have him now, follow to the plant exit and make a U-turn at the Howell exit," Sean instructed. "Wait at the Howell exit until we give you the word that he's left the plant."

"Roger that, Sean, you need to know that he's slowed down and I'll have to pass and leave him," Bill reported.

"Why's he slowed down?" Sean asked Tom Goodsell.

"He's early," Tom told him. "At his current speed, he'll be at the plant fifteen minutes early."

"Frank, how far back are you?" Sean asked.

"I have him in sight," Frank reported. "But I can drop in behind him; I borrowed a UHP cruiser, so can act like I'm wondering why the heck he's dogging it on this stretch of freeway."

"Okay, Frank, if he slows down even more, pull him over and ask him what the problem is," Sean instructed.

"No need, Sean," Frank reported. "As soon as I dropped in behind him, he sped up like a good boy. He should be at the plant exit in five."

"Where did Frank manage to borrow a Highway Patrol cruiser?" Sean asked Tom.

"Who knows," Tom said, trying to project an air of ignorance. "But, great idea, the UHP guys are known to cruise this stretch of highway, and anyone doing anything out of the ordinary would attract their attention."

"Sean, he's left the highway at the plant exit," Frank reported. "I'm going to go to the Howell exit, U-turn and then come back south to the 15/84 split."

"Okay, Frank, I have him," Sean told him. "He's pulled off and is just waiting in his car now, probably killing time." Sean could see him because he was perched on one of the hills above the road to the plant in a stand selected by Tom Goodsell. Tom had gotten involved when James had reported to Sean that his people had picked out the teams that had been placed earlier. Now they were much better hidden, and Tom was confident that they would not be spotted.

"Okay, people, he's moving again up the plant road to the gate," Sean informed them all. "Stand by; I'll let you know when he leaves."

*   *   *

In James's office, Isabella stood poised with her camera. There had been one other visitor that morning, but they knew him; he was the representative of the crane company from which they were going to rent a crane for the mixer placement. He was currently on site with Simon, checking out the area around the mixer building to work out where to put the crane and how large a crane they would actually need. James knew from his days at James and Brown. He had worked for them when he had first come to the United States, and among their product line were cranes. So, he knew that history was replete with circumstances where a crane had been selected without allowing for the boom angle and the fact that the ability to lift safely was largely governed by the boom angle.

Isabella saw the maroon Mercury Sable pull up, and she started taking photographs. She noticed as she was taking them that Commander Reinsch was leaving the plant and watched her pass their visitor on the way to her car. Isabella ignored her and focused on their visitor, or the man she presumed was their visitor. She lost him from view as he entered by the front door to the visitor's lobby. A minute or two later, James received a telephone call to tell him that Mr. Geoffrey Miller had arrived. He told the guard that he would be down directly to collect him and asked Isabella to get coffee and tea ready. James went downstairs and greeted their visitor.

"Mr Miller, welcome to Utah," he said. "I'm James Martin, the general manager here. "I'm so sorry we have to meet under these circumstances."

"Please, call me Geoffrey. Thank you for taking the time to see me," was the reply.

"How was the drive?" James asked.

"Easy enough," Geoffrey replied. "Your directions were spot on."

"Please come this way," James invited. He led Geoffrey to the conference room and showed him in. "Excuse me a minute," he asked Geoffrey. "I need to quickly call someone."

"Ruben, this is James. I thought we were going to replace the tacky mats in the main building more often. Could you see to that?" he said, making the call that he and Ruben had agreed to before.

"I'm sorry," he apologised to Geoffrey. "We are trying to keep this building clean, and because we are spread out so, it is sometimes a challenge because people track all kinds of mud, soil and other materials in on their boots and shoes."

"No, please carry on," Geoffrey asked. "I don't want to be any bother."

"It is no bother," James assured him.

"You're not an American?" Geoffrey asked.

"I'm a citizen," James told him. "But, I grew up in England and only moved to the US in the mid-seventies."

324

"You've not totally lost your accent," Geoffrey commented.

They were interrupted by Isabella, who came in with a tray with coffee and hot water for tea. James introduced her and then offered Geoffrey coffee or tea.

"Coffee, I think," Geoffrey said. "I do not intend any slurs, but my experience with tea in America has not been good."

"I've also heard that about the coffee, too," James said. "Isabella is a coffee connoisseur and keeps us on the straight and narrow, no old socks coffee here."

"Is this all Michael's belongings? I rather thought that there might be more than this?" Geoffrey asked, pointing at the boxes on the table.

"That's most of what we found in his desk and his locker," James explained. "There were some papers that relate to the manufacturing process that I'm sure you will understand we cannot let outside the company."

"Of course," Geoffrey agreed.

"You have not heard from Roberta Miller?" James asked.

"Not a dicky bird," Geoffrey said. "I've absolutely no idea where she has gone."

"In that case, we would be happy to turn these belongings over to you," James confirmed. "As a formality, do you have some identification on you that we can refer to so that in case she does appear in the future, we can show that we made a good faith effort to deliver his things to a family member?"

"Of course, a passport do?" Geoffrey replied, proffering his passport.

James took the passport and handed it to Isabella, who briefly looked at it and then handed it back. She made some notes on her pad and then filled in a line on the forms she had printed up earlier. She noted on the forms the passport number and name.

"How is it that you're on a British Passport and yet Michael was an American?" James asked.

"His father moved over here right after the War," Geoffrey explained. "He became a citizen, and Michael was born here."

James then explained that the forms included an inventory of all the documents and belongings they had found and that they would turn them over to him upon receipt of a signature. Geoffrey quickly looked through the list and then poked through the boxes. He took out the hard hat and coveralls and commented to James that they would take up too much room in his luggage. Isabella struck through those items on the list, then Geoffrey signed on the dotted line.

"Would it be possible to see the place where Michael died?" Geoffrey asked.

"Of course," James agreed. He had, in fact, anticipated this request and had made arrangements. "I'm afraid that there's not much to see," he continued. "The explosion destroyed the building, and we finished the job and are now in the process of putting up a new building."

"If it's possible, I would just like to see the area?" Geoffrey asked.

"Of course, please come with me," James offered. He led the way out of the building to a truck, and they drove out to the construction site. James handed Geoffrey a hard hat and led him to the building.

"This is what the building would have looked like," he said. "Except where that big empty space is, there would have been a mixer. We are almost ready to install the replacement mixer; it will be here early next week, so we're planning where the crane should be sited."

"Fascinating," Geoffrey said. "I never imagined that Michael would work in such a place. I thought he was permanently tied to Pittsburgh."

"Well, I suppose we go where employment takes us," James said. Outside the building, they stood just looking around. It was quite difficult to see much of the rest of the plant because of the hills and valleys, and the fact that the mixers were sited in little canyons to isolate them from the rest of the plant. Geoffrey looked all around at the various hills surrounding them, almost as if he were looking for something. Finally, he seemed to be satisfied and returned to the truck.

"Well, thank you for bringing me out here," Geoffrey said. "I really appreciate you taking the time to see me, and you've been more than kind."

"I'm just sorry that you had to come out here under these circumstances," James said. "I'm also sorry that we can't tell you what actually happened. Perhaps one day we will understand."

"The mixer blew up, right?" Geoffrey asked.

"Yes, we've established that and the fact that it was a foreign object in the mixer," James reported. "What we cannot explain is how the object got in there and why all the people were there."

"As you say, perhaps one day," Geoffrey agreed. "Well, I've taken up far too much of your time."

"I'll drive you back to the office, and you can collect Michael's belongings," James said.

Back at the office, James led Geoffrey back to the conference room where Isabella was waiting for them. Geoffrey walked over to the table and picked up one of the boxes. "If you could just help me lug this stuff out to the car, I'll get out of your way," Geoffrey promised. "I'm going to try and make it back to Aspen tonight."

"That's a long drive," James cautioned. "Drive carefully and watch out for the Highway Patrol, they're generous, but not that generous. If they see anything unusual, they will investigate. In the winter, that's a good thing out here because a breakdown could be serious if it's really cold. Watch out particularly near Nephi, there's one chap there who lurks on the outskirts of the town waiting for unwary people."

"I noticed that about the Highway Patrol chaps," Geoffrey said. "I was getting here early and slowed down on the motorway, and one pulled in behind me."

"He was probably wondering just what it was you were looking at out here. There's not a lot to see," James said. "Or he thought you had car trouble and was going to call in help."

"Anyway, when I resumed a more normal speed, he left me, even waved to me," Geoffrey said. "Oh, and thanks for the warning about Nephi."

"Let's get this stuff out to your car then," James suggested. He picked up the second box, and Geoffrey balanced the rolled-up posters on his box. Isabella held the doors for them, and Geoffrey led the way out to his car.

After Geoffrey had gone, Ruben picked up the tacky mats again and then got James and Isabella to walk across new ones. That done, he called in Zan, who looked at them all and told them that it was definitely Geoffrey Miller who had been on the plant site the last weekend. His footprints were distinctive enough for Zan to categorically state that they were a match. Isabella then carefully removed the cups and the documents and bagged them for the FBI to dust for fingerprints. She commented to James that Geoffrey had

327

travelled a fair bit. Her quick flick through his passport had shown her stamps and visas for China, Brazil, Jordan, France, Germany, South Africa and several other countries. James was amazed that she gathered so much with such a quick review, but then she surprised him even more by writing out for him all the particulars from Geoffrey's passport. She then left, telling James that she was going to get the pictures she had taken developed.

* * *

Sean watched from his vantage point as Geoffrey Miller drove back down the access to the freeway. He called Bill waiting at the Howell exit and told him to start south. Sean then watched Geoffrey cross the freeway to pick up the southbound on ramp and was then horrified to see him make a U-turn, re-cross the freeway and take the northbound on ramp. He frantically called Bill, but it was too late; Bill was already well on his way.

"Bill, Sean, subject has switched on us and is headed north. Can you make a turn without being seen?" he asked.

"Not a chance, Sean, it's open here and the access road goes over the freeway, so I'd stand out like a butte on a plain," Bill replied.

"Okay, plan B, go south to the next exit and turn and see if you can catch him," Sean instructed. "We'll try and re-acquire him from here."

Sean and Tom hurried down to their car and bumped their way down the jeep trail to the frontage road and then the on-ramp. Sean was cursing himself for a fool. He had been so confident that Geoffrey would go south to get back to Salt Lake City that he had dismissed the obvious alternative that Geoffrey would go north, perhaps to Boise, perhaps all the way to Canada. He sped up the freeway, confident that he would soon catch up with the maroon Mercury. He was fifty-plus miles into Idaho at the intersection of the I-84 and the I-86 when he finally admitted that they had lost him. He could have exited at any of the ten off-ramps they had passed, but Sean was placing his money on the first two or three. He had been travelling fast enough that he should have caught up with him long before they reached the intersection. The next question was, did he go north or south at the exits? North would take him into Idaho, south back into Utah and then perhaps Nevada.

"Sean, do you think that our subject just chose to change direction on a whim, or was it part of a plan?" Tom asked.

"What?" Sean asked.

"A plan, if he was out here on Saturday, he would have had time to scout the area," Tom suggested. "That to me suggests that he has a plan and is now following it. I doubt that he saw any of our tails; he's just executing his plan."

"You could be right," Sean agreed. "What did James tell us about his Saturday visit? He used a Bronco or something similar, now he's using a Sable, where's the Bronco?"

"I think we should look for the Sable," Tom suggested. "He's probably made or going to make a car switch, so if we find the Sable, maybe someone saw him make the switch."

"If he stashed the Bronco, that suggests a confederate," Sean thought. "I doubt that he stashed it somewhere and then hitched it back to Ogden or wherever he was holed up."

"Maybe we should check out that temple that Michael Miller used to go to," Tom suggested.

"Good idea," Sean agreed. He then radioed in and asked for help from the state and local police forces of Utah and Idaho in finding the Mercury Sable. They at least had the make, model, number and colour of that vehicle. Of the Bronco, or whatever it might turn out to be, they had no particulars whatsoever.

Three hours later, Sean got a call from the Idaho State Police. They had found the Sable in Malad City, parked under some trees in a vacant lot off 4th West Street. Some teenagers had seen a man pull up in the Sable and leave in a blue Bronco. So Geoffrey had gone north, probably from the Howell exit, to get to Malad City. The question now was: where had he gone from Malad City? The I-15 freeway was right there, and he could have taken it south to Salt Lake City or north to Pocatello and thence Butte, Great Falls and Canada, or he could have ignored the freeway altogether and taken a different route. For now, Sean had to content himself with the fact that they had the Sable, which they would go through with a fine-toothed comb. He detailed Frank and Heather to Malad City to collect the car, and they made arrangements with a recovery firm in Tremonton for a flatbed truck on which to transport the car back to Salt Lake City. Sean also issued a travel notice to all airports and border crossings in Montana, Idaho and Washington in case Geoffrey tried to leave. He was not sanguine about the chances of actually apprehending him at the border. There were a number of small border crossings where he could slip into Canada. But, he reminded himself, Geoffrey had a plan and was probably still following the plan, so what was the next move?

*　　　*　　　*

James called it a day early and went home. Geoffrey Miller had been interesting, and James was still trying to place where he was from. His accent was near perfect, but not quite. There were tiny intonations that did not belong even to any of the regional accents in England, and certainly not in Scotland, Wales or Ireland. Katrina was happy to see James home and asked him about his day.

"I think it's out of our hands now," he said. "The FBI has taken over, and they were going to tail him and pick him up at their leisure."

"Do not leap to conclusions," Vincenzo warned. "Operations have been known to go wrong."

"What can go wrong?" James asked. "There's one way in and out of the plant, and they were stationed to cover that road. They would have to seriously err to lose him out there."

"I will check the area," Vincenzo stated. He disappeared, and Katrina said, "James, I love Vincenzo, but all this skulking around makes me nervous. He just appears and disappears, and I don't know where he is half the time."

"Well, it should all be over soon," James said again. "I should imagine by now that the FBI has picked up their man and is interrogating him as we speak."

"I hope you're right," she said. "You look like you could do with a break."

"I never thought when I signed on with LST that there would be anything like this," he said. "It's not quite what I expected. I was thinking of a job where we looked into the incident, worked out what happened, fixed things and went back to production. This is more like a novel. I told the FBI people that I met that it was beginning to sound like a second-rate novel, and I still think that."

"Well, sometimes life is stranger than fiction," she reminded him.

"True, but I never thought that my life would have anything in it that even hinted at fiction," he laughed. "Maybe one day I'll write my memoirs, at least now I'll have something to write about."

"I don't know," she commented. "We've had a fairly interesting life, so far. Perhaps someone might be interested."

Vincenzo came back and reported that the neighbourhood was quiet. There were no parked cars in odd places; his telltales that he had left in odd places were undisturbed, and the small children from down the street, Vincenzo's Baker Street Irregulars, reported nothing new. James was grateful to him. He knew that his brother-in-law was with the Italian authorities, but he had never really seen him in action. He was glad that he was an ally and not an adversary. Katrina told them both that dinner would soon be ready and asked if either of them wanted anything to drink. Vincenzo declined, but James took a large glass of wine; he felt he needed it.

*   *   *

Isabella collected her photographs from the developer and took them back to her house. She laid them out on a table and started to look through them carefully. The early ones that were taken before Geoffrey Miller arrived, she discarded and stacked into a small pile. The others she grouped sequentially. Colleen arrived home and came in, saw that she was busy with pictures and asked her what she had.

"These are pictures I took at the plant today," she explained.

"Who is the guy?" Colleen asked.

"Geoffrey Miller, supposed cousin of Michael Miller, the guy who died in the incident last year," Isabella explained.

"Quite a good-looking guy," Colleen commented. "Who's the babe in the uniform? Why did you say supposed cousin?"

331

"That's Commander Reinsch," Isabella told her. "She's with the Navy, and she's been out at the plant for a while."

"She's got a figure to die for," Colleen remarked. "Can't see her face, what does she look like?"

"Very attractive," Isabella reported. "She turns heads. That's the problem I'm having."

"What do you mean, you fancy her?" Colleen asked.

"No, look at this guy," Isabella told her. "Look at this sequence of pictures. He walks right by her. She's good-looking, as you say, got a figure to die for, and what does he do? Nothing!"

"Maybe he's just not into women?" Colleen suggested.

"Not a chance, he was busy undressing me in his mind when we had our meeting," Isabella disagreed.

"So, what's the explanation?" Colleen asked.

"They know each other but don't want anyone else to know," Isabella announced. "Look how they both studiously ignore each other. We can't see her face, but there is no head turn, nothing. Look at his face, not even a sideways glance with his eyes. He walks past her as if she isn't there."

"You're right," Colleen agreed. "I've never walked past a guy, but he didn't check me out, even if he did the Italian thing and waited until I'd gone by and then checked out my butt. So what does this mean?"

"We were expecting this Geoffrey Miller today. James has been working with the FBI because the FBI thinks he's a spy," Isabella explained. "What they really wanted to know is, who is his contact in the Pentagon? It looks like we're looking at his contact."

"Spies, do you think so?" Colleen asked. "Does that have anything to do with you saying supposed cousin earlier?"

"Yes, we don't think Michael Miller was Michael Miller if you see what I mean," Isabella said.

"I do, it explains so much," Colleen said. "He changed in Pittsburgh, but perhaps he really didn't change; it's not him at all."

"Right," Isabella agreed. "We got a phone call one day looking for a Samuel Levin. James did not say much, but I know he was thinking that there was something wrong. For today's visit, he had us collect prints, both fingerprints and footprints, and he wanted me to take pictures of this guy at the plant."

"So what do we do now?" Colleen asked.

"I think we'd better take this to James and show him and see if he has the same conclusion," Isabella said. "Come on, Colleen, we need to hurry."

*   *   *

Partway through their dinner, Vincenzo suddenly got up, gathered his plate, utensils and glass and disappeared. James heard a car pull up near their house, then a knock at the door. He opened it and was surprised to see Commander Reinsch.

"Commander, come in. What brings you out here?" he asked.

"Thanks, James, I'm sorry to bother you, but the admiral has given me some odd instructions," she said.

"Come in, come in," James repeated. "Can I get you a glass of wine or something?"

"Wine would be nice, thanks," she agreed. "Oh, I'm sorry, I didn't realise that you were in the middle of dinner."

"Katrina, this is Commander Josephine Reinsch," James introduced her. "My wife, Katrina. So, what may I do for you?"

"As I said, the admiral gave me some odd instructions. He said that you had come across some documents relating to our program and that you were holding them," she explained. "He has instructed me to collect them and transport them back to Washington."

"Well, I don't have anything here," James told her. "I try not to bring anything home that I don't have to."

"So, are they at the plant then?" she asked.

"Yes," he lied. "I have them stored in a safe place at the plant and can get them for tomorrow if you wish."

"I need to get them today," she insisted. "I was given very specific orders."

"I understand," James said. "But I'm having difficulty understanding why tomorrow would not be soon enough. The documents are not going anywhere, and only I know where they are deposited."

"I'm afraid I must insist, James," she said. "My job is on the line here."

"Commander, the admiral will understand when you explain that the documents are an hour's drive away and I've had too much wine to start driving out there tonight," James pushed back.

"If you can't drive out there, I'll do the driving and then you can show me where they are," she suggested.

"I don't think that's a good idea," James told her.

"Look, either you let me drive you out there and show me where they are, or tell me where to find them, and I'll do the job myself," she said.

"I'm sorry," James said. "I can't do that."

"Well, I'm sorry too," she said. She pulled a gun from her pocket and pointed it at Katrina. "Either you tell me where the stuff is, or I shoot her."

James was at the point of replying when there was a knock at the door. It was a very insistent knock, and Commander Reinsch motioned for James to answer it. He opened the door, and Isabella and Colleen rushed past him into the house.

"James," Isabella said. "I know who the contact is. It's Commander Reinsch. Look at these pictures; you'll see what I mean." Isabella then looked at James and Katrina and realised that all was not well. Commander Reinsch pushed the door shut and waved her gun at the two newcomers, motioning them to join James and Katrina.

"Well, Ms da Silva, aren't we the clever girl, not just a pretty face after all, how did you work that out?" she asked Isabella.

"When Geoffrey Miller came to the plant and walked past you, there was no looking, no backward glances, nothing, you tried too hard not to know each other," Isabella explained, looking to buy time.

"I told Geoffrey that he should have given me at least one lewd glance," Commander Reinsch complained. "But, men, who can rely on them? Now I'll count to three, James, and if you don't agree to come with me, I'll have to blow a hole in that pretty wife of yours, one, two."

Her count was interrupted by a gunshot that sounded like an explosion in the confines of the house. James looked at Katrina in concern, but she was fine and was in fact staring at Commander Reinsch. She was gasping and looking at her arm. She dropped her gun from her now useless hand, and it went off, sending a bullet through the front door.

Then Vincenzo strode up and quickly hit her twice, knocking her out cold.

"You had better call Sean," he told James. "Tell him to come and collect her and Geoffrey Miller, and he'd better get an ambulance as well. Also, tell him to alert the local police before people start calling in."

"Okay," James agreed. "Shouldn't we bind up that arm?"

"I'll do that," Vincenzo told him. "You just make the call."

James called Sean Booth and told him that Commander Reinsch had been identified as the confederate of Geoffrey Miller and that she was at his house with a gunshot wound to the arm. He also told him that Geoffrey Miller had been detained. How Vincenzo had managed that and where exactly Geoffrey Miller was, James did not know, but he was sure that by the time Sean arrived, things would be clear. Sean went into action and called the local police dispatch, telling them that an FBI operation had just gone down and that there was a casualty. The dispatcher called an ambulance, and the police sent a couple of cars.

For the next hour or so, it was chaos at the house. First, Vincenzo handed out large quantities of spirits to everyone in an effort to calm frazzled nerves. Being threatened by a woman with a gun was not an experience any of them wanted to go through again; the first time was stressful enough. Then the local police arrived, followed shortly afterwards by the ambulance. While the paramedics were treating Commander Reinsch, Sean arrived with several agents, and he took charge. The local police then set up barriers to keep casual onlookers away.

Vincenzo disappeared for five minutes, then came back with the bound and gagged body of Geoffrey Miller. Duct tape does wonders when liberally used, and Vincenzo had not been shy to use it. Sean asked Tom Goodsell to first handcuff Geoffrey Miller and then remove the duct tape, which was fine until it came to the gag, and Geoffrey actually cried out in pain when Tom ripped it off.

"You can't hold me," Geoffrey protested. "I'm a British Citizen, what right do you have to treat me like this?"

"Save it," Sean told him. "Frank, get him out of here."

335

"But, I have rights," Geoffrey protested. Frank was in no mood to listen to protests. He had been part of the wild goose chase running around northern Utah and southern Idaho looking for Geoffrey, and was still upset. He hauled Geoffrey out and drove off to Salt Lake City. The next to go was the now conscious Commander Reinsch, who was taken out by the ambulance crew and transported to a hospital in Salt Lake City under the watchful eye of Heather, one of the other agents who had been involved in the pursuit.

When the ambulance crew had departed, Sean then turned to James and asked, "Perhaps you should tell me who everyone is?"

"My wife Katrina," James told him, indicating Katrina. Then he motioned to the others, "Isabella da Silva, my Human Resources Manager and Colleen Richards, researcher for the Salt Lake City Star."

"Thank you, we'll get statements later. How did you know it was Commander Reinsch?" Sean asked.

"I didn't until she came to me with some story that the admiral had given her orders to collect the materials," James replied. "As we both know, the admiral knows very well that you guys have all the stuff, so she and or Geoffrey Miller must have assumed that I had found it and stashed it somewhere. She was about to start shooting when Isabella and Colleen arrived. Isabella had figured out it was her from the pictures she took at the plant."

"How do you mean?" Sean asked. Isabella laid her pictures out on a table and went through her explanation again. James noticed both Sean and Vincenzo nodding; they obviously agreed with her. "Unfortunately, that would never hold up in a court of law," Sean bemoaned. "But, I agree they know each other and were at pains to disguise the fact."

"How did you lose Geoffrey Miller after he left the plant?" James asked.

"He crossed the freeway as if he was going south, then did a one-eighty and came back over to go north," Seam explained. "We were caught on the wrong foot. We figure he got off the eighty-four at the Howell exit and went north to Malad City. He switched cars there, and we weren't able to catch up with him."

"I told you, James, that operations often do not proceed as planned," Vincenzo reminded him. "No matter how much you plan, there is always something."

"How did you know we were going to have visitors?" James asked him.

"I saw the car coming near, then they turned off the lights and parked down the road. Why, if someone was coming here, wouldn't they drive into the driveway as Isabella did?" Vincenzo explained.

"So, how did you get Geoffrey Miller?" Sean asked.

"I paid my Baker Street Irregulars to throw snowballs at the car," Vincenzo said. "While they were doing that, I approached from the blind quarter and took him by surprise."

"Baker Street Irregulars?" Tom Goodsell asked.

"Vincenzo is a fan of Sherlock Holmes," James explained. "In the books, Holmes often uses children to gather information for him."

"So, what about Commander Reinsch?" Sean asked.

"After I had suitably restrained Geoffrey Miller, I saw Isabella arrive and took advantage of the distraction that she created to gain entry to the house again. I was in time to see the commander threaten to shoot Katrina, so I disabled her," Vincenzo explained.

"One shot to the arm, that's pretty good shooting," Sean remarked.

"Not really," Vincenzo said. "I was less than five meters away; it was an easy shot."

"You'd better let me have that gun," Sean said. "If this ever gets to court, that might get messy."

"What do you mean, ever gets to court?" Colleen asked. "I thought that you'd all decided that they were both spies, aren't you going to prosecute?"

"That's not for me to decide," Sean told them. "That decision would be for the Federal Prosecutors, and we may do a deal with her to get the rest of the network, who knows? She may just confess and plead guilty, in which case no trial, no evidence hearing and all the other messy aspects of an espionage case."

"So, if she goes free, what's to stop her coming back here and taking revenge?" Katrina asked. "I don't want some mad woman running around pointing guns at me."

"A deal wouldn't be that simple," Sean explained. "She'll do time for sure, the question will be, how much and where? The admiral is going to be royally pissed when he discovers that his fair-haired girl was the leak."

"Why did she do it?" Katrina asked.

337

"That we don't know," Sean admitted. "We'll have to do some digging into finances and all the usual things to try and work out why, or she may just tell us. It might be conviction, it might be money, it might be love. My bet, for what it's worth, love in this case."

"You had said before that the Pentagon had some suspects," James reminded him. "Was she on that list?"

"There's the problem, I can't tell you that," Sean apologised. That to James meant that she was not on the list and that the Pentagon and the FBI were now going to do some serious digging into the lives of those on the list to see why they had attracted attention in the first place.

"It's a pity Bernard wasn't here," Colleen said. "He would have loved the idea of a spy story."

"Ah, yes, Mr. Rasmussen," Sean said. "We've been following his moves for a while; he plays very close to the line sometimes."

"When are you going to go public with this?" James asked.

"It depends on how much more of a network there is and when we round them all up," Sean replied. "Obviously, with the events here tonight, it will be hard to keep it quiet for long."

"Would you consider giving Bernard Rasmussen a briefing just before your big news conference or whatever you will do?" James asked.

"I'll think about that," Seam promised. "I'll have to get the Director's approval. Now, if you all don't mind, we really need to get statements while events are fresh in everyone's mind. Tom, would you take Ms. Richards, Bill, maybe you could take Ms. da Silva, and I'll take Mrs. Martin, then we'll take James and Vincenzo later."

Three hours later, all was essentially over. It had been a long, stressful and eventful evening, and James and Katrina were happy to see everyone depart. Sean had called in an evidence team who recovered Commander Reinsch's gun and the bullet that had been fired from it, and they had also taken possession of the Ford Bronco. There was little else at the scene, so they departed to turn over the hotel room that had been used by Commander Reinsch while she was on assignment at LST. The same team was also going to make a more thorough search of the room that Geoffrey Miller had used in case the agent who had quickly looked it over had missed anything. James thought that the Marriott would be thrilled by that, two of its rooms closed to any potential guest for who knew how long.

James called Robert Warner and told him what had occurred. Robert was most concerned that someone had been shot, as he put it, it could have so easily been James, Katrina or one of the others. James was deliberately vague about who had actually done the shooting, just telling Robert that it was an agent who had brought the commander down. Robert told him to take the next day off and just spend it with his wife. He needed the time and space to decompress from the experience. James agreed and called Isabella and told her to take the day off as well. He then called Simon and told him to act as general manager for the next couple of days. Now all they had to do was wait until Sean told them he was ready for the announcements and the revelation to the world of what had transpired.

*   *   *

Bernard Rasmussen arrived at his office on Friday morning to find the editor and two other men already there. "Can I help you?" he asked.
"Special Agent Sean Booth," Sean said, introducing himself and showing Bernard his FBI identification. This is Agent Tom Goodsell."
"What can I do for you?" Bernard asked.
"You met with a Susan Watson recently," Sean said. "And she gave you certain information."
"And if I met with this person, I'm not sure I understand what this has to do with the FBI," Bernard said.
"The information you received is germane to an ongoing investigation," Sean told him.
"What information?" Bernard asked.
"The information that describes a Navy decoy system," Sean explained. "I think the time for dissembling is over. We are not here to arrest you, but we would like to hear about your trip to Washington."
"You seem to know it all already," Bernard remarked.
"True," Sean told him. "We have you photographed meeting the Congressman by the Washington Monument and then your subsequent meeting with Susan Watson. We're here to make you an offer."

"What kind of offer?" Bernard asked.

"An exclusive first look at a major story," Sean promised.

"What kind of story?" Bernard asked.

"It entails your research into the life and times of one Michael Miller," Sean explained.

"What about Michael Miller?" Bernard asked.

"We cannot discuss that now, but if you would agree to work with us we can offer you the opportunity that we believe you have been looking for," Sean suggested.

"When?" Bernard asked. "I don't want to dump everything and then sit tight for six months while you guys do your thing."

"Within the week," Sean told him. "We are at a stage in an operation that will conclude within the week, and then we will be making a public announcement. We are prepared to give you the exclusive preview the day before the general announcement."

"And what do I have to give in return?" Bernard asked.

"We would like you to cease and desist in your investigations into the programs at LST and to surrender to us the documents given to you by Susan Watson," Sean explained.

"And if I don't?" Bernard asked.

"That, of course, is up to you," Sean assured him. "But then, we would not include you in any briefing of the events that are unfolding as we speak."

"How do I know I can trust you?" Bernard asked.

"I am satisfied that Agent Booth means what he says," the editor said, uttering his first words since Bernard had first walked into the office. "My put is that we go along. All your other attempts at stories have led nowhere, and this promises to be something we can finally use."

"Okay, I'm in," Bernard agreed.

"Thank you," Sean said. "Now, if you have the documents that Susan Watson gave you?"

"Sure, here you are," Bernard said, handing over the papers. In truth, he was happy to be rid of them now. The idea of pursuing that story had seemed attractive, but now he was not so certain, unless of course there was an even bigger story relating to the indiscretions of a Senator.

At last, a story!

Sean Booth called James and told him that they had made several other arrests and that they were now ready to go public with the story. He also asked James if he would be available to meet with Bernard Rasmussen and suggested a time and place. James then called Isabella and asked her if she would be available for the meeting, to which the only real answer was going to be, yes. Robert Warner was next on the list, and he delegated the task to Ron Simpson, the external affairs point man for LST. Sean had set the meeting for three the following day at the Marriott in Ogden, which was not quite midway between the plant and Salt Lake City, but close enough. James met with Isabella and Ron Simpson to review what they would discuss. He was hoping that Sean would take the lead and do most of the talking; after all, the story was much bigger than just the incident at the plant.

At three the next day, James and Isabella were waiting at the Marriott for the others to arrive. Sean came first, then Ron and finally Bernard, who arrived with Colleen. Sean made the introductions to Bernard and led the way to the conference room he had reserved for the afternoon. Bernard was a little taken aback when Sean introduced Isabella to him as Colleen's partner. He had always thought that she had a roommate, but he had always thought in terms of a platonic relationship based on rent and expense sharing, nothing else. But as he thought about it, things began to make sense, and he pushed the matter to the back of his mind and focused on the reason he was there.

For the next two hours, Sean disclosed to Bernard the history of the FBI investigation and the subsequent events and arrests. He gave Bernard a list of those arrested and in what cities. It truly was a nationwide operation. He also disclosed that Michael Miller, one of the victims of the earlier LST incident, was merely an alias for Avi Ben David, an Israeli spy who also used the name Samuel Levin at times. The real Michael Miller was alive and well and in Brunei. Sean told them that the FBI had interviewed him extensively and he had admitted to helping Avi Ben David in return for several hundred thousand dollars and help disappearing to Brunei.

Bernard then had questions for all of them, most of which were answered. Some items Sean said that he was not at liberty to discuss, and for other questions that were asked of James, Ron stepped in and gave Bernard a nice roundabout answer that actually said nothing. Bernard asked about the ersatz Air Force major and his cohorts who had threatened him outside the diner, and Sean told him that his best guess was that the CIA had used one of their independent contractors to get him to back off digging too deeply. That, Bernard said, warranted much more explanation, but all that Sean would tell him was that he thought it was occasioned by Bernard's contact with the Congressional Aide and that it was something best left well alone. By now Bernard had begun to realise that spies play for keeps, and whereas it was a nice idea to be principled, there were times when it was better to use discretion.

The meeting finally broke up at about six, and Bernard left to write up his story. He had been thinking about the outline that he had put together earlier, and it was obvious that that would just be discarded in favour of this new material. Best of all, the FBI was giving him a head start in that they were going to make their public announcement the next day, by which time he ought to be able to have a story on the front page of their paper.

The important thing was that he finally had a story. He had started with the incident and had tried to find a story in that, only to be frustrated at every turn. Then he had been thrown a bone by a Senatorial aide, whom he now thought was just trying to use him for her own purposes. Whether or not the decoy story had any basis in fact or truth, he would never know, and it hardly mattered now. A spy ring, particularly a spy ring from a supposed ally, was a story that would shake things up royally and provide grist for many mills for weeks to come. He was quite prepared to drop his digging into the incident at LST and what might or might not be the involvement of the Navy in the programs at the plant. That was always going to be speculation; this was real.

Sean waited until Ron, Isabella, and Colleen had left, and then he thanked James for his help. It had been a strange case and, fortunately, they had not had to reveal in any way what the Sagitta Program really was. The smoke screen thrown up by Senator Baker, Sean suggested, was just a ploy to gain attention for her own agenda. The Senator was on one of the committees that were briefed regularly on all programs, and the rules surrounding disclosure of any information from those briefings were well understood by all and usually respected. The fact that she had disclosed the existence of the program, albeit under another name, was disturbing, but he would leave that to his boss to decide if any action was warranted. The real problem was that the Senate policed itself, and in his mind, that was a certain guarantee that nothing would ever be done. Even the most egregious sins were normally treated with at most a mild rebuke. They considered themselves above the law and did not welcome any criticism or enquiry. Sean knew that criticism of Senators' actions by a mere FBI agent was tantamount to heresy and would be considered by some of that august body as almost treasonable, so he told James that his opinions should not be shared with anyone.

Sean also told James that the Pentagon was turning things upside down in an attempt to ensure that there were no more traitors among their ranks. That would be a hard one to pin down, because the sheer number of employees there made it statistically possible that there was someone disenchanted enough to spy for someone else. But that was for the future. Now, at least, they had uncovered one spy ring and had arrested all those that they could identify. Any left would be without a source and without the cohesion provided by their control, Geoffrey Miller, or, as he was otherwise known, Isaac Horowitz. If those left felt exposed, they might try and establish new identities, or they might simply leave and go elsewhere. Whatever the circumstances, it would be a little while before they might be effective again.

One thing Sean did tell him was good news. Commander Reinsch had been offered a deal and had pleaded guilty and was, as the expression went, singing like a canary, so there would be no long drawn-out trial and no need to reveal that she had been shot by a member of a foreign government agency. She was the one who had given them the names of the rest of the ring, and she was also detailing other activities. As Sean had said before, she would do time, but it would be relatively short. She had given them details of the involvement of Senator Baker and Susan Watson. Senator Baker had been concerned that the FBI was investigating the Pentagon leak and was getting too close to the Israeli ring, and had created her own diversion to deliberately confuse things. In retrospect, she now probably considered her actions as ill-conceived and unnecessary. She was now covering her tracks with pro-Palestinian statements to draw attention away from her strong ties to the Israelis. She would probably quietly retire by resigning her seat due to some 'family issues', but she was finished in the Senate. George Adams had met with the Senator and shown her the pictures and the evidence recovered from Bernard Rasmussen, and she had bowed to the inevitable. Congressman Wheelwright, on the other hand, had blustered about being used by the Senator and was not about to admit to anything or resign, retire or in any other way indicate that he might have the slightest iota of complicity in this affair. Susan Watson had dropped out of sight and would probably emerge later under another name.

Sean did caution James that now there were going to be Congressional hearings, the truth behind the Sagitta program might leak out beyond the damage already done by Senator Baker, and, in his opinion, if that happened, the program would probably be quietly cancelled. His reasoning was that the Government would not want to explain to the populace that merchant ship captains, no matter in whose employ, were sailing around the world with nuclear weapons on their boats. There was also the issue of foreign ports that simply barred the entry of any vessel with nuclear weapons aboard, US warships included. Nothing good would come of these hearings, and he counselled James to start thinking about what the division would look like without the program. James believed him. If the truth about the basing mode of the Sagitta Program ever got out, there would be a hue and cry such as had never been heard before. Waterway Chemicals would be identified and all their vessels would be suspect and therefore likely to be subjected to customs searches in whatever port they put into. It would not matter that the hearings were supposed to be closed. There were likely to be just too many people involved, and someone would leak the information. It looked like Sagitta was going to die.

It was a relief to go back to the plant and relative normality for James. At his staff meeting, he gave his team the bare bones of the case and told them that Commander Reinsch would not be back. He was amused when Simon commented that Craig Robinson would be happy to hear that and might even make some comment about Navy people. James doubted that; she was, after all, an officer in the Service, as was Craig, and it could just as easily have been an Air Force officer. After the meeting, James called Simon aside and told him that he was guessing that there might be a cancellation of the Auriga Type B program in the air. They then sat down and started to look at how they would restructure the division without that program. It would mean some significant changes, but by lunch time, they had the basis of a plan and would be able to execute if and when the cancellation occurred. All they could do now was wait.

Epilogue

DATE-TIME 03/08 – 21:18 COPY 01 OF 03
FBI ROUNDS UP SPY NETWORK
    BC – Spy network broken by FBI · FL ·
FBI rounds up an Israeli spy ring seeking information on US
rocket programs · FL ·
By Bernard Rasmussen · FC ·
Salt Lake City Star

SALT LAKE CITY, UTAH – Following months of investigation, the
FBI announced today that it had arrested ten members of an Israeli spy
ring and had detained for questioning a US Navy commander
suspected of espionage. The spy ring had been operating within the US
for some time and was working to get information on ballistic missile
programs. The FBI identified those arrested, including Isaac Horowitz,
who was in the country under an assumed name and travelling on a
British passport in the name of Geoffrey Miller. Horowitz was identified
by the FBI as the coordinator or 'control' of the group, and it was he
who gave instructions and passed messages and information back and
forth. Others arrested were John Philips from San Diego, David Jacobs
of Chicago, Steven Cole from Washington, Lamar Evans from
Birmingham, Peter Black from Atlanta, Geraldine Andrews from
Charlotte, Alec Gardiner from Seattle, Heather Decker from Denver
and Patrick Hayes from Columbus. The FBI categorised these spies as
'illegals', people posing as innocent civilians while trying to gain access
to information on the most secret of US ballistic missile technology.
The term 'illegals' is used in the intelligence community because they
are deep-cover agents who take civilian jobs that have no connection
with foreign governments. Other agents are often run from embassies
and trade, or other missions.

The detained US Navy commander, Josephine Reinsch, has been
working in the Pentagon and is accused of passing information to the
Israeli spy ring. Horowitz and Reinsch were arrested in Utah last
Wednesday by the FBI as they were attempting to obtain information

on ballistic missile programs managed by Locomotive Springs Technologies, a local Utah company. The FBI commended LST for their cooperation in apprehending the two. The balance of those arrested was taken into custody this morning, early and represents one of the largest sweeps of foreign agents the FBI has made in some years.

The story does not end there. Several months ago, LST featured in the news when a building exploded and thirteen people died in the incident. It was disclosed by the FBI that one of the thirteen, Michael Miller, was in fact Avi Ben David, another of the Israeli spy ring. The circumstances of the incident are unknown, and perhaps are unknowable, but the FBI speculates that the other twelve employees of LST had discovered the activities of Michael Miller and had confronted him. They speculate that in an ensuing struggle with one of the LST employees, a foreign object was dropped inside a mixer, causing it to explode, killing all those in the building. The FBI further disclosed that it had executed a warrant to search the premises of Temple Beth Shalom, south of Salt Lake City, for materials that Miller may have concealed there. Miller frequented the temple under the name of Samuel Levin, often standing in as Cantor. Not arrested in the sweep was Roberta Miller, the supposed wife of Michael Miller, who, in fact, is Ruth Avraham and is now wanted for questioning by the FBI.

Here in Utah, people in Logan are shocked by the news. Neighbours of the Millers knew them as good Church going people, ever ready to help anyone in need. Their landlord, Warren Anderson, said that they always paid their rent on time and that, although Roberta Miller disappeared right after the LST incident, the house was left spotlessly clean and in perfect order. She also chose to forego recovering the security deposit normally required by landlords, which, now, is seen by Warren Anderson as a signal that all was not as it seemed.

LST stated that Michael Miller passed all the usual pre-employment checks and, for all intents and purposes, was who he said he was. Their check with Penn State revealed a Michael Miller who graduated as a chemical engineer. LST stated that Miller presented a US Passport in that name when he signed on, so they saw no reason to doubt his bona fides, and as far as they were able to tell, the passport was genuine.

The FBI briefed members of the House and Senate yesterday, and now various Committees in both houses are pressing for hearings to determine how such a spy ring could have operated undetected for so long and what information it has already passed on. The political implications are complex, and the wrangling is likely to continue for some months. Not known is how this latest event will affect relations between the US and Israel, but the Israeli Ambassador was summoned to the State Department today and given a note. Notes in the diplomatic world are the means of formally passing on information or views about incidents or events, which can be interpreted in this case that the US was expressing its displeasure formally and would expect a formal response.

Unless the conflict in the Middle East is somehow resolved and there is a formal recognition of Israel by the PLO and the surrounding countries and a Palestinian homeland that exists side by side with the State of Israel in true harmony with mutual respect, it is difficult to see an end to it all. Lack of resolution will drive additional attempts by both sides to acquire more and better weapons. It is generally believed that Israel already has nuclear capability, and the latest espionage scandal would appear to be an attempt to acquire an effective delivery vehicle other than aircraft. This would give them the capability to strike at their most belligerent adversaries in Saudi Arabia and Iran.

This incident needs to be seen against the wider context of not only the Middle East Conflict but also the continuing struggle for supremacy between the world's two superpowers, the United States and the Soviet Union. The Soviet Union has, of late, cast itself in the role of a major player in the Middle East conflict and has been promoting the efforts of the PLO to gain the upper hand diplomatically. Unfortunately, Israeli Prime Minister Mr. Shamir is being cast as Mr No by Mikhail Gorbachev, as he says no to everything, which is unfortunate as it lends credence to the image that the PLO is trying to now present as a viable political entity, not just a violent liberation movement.

The United States continues to support Israel, which has seen its share of conflict. Since the creation of the State of Israel in 1948, there have been major conflicts in 1967, 1973 and 1982. There has also been an ongoing conflict with the PLO, which, until the Gorbachev doctrine of perestroika, was intent only on 'driving the Jews into the sea'. The problem does not end with the PLO. Many of the neighbouring countries of Israel have policies aimed at the elimination of the State and have been building up weapon systems to this end.

It seems, for the moment at least, that both sides in the conflict have become unwitting, or perhaps witting, pawns in the power struggle between the United States and the Soviet Union, with both superpowers seeking to be seen as the broker who will bring about peace in the region.

Will this latest effort by the Soviet Union help or hinder the peace process, and will there be a solution to the Middle East Crisis? Only time will tell.
AP-BA-03-08 2125MST ·